—THE—
SILVER
BOUGH

D1464603

THE
SILVER
BOUGH

NEIL GUNN

Chambers

First published 1948 by Faber and Faber
Second edition published 1985 by Richard Drew Publishing Ltd
Reprinted 1987

This edition published 1992 by W & R Chambers Ltd,
43-45 Annandale Street, Edinburgh EH7 4AZ

© Foreword Dairmid Gunn 1985

All rights reserved. No part of this publication may be
reproduced, stored in a retrieval system, or transmitted, in
any form or by any means, electronic, mechanical, photocopying,
recording or otherwise, without the prior permission of
W & R Chambers Ltd.

British Library Cataloguing in Publication Data

A catalogue record for this book is available from the British Library

ISBN 0-550-23002-5

Printed and bound in Great Britain by Cox & Wyman Ltd

FOREWORD

Neil Gunn, one of Scotland's most distinguished 20th century authors, wrote his first book in 1926 and his last thirty years later. Although certain themes remained central to Gunn's writing, the author's emphases and interests changed with the passage of time. External influences had a significant effect on him – the emergence of fascism in Germany and Italy, the development of communism in the Soviet Union, the misery of the Depression and, of course, the ravages of the Second World War. Throughout the War and until 1949 Gunn lived in hill country in Easter Ross in the north of Scotland and enjoyed his most creative period of writing. The ambience suited him – access to hill, moor, mountain, stream and the rhythm of life in a crofting community. His essays on his life there, which eventually appeared in collected form in 1949 as *Highland Pack*, had a cheering and restorative effect on a reading public tired of the restrictions and dreariness of wartime and post-war Britain. One of these essays concerns four standing stones on the moor beyond the crofting land near his home, and their significance. This subject is pursued persuasively and imaginatively in *The Silver Bough*, published in 1948.

The late 1940s may have been depressing years for the people of Britain, but there was much about those years that was both stimulating and exciting. Political developments aside, there was plenty on which to speculate regarding progress in nuclear science. Gunn, who had a mathematical bent, was as fascinated by nuclear physics as he was by archaeology. He shared an anxious hope with many that man would develop the potential of nuclear science for peaceful ends alone. The dropping of the bomb on Hiroshima, after all, was then an event of the recent past. Paradoxically, he saw the way ahead for mankind through looking back, not just a few centuries but thousands of years, for perspective and meaning.

At the heart of *The Silver Bough* is a cairn on a knoll surrounded by standing stones. It is of obvious professional interest to Grant, the archaeologist, round whom the story revolves. During excavation he finds that he is satisfying a yearning within himself for spiritual renewal. The life-enhancing qualities of the crofting family with whom he lodges and the quiet tenor of Highland life bear a curious similarity to his speculations on how 'the cairn people' lived in the distant past. On seeing at a distance an old man and his dog, he muses, 'There were no other figures to be seen and in a moment the little drama with the old bent figure might have been of any Age back to Neolithic times.' It is as though Grant, the sympathetic outsider, is at once pondering on what 'was' and relating his speculations to what he finds around him, or vice versa. His ideas spread outwards like ripples in a loch, fascinating his colleagues and giving some meaning to the life of a neighbouring landowner, who is mentally scarred from his experiences in the War.

As imaginative as Grant's ideas is the plot of the book, which is intricate. To the mystery of the skeletons of a woman and child found in a cist in the cairn is added the question of the background of the landlady's beautiful grand-daughter and fatherless child. A crock of gold is found, and lost – a loss eventually accepted 'philosophically' by the archaeologist. The whole story is on two levels, the seen and the unseen, between which at times there is a startling similarity.

The Silver Bough underlines Gunn's belief in the importance of preserving the continuity of life from antiquity to the present – a continuity that can only be maintained if the wisdom of the past is neither forgotten nor forsaken. History for him is not a list of dates and names of leaders, good and bad, but rather an evolution in terms of community life, reflected in myth and tradition. Perhaps a sentence from the preface of Frazer's famous *Golden Bough* quoted in the book sums up Gunn's view most accurately. 'Compared with the evidence afforded by living tradition, the testimony of ancient books on the subject of early religion is worth very little'. To that Gunn through the central character has added, 'And not only of early religion.'

Dairmid Gunn
Edinburgh, 1985

To the memory of
JOHN ROSE FREW

I

Simon Grant, who had handled many skulls in his time, was immediately taken by the shape of the head, the colouring, and the fineness of the features. He got a close view of it as he turned to lift his rucksack off the seat and make room for the man beside him. "Lovely day," he said, with a friendly smile.

The dark eyes steadied upon him for an incurious moment. "Yes." Then the man settled himself and the old country bus rattled on.

Grant turned his face away and stared through the glass, disconcerted by that objective look. There had been no feeling in it, no human interest, yet a very little more of it would have scattered his wits. A demobbed officer of his county regiment, he thought . . . descent through Highland landowners . . . definitely archaic, he decided, using a vague word for a start. They had entered on a vast stretch of vacant moorland, backed by mountain ridges of no particular height in the flattening summer heat. The heather was a dead dark brown and, in the clear sunlight, held the tone of the man's eyes.

Every seat in the bus was occupied, with two young fellows standing near the door, talking to the conductress in low voices and laughing now and then. He had been enjoying their country mannerisms, the Highland drawl, and had particularly observed the way they flattened themselves against glass and woodwork as the man beside him had entered.

Like himself, most of those on board were clearly visitors or tourists and it had been interesting to watch their behaviour,

9

to glance at the shape of their bones, their colouring; to time, as it were, their reactions; for all this required no conscious effort, but on the contrary was once more a familiar amusement for one who had been ill and was restored to the sunlight—with a pleasant and possibly exciting gamble ahead. For from the given facts—and Colonel Mackintosh, his chief, was celebrated for his scientific caution as an archaeologist—there was at least a sporting chance of finding a small hoard of skulls, each one of them, except for the possible "intrusion" of a round head, as long as—and now the word came to him—the *Neolithic* one on the man beside him.

His happy discovery was interrupted by two young women who suddenly saw a distant cow and a solitary cottage in a green depression of the moor where water meandered, and in the hubbub of wonder created by the word "lonely" Simon Grant said, "Excuse me, but I am going on to Kinlochoscar, and I just wondered if you might know Mr. Donald Martin of Clachar House."

The dark eyes considered him. "Yes."

"Can you tell me if he happens to be at home?"

"Not at the moment, I believe."

"Ah. Thank you." Grant moved on his seat, flustered a trifle, and said, as he glanced out of the window, "I have a letter of introduction."

The laughter over the cow and cottage ceased as amazement at the reality of loneliness held eyes to a long unwinking stare. He saw one of the two lads in front turn his back, lower his head and whisper something to the conductress. She gave him a short jab with her elbow, which he seemed to enjoy; but presently, as she turned to cast a negligent glance over the bus, her eyes steadied for an instant on the man beside him. Her face was noticeably flushed.

Grant was not upset by his companion's manifest desire not to engage in conversation. For himself, he never quite understood this silent mood of long-suffering which seemed to afflict so many of his countrymen when travelling, though he had often pondered it. In the present instance, however, it was something more, even quite other, than a taciturnity. The dark eyes had seemed to move over his face in an inscrutable guessing, a detached courtesy, yet set far back in them there had been for a moment something hard and solitary like a standing stone in an arid waste. This was what had flustered him, even if he now realised that he had probably seen no more than his own reflection. Besides, his thought was inclined to run to standing stones!

Slowly, mile by mile, the moor rose to its height, to a loch with pines and a gamekeeper's house, the entrance to a concealed shooting lodge, and then the road tipped over as it passed between the mountains and began the descent of the gorge. The scenery was magnificent. An hour later they drew up before the hotel at Kinlochoscar.

Simon Grant had not written to the hotel, which was quite a large one, as early June had never been part of the "rush season"; but for the last few miles he had overheard enough talk to worry him. When he got out of the bus, he slung his rucksack over his shoulder and made for the reception office.

"No. I'm afraid I haven't booked. I didn't think——"

The tall dark-haired manageress smiled and shook her head. "We're absolutely full up."

"Not even a corner—anywhere—until I look round?"

"No. We have quite a few sleeping out."

"You mean—no chance even of a private house?" And now he was visibly concerned.

"Afraid not. But you could ask the postmaster. We have had to refuse many bookings."

"Really," said Grant. He scratched his close-cropped pointed ginger beard; his blue eyes quickened and glanced; his short slim body, his arms, moved with a restless energy.

"Since the war . . . people can't get abroad . . . the same everywhere, I hear . . . unless you book it's quite hopeless . . ." Recognising something unusual in the middle-aged figure before her, she was doing her best to explain; but now other travellers were pushing up to the desk. Grant suddenly awoke to them, smiled, thanked her, and then from a yard or two called, "The postmaster?"

She smiled to him between the heads of her guests. "You could try."

The postmaster stopped serving a small girl with groceries and also shook his head, but ultimately told him to try Mrs. MacPherson. After Grant had been to four houses, he realised that he was taking part in an old Highland game: no one liked to leave him without hope. It was a haphazard attractive village at the head of a sea-loch. When he got back to the hotel he saw a solitary suitcase on the stretch of gravel where the bus had drawn up. He had quite forgotten that he possessed such a thing. Having wiped his forehead and resettled his hat—an old tweed affair—he picked up the suitcase and struggled with it towards the hotel entrance where a porter was good enough to take it from him. He intercepted the manageress in the hall; she smiled sympathetically and said she had feared all along that his hunt would be hopeless. He wiped his forehead again, dropped his hat, and smiled. They discussed the situation. His only hope, it appeared, seeing, as he said, he did not mind where he slept, was at the small township of Clachar, which, unfortunately, was three miles away. That, Grant assured her, would suit him excellently. "Remember, I'm promising you nothing——" she was beginning to explain, when he responded with a certain eye-flash: "But I could try?" He had a rather high-pitched but pleasant laugh. In the end it was agreed that he could partake of the early afternoon tea provided for guests arriving by the bus, leave his suitcase in the hotel, and then set out on foot for

Clachar, seeing he would rather not wait until six o'clock—
"or maybe a little later"—when an hotel car would be
available. She turned back to him, "If you're absolutely
stuck for a bed for the night—I'm promising you nothing,
remember, for, to tell the truth, I'm frightened to ask how
the maids are sleeping in the attic——" "But I shouldn't
mind an attic—even though—even if——" His momentary
earnestness broke as he stumbled, and they both laughed.
The touch of colour enhanced her appearance, and as he
went to wash he decided that for one so busy the manageress
was a charming woman.

Refreshed and with the rucksack firmly settled on his
back, Simon Grant apologised to the manageress for
troubling her once more but wondered if by any chance she
could tell him where he might find Mr. Martin of Clachar
House.

She gave him a glance. "Why, yes—I saw him about a
few minutes ago." She walked to the hotel door. "There he
is," she said quietly, drawing back a pace. And Grant saw a
man coming round the corner of the hotel and setting out
alone along the Clachar road. It was the man who had sat
beside him in the bus.

2

More than odd, thought Grant, as he continued to follow the man along the narrow road to Clachar; in fact it's absolutely absurd, he decided, laughing silently to himself at something fantastic in their solitary progression, but sobering quickly, for he must act resolutely right away or he couldn't go ahead with his project at all. The Colonel, he felt, might at least have given him a personal hint about the fellow. But then the Colonel would never notice a little thing like that! For a few minutes he became self-conscious, heard echoes of the Colonel's talk about the unfortunate tendency among certain archaeologists to rush into theory, to construct whole civilisations, evoke races and all their wanderings, from a chance bone, a chipped flint, or a piece of baked clay. But then Grant always knew when the Colonel was getting at him.

It was very hot, absolutely boiling, he concluded, now sweating profusely, for the 'flu had taken it out of him—temperature over 103—and his body, like his mind, felt light and sensitive. Would he put a spurt on and overtake him and be done with it? If he suddenly looked round, would he wave to him? They had left the sea, but now as they came up on the ridge, Grant saw it again in the distance, a glimmering sheet set with islands; a bay rather than a sea-loch; croft houses dotted about, a stream—but the man in front had stopped, was standing quite still, staring ahead, like a figure in a film. Grant, who had involuntarily stopped, began to go forward again, aware of a sudden nervousness, an uncertainty. His footsteps at last aroused the man, who turned his head slowly.

"I believe you are Mr. Martin?" and Grant smiled in his friendly way.

"Yes."

"I'm afraid I did not make it clear that I have a letter of introduction to you from Colonel Mackintosh, the archaeologist. Do you mind if I——" And, pulling the letter from a breast pocket, he presented it.

"Oh," said Martin without any expression as he took the letter, then he looked again at Grant.

"My name is Grant. I work with the Colonel—with Colonel Mackintosh. He suggested that I might call on you, in connection with a certain cairn on your land. I hope it's not inconvenient?"

"What cairn?"

"It's a cairn—uh—not far from Clachar House—near the sea. I could show it to you on the map." He began fumbling at his pockets.

"I know it," said Martin.

"It's a matter simply of opening up the cairn, just to see what's inside. But it means entry on your land, though, of course, I should see that nothing was really—uh—messed about." A frank flash came from the blue eyes.

The flash was not acknowledged and the letter was quietly shoved into an outside pocket. "How is Colonel Mackintosh?"

"He's very well; only wishing, he said, that he could come up himself to see you—and get the job done properly."

Now a faint dry humour gathered about Martin's eyes, a certain irony, which gave the face an aloof attractiveness. Grant heard the slight expulsion of breath from the nostrils and caught the smell of whisky. Presumably Mr. Martin had had his afternoon tea not in the lounge but in the public bar behind the hotel.

"You're going on there now, to the Stone Circle?"

"Yes. There is a stone circle round the cairn, but the actual work, of course, will be on the cairn—I mean, I shan't interfere with the standing stones."

"I see," said Martin, the dry humour already gone. The jet-black hair, a certain pallor, the fine features—it could be a very expressive face. But the mask was habitual, indifferent, and quiet as stone.

Grant had nothing more to say.

"Well, shall we go on?" With that objective look which seemed to pause and contemplate its object, Martin moved on.

"I hope you really don't mind," said Grant, his own tone firming.

"Not really," answered Martin. "To tear the guts out of everything is characteristic, I suppose." His tone remained uninterested.

"Characteristic of what?" inquired Grant.

"Of our age." He half turned his head. "Or don't you think so?"

"It all depends on the point of view." Grant smiled ahead, for he could be angry as he could be merry, and as quickly.

"And your point of view?"

"Is that knowledge helps."

"Helps what?"

"Humanity," said Grant succinctly.

They walked on.

"Are you to do all the digging yourself?" inquired Martin presently.

"I hope to find some labour, though I had supposed that may be difficult."

"Very difficult, I should say, if not quite impossible."

They had come down the slope and now a winding belt of small birch trees ahead indicated a stream of which Grant presently caught a glimpse.

16

"I don't suppose you could suggest," he said politely, "any possible source of labour? A man of any age would do, so long as he can lift stones or dig."

"I'm afraid—not. The old here cultivate their crofts or go to sea to fish occasionally. Productive labour—which they might be unwilling to forgo."

With an effort Grant said nothing. The road came within a hundred yards of the stream, on whose bank he saw a woman knitting, a dark-brown shawl round her head. A man was staggering about in the water below her. A motor car came noisily towards them and Martin stopped. "You might," he said, "get the man in the burn there to help you. I rather think the job he's on is about finished. But the woman will tell you." His talk was now easy and cool as his courtesy. The car drew up beside them. "Got her right?" he asked the driver.

"She needs a new gasket," answered the fair-haired young man who seemed to have acquired some of his employer's expressionless manner. "I'll turn her here." A rough cart track went from the road towards the stream, and while the car was being turned, Martin said to his fellow-traveller, "If you care to come along and see us, do."

"Thank you." Grant's nod was nearly a bow, but as the car drove off, he said to himself, " 'Productive labour'— damn him!" He hitched up his rucksack, wiped his brow, and started for the woman by the stream. All at once he found himself in a furious temper. He paused for a moment to let it rip, then, much relieved, he went on and removed his tweed hat with the friendliest gesture.

The aged face, framed by its shawl, was heavy and solemn, the unwinking eyes a faded blue. The expression was that of a woman quietly on guard, waiting to hear what had to be said. Grant said it straight away, and did not omit the fact that he had been directed to her by Mr. Martin. It would be perfectly simple labour, he explained; neither so

17

heavy nor so wet, he added with his engaging smile, as heaving these boulders from the stream. The crack of one boulder on another drew his startled attention. The shambling figure in the stream had now turned his face towards them and Grant saw that it was an idiot's face. The trousers were tucked up to the thighs and the body staggered on bare feet.

"My son," the woman said, "is engaged under the County Council for road work. But just now he is only taking the stones up to be ready for the breaking. There is no hurry for this. Indeed he has taken enough and he is only going on now in case they will be needing it all."

"I see," said Grant, quietened, hardly knowing where to look.

"So we would be very glad if you could engage him. He is a good worker and very strong."

Grant felt the eyes on his face. The woman had talked in the matter-of-fact tone of one used to conducting such business, but there was a patience somewhere, a dumb waiting, that swept all anger away and left him uncomfortably but deeply moved.

"Very well," he said, nodding. "We'll see. Yes—I'll think it over."

"Five shillings for the whole day, if that's not too much, though indeed he will be making much more when he is at the stone-breaking."

"I think it's too little," he declared, hitching up his rucksack. "However, I must be going now. Could you tell me the nearest way to the Stone Circle?"

She was pointing to a footpath that left the road, when her son intervened. The face was upturned directly below them and through the thick protruding lips of the large mouth came sounds like "Gu-gu-gu——"

As though she perfectly understood, she pointed to certain stones. "Take them, and that should about do." His gaze followed her pointing finger and saw the stones, then he made for them earnestly, his broad shoulders dipping to the wading shambling gait.

"Very well, then," said Grant. "I'll let you know. And thank you very much."

"We stay in the first house, on the way in. You can just see it."

He followed her hand and saw it.

"You will find him a good worker," she said. "And I am always with him myself."

"I can see he is a good worker," he answered, smiling and touching his hat. "Good day, and thank you again."

3

He muttered to himself as he walked away and gave small embarrassed laughs. Hang it, it had been awkward! And oh lord, that look in her face, knowing he was wanting to clear out, to make no arrangement, having stumbled on the unmentionable. Her son!

Life is pure mystery, he said in marvel, thinking of the woman, aware again of the dumb patience, the silent knowledge, her face beside him on the air. Like a guilty schoolboy, he hardly knew how to contain his smile or where to look; so he looked for the path, saw it ahead, joined it by a short cut, followed its zigzag up the slowly rising ground, and emerged on a broad back of land whence Clachar in all its dimensions lay before him to the north.

It was still and somehow very old, caught by the sunlight and held, as in an ancient almost wearied enchantment. Two of the three islands were flat and green, unexpectedly green, and the sea between them and the land was a deep blue, changing inshore to patches of bottle green and of purple. The stream found the sea through a breadth of hummocky land where houses faced about in many directions, before they spaced themselves out in more orderly fashion as they came up the valley with the road to Kinlochoscar. Not more than about a score of them all told, but from the configuration of the land and the islands of shelter and retreat in the sea, Grant knew that human life had indeed been here since prehistoric times.

His eyes moved westward from the houses, from the little fields with their green crops, the grazing land dotted with lying cattle, to a belt of trees about a large house; concentrated, with a sudden knitting of eyebrows, on the stone walls, the roofs, the outhouses, the narrow sea inlet like a private harbour; and withdrew over the brows of cliffs, upward towards himself, until they paused where the land flattened, and saw the circle of standing stones with the great stone mound in its midst. His eyebrows grew smooth and his eyes round and steady. "That's it," he said softly to himself, as if the stones were waiting for him to come home.

Forgetting to look where his feet went, he put one of them in a rabbit burrow and might easily have broken his leg as he fell headlong, but though it was fifty-two years old his body was light and even nimble. He sat for a little while, however, ignoring the tweed hat which had rolled on, because now he felt extraordinarily happy. I might easily have broken my leg, he thought, trying to sober himself. But it was so exactly the kind of place where he wanted to work, the very kind of world where he wanted to be. The time and the place and the adventure together. Lord, I'm lucky! he murmured, in slow wonder and gratitude as he rubbed a muscle. Then he went down more soberly to the circle of stones.

Except for one tall monolith in the south-west, the standing stones were of no particular height, but the size of the cairn excited him. For a long time he wandered about in a restless way; occasionally he paused to touch a standing stone, to scrape the lichen off, to feel as well as to see the texture; he took out his pocket compass; he got on his knees; he studied alignments, real or imaginary, head to side like a connoisseur before a masterpiece; and once when he obviously and deliberately looked for something and found it by kicking some turf off a small hummock, he sat down on it. But in a minute he was up again, walking away from the cairn, head bent, as if he had lost money through a hole in his trousers pocket on an imaginary avenue. Actually, however, he was wearing knickerbockers of a greenish Harris tweed, which, being cut to the design of an older day, were not noticeably baggy about the knees and in fact clearly showed the buckle-fastening over the stocking. Money, indeed, was about the last thing to worry him, not that he had much of it, but what with a lectureship and a banker who could be utterly relied on to look after a bachelor's modest investments with discretion, he had enough. At last, turning round, he gazed back into the circle, standing very still now, his mouth open and the lower jaw with the clipped pointed beard twisted to one side. The blue eyes caught a glint as the eyelids quivered, for his concentration was considerable; then the jaw came back into position, the lips met and pressed, and just perceptibly the head nodded—not, obviously, in perfect assurance, but with that remnant of doubt which produces the true suppressed excitement.

After these and other preliminary skirmishings, including a diametrical spanning of the outer circle of standing stones in which he lost his hat without losing count of his yard-long paces, he approached the heart of the matter which was the cairn. Herein lay what mystery there might be, what treasure, archaeological or literal, time might have hoarded for this hour.

One thing at least was clear; the cairn had never been opened up. It would contain a chamber or chambers built and roofed over in the Neolithic Age, when man used stone implements and weapons. It might be many many centuries older than Stonehenge. It might contain—what no chambered cairn had ever contained before. It was like a book that had never been opened—and might be a masterpiece. To skulls and bones there might be added something that his fingers would feel and his eyes look upon in revelation and in triumph. There is a sense, he had once argued (when

22

his chief, Colonel Mackintosh, had called him an incurable romantic) in which all scientists, and particularly arch-aeologists, are romantics of the purest dye, indeed childish romantics (he was an impassioned arguer when roused), because why?—because they are forever hunting the unknown; even the aristocratic mathematicians hunt *their* unknown, the X in their algebra. X is their treasure trove (shouted Grant, growing warmer) and if there wasn't an X, damned the hunt would they do at all. And that's why (and with a sweeping gesture he interrupted his chief) when they do find it, like the mystery in the heart of the atom, that's why they are so astonished when the other fellows, who are *not* romantics, use it to blow us all to blazes.

A yard was a longish stride for a man of his height, but when, pacing along a straight line by the cairn in order roughly to estimate its length, he was occasionally thrown off his balance by the uneven ground, he held to one rocking leg with a wonderful pertinacity. With a hesitating count of thirty-eight, for end stones were splayed out somewhat, he decided that, as cairns went, it might, without undue exaggeration, be called a whopper of a cairn. He climbed up it and down it; he walked round it; he climbed up it again and from his geological knowledge came at certain topographical and social conclusions as he gazed around, noting the shape of the hills, the alluvial flatness around the lower stretches of the small river, and the islands —one in particular now green as an emerald, with pearls that were sheep on it. Finally he began to poke and pull at deliberately chosen spots in the cairn itself until he began to evolve such theories that he felt it was time to stop. Even phantasy should be come at from rock bottom.

As he was shouldering his rucksack he missed his hat, retrieved it, and with a last lingering look at the cairn murmured happily that it was pure virgin. Then he went ahead towards the houses of Clachar, confident now of wheedling a bed out of an aged cripple. The ground began to descend and lo! here was a vast stone like a rock. The whole place was clearly reeking with prehistory. His approach, however, grew more tentative as he perceived something curled in the shadow at its base. It was a young woman with dark-red hair and a child of about four snuggled against her breast. They were both fast asleep. The child's face had the dreamlike beauty that is hardly of the earth; the hair was amber, the skin fair as fine beeswax; the lips were parted in the innocence that comes by nature to the female child. The woman's hair had a tawny depth, her face a strong but regular mould; a still, generous face and mouth, a straight nose and real eyebrows; but what took Grant was a fairness of skin which gave the odd impression that its light came from within, though perhaps the impression was enhanced by the freckles.

He was suddenly moved, and at the same moment, as if his thought had touched her, she opened her eyes. After her first bewildered stare, her thought was for decorum, but she was all right and sat up.

"I beg your pardon," he said, turning away. So natural had her instinctive movements been that she had not awakened the child, and Grant stopped. He was ashamed to stop, but he stopped. "I am very sorry," he said in a quiet voice, "if I disturbed you." He had a habit at such a moment of touching his hat, or rather of catching its brim between thumb and forefinger and giving it a tiny up-down movement, as though the total removal of the hat would be altogether too arrogant a gesture.

"It's all right," she said and smiled with a warming smother of confusion, which enriched the skin as she bent her eyes on her child.

"To tell the truth," he said, coming back an uncertain pace or two, "I was wondering, when I saw you, if anyone could tell me if it's possible to get a room anywhere in

Clachar. I tried the hotel in Kinlochoscar and several houses, but every place is full up. The manageress of the hotel said I might find a room here."

She supported herself with one hand as she answered thoughtfully, "I don't know."

"Any kind of place would do, so long as there's a bed."

"There are two houses—but they have visitors." She hesitated.

"I'm afraid," he said, "it looks as if I'm fated to sleep out all night." And he smiled.

"My grandmother, sometimes . . . but we have no water in the house."

It was on Grant's tongue to say joyously that the whole world was his bathroom, but he had a natural modesty before women, so he said, "That's nothing. I have been in countries where water is scarcer than wine, and as for a—water-tap——" He dismissed it as a fabulous wonder. "Please don't let that trouble you."

"I—could ask my grandmother. But——"

He thanked her a thousand times and asked her grandmother's name.

"Mrs. Cameron. That's the house—the one with the white gable to the burn." Once more he followed a pointing hand. "But," she continued doubtfully, "I am not sure——"

"What an attractive cottage!" he cried so loudly that the child woke up. "And now I have wakened your child."

"It's all right," she said, gathering the bewildered child towards her. "My grandmother was going up the road to a neighbour's house, but if you cared to call in an hour or two——"

"I'll do that. Thank you *very* much," and this time he caught the crown of his hat, removed it wholly, and walked away.

Now as he walked what he saw were her fingers spread flat against the child's back, each as naked of a ring as when it was born. "Your child," he had said. Not that that would really have mattered, if in fact it weren't her child. But even to a confirmed bachelor real motherhood has its signs. It was when the child had grown petulant and the mother had bent her head, that the naked hands had so to speak looked at him.

4

Realising he was blindly heading for Clachar House, he decided all in a moment to head on. It was high time he had this business settled definitely with Mr. Donald Martin. The whole way the fellow had behaved left much to be desired, apart from any question of manners. Even his invitation to call round had about it now not so much the air of a polite afterthought as a studied intention. He may have wanted time to make up his mind as to whether he should allow anyone to—to—what were his words—"to tear the guts out . . ." Pretty cool, not to say insulting. It was, really. As if these blessed fellows owned the earth itself! And then they wondered why there were socialists! He staggered, for he had had no lunch and his body felt feather-weight. But his mind was wonderfully clear, and was now strengthened at the prospect of a bed in a cottage. Hotels worried him, for the things inside them got in his way. In any case he had fully intended, after a night or two in the hotel, to find a cottage. Two guineas a week instead of seven made a difference over two or three months; more than enough to take one on a tramp steamer to Greece and back, or even Egypt, though things were getting a bit messed up thereabouts these days. Perhaps the old Colonel mightn't get East after all! Grant's good humour returned, and he thought the young woman's face had something generous, spendthrift, beneath the firm bone. Too much so, possibly. Enough anyhow for someone to have taken advantage of it. Then the explanation came in a flash:

the father would have been a war casualty; no time to marry—and he didn't come back.

That's the way it goes, he thought, remembering the quality of her voice which—and he recognised it suddenly—matched the tawny in her hair. A soft but firm voice, fatally kind.

From the curve of the short drive, he felt the house approach, then there it was, a grey stone, plain, with flat windows, a pillared stone porch, some weeds in the gravel, and a faint air over all of tiredness or disuse. When he pulled the bell he listened, like one who did not expect it to work, but an elderly woman appeared, thin, with high cheekbones and an anxious restraint.

"I don't know if he's in," she answered, appearing to think the matter over. "But I'll see. What name will I say?"

"Grant, Mr. Grant. He asked me to call."

"Oh, did he?" She seemed relieved and turned away, but came back after a few paces and showed him into a front sitting-room. There were chintzes on the chairs, old prints on the walls, and the air seemed to have been exuded in still-ness from the dead ivory of the wallpaper. It was not stuffy but he needed moving air. No one came. All of a sudden he felt extraordinarily tired, so that his muscles trembled as he took off his rucksack. In a moment he was angry with him-self for feeling dizzy. This was appalling! He must get out. The door opened and a woman came in.

She was so obviously Martin's sister that she looked to Grant at that dizzy moment like his female apparition gone neurotic, such a whiteness in the pallor of her face, a ghostly brightness about the dark eyes, beneath the black hair. "I am sorry, but my brother is out at the moment." Her voice was hurried but attractive, then anxious . . . He was aware of her eyes on him. They seemed extraordinarily large and to be coming nearer.

"Excuse me," he said, "but I feel a little——" My God, I

28

am going to faint! he thought. He felt the grip of her hand as the deep chair took him. Then she had the sense to fly and he closed his eyes. But no, he was being joggled and rained on. Through the dark mist he saw the face; it was Martin's. A glass was at his mouth; he let it clink against his teeth and then sucked; the spirit went down and he choked a little and gulped, feeling the breath coming back into him in great heaves, his heart thumping, while he stared at the crystal liquid in the tumbler and gradually got control. "I'm sorry——" and he started coughing, grew utterly exhausted, and came round.

"Sit still," said Martin. He handed the tumbler to his sister.

Grant let his head fall back, looked at them, and smiled. "I thought—I was going—to pass out."

"You did," said Martin.

"Ah, did I?" murmured Grant unconcernedly. "The sun —too much sun. I—lost my hat."

"Try some more of this."

"Thank you, I will." He took the tumbler, and, though it shook, got down a good mouthful of the clear liquor. After a few moments he was able to find his voice. "Vodka?"

"Vodka," said Martin, with that dry humour which seemed to seep into his features at ironic moments. "It's the only spirit we have."

Grant was amused also. "That's one thing they make," he ventured.

Martin's sister had now got the window shoved right up and, coming back to Grant, said, "I'll have a cup of tea made for you at once. Then you will stop to dinner."

"No, please——"

"But you will," she said in a white flash and went out.

"I had no intention of troubling you," Grant explained. "All I wanted to say—was just to confirm the—the business about the cairn. I really do not wish in any way to intrude,

and therefore if you would please——" He got to his feet.
"—If you would please," he repeated, gripping the back
of the chair, "tell—uh——"

"Mrs. Sidbury."

"Your sister——"

"She is my sister."

"I beg your pardon. I——"

"I think you had better sit down."

"I'm practically all right now. Thank you very much.
Been very good of you."

"In any case, I think you had better wait until my sister
comes back. Don't you?"

"Well, perhaps," said Grant and he sat down.

"Another drink?"

He deliberately shook his head. "I rather fancy—it's gone
to my head—already," but he hardly smiled.

There was the objective look, which Grant felt on his face,
then Martin went out.

Eyes shut and head back, he blew out gusts of breath
noisily, as if the alcohol had momentarily poisoned him.
Vodka! It was the sort of stuff he *would* have! But now he
was concerned with himself, with cursing himself for being
such a feckless ass. Then suddenly he didn't give a hoot, he
decided, and just rested.

The housekeeper brought tea on a tray, arranged it on an
occasional table before his chair, and withdrew.

It was the simple truth that he preferred tea to any drink
man had invented, though he was appreciative at the proper
time of many wines and pinned his faith to whisky when
life was cold and wet, if always in small quantities, for
alcohol in any guise made him talk excessively, and he
reckoned he knew his weakness. He blew on the tea and,
after hearkening a moment, poured it into his saucer. Now
he blew more carefully, then gulped the lot, just catching a
dribble before it left his beard. Good stuff, excellently

brewed! Life flowed down into him, and slowly up. When Mrs. Sidbury appeared he got to his feet with some assurance.

"Please," she said, with a gesture to his chair. Her movements were both quick and charming, and as she sat down he saw that her face had indeed a marked pallor, but it seemed now almost a natural pallor and he forgot to think that she was neurotic. "Feeling a bit better?" she asked.

"I don't know what came over me," he tried to explain. "Too much sun, perhaps. I was laid up recently. Doctors warned me to take it easy for a while."

"It was hot to-day," she said, "enough to overcome anyone. Have you walked far?"

"No. Only from Kinlochoscar, but I've been pottering about the cairn up there for a while. I—excuse me——" and he got his gold watch out of a waistcoat pocket. His astonishment was ludicrous. "Twenty minutes to seven!" He looked at her as if she had played a trick on him.

She laughed quickly; all her movements were quick and bright, like those of a highly strung person determined to be gay. "You forgot the time!"

"I'm afraid I did!" He laughed also. "That's the worst of archaeology. Sometimes you—you walk out of time; at least, out of the present."

"Oh, are you interested in the Stone Circle?"

"Yes. At least I should like to have a look inside the cairn. Colonel Mackintosh, an authority on this peculiar subject, gave me a letter of introduction, as a matter of fact, to your brother——"

"Oh but I know Colonel Mackintosh! He was here last year!"

"Yes. They were having a look over these parts. He was particularly taken with Clachar."

"And did he tell you that the cairn is haunted?"

"No. It's the kind of—ah—unverified experience that he would be inclined to forget."

She laughed again. "And where are you staying? At Kinlochoscar?"

"No. I couldn't get in there anywhere. So I have arranged to stay in Clachar here. It will be much more convenient. And that's why, though it was so good of you to ask me to stop to dinner, why I——"

"But you must. We are eating in a few minutes. And you'll want a bath." She got up.

As he lay thoughtfully in his bath, Grant decided there was something odd somewhere. She was in her early thirties, he reckoned, and obviously anxious that he should have the meal with them. Perhaps her husband was here—and others. A guest might be a centre of interest—in certain circumstances. He grew more thoughtful. It might not be the cairn that was haunted—not exclusively, anyhow, he decided, feeling much refreshed now and even kicking the water into a gentle wave that lapped his chin. Moods had a habit of invading him with a quick irresistible boyishness. And he was not going to lose his adventurous holiday feeling for anyone.

At dinner, however, there were only the three of them. She talked about the food difficulties, hoped he liked curried rabbit, and, when he refused the beer, made no reference to vodka. Martin poured himself a bottle of beer and seemed more agreeable, though his talk had its easy automatic quality, like something that was intelligent but not felt.

"And where are you staying in Clachar?" Mrs. Sidbury asked.

"Actually I haven't been there yet. It was arranged indirectly: that's why I felt I should have pushed on. But this has been—very kind of you. To tell the truth, I was so taken with that old cairn, that I felt—I thought—I had better make sure there would be no intrusion on my part. I hope," he concluded, looking directly at Martin, "that you don't really mind my doing a bit of excavating up there?"

"Why should I?" said Martin smoothly. "It's in the interest of science, isn't it?"

"Do you expect—I mean, will it take you a long time?" asked his hostess with a quick smile.

"That's just it," said Grant. "It may. I'm not going back before the summer recess. So I have pretty nearly as long as I like."

"How fortunate for you!" said Mrs. Sidbury. "I suppose you have to dig up things very carefully?"

"Yes. Measurements, and photographs, and what not. Colonel Mackintosh will believe me if I say something is three feet five inches, but will look bothered if I record that it's a yard or so."

She laughed. "I must say I rather liked him. When I said it was a pity it had been wet, he felt his sleeves before he agreed. But he has a twinkle."

"And his own bee in his bonnet," added Grant. "When you hear him clear his throat—grumph! grumph!—that's the bee getting under way."

She was clearly delighted with her guest, who, because he was nettled by Martin, set himself to entertain her. The vodka and the bath helped. But over coffee, he asked in direct challenge of Martin's implicit scepticism, "Is it your contention that all archaeological knowledge is valueless?"

"Shall we say," Martin suggested, "rather far-fetched at this time of day."

"It doesn't strike me like that," replied Grant. "On the contrary, I think it is extremely important. I think what is really wrong with us all is that we don't know our own history as human beings, and particularly our earliest history. If we knew that, there—there might be less bees about," he finished in a rush.

"Even atomic bees?"

"Even atomic bees."

"You think so?" Martin spoke without any stress, but with that steady look as if his guest were some particularly large kind of bee complete with legs, antennæ, and other curious features. Then unhurriedly he lit another cigarette.

"But surely knowledge helps, of whatever kind," said Mrs. Sidbury.

"Helps what?" asked Martin, not troubling to look at her.

"Helps everything," she said.

"Everything is nothing," and he dismissed the words with the smoke.

Grant saw in a moment that she could never argue in her brother's terms, that he had her defeated before she opened her mouth, intellectually defeated; the instincts were another matter. Sparks would fly on occasion; her sparks, anyway: he was simply deadly. She had plainly arranged this meal against her brother's wish.

Martin's eyebrows moved, remarking as it were: Really? This would have been sufficient to stir Grant like a lash, were it not for something genuinely uncaring in Martin's deeper attitude. He was not being cynical or supercilious; he was just uncaring and polite as need be. Yet deep beyond plumbing, Grant was aware of an annihilating insult to the basis of human living.

"How can everything be nothing?" asked Mrs. Sidbury. "I may be dull but I think that's absurd. Donald has merely a habit of making those sweeping statements," she explained to her guest.

"In a sense, I suppose, there's got to be selection," her guest admitted. "If I find nothing new in the cairn, then the everything that is the cairn might be deemed nothing much by Colonel Mackintosh. In that sense, everything might be nothing. But—to say that everything is in fact nothing——" He was amused and plucked an elusive piece of cigarette tobacco from his lower lip.

34

"Do you really expect to find something new?" asked Mrs. Sidbury.

"Of course," he answered. "I hope to find something quite astonishing."

"Splendid! May I ask—what?"

"Ah!" Grant was mysterious. "The truth is," he went on confidentially, "I never do open anything—much less a cairn—but I find something, *if* I'm looking for it. That's the whole secret."

"You find what you look for?" asked Martin.

"Yes," replied Grant at once, "and I don't place it there beforehand, actually or metaphysically."

Martin glanced at him and smiled slowly. "For instance?"

"We had been discussing the possible proceedings when a place like the cairn up there was being ceremonially used, and a colleague asked me, 'Have you read the Iliad lately?' The question stuck in my head. So one night I opened the book—at the last paragraph. It's the description, you know, of the burial of Hector. They burnt his body on an enormous pyre of wood; then, when they wanted to get at his bones, there were still burning spots so they subdued these *with bright wine*. Then it tells how his comrades gathered his white bones, with tears running down their cheeks, and placed them in a *golden urn*, wrapped in soft purple, and placed the urn in a grave and piled over it a *huge cairn of stones*; and after that they went and feasted right well in noble feast at the palace of Priam."

"How remarkable! And do you really think something like that happened—up there at the Stone Circle?" asked Mrs. Sidbury.

"With the noble feast afterwards down here? Who knows?" said Grant.

"The same period?" asked Martin.

"It might be, if not the same Age. We were always a few centuries behind. The Iliad is clearly the height of the

Bronze Age. The cairn up there was the Age before, the Neolithic. But whether the axe-head was made of polished stone or bronze may not imply a vast difference in the human head. I am inclined to think not, for reasons which I could elaborate."

"You could?"

"Yes, I could," replied Grant at once. "I crossed over the Highlands from east to west last time I was up, and saw on the east coast a four-plough tractor in operation and on the west a foot-plough that, but for its iron tip, might have come straight from the Stone Age."

"Tell me," said Mrs. Sidbury, "do you really expect to find a golden urn?"

Grant laughed, his mounting intensity at once broken. "I may find a pot—but perhaps not of gold!"

"But, as you said, who knows?"

"Who knows," he repeated.

"Some more coffee?"

"No, thank you. And I really must go now."

"Well, we mustn't keep you. But please do look in and tell us how you are getting on. I am quite thrilled. And if we can possibly help——" She looked at her brother.

He nodded just perceptibly.

As he went on his way towards the houses of Clachar, Grant knew that it was something far other than a cairn that worried Martin. Colonel Mackintosh had said that Martin's father, for some local or sentimental reason, had hoped that no one would press for the cairn to be opened up, but that with young Martin it was different. It was! The fellow merely doesn't want anyone around, thought Grant, but I'm here and to blazes with him! It was a lovely evening for such an invigorating and adventurous thought, and he proceeded, refreshed and in good spirit.

5

Perhaps the exhausting and exciting nature of his day had induced a certain heightening even in his vision, for the houses of Clachar had, it seemed to him, a remarkable aptness to their location. Each had grown up in its own place and was well content, taking to the lie of the ground as a man might who had time to sit down, turning a gable here like a shoulder and a front there like a face. Where the ground tumbled in antique frolic the grass was thick and lush with wild flowers, and the scent from uncountable blossoms came to his nostrils like an immortal essence. An old tethered dun cow stared at him over a knoll. The wandering footpath found in the end a wooden footbridge and he looked down into the clear water that seemed a warm brown. Some way below him boys were wading in a pool, perhaps looking for sea-trout which the tide had left behind. Their voices were shrill and yet strangely harmonious in the flat long-shadowed evening light. All at once, as, having straightened himself, he stood still and involuntarily listened, he had the odd illusion of that extra dimension into which our solid world stands back, and this experience, as always, had for him an air of beneficence and strange beauty.

His face turned to the west and for a moment an orange light shone on it, then he crossed the small bridge and went up towards the house to which the young woman had pointed. A big red cock by the gable-end lifted a yellow leg in high and brittle dignity, said "Kok—kok?" and winked. Along the front wall ran a narrow strip of flowers, hedged in with boxwood, a miniature border of colour all weeded and tidy, broken by the blue flagstone before the door. As he stepped lightly on the stone and raised his hand to knock, he heard an old woman's voice say, "Now will you go to sleep! It's ashamed you should be of yourself at this time of night and you not sleeping."

"Granny, tell me, does the standing stone stop standing when it's dark and go walking and walking away off?"

"Perhaps it's not away off it goes. But one thing is certain: it never comes near little girls who are good and go to sleep."

"I'm good, amn't I, Granny?"

"You're only just middling good. But if you went to sleep, then you would be good indeed, and it's the other way the stone would go altogether."

"Tell me a story, Granny."

As the old woman was asking the young one what story she would like, Grant's fist slowly fell and he looked around to make sure he was not being overseen, standing there as the queer stranger who didn't knock. The blue cat on the low garden wall had closed its eyes, and now with its whiskers sticking out from its squashed features it looked for all the world as if it had laughed in its sleep and forgotten to put its face right.

"The Silver Bough," answered the child.

"Is it that one again? Very well," said the old woman. "Once upon a time there was a king and he was walking by his palace wall when who should he see but a young man passing by, and the young man held in his hand a silver branch—all right, all right," the old woman interrupted herself as if she had been corrected, "a silver bough. He held in his hand a silver bough, and it was the branch of an apple tree, and from it there hung nine golden apples, and when he shook the branch, the nine golden apples hit against each other, and made the sweetest music the king had ever heard in all his life. So sweet was the music that the king forgot all his cares, and they departed from his mind, and he thought

38

the world was fresh and beautiful. The king asked the young man if he would sell the branch to him, and the young man said he would, but if so it would not be for money he would sell it. What would it be for? asked the king. And the young man said it will be for your wife and your son and your little young daughter. And the king said in the end that he could have his wife and his son and his little young daughter, and so it was agreed between them, and the king got the silver bough. But when the king went and told his wife and his son and his little young daughter what he had done, then they were very sad, for they liked being with the king in the palace and didn't want to go away. It was the sadness that came upon them then, but in the middle of it what should the king do but shake the silver bough, and the sweet music sang from it again, and all sadness and sorrow departed, and the king's wife and his son and his little young daughter went willingly away with the young man. Now it was all right for a time, and for another time, because the king had his silver bough, but by the end of a year and a day he was missing his wife and his son and his little young daughter, and missing them very much he was, and soon he could not do without them any more, and so he set off to find them. Off he went, and on, and far away, and when at last he was very tired, a cloud came about him like the darkness and he fell into a deep sleep. Then he awoke and lo! there was a palace, and a wonderful palace it was, set on a great dim plain, and he went into the palace and who should he meet but Mananan himself, the one who looks after the seas of the world—for wasn't it Mananan who had come in disguise as the young man with the silver bough in his hand. So the king knew he was on the right track now, and he spoke to Mananan, and to Mananan's wife, for she was there also, and told why he had come. And they understood that, for they were not bad people but only the great ones who can do what they like, except for the one thing they mustn't

39

ever do, not even the greatest though he is a king itself or a lord of the seas, and that is he must never be unkind to the stranger who enters at his door. So they listened to the king and nodded and gave an order to the palace servant, and soon walking down the great stairs towards them came the king's wife and his son and his little young daughter, and right glad he was to see them, but no gladder than they were to see him. Well, at last the time came for them to go to sleep, and to sleep they went in Mananan's palace, for what would anyone be without sleep? And then—and then—the morning came, and lo! there was no Mananan's palace, it had all vanished away, and the great dim plain had vanished away, too, and where were they but back once more in their own palace, all of them together, as if they had never left it, but behold! hanging on the wall in the morning sunlight was the silver bough with the nine golden apples on it."

"That place where the palace of Mananan vanished away, was it like a moor and stones on it?"

"It was a bare moor and there was no stones on it as far as ever I heard."

"Granny—sing the song of the Silver Bough."

"Only if you promise to compose yourself and keep your hands in. For if your mother comes home and finds you still awake, it's not music you'll catch."

The lullaby the old woman crooned was about as old as the soil the Silver Bough grew out of and as deep, and Grant knew when it had taken the child away by the slowing of the old woman's voice. In the silence, he knocked gently.

She came to the door with a wondering expression which steadied on him as he greeted her, then her eyes brightened, but at the same time with a quickened concern she asked, "Were you knocking before?"

"No."

She nodded, relieved at that, and hospitably invited him into the parlour, where the light was dim but soft, with a round table in the middle of the room, gilt ornaments on the mantelpiece, and an armchair of slippery horsehair upon which he was invited to sit.

"My grandchild was telling me about you," she said, and it took him a moment to fit the word 'grandchild' to the red-haired woman, but already he felt at home. There was a kindliness about the old lady, a brightness of eye and movement, and at the same time such an air of practical good sense that he knew he could go on talking to her with ease and pleasure.

"Anna was thinking the place was not good enough for you, what with water no nearer than the well and food that's difficult to get, but I said to her that you would be the best judge of that. We can't have what we haven't got."

He laughed. "And I wouldn't be surprised but you may have some things that we haven't got. I haven't eaten a fresh egg for three months."

"Fresh eggs, is it? Och!" She lifted her hands and dropped them. "There's as many eggs as you can eat, and we have our own cow, so there's milk and cream, and butter and crowdie. Indeed when sometimes the milk is going wrong on me I'll be thinking of the starving children in the world, and sad I'll be, and wishful I could give the poor things some of it."

Now his doctor had told him to stuff himself with as many eggs and as much fresh milk as he could naturally accommodate, and when he told Mrs. Cameron this, she made a dramatic little gesture as though words failed her, and he laughed again. But something had also been worrying her and now, emboldened, she said, "Won't you let me help you take that thing off your back?"

He dropped the rucksack to the floor and she said, "Before you make up your mind, just come and see your bedroom."

"Could I have this sitting-room to myself?" he asked. "I'll have a lot of writing and——"

"Surely, surely," she said. "And no one to trouble you."

Before the steep narrow stairs, she waited for him to go up, but he bowed her before him. She was a small woman and climbed actively. At the top he complimented her on her youth. "I feel as young as I look," she said, "and I won't be seventy until next month."

"Good for you! And you don't look it."

"Och, I'm only a great-grandmother so far. Now this is your room."

It had a light-coloured wallpaper, a wash-basin and ewer in brightly-patterned blue, and a solid old-fashioned wooden bed. The window was open and the linen smelt faintly of wild thyme. "Perfect," he said.

"There's a little placie here." She opened what looked like a cupboard door beyond the bed in the wall towards the stairs. It was a tiny room with a skylight window and he thought of it as an impossibly small dressing-room. His eye landed on a low boxed-in piece of furniture that looked like an antique in commodes. When he saw that it had a lid on top, he smiled with his back to her.

"We are glad to do what we can," she said as he closed the door.

"Well, it'll do me fine, and I'll be very glad to stay with you, Mrs. Cameron, if you'll have me."

"If you take us as you find us, it will be a pleasure," she assured him. "And now I'll hurry and get you something to eat."

But he explained that he had had supper and they settled on a glass of milk. She brought it to the sitting-room on a tray with a plate of biscuits.

"I might be staying a long time, perhaps two months," he said. "I hope that's all right?"

"I hope so indeed," she said. "But you'll see how you get on with us."

"I'll risk that! And now about paying you, for we may as well settle that, too."

"Och, never mind just now. We'll be seeing later what you think it's worth, for it's not much we'll have for you, I'm warning you!"

"Have you never had anyone staying with you?"

"Oh yes. The last I had was two years ago, but there was the long spell of the war when I had nobody, though Anna was good to me and made me an allowance. She was in the A.T.S., but then—she had to come home."

He immediately thought of the child.

"She should be home now, but she went in to Kinlochoscar for some things. She knows how to attend to a gentleman, because she was in service before she was called up. And she's been working in the hotel, but she always wanted to come home at night to see the child, and that was not easy and she got run down, but she's better now, and, to tell the truth, I would rather see her occupied at home, for a spell whatever. She has ever been a good girl to me."

"In that case, we should all be suited," he said lightly but with understanding.

"Indeed that's what I was hoping," she responded at once. "And next month, as I'm always saying, I'll be independent."

"Really?"

"Yes. My birthday falls on a Friday, and they're telling me I'll be able to draw my first old age pension on that day."

"We'll make it a spree!" he said.

When she had gone he stood looking out of the window, touched deeply by something brave and nameless at the end of his long journey.

6

In the morning Simon Grant felt fresh and sprightly. The middle part of the night hadn't been too good, but now he realised that he had fallen into a second deep sleep, and that, against the chances, was enough to make him more happy than if he had been victorious in a difficult argument. The cat had obviously licked up her porridge and milk and been shooed to the wall on which the sun was shining. It was going to be another glorious day. "And where were you all night?" But the cat bore his attentions with a sleepy indifference, arching her back only when she had to. The cock, in his polite fashion, was finding imaginary grain beside the peat stack for those members of his harem who wished to believe him. Grant wandered to the byre and found that the cow was already out at pasture. After a look behind him, he entered. The stall had not yet been cleaned, and the manure smell had a certain prehistoric thickness which he found not altogether disagreeable, reminding him as it did of the affiliations of *homo sapiens* with the animal kingdom.

Wandering happily back, he encountered Mrs. Cameron on the doorstep. There were pleasant good mornings, and inquiries about sleep, and she told him that his porridge was in. He had insisted on porridge, and not entirely because it might help his hostess in her food problems. Beside the plate was a bowl of milk distinctly yellow in colour. It stuck to his spoon. As it happened, he was fonder of cream than a cat, and the porridge was well boiled.

When Anna came in with bacon and two eggs, he

chuckled, excused himself, glanced at the plate and laughed. "I can't," he said, "I just can't!"

The warmth came into her face. "We have plenty of eggs."

"But I couldn't. You must take one back at least."

Mrs. Cameron appeared and asked what was two eggs for a grown man, and besides there was the old rule: one could just leave what one couldn't take. But one couldn't leave an egg! The thing, as he suddenly saw, had become moral. But Mrs. Cameron saw it differently. "They first shrink your stomach," she said, "and then make it a sin to leave an egg." Laughter stayed with him.

The meal over, he explained to Mrs. Cameron that he now wished to go to Kinlochoscar for his suitcase, in which were his ration books. She assured him that the bus could bring it to-morrow, for it ran three times a week between Kinlochoscar and Clachar. When they had discussed the local travelling and postal arrangements, he came at the matter which was nearer his mind. In a few words he explained why he needed labour to help him in digging up old cairns. Was there any such labour available? While she was being thoughtful about this, he said, "As a matter of fact, I was recommended to a woman who has a son working for the County Council, taking stones out of the stream. Do you know her?"

"You mean Mrs. Mackenzie and her son Foolish Andie?"

"I could see he was a bit—foolish, yes."

She was looking at him. "Who recommended you to that?"

"It was Mr. Martin of Clachar House."

A curious reserve invaded her face.

"Do you know him?"

"I met him yesterday. I had to get permission from him, seeing the cairn I want to open up is on his land."

45

"I see," she said, and she stared out of the window. "Did you get the permission?"

"Yes, I think so."

"You have spoken to Mrs. Mackenzie?"

"I'm afraid I have. It's rather been worrying me off and on, because—it makes one feel sort of awkward."

She nodded. "He's a good worker. You need have no fear of that. And she's a deserving woman. She'll get him to do just what you want, if it's simple digging or stone-lifting. She has had a very hard life, very. It's a sad story. If you could give him something to do it would help her, and she needs all she can get."

"Well, if you say so, I could take him on for a week and could see how he did."

"That might be the best plan," she agreed. "And if you needed better help, I could see what I could do."

"Thank you very much. That's fine."

But as he went up the road he wondered why she had quietened so unexpectedly. It clearly had something to do with Martin, and his dream and restlessness in the middle night came back to him. Martin had had a brown bear on a chain and as he made it perform, the bear turned its head and it had the idiot's features. It was not, however, the monstrous grotesque beast that had worried him, it was Martin's face. There was something in the face that was—the word or thought now came spontaneously—annihilating, and the more so because, in a way beyond explaining, it was not actively annihilating. The face had wakened him.

That Martin clearly did not want him about the place did not worry him; on the contrary, it made him all the more determined to go on with the work, for Martin's attitude was an insult to the spirit of archaeology which was concerned with deciphering the hidden part of the story of man's invasion of the earth. It was the fundamental story, the central drama, round which all the other sciences were

46

grouped as lights about a stage. That any man should arrogate to himself the power to switch off the central bulb. . . .

He should have got his permission in writing. So much was axiomatic. I am making a bad beginning, he thought. And now there was this business of the idiot. Excruciating! For what would they think, the Colonel and the others? It would be the joke of the club. Gales of laughter. Did you hear the latest about Simple Simon? He knew they called him Simple Simon. Blair, the petrologist, made a cult of retailing titbits about Simple Simon which he hadn't the wit to make up himself. Usually he was more than a match for Blair, but they all knew, with a schoolboy cunning, how to work up to his weakness, which was a sudden consuming wrath in a torrent of spluttering language. With a touch of pricking heat, he dismissed them—for he was never inwardly dominated by them—and came back to his immediate problem.

To employ an imbecile on work requiring so fine an exercise of care and discrimination was, he realised, despite his extraordinary thoughts during the night, quite impossible. That Martin, who obviously suffered from too much intelligence, should have suggested it was enough to make wrath bubble. He had never really intended to employ him—until he had had these fantastic night thoughts, about the idiot as a prehistoric personation. Now, in the daylight, he could afford to show some ordinary sense for a change.

Every now and then his eye had been lifting to the stream, and at last he saw them. A primitive grouping right enough! A Paleolithic hurtling of stones! The glottal stops of the missing link! . . . There *had* been something in his dream! He was smiling vaguely in an embarrassed way as at last he approached the woman. Except for the automatic movement of fingers and needles, she sat watching his approach like a figure in softstone. Her still, heavy face was a dumb question in the distance. He waded up against it and cheerfully bade her good morning. She got up but he made her sit down again, aware that she had read his face. That she had had to become skilled in this art was more than embarrassing, it was pathetic, a tragic comment on life. He moved about, considered the stones geologically, and saw the idiot pause to stare at him and then shift his glance to his mother with a sort of wondering cunning or gleam of primitive intelligence and vague noises. "It's all right, Andrew," she said in a quiet natural voice, with a simple nod and a glance of her eyes that set him to work again.

"Well, Mrs. Mackenzie, I don't think really that I'll need your son's help. I—I have been thinking it over, and actually I would need someone with some knowledge of the work. It's special work and—and therefore I would need someone who knew just what to do." He went on to express the same idea in other words, for she remained completely silent.

"Very well," she said when he had finished. Her fingers began to work of their own accord; she did not look at them as they worked.

Five minutes later he left her, smiling vaguely as he called himself a Mousterian ass, for he had engaged Foolish Andie for a week's labour beginning next Wednesday, which was five days hence. Also he had engaged her to knit him two pairs of stockings and promised to provide the coupons for the wool.

Presently he was enjoying the joke himself and felt oddly relieved. The only thing to do with colonels and petrologists and landowners was to challenge them on their own lake middens. And after all there *was* a psychological or realistic argument in employing someone of primitive intelligence inasmuch as one might test his reactions, if any, to a primitive creation like the chamber inside a cairn! That might put at least the unimaginative Blair on his back—even if the fellow hadn't a real back to be put on.

The internal argument grew until it burst, for it was a lovely morning and the sky serene. These five days would give him time to do preliminary mapping and hunting for local lore on an exhaustive scale, while by the end of them a telegram should have brought him his box of gear. Blessedly, there was no hurry in the world, and he was going to prove himself no "barrow-digger", that term of abuse for the old antiquary who thought he could tear the secret out of the heart of a barrow or cairn in a few hours by digging a hole in from the top!

The eye that now kept lifting to the landscape was the archaeological eye, the trained observing eye which found the most delightful interest in its exercise. Nothing was too large in mountain conformation nor too small in rabbit scrape to fail to be read like print. His research had in fact been mostly field-work, and in map-making he excelled, being surprisingly ingenious where correlations were involved. He could speak with warmth on the geographical approach to his subject, and here he was to-day with a spot of actual digging on his hands and all to himself. It made him feel like a small boy with a tight secret.

The postmaster at Kinlochoscar accepted his telegram and inquired how he had fared in getting a lodging. Grant told him he had fared extremely well. When the postmaster had extracted the detail he said, "She has the girl and the child staying with her. Ay, a sad business." "You don't feel it's sad," replied Grant, "but I must be off. I want to get a car. Thank you and good day."

The hotel manageress was delighted to hear of his success, but when she had got the detail she said, "Anna Cameron is a very nice girl and you should be all right there."

"I'm sure I shall," replied Grant so genially that he dropped his hat.

She had a car, too, which she could let him have at once. "Or are you staying for lunch?"

"No, I said I would be home for lunch," He looked at his watch. "But perhaps—a glass of sherry?"

"Certainly." She pressed a button.

"Oh and by the way, I've just sent a telegram for a box, a wooden trunk. It has some of my working gear. If you happen to see it lying about anywhere, would you——"

"Surely."

"Bless you!" And he went to the lounge to await his sherry.

7

"Y ou must always come round by the boathouse,"
said Mrs. Sidbury.

Simon Grant thanked her very much. "I did not
realise it was so steep."

"The local people use it occasionally," she said with a
glance at the path which came tumbling down to the beach.
"But if you go round by the boathouse, it's quite simple."

"I was just wanting to have a look at the caves," he
explained. "I find the whole place remarkably interesting."

"Good! We enjoyed your visit. I hope you are quite——?"

"Absolutely. I merely overdid it. Very sorry to have
troubled you."

"No trouble at all, and I like to shake up Donald occasionally!" She had a quick fly-away manner which at the
moment was attractively irresponsible. She swung a green
bathing cap round her right hand. A towel hung from the
crook of her left arm.

"It was very good of you," he murmured, uncertain now
about going on, for she was obviously on her way to bathe.
But she smiled at his hesitation and said she would act as his
guide. She spoke rapidly, telling him how as children they
always bathed from the Monster Cove. "Donald once said he
saw a mermaid there. It was a summer twilight and he was
all alone, aged eleven." The memory gave her a pleasantly
perverse delight, and Grant could not help observing that
she had no visible bathing costume. "See those low rocks?"

"Yes," he replied, noting what looked like a few yards of
skerry.

"She was sitting on that rock combing her long golden hair."

"The mermaid?"

"Yes." Her quick bright laughter had something in it nervous and brittle. He wondered if she was deliberately exaggerating.

"They always do have long golden hair," he suggested.

"Yes, too bad, isn't it?" She was black as a blackbird but her face was white and vivid. "It's nice all the same to sit on the rock and sun-bathe. We had a game, too. We would stare and stare into the Cove until the monster formed in the dark cavern."

"Why the monster?"

"Goodness knows," said Mrs. Sidbury. "But I am still a little uncertain. I wouldn't, for example, even now sit with my back to the Cove the whole time."

"No?"

"Oh no! Whoo—no!" She swung away nimbly on her white canvas shoes, her light dress with its green dragons throwing a dancer's whirl about her bare legs.

Grant, though embarrassed, was definitely not afraid of her. Indeed he joined in her laughter, if, as it were, separately. And presently when she asked him if *he* had any notion why it had been called the Monster Cove, he said he might have. Hitherto she had hardly looked at him, but now she gave him a questing glance. Indeed he felt her glance steady for a moment on his face. Her dark lashes were long as spiders' legs.

"You see, away back in Paleolithic times, in a place like this, men would naturally stay in caves. The first men did whenever they could."

"Paleolithic?"

"Merely the name for the Old Stone Age. We have picked up chipped bits of flint or stone that they used as tools or weapons. As time went on, they learned to chip more neatly, until at last in the New Stone Age or Neolithic Age they not only chipped but ground their stones and made a very nice job of them, too, a real craftsman's job. They also domesticated the farm animals. They were the fellows of the Neolithic Age who built the cairn up there."

"Really?" She was now quite serious. "And how long ago was all that?"

"Well." He smiled. "Talking generally, the Paleolithic Age goes back—what?—200,000 years? Or half a million, if you like. But the Neolithic Age lasted only six or seven thousand years and finished before the Bronze Age, which began, let us say, about 1800 B.C. in Britain. All very rough and ready, with different times for different places, and an odd thousand years or two before the Bronze Age might hardly be noticed anywhere." He glanced at her and she smiled, but quickly as though to get the smile over.

"So——"

"So I should say it's fairly certain that this place has been continuously settled from Neolithic times. It's that kind of place."

"It is," she agreed with a look at the cave mouth.

"From living in caves, some men—the more progressive, shall we say—would move over to Clachar and build huts there, round huts. We know quite a lot about the sort of huts they built. And that would ease the housing problem."

"A housing problem even then?"

"The housing problem and the food problem—the eternal twins."

"We don't seem to have advanced much, do we? That's the Monster Cove."

The entrance was an irregular arch some twelve feet high and the eye went in over the shingle until the light grew dim.

"It turns to the left after a bit," she explained. "We always took candles."

"So you have been in?"

53

"Oh yes. As children, yes, but—there's a smaller cave, with a sort of ghostly gleam——"

"You mean white? A limestone white?" He looked incredulous.

"It was our ghost anyway, by the entrance. I never went in."

"Do you mind if I do?"

"But you haven't a candle."

"I have an electric torch."

"May I go with you?"

They went forward on the noisy shingle. At first there were ledges on the left, and they were rounding these to face the inner darkness when the roof was split by a rocketing sound, terrifying in its reverberating swiftness. She cried out before she could stop herself.

"The pigeons," she gasped, "I forgot!"

As Grant's own heart had gone into his throat, he smiled back. He switched on his torch and moved its beam in circles. No more pigeons. As they went forward, the roof came down to meet them, the dark walls narrowed in. They waded heavily against a wave of shingle that slithered and cried with an echoing cry and the roof came so low that they stooped. Then the shingle went more quietly the other way and there was no roof but only an inner darkness.

They involuntarily stood, the cave swelling out from their breasts into a largeness that was quiet, with eyes in the cave that could pierce the dark, watching the two vulnerable creatures adventuring between the two worlds.

As the beam of light crept along the wall, Mrs. Sidbury stood very close to Grant. In the moment when she saw her girlhood's ghost, something invisible moved with so heavy and ominous a noise—a slap and stone-crack—that she cried out in real terror and gripped his left arm. He made raucous yells as he backed away, defiant and repelling, and caught two gleaming eyes against the beam. In over-swift anxiety to check the sweep of the beam he hit his leg with the torch and it fell to the ground and went out. He groped about, yelling louder than ever, became aware of Mrs. Sidbury's condition, got a blind clawing grip on her breast which all but demented her, and then had her by the arm, making for the dimness, slithering down the wave of shingle, stumbling, getting up, and entering once more the blazing sunlight.

She looked ravaged and, leaving him, staggered towards the low rock, and sat against it with bent head as if about to be sick. Grant felt very ashamed of himself. It had probably been nothing more than a damned seal. But panic had got him for a moment! His hands were trembling. Disgusting, absolutely disgusting! A seal—or some such timid brute. All at once she lay over. He went towards her.

She lay on her right side, her knees towards her chin, eyes closed. But despite the dead pallor of her face, she had not passed out. Her eyes opened, she smiled faintly and murmured, "Leave me, please."

He straightened himself and withdrew.

Not knowing what to do, he stood looking at the sea. glanced back at her, moved restlessly, began to smile, to screw his face fiercely, deeply embarrassed, ashamed of himself, aware that he did not know what on earth to do with the woman. She was highly strung, but there was something taking about her, an overlaid innocence somewhere that nothing would ever quite kill until it killed her. His anger getting the better of him, he approached the cave, entered, went up the slow wave of slithering shingle and stood on the threshold of the dark; felt in his pocket for matches, struck one and brought the solid darkness against him. As he lifted the match it went out and he was blinded except for gleam-points that it took him a moment to realise were after-effects of the flame. He struck two matches and more slowly held them aloft. White on the floor in front; the flame burnt his fingers; the matches scattered and went out, and the box dropped from his left hand. He made a noise that was a challenging growl and hearkened with every hair on his head and bone in his body. Then he knew, as by a memory of its twisted shape: it was her towel. On hands and knees he went forward like an animal, listening, waiting for the pounce, his mouth as dry as leather. A hand landed on the towel, drew it to him, against his breast; he got up, began to back away, and presently was roaring down the stones. She was standing by the rock, and the tumbled black hair about the white face gave her in his blinking eyes a sort of still madness, the stillness of a figure on another and stranger shore.

After the pitch darkness, the light, intensified by reflection from the calm sea, was certainly very strong, so strong that the calmness of the sea itself was strange, as was the shore, and the low dark skerry. Slim and vulnerable, fragile and looking over at him, with a tragic spirit-face. He blinked hard and went towards her. The green things on her light dress *were* dragons; then his eyes lifted higher. "You dropped your towel."

As she caught the towel it unrolled and two negligible pieces of green bathing costume fell on the pebbles by the rock. "Where?"

"Inside."

"How did you find it in the dark?"

"Feeling all right now?"

"Shall we sit down?"

They sat down. "It was probably a seal," he said. "The bulb in the torch must have burst, but I have another one. In fact, two. One acts like a lantern. You carry it by a handle. It's very handy."

Her head moved in acknowledgement.

"There are other caves, I understand?" he said.

"Two more, but they do not go so far in. They are quite innocent . . . That's the old word we had."

"It's quite a good word."

"Whatever it means." She added, not looking at him, "You must not mind Donald. I wanted to say that."

He had the feeling that was what she had wanted to say—and all she had wanted to say—from the beginning.

"I don't. Only I'm not quite sure whether in fact I have permission to open the cairn. I feel he does not want me to."

"That doesn't matter. He would never interfere. So please go on."

"Thank you. But—why doesn't he want me to?"

"He doesn't care whether you open it or not. It's just that he doesn't want people around. He—he—he doesn't want anybody interfering. There is that, still. That's something."

"You want him to be interfered with?"

"Yes. And I don't care how!" Her voice rose slightly.

The role being cast for him was not a very high or complimentary one. "Not too pleasant for me, is it?"

"But you don't mind? If you could help . . . but perhaps you would mind . . . Yes, I see."

"I would help if I could. Only, I'm not very good at—psychological situations. I get worked up sometimes."

"That wouldn't matter. That's all to the good." She began picking pebbles, growing bodily restless again, nervous, after her strange calm.

His admission that he got worked up had embarrassed him in the moment of its utterance, like an unexpected confession. He watched her picking the pebbles and throwing them away; observed her profile. Her silence was a suppressed cry which he almost heard.

"You see," she said, "he's not interested in anything, least of all himself. He just—goes about. It's terrible. I hope you don't think it's too awful of me talking like this."

"No," he said, "no," and he picked up a pebble himself, but did not throw it away; he automatically examined it. Water action had made it beautifully smooth. "Did something happen to him?"

"Yes. It was the war. Finally—a prisoners' camp." She looked up and away. Her fist gripped a pebble and he read the fine bones of the knuckles through the skin.

"Where? In Germany?"

"No. The East."

He waited, but she could not wait long. "I don't know what they did to him—or what he did." She could not bear it and jumped up with a cry and a wild gesture as if she had been hit. "Forgive me!" she cried and walked off.

He looked at the towel and the two pieces of costume strewn about the stones; he looked at her back, her bare legs, at her head which bent with the movement of a wild filly about to bolt. Her footsteps did actually quicken; then they slackened and she drifted on, the sea beyond her, the green islands in the blue. At last she stopped and looked back along the shore. He picked up the towel, tucked the bathing costume inside its folds, and went towards her. Before he had gone very far the lower part of the costume fell out of the towel. He poked it in again, with an increasing sense of strangeness, of impossible intimacy.

"I'm sorry to have troubled you so much," she said, smiling, not looking at him. As she took her belongings, he observed that her hands quivered. "It was that Cove."

"Never mind about it," he said. "There's still your cap, but I'll find it when I go back with a torch."

"Oh yes, my cap!" She laughed a broken note or two. "I'm ashamed of myself."

"Never mind about that," he said in a spontaneous way, smiling, feeling friendly and kind.

She gave him a quick glance. "Thank you very much." Then she went on.

8

That evening he found Mrs. Cameron prepared to talk about many things, including the caves, but when he came to the folk in Clachar House, at once she showed reserve; in fact, she distinctly listened as though to make sure Anna wasn't within hearing.

She began with "the family", for it was an old family and a good one, she said. She spoke with a curious solemnity; there was something beyond her words, far off, and though this was mystery to him, he did not dislike it; on the contrary it built up forms and shapes distant but strangely objective and he had the odd illusion of seeing them moving about as figures move under destiny. Never a big family, never a chief with a clan, yet "a good family", and always in their generations there were those of them who fought in wars in distant lands. One of them, who was a general, fought in the Peninsular War and married a Spanish wife. It was at this point that Grant became slightly excited, but when he asked her what part of Spain the wife came from, she replied that she did not know. "It must have been the north of Spain of course!" he said. "Perhaps it was," she answered. "All I know is that they said she was very dark and very beautiful and she came from Spain." "Quite so, quite so. Don't let me interrupt you." But he interrupted her several times, for he was deeply interested in the question of race, not in the modern national sense but just in race, and at the moment in the prehistoric tracing of race along the line of the megalithic culture, all the west-coast seaway from Spain to Clachar. He expected to find a skull like

Martin's or his sister's in the cairn. Discreetly he regarded the shape of Mrs. Cameron's head. . . .

With a slight sense of shock he realised she was now talking of Martin. " . . . a brave soldier, though never a regular soldier, like those before him. But he was in the Territorials, and some liked him as an officer and some didn't. They said he was not too reliable—I don't know. He had some queer opinions they said, and once there was a terrible row between him and the old Colonel of the regiment, but I don't know." She suddenly stopped, as if her objective vision had blurred. He looked at her quiet but strangely mournful expression and felt baffled.

"He was a brave soldier?"

"Yes. He was decorated."

"What for?"

"Bravery on the field. They say he should have got the V.C."

"What did he get?"

"The M.C. He saved the life of a local boy, he carried him on his back."

Though it remained quiet and contained, her expression was now beginning to embarrass him.

"He wasn't captured at Dunkirk?"

"No. He fought through that and came home." She lifted her eyes to the window.

"Then he went out East?"

"After a time, yes. Since he came back he has been strange. They say he walks at night along the shores." She was going to add something when Anna passed the window. "I have been keeping you with all my talk," she said apologetically.

"I have enjoyed the talk very much. You have no idea how interesting I find it."

"Have you been talking with old Fachie yet?"

"Yes. We've had a few words."

"A few words! Do you mean to say you were able to get away from him?"

She was herself again and he chuckled.

But when she had gone out, he could not help wondering what other odd things Martin did besides wander along the shore at night. For a time he stood staring through the window, aware of the silent wash of man's history as of tides on shores, all the shores of the world. The evening was calm and silent, and its green light mounted the tumbled ground beyond the stream and caught the stone chimney of a concealed cottage, from which a clean blue smoke rose untroubled. The blue evoked a memory of the sea around an Aegean island. A woman's voice in the distance cried her young son home. A dog barked. He looked about him, saw his hat, and went out.

Fachie was going round the gable-end of his thatched cottage, his small old body bent like a bow, moving slowly as if shepherding invisible things into the house for the night. It wouldn't be dark until after eleven, and even then a very deep dusk rather than a true darkness. The half-light, with its glimmer, had always had for him a curious historic reality, as though the world in this quiet hour turned itself into a stage whereon all that had been could once more be, but invisibly now and therefore magically. The word "magic" was as professionally real to him as the word "atom" to a physicist. He knew his learned theories. But, unlike the physicist, he had to translate his concepts in terms of human behaviour. He did not dislike doing this but he had to be very wary in doing it, or they would not permit him, even in method, the use of the word "scientific".

The trouble with this half-light was that it made the word "scientific" magical, and as the mood of the twilight grew in its airy and subtle delight, a silent and delicious mockery translated "scientific" into a mumbo-jumbo word, stripped its portentous solemnity from it and left it naked as any totem-pole. Once he had written an essay called "The Heresy of the Twilight", but feeling that its irony was insufficiently concealed and its wit concealed only too well, he had modestly refrained from offering it for publication.

From his medley of self-evolving thoughts, he awoke to find himself well away from Clachar, having followed a path which had brought him near the base of the first inland hill. Perhaps the sight of Fachie had unconsciously been heading him towards what that little old man had described as "the robbers' glen". He had got some old lore out of Fachie, though most of his talk had been of boyhood happenings, interesting but of no archaeological value. In talking to old inhabitants, one often went through the whole midden without unearthing the smallest of small finds; yet one had to be as patient and attentive as though excavating a real midden. But he had not properly begun on Fachie yet. So far, two points of interest had cropped up. The first referred to an uncouth human figure which haunted the Stone Circle. Mrs. Sidbury had said something about this, which, though he joked about it at the time, he had mentally noted. Fachie had not been too willing to talk, apparently because it was "just old blethers", but he had given the figure a name—*Urisk*. This hairy monstrous man of popular Gaelic legend lived in the cairn and came out only at night. "Ach, they would believe anything in the old days," said Fachie, with a side glance at the learned one beside him. "No one believes it now at all at all. There was a lot of superstition about such things in the old days."

"Perhaps there is more in superstition than always meets the eye," Grant had suggested. And the little old man had asked, with the same quick sidelong look, "Do you think so now?"

It had been an interesting half-hour, cram full at least of primitive psychology! But after all, the important point did emerge, namely, that such a superstition would have inevitably helped to keep the cairn intact. No natives of past generations would ever have had an urge to liberate an urisk! The boldest of them, the warrior who freed maidens from monsters and giants in castles, would merely have put more stones on his cairn to keep him down. They did stranger things to ward off the spirits of the dead.

But the mention of a robbers' glen had sent him back to his six-inch Ordnance Map in the hope that he might find thereon some reference to an antiquity. He had, however, found none. "In olden times they do say it was a terrible place for robbers. I remember my old grandfather saying they had a den there. No, no road went through that place, but they hid there, and came out to rob travellers. That was the story." And it was clear from Fachie's tone that he felt himself on much firmer ground with the robbers than with the urisk.

"Has anyone been robbed by them in your time?" he had asked.

"No, I wouldn't say it was in my time; no, not in my time; though the place had an evil name, and as boys we wouldn't readily have gone that way, no, not that way."

He would talk many times with old Fachie were it only to be enchanted by the rhythm in his voice. The rhythm went on like the ridges of the hills or the slip and slide of the waves, and could use repetition for solemnity or wit, together with a light in the eye. Was he physically a stunted growth from Paleolithic times? One of the little folk who followed the receding glaciers in the last Ice Age, while the island of Britain was still part of the continent of Europe, and the Thames flowed northward up through the middle of what became the North Sea and was joined by the river Ness from Inverness somewhere off the coast of Norway? Hunting reindeer in the Robbers' Glen like any Lapp?

Sweating by the time he got to the first ridge, he hardly

noticed it, he was so interested in checking what he saw by the contour map in his head. He dipped down, to rise along a slow shoulder of dead-brown heather, with occasional pale-pink blooms of the cross-leaved heath and other growths that sometimes brought him to a standstill. For everything interested him, a flower, a bird, grass or moss, in a natural factual way that was friendly rather than emotional. He knew them as familiar things come upon; now and then his eyes lit up.

The Robbers' Glen was nothing much to look at; it was indeed as bare as a scoop, except for some small birches on a steep slope in its lower reach before it faded out where its tiny tributary ran almost at right angles into the Clachar burn.

The old drove road (long disused) went up by the mountains. Doubtless it was this cross-country traffic of the old days which the robbers had attacked! But where was their stronghold? At least, where could it possibly have been? For there wasn't even a croft ruin to Grant's practised eye, and his eye saw the whole two or three miles of the simple glen as it rose slowly towards the mountains. No life moved on it; not even a sheep. Indeed it seemed too deserted, too silent, with something dimly ominous in its air. Feeling he was now being moved by Fachie's long-pondered fancies, he smiled and turned to the west.

The sun was sinking beyond the rim of the western sea in a stupendous glory. Fiery cloud convoluted in a slowness that matched the majesty. A red visor veiled the sun-god's eyes; the wide-spaced shoulders humped; the great arms flattened and came to rest upon the horizon bar. Behind the red visor, seeing but unseen, the eyes. From them, Grant's own eyes ran along the floor of the sea, tripped over the islands and fell into Clachar. Quieter the place was than the god's thought; more secretively subtle than that thought's vast extension might encompass; more innocent its mask than one who had never lost innocence might know. In stretching himself upon the hill-top, he slid happily behind the mask, behind the still faces of the cottages that gave nothing away; then quietly, invisibly, moved hither and thither, until he came to rest by the cairn in its circle of standing stones.

The stones were like men turned to the cairn in homage or worship; but they were also like men guarding the cairn, motionless as soldiers he had seen guarding the tomb of a dead king, one tall like a leader, the others squat; and then in a moment he perceived, with a strange and disturbing twist of thought, that they were not only guarding the tomb, they were also hemming it in.

No one really knew why these stones had been set in a circle; and it might now be taken as fairly certain that no one ever would. He had long ceased to wonder about it. Before some ever-youthful theory of sun-worship, he smiled, with a tolerant "Perhaps—who knows?" All he did know was that man's worship was devious beyond following and vastly more ancient than the mystery of the stones.

Then, as always in such fluid fancy, a knot formed about the one solitary fact, namely, that the cairn was a great tomb; and instantly, as if his mind were indeed a radioactive substance emitting thoughts of an inconceivable swiftness, he completed the destruction of the world by atomic bombs, saw the cairn of Westminster Abbey and a future race of archaeologists opening it up. The evidence would disclose that this had been a chambered tomb in the Pre-Atomic Age. And to the inevitable idealist who would put forward the theory that Something—perhaps an Ancestor—had been worshipped here, a future Simon Grant would tolerantly reply, "Perhaps—who knows?"

Westminster Abbey and Stonehenge, the Kremlin and the Stone Circle in Clachar. Up swooped his thought upon its metaphysical air and he comprehended in a flash that idealist and materialist were both right, that they separated in order to gather their strength to come together in a higher fusion; to separate and come together again. And then, induced like the flash between positive and negative, his thought apprehended that they were never really separated, that the famous dialectical process was merely another of man's illusions, helpful as crutches or Euclidean figures were helpful but essentially an illusion; much as the physicists, long contending between their theories of waves and particles, were now accepting the notion that waves and particles were but different aspects of the same thing.

He gave an involuntary shiver, for he had been heated in his climb and an air came coolly from the sea. Swivelling round for a last look at the Robbers' Glen, he was stilled on his supporting palms.

A man was walking down there who had come from nowhere.

Shocked beyond thought he lowered himself to the heather. The figure was too solid for an apparition, yet had all the solitariness of one. He watched him for quite a time, just watched him, fascinated. The man continued in his purposeful way down the glen.

During the few minutes he had been fancifully contemplating the west, the man could not conceivably have come from the mountain and down the glen to where he now was. The place had been empty, and lo! there the fellow was with a small bundle over his back, held by one hand, walking away down below by the side of the stream.

He must have been sitting down resting. But the thought was not convincing. He did not move like a figure that had been resting. Besides, he never looked up, and Grant had been striding about on the skyline.

When he had passed by him, Grant crawled forward a little. His long sight was good, but he now made a small funnel of his fist and peered through it with his right eye, and at once the movement of the figure was vaguely familiar.

It's Martin! he thought.

There could be no certainty, because the distance was long and the light beginning to go, but all the same he was quite certain. He followed the figure until it dwindled at the glen mouth and turned away out of sight by the Clachar burn. It was a very roundabout way of going home to Clachar House!

For a long time he wondered; then feeling like a spy who must not be seen, he retreated down the hillside to his lodging.

9

It was Tuesday, blue-skied, and Simon Grant was enjoying himself with the earnestness which time leaves alone. He had his reflex camera, with large focusing-screen, whose reactions were known to him intimately, naked or in filter, together with its head-like movements on the universal joint of its telescopic tripod, and he called it, with obscure but pleasurable irony, his innocent eye. Before its pictures, the scientific critics bowed down. His prismatic compass, which he could carry before him as a deacon his church-offering, gave him his ground angles, and his Abney clinometer his vertical angles. He had his linen measuring tape, his rulers, his numbered pegs, and many odds and ends besides. He had his day-book for recording both his actual doings and his vagrant ideas. And finally there was the drawing-board, with its squared paper, upon which were set down in their true spatial relations all things that he deemed necessary for an accurate plan of cairn and circle.

It was exciting work because he made it exquisitely exacting; he was so happy that he looked stern; and not, indeed, until he was finally rough-checking the height of the cairn, as ascertained by line and angle, did his world collapse. The check consisted in the simple process of measuring the cairn against his own eye-height: thus, he climbed up until he got the top of the cairn on a level with his eye and then noted with care the stone upon which he stood; having climbed down backwards until he got this stone on a level with his eye, he now noted the next stone upon which he stood and saw that when he got to earth he could measure

68

its height from the ground against his yard rule; but as he kept his eye on this final mark and stepped down an unstable stone threw him backwards and, but for the luck that was with him, he might have dislocated his spine.

Anna found him lying twisted on the grass, but when she kneeled and put her hand on his brow, he opened his eyes at once, stared at her for a moment with an odd remoteness, and sat up. Slapping a hand to his side, he yet smiled as he saw the death fear fade like a frost from her face.

"I had a tumble and felt a bit sick," he explained. "Am all right. Absolutely."

"Granny was wondering why you never came home for lunch." Warmth was invading her face.

"It's not that time!" He looked at his watch. "Three o'clock! Good gosh!" He had anticipated being finished with his map-work by one, and had hoped to spend a pleasant afternoon at home inking-in the pencil on his plan and having everything ready for a working start on the cairn in the morning when Foolish Andie and his mother were due to appear. "I'm sorry, Anna." He looked at her with mirth in his eyes, for in his five days at the cottage he had grown fond of her in the friendliest way.

"It's all right," answered Anna smiling, for it didn't matter how many hours he was late if he was all right himself. It was that kind of blessed cottage. "Are you finished?" The reserved politeness of her voice had its unvarying charm.

"Yes. Do you think you could give me a hand home with some of the gear?"

"Yes, sir. Surely."

He got up carefully but was all right except for a bruised feeling down his right side. He stretched himself exaggeratedly, saying, like an embarrassed schoolboy, "Don't call me sir, Anna. I have a great respect for your granny and yourself—and especially for Sheena. If we left these pegs

69

in the ground I don't suppose anyone would touch them?"

"I don't think so. But I could easily——"

"We'll chance it."

They went home together.

Later that afternoon, with his plans and inks before him, he found himself thinking about her as he stared out of his sitting-room window. The Colonel might say he was a romantic, but he knew himself as very shrewd. Her unfortunate predicament naturally drew his sympathy but did not cloud his judgment. She was no wanton. That was certain. But she had a softness, a kind deep softness. Yet even that lay, as it were, like a beauty between her strong bones. There was a certain light in her eyes, when she was momentarily embarrassed and glanced away, which had something beautifully tragic in it. She was no wanton, but, with her affections stirred, she might be misled, wholly and fatally, and, he concluded, perhaps with no vast difficulty.

He nodded, pressing his lips together, and a frown came between his eyebrows. He had a hunch that some soldier had done it who wasn't engaged to her and wasn't killed. Had it been a true case of her boy being killed, he would have heard the story before now. This was the kind of cottage that did not make up such a story for appearance' sake. And from many signs—the postmaster's expression in Kinlochoscar, to begin with—he had come to know that there was no story but the very ancient one of a lassie being left with the baby. His frown deepened as anger probed, for it still remained amazing to him how any damn fellow could have deserted a girl like Anna. She was a practical, hardworking, kind-hearted girl, but she was also at moments a distinguished woman, who, dressed up and bearing herself with her natural reserve, would stand out in any company. I should think so! And not much of the right company left for her to stand out in, by God! he concluded with some spirit and wrath.

He got up and poked at his side, which was still bothersome but not much. Her face came before him with the fear on it, the lips parted, the eyes wide, and—the solicitude. It was the only word he could think of. Care and thought, a natural kindness, for other people, that was what distinguished them, what was innate, he decided. And from them his vision jumped to social levels where this quality was not so innate, where on the contrary it was eaten up by an egotism that lived on itself like a rotten cheese.

The happy image restored some of his good humour and he got back to his inking-in. But after supper, with Anna gone to Kinlochoscar, he was in the mood for talk with the old lady, for he had noiselessly opened his door and overheard a new magic story and a new lullaby.

"No, it's more than bairns' talk," he assured her. "It's out of stories like these that we try to reconstruct the past. For, after all, why should there be magic stories, why should man have been *pleased* with a magic story? What is it in Sheena that makes her *want* a story like that above all else?"

"I'm sure I don't know," said the old lady.

He laughed, as if her smile had communicated something esoteric, instead of showing an inaptitude for speculative discourse.

"But you see what I mean? Why is man haunted, for example, by the story of the Fall? Why should it have come into his head at all that he had fallen from anything? If we haven't fallen, but actually climbed, why isn't it the climb that—that's the thing?"

"When you fall you hurt yourself," she said, "and you remember that. Are you feeling quite well now?"

"Yes," replied Mr. Grant in mazed mirth. "Quite well." He glanced at her to make sure his ebullience was not misunderstood. "And Anna was so kind to me."

"Yes, she's a kind girl."

The quiet tones did not nearly express enough for him, and when he heard her even quieter tones, saying, "She was in the A.T.S. when she fell," he was so full of his own fall and Anna's solicitude, that he cried:

"Oh! Did she hurt herself?"

In the gaping silence, the true meaning of Anna's "fall" and the birth of Sheena came at him, and he stood appalled, his hot blood flooding his body, which went stiff as a grotesque figure in a magic story.

She was now looking at her knees, which her hands smoothed nervously, smiling in a strange way. The sad smile was being invaded by a queer earthy humour. She got up, muttering something about "keeping him", and went out. Still transfixed, he listened without breathing and heard what sounded like cackles of laughter.

He moved about, stretched his legs and felt himself stretch longer, choked back his laughter and doubled over his bruised side. The choked laughter was grotesque and tragic; charged with a wild humour he wanted to let rip. "What an idiot!" Ashamed of himself beyond thought, he shook in the armchair.

10

Suddenly he saw the idiot and his mother sitting on the edge of the cairn, its grey bulk behind them, waiting for him. Pausing to take his breath, he turned towards the sea, which was a living blue, a deep sparkling blue, for the sun was still behind his left shoulder on this June morning. Fresh as Creation's dawn, he tried to murmur to himself, but with no great success, for if anyone could tie himself in knots he was the man, though why this should happen to him, this labour force, this lunacy, the dark gods alone knew. More grimly he approached them, more smiling.

When he saw her bring her son and herself to their feet in respectful attention, he cried "Good morning!", waded in, and lowered his gear to the ground.

Her grave manner was a help. She had the dignity that made the occasion as natural as it could be. She listened but not anxiously. He began to walk round the cairn, pausing now and then to regard it. "You see, this is a place where in prehistoric times they buried their dead. I want to open it up to get at the graves which are inside."

She nodded; and, knowing how superstitious local folk were about opening graves, he realised that if he had said he was going to open up the entrance to hell itself, she would have nodded in the same way. It was work. He was flicked by a chilly thrill. Enlivened, he continued, "Now the problem is: Where is the passage that goes into the heart of the cairn where the chamber is with the—uh—the remains, the bones and things? For there is a passage, and if we can find it we can then go straight in."

She nodded.

"Now usually," he continued, coming to a definite standstill, "the passage goes in somewhere about here, for this is the east side, but not by any means always. Sometimes it's in the south or the south-east or even the west. So we may have to do a lot of clearing before we come on it."

She nodded.

"It's a big pile as you can see. It's over a hundred feet long and though not so broad as it's long, it's still roundish, and I have found that interesting for various reasons. However, I thought we might make a start here to-day and see how we get on."

She nodded, but with a quiet movement now, preparing for action.

"There's just one thing," he said, and at once she grew still so that he heard her mind feel: Now it's coming. "Just one thing," he repeated, for, being a shrewd man, he had worked everything out, "and that is, if you don't mind, I'd like you to stand by your son. I mean you can go on knitting, but I'd like you to watch what he comes on. For it's absolutely important to me that nothing unusual should be moved before I see it. You understand that, don't you?"

"What sort of thing?"

He met her steady pale-blue eyes in the oval of her shawled face. "I'll tell you." And with some animation he proceeded to tell her which stones didn't matter and which did, together with the absolute importance of at once calling his attention, if he were not on the spot, to any unusual feature or find whatsoever. When he had finished and she had nodded, he proceeded to remove the first stone.

He laid it on the ground several feet from the cairn. "I want a row here first to contain the stones, to keep them in, because we must make a tidy job. Then when we have found

74

what we want, it will be easier to put all the stones back where they were, for we mustn't have Mr. Martin complaining that we are making a mess of his ground."

Moving back, he watched them go into action.

"Andrew," she said quietly, "take that one," pointing to a stone at her feet. His head jerked to her face, from her face to her hand, from her hand to the stone, and, making his throaty sound, he at once stooped and lifted the stone. She walked with him to Grant's stone and got him to place his beside it. "Another," she said, pointing to the cairn. Off he set with shambling haste, while she waited. The next time, she didn't speak, she just pointed. The third time she didn't even point.

Unable to stand stolidly watching, Grant peered here and there at the cairn wisely. He had intended, of course, to do some carrying himself, but his side had given him a twinge as he had stooped to lift the first stone, and besides there was something so unusual in the scene that he wanted to have his face to himself. With his Leftish tendency in politics, he could not help feeling that Labour had been given a peculiar signification. It was so sudden a feeling that his smile to the cairn held the self-conscious twist of one who had committed an unexpected misdemeanour. And he couldn't laugh. A sudden vision of the Colonel's rather puffed face with its brown moustache, jutting somewhat in a scoffing irony, nearly undid him.

As he turned round, he saw that she was shaping the growing row of stones into a slight curve to follow the base of the cairn. Intelligent of her! And now she was going back with her son to the cairn. He was wearing a leather jerkin, of the sleeveless kind Grant had worn in the 1914 war, only she had manifestly reshaped it, and he wore it back to front, buttoned behind. Her object now was to get him to carry not one but two or three stones, according to their size. She succeeded.

75

He had a head so round that it seemed to be pushed in behind to keep the shape. The sand-brown hair was cropped short all over except for the fringe that invaded the brow, which was of normal height if narrowed somewhat from east to west. The mouth was pushed out as if the lips had been stung by bees. The eyes were small—and suddenly Grant saw that they were cute, which, locally, was not quite the same as cunning. This astonished him in a breath-taking way. Foolish Andie was enjoying his new game with the stones!

Not at all the usual picture of the hang-dog brutal prognathous primitive, this. Merely a shambling half-giant with a childish intelligence that had no utterance. And Grant had his moment of confirmation of his theory that the early primitives were wont to enjoy themselves immensely and gossip and laugh half the day. African pigmies were full of laughter. Primitive man, when not bedevilled, threw laughter about as naturally as flowers threw their scent or birds their songs. It was in the nature of things. A book should be written about it. Foolish Andie might not be a good example, still. . . . He strolled across to the woman.

"That's fine," he said. "We'll have to put you on the pay-roll."

For the first time she regarded him with uncertainty. Perhaps his words represented an order of intelligence beyond her customary grasp; perhaps she simply could not believe him. But when he had made himself clearer, she said, "That's too much." He turned away with the uncomfortable feeling that she had been moved by more than the monetary recognition.

But the fun really started when the few yards of containing wall were high enough for him to suggest that the stones could now be thrown from the cairn. Thrown they were, and shot and hurtled, to an accompaniment of guttural sound that was splendid. When the stones were small boulders, the staggering action was stupendous and the grunts in keeping.

Grant smiled, and skipped out of the way, and laughed, and laughed louder. Foolish Andie saw, and stopped, and looked at his employer with a light in the dark-blue eye and the mouth open. "Gu-gu-gu? . . ."

"Ga! Ga!" cried Grant in the happiest agreement.

Foolish Andie's face crushed into a grin that broadened until the eyes all but disappeared.

Grant waved an arm and went round the cairn, his face hot and his mind off the record. It beats the band! he thought. It beats two bands! Ga! ga! he confirmed himself, and subsided by his gear.

But it *is* damn funny, he cried as he fumbled in his haversack. He saw life as God's happiest piece of fun. He also saw his camera. His hand landed on his day-book. Would he take a snapshot of life in action or enter his happy thought in the book? An obscure feeling or shyness about intruding too far too soon on his labour force made him open the day-book. He had got the length of (c) under his heading *Primitive Social Behaviour* when Mrs. Mackenzie appeared round the cairn. Would he come? He jumped up and went.

It was no more than the cairn's peristalith, but it interested him immensely. The upended stone was about three feet high, a small "standing stone" or orthostat. Loose stones were soon cleared away from it and from its neighbour on the right which was much the same height and distant about a foot and a half. Between them, the ordinary-sized stones of the cairn had manifestly been built up drystone-dyke fashion. These upended stones or orthostats would go right round the cairn forming its containing wall or peristalith. There were theorists who said that the great stone circles themselves were but a later development of this peristalith which kept back the cairn—or kept in the dead. But the true field worker was now leaving theory or hypothesis to wait on evidence. When he had cleared three of the upended stones, he decided to take a photograph, went to get his camera, and returned with all his gear. The overlap of loose stones seemed to him remarkable and he wanted to show its depth.

Foolish Andie regarded the camera with great interest and followed Grant's movements with solemn open-mouthed attention. The sun was not quite where the photographer wanted it, having moved too far round, and as he was mounting the cairn itself in the hope of getting the northern side of the excavated bay square-on, he heard Mrs. Mackenzie speak rather sharply. He turned his head. She was shooing Andie away from the prismatic compass which was lying exposed.

"Don't let him touch that!"

"No, no," she answered. "It's just that he likes bright things."

"Sound fellow!" he called, as he got into position.

The work went on, and but for the angle of the light he might have forgotten the lunch-hour. "Yes," she answered, "we have our piece with us," and straightway she and her son withdrew round the cairn, leaving their employer to his sandwiches and his reflections.

And things were going very well, he decided, even fantastically well! They coincided in some hidden way with the notion of holiday, freedom, and mirth. Compared with Cnossos in Crete, a chambered cairn in the Highlands, where many cairns had been opened, was hardly a matter of exalted archaeological importance! But the grey stones lay there in the sun, and one of them, as his head moved, winked.

Munching his sandwich, he scratched the glazed spot on the stone with a thumb nail, stood back, and decided he would clear the ground for at least a couple of yards inside the peristalith. It struck him there might not be much sense in doing this, for the passage, when found, would go through the peristalith, but still he decided he would do it, moved by an impulse to finish tidily what he was at, rather than hurry ahead after any preconception.

His reward came the following afternoon just after lunch. With pursed features he was contemplating the next spot for an exploratory incision, when she came to him hurriedly.

"He's found it," she said.

He did not speak but went before her. There it was sticking through the loose boulders—an edging of flagstone.

"Gu—gar—r—r," muttered Andie.

"You're dead right," said Grant. "Just dead right. Now— carefully now—we'll clear the loose stuff away." He began pitching the small boulders with a tremendous industry which Andie tried to excel. In no time the upright face of a flagstone or slab was completely revealed. It had a slab on either side of it, and another, as lintel, on top. But it looked small for a passageway. Yet passages *were* low and narrow. He tried to wrench, to move, the upright in front, but it was solidly embedded. He had to pull Andie from it. "Steady! We'll clear all the stones off the top slab and then we'll be able to lift that."

There was a nasty moment, when, having undermined the cairn above, they let it come roaring down on them. Grant leapt off the ledge, fell, and rolled over, but Andie's reactions were always slow. The first stones knocked his heels from under him so that he fell back, slid, and came to rest with his feet in the air and boulders on his belly. For a moment he lay still, then he scrambled up, shaking the stones from him, grinning noisily, as if he had had a paradisal ride. Breathing heavily, Grant went and clapped him on the shoulder. "You'll have to be more careful," he shouted, laughing and feeling guilty.

The work now was nothing and soon they had the whole lintel exposed. But, unless the next one had collapsed, there was only this one. And, by heavens! he thought, it looks

79

more like a box than a passage, it looks suspiciously like the intrusion of a short cist. In his excitement he became very businesslike and saw that every threatening stone was removed from the face in front and all stones sufficiently levelled on either side. "Now then!" he said.

It was beginning to move when Andie slipped. Mrs. Mackenzie said, "Let me." They let her.

"Now then!" The lid lifted up and over and fell clear with a clash. In the short stone coffin were two skeletons.

II

Grant paid no attention to Andie's excitement, for the skeletons and their disposition fascinated him. On his knees he peered, knowing enough to realise that they were those of a mother and child, a growing child, perhaps of four or so. The mother had been laid to rest on her right side, with her knees tucked up, and in the bay of her body her child had been placed. The sight affected him even at that moment in the exultation of his find. The skulls were fine and fragile, the bones slender; a grace was in this slenderness, like an immortal story. Then he noticed specks like blackened oats. He bent right down but did not touch. Jet beads from a necklace. His eye caught a faint gleam from under the edge of the pelvis, and his heart hurt him, for it was the gleam of gold.

He got up and Mrs. Mackenzie said, "He was just excited."

"What's that?" But he wasn't interested. Very few people liked skeletons. Many found them depressing. Mr. Grant, however, had met some beautiful skeletons in his time. He came back with his camera and drawing-board. He was excitedly preoccupied and fiddled about with the drawing-board trying to reflect some extra light into the cist. Far from satisfied, he nevertheless got Mrs. Mackenzie to hold it in a certain position while he first lightly dusted the bones and then worked his camera through a variety of angles. When he had taken three photographs he said with great earnestness, "Now you watch here and let no one near it until I come back."

"I'll do that," she promised.

But when he had gone a little way, he turned back. "Come along!"

"Go with him," said Mrs. Mackenzie to her son, and he went.

The archaeologist was already moving at a brisk speed and Andie seemed tied to him by an invisible string. Andie took long low strides, the edge of his heel hitting the ground first, in the peculiar motion of a rocking horse that could only rock forward. Gradually, however, he began to overhaul his employer and presently Grant was aware of the face beside him, excited and smiling, and obviously saying that things had come to a mysterious pass. Grant agreed. Andie was delighted with the agreement and became a trifle more expansive. "Yes, yes," said Grant. "I want you to carry a box for me." The sounds seemed so good to Andie that his small twinkling eyes disappeared for a laughing moment.

At the gable-end, Grant said, "You stop here."

Andie stopped, followed the hand, saw the spot of ground to which it happened to be pointing, and sat on it. The eyes twinkled upward.

Mrs. Cameron was at the door.

"I have come back for some things," Grant explained, "and I was wondering if you had a big board . . ." They disappeared into the house.

Presently they came out. Mrs. Cameron called to Andie, "My word, but you're the important man now! Do you think you can carry this?" It was the large lid of a wooden chest. His arms went out and caught it. "No, no," she said, and put it on his back. "He has fairly taken to you, and it's not to everyone that happens," she called to Mr. Grant, as he walked away, a longish rectangular box under his arm which he had taken from his wooden crate. She stood watching them until they had passed from sight, then laughing softly to herself she looked about the landscape.

The shining silver paper, which Grant pinned to the lid of the chest, winked at Andie so effectively that they had some trouble in getting him to give way to his mother in the matter of holding the lid so that it reflected light into the grave while Grant once again took photographs, including a couple of snapshots with a small pocket camera.

The discovery of a mother and child in a single short cist was rare enough for him to work with the utmost care and precision. The skulls, the ancient and fragile bones, he handled with great delicacy and close attention, before depositing each on a tray in his rectangular box; then, and only then, he lifted out the gold ornament. It was a bracelet, of, to him, the familiar penannular shape of the Bronze Age; rounded and thick as a slim pencil, but it was not hollow, it was solid, and its terminals were not flattened into any kind of trumpet shape, one indeed was rounded into a slight boss. He examined it with minute care, for he knew that already, some hundreds of years before Christ, cunning craftsmen could cover bronze with finely beaten gold and thus deceive the unwary with imitation jewellery. There was no doubt in this case, however, that the Highland goldsmith had worked the pure metal. He fondled it delicately in his silk handkerchief and when it appeared again, it so shone that Andie made a commotion. Grant turned his head and laughed. "You would like it, wouldn't you?" With loving care and a beating heart he slid it into one of his brown paper bags and placed it in the box. Then he started the lengthy process of recovering every small seed of the jet necklace, finally combing the dust of the empty cist with infinitely patient fingers.

It was a great day's work and enough for a day. When he had got the stone lid replaced on the cist, he turned his back for a moment, fumbled in his pocket-book, and, going up to Mrs. Mackenzie, slipped a pound note into her hand. "You have brought me luck," he said.

Her silence was more than speech, for he added, "Shush! That's nothing." Then he stamped about a bit. "He has worked like a trojan, grand! Haven't you, Andie?"

"Whu—whu——"

"That's the lad! And, by the way, Mrs. Mackenzie, you needn't say anything about what we find here. We don't want anybody poking their noses into our affairs. We get on nicely together. Mum's the word!"

"Thank you, sir. You're very kind."

"Poof! Nothing. And now we'll be off."

She had even contrived to suppress her emotion with dignity, a decent simple woman, who had borne her burden in a way that the great might emulate to their advantage, he concluded with no less precision in thought than he had just exhibited in action.

But that night he could not go to bed. Once more the story of the Silver Bough had been told in a way that set him dreaming before his day-book in front of his sitting-room window, the gold bracelet beside him. It would be exciting to get the child a real Silver Bough, just to see the reaction! A catspaw of mirth invaded his face. His eyes chimed. He began a conversation with a man he knew, a craftsman who had a workshop behind a little shop of great disorder in a side street. It was really a dirty little shop with an acrid smell, but now he saw that it was a fabulous shop and that dirt was its mask. He suddenly understood why so skilled a man could spend hours repairing a silver ornament for a silly rich woman; or, worse, doing the repair for a front-street jeweller who himself could make nothing but money, especially out of the rich woman. He saw it all with the revelation of a grotesque medieval story. Beyond that! beyond that! he saw that the grotesque story was *true*. His urgent chest moved the small table to a squeak. Any little hollow brass rod—so long—would do, and you could bend it slightly, very slightly (he explained to the craftsman) and

84

then paint it silver; the nine hollow balls, about as big as little apples, but each one with a different note of the scale in it and you would paint them gold and hang them along the bough. You understand? . . . And the scene in the little shop faded to the scene "ben the house", and the child was looking at the Silver Bough, but could not yet stretch out her hand for it, so great was the magic, and then he tapped one ball here and one ball there with a finger-tip and lo! the lullaby chimed its own song sweetly in the great silence of the kitchen.

He glanced behind him, but there was no one in the room to overlook his childish phantasy, so he laughed silently at himself, and said he had a good mind to write a letter to the craftsman there and then, and his eye landed on the gold bracelet. He picked it up and once more went over it with his magnifying glass. So far as he could recall, its terminal finish at least was something new, and indeed the boss looked like a flattened head, even a primitive attempt at a serpent head, while the other terminal perceptibly tailed off. What! Was he deceiving himself? or could this possibly be a fumbling after the serpent motif? And suddenly, his mind taking a leap into myth, he asked himself: why *did* women (men too) in the first instance wear a bracelet? . . . Decoration? But what *was* decoration? . . . Sex appeal? But what *was*—wait a minute, just you wait a minute, said Simon Grant. . . .

When his argument, after winding its way through spells and charms, had finished its subtle traffic with primitive forces or gods as elusive and potent as the nuclei of the physicists (for his reading was varied and he knew that the mention of physicists made even argumentative archaeologists hesitate) he came back to the gold. Once on a northern trip to have a look at the cairns and brochs in Caithness, he had dropped off the train and gone up the valley of Kildonan in Sutherland to inspect the old gold diggings. In living memory, nuggets had been found there. . . .

When his mind came back to the stone cist he wondered why there had not been certain grave-goods, even a pigmy food vessel . . . and wondered how it had happened that just these two had been buried like that. The bones showed no signs of violence. How together? at the same time? Had the child died—and then the mother gone to keep the child company in that afterworld where there would be no one to look after the child properly? Had the mother asked to be despatched? Had she—despatched herself? Or had the mother died, and the child been sent . . . ?

His questioning raised human values of so profound a nature that his ghost wandered through all his anthropological knowledge for some material point to fasten on, and suddenly, and quite on its own, it found itself regarding Anna and her child, as he had first come upon them, asleep in the shadow of the rock. The very attitude, to the disposal of the limbs, was the same! Time, the cameraman, faded out the bones in the stone cist and faded in the sleeping figures by the rock. That was all. Simply—that was all.

A cold catspaw went wandering about his spine, stopped his breathing, and made him listen as though he might over-hear the ineffable meaning of what he had seen.

For what he had seen seemed in that moment all of man's story under the sun. And instantly it was strangely close to him and valiant. They fell asleep and they woke again. The overarching sky and the plain of the world, and the human story moving over that plain. Moving over that plain, light upon the faces, on a journey with no known end and no meaning, and because there was no known meaning intimacy and valiance came in warmth about the heart. The journey from the far past into the farther future; and how-ever the gods of the sky or the demons of the underworld contrive to beset it, the journey continues to no known shrine; and always because there is no known shrine, the warmth deepens and the valiance grows precious with understanding one of another. Faces taking the light in warmth and courage and understanding, and creating in that very act, on this mysterious journey, that with which the unknown may be faced, may be challenged; for what can be contained in the utmost essence of the unknown that could of its nature surpass this? The woman frolicked with her child on the earth. . . . The skeletons fade out in the cist and Anna and Sheena fade in. . . . There came upon him a faint beating, like the slow beating of a heart, the heart of the earth, beating more firmly, like a padding of feet . . . and Anna passed his window carrying a pail of water from the well.

Breath packed his chest, then eased away, and he decided that myth is an extraordinarily potent business. Time and space are its plastics which shape and dissolve in essential meanings, like movements from the Creator's hands. The Creator's hands, as the local folk said. For you could talk of the Creator in a natural way, but not so of God, who was religious. But already his mind was fumbling and disconnected. The thing behind was too much and too big. He got up.

The light was growing green outside and fading away in the room. Things were settling down for the night, rocks and stones and the little pathway. The fowls were silent. The cat jumped up on the garden wall, turned its head slowly with an inscrutable air of dominion, sat down and folded its tail around its haunch. It looked bored with its own mastery. But he noted that the tip of the tail moved up and down in a quivering life of its own. For no reason, quietly, softly, the cat arose and jumped out of sight. Grant went up to his bedroom.

Presently he heard Anna come up the stairs. Sometimes the child, half-wakened, whimpered petulantly as she hushed and carried her. To-night, too, there was drowsy protest, but Anna's hushing voice was soft as a wind-rhythm, rising and falling in the lullaby of the Silver Bough, ignoring the protest and carrying it away. Her door closed.

Noiselessly he took the long box out of the tiny dressing-room and placed it on the floor of his bedroom. He lit two candles and his electric lamp, then opened the lid of the box. With gentle care he placed all the bones in position on the floor till the two skeletons lay extended side by side, and went downstairs very quietly for his measuring tape.

During the night he dreamed so vivid a dream that it wakened him and for a few moments he still saw the two figures moving in the grey light, but even as he blinked they dissolved, though he still heard the little one's cries—until they passed into Anna's room. Sheena had merely wakened up; that was all. He looked about the vacant floor and listened. The grey still light of the morning was in the window and he had the odd feeling that it was watching him.

12

"I hope Sheena did not disturb you last night?" said Anna as she removed his porridge plate.

"Me? No! Why, was she restless?"

"Yes. She must have been dreaming."

"Do they dream so young?"

"I think so," she answered smiling.

"Interesting. Did she tell you what she was dreaming about?"

"No. I think she just thought that I had left her. She was calling me so loud that I was afraid she might have wakened you."

"Even if she had done—what of it? We were all that age once!" He liked Anna's voice. "I suppose she just clung to you and explained nothing?"

"Yes," said Anna.

In the afternoon, while he was directing a new opening into the cairn on the south-west side, Mrs. Sidbury appeared. She moved with a wind-blown erratic lightness that had its grace, but in an instant he knew that he hated visitors on the site.

She greeted him, went and spoke to Mrs. Mackenzie, and had a few words for Andie. There was obviously no slightest trace of snobbery in the woman. But he knew that already he was becoming over-sensitive to place and atmosphere, and so to people. She suddenly struck him as a gay woman who had once been nearly strangled.

"No, nothing much yet. It may take a little time," he explained. The cist had been covered over.

She peered about the stones, balancing lightly. "We should like very much if you could come to dinner to-morrow night."

"Thank you," he replied, confused by his momentary hesitation. "I shall be very pleased."

"Donald hasn't been to see you?"

"No."

"He was going to, I think."

"At least we could show him we are trying to be tidy! All these stones out there will be put back."

Her dark eyebrows arched. "But won't that be a lot of extra trouble?"

After a little while, she left.

Later the schoolmaster appeared. Grant glanced at his watch. In half an hour they were due to stop work anyway; but he gave no order. Better bear it for half an hour.

He had been told that the schoolmaster was a clever man who knew all about everything in the place, including the olden days, and had spent an interesting evening with him, for the man had a considerable amount of Celtic scholarship of a kind. In fact it was made clear that he had come to the small Clachar school, which had but a handful of pupils and in which he was the only teacher, in order to pursue his studies along certain empirical lines. There were times when Grant thoroughly enjoyed theories, and to an enthusiasm he naturally responded, but this was not one of the times. Mr. McCowan was tall, thin, dark, with spectacles and a deep impressive voice.

After five minutes, Grant was objecting: "But these Neolithic people were not Celtic. This cairn was already ancient before your Celts or Goidels appeared on the scene."

"You are quite certain of that?" Mr. McCowan had a way of holding his smile.

"Quite certain," replied Grant without any smile.

When the discussion became involved, Grant swept the

whole of Scotland clear of all humans in the last Ice Age in order to start from scratch. Then he introduced man as the ice receded, and in particular he brought Azilians to Oban who lived in caves, had barbed harpoons of red deer's antler or bone for spearing fish, had hammer stones, bone fabricators, some flints; who hunted seals, boars, otters, wild cats and deer; who lived on crabs, oysters, winkles, limpets, and cockles and mussels alive alive-o, concluded Grant suddenly on a lighter note, for he had been growing earnest and lengthy.

"And these Azilians?"

"Come before the Neolithic Age. Fishing folk to the West Coast. It even sounds familiar!"

"And where did *they* come from originally?"

"Perhaps up from England," answered Grant with a sly twinkle, refraining for the moment to bring them in slow stages from France. Ten minutes later, he said, "Upon this scene your Gaels were mere newcomers, parvenus—of whom I have the honour to be, perhaps, a somewhat mixed sample." And his eyes considered Mr. McCowan's head.

Mr. McCowan helped him home with his gear, still arguing, and they parted with smiling heat. It had been a dry day. They hadn't even struck the peristalith on the south-west side. These silly racial arguments, said Grant to himself, were exactly like the cracking of cairn stones hurled by an idiot, not forgetting the diffused smell of brimstone.

But he grew calmer in the evening as on a square of plate glass he began to build up the necklace with the pieces of jet. Soon he was entirely lost in this fascinating jig-saw puzzle, of which, however, the final picture was clear in his mind. It was that of a crescent moon whose horns were pulled together to fasten in a point at the back of the neck. The shape was defined in the main by three circles: the outside circle of the crescent moon, the inside circle, and a circle that ran midway between; and all three circles were made up of these small barrel-shaped beads of jet strung together; the very smallest, for the inner circle, had looked to him in the cist like black oats, the largest were about an inch long. These circles were kept apart by beads of the same shape placed diagonally and spaced out. Four large lozenge-shaped pieces gave a stiffening and dignity to the whole, while two triangular pieces linked the circles together to meet in a catch behind the neck. It was not only a pretty pattern but, as he knew, for even these ancient days, a distinctively native one. A Scottish contribution to the Bronze Age. Again, the material was not true jet, but lignite such as would have been found among the Sutherland coal measures (coal-mine to-day at Brora; gold diggings yesterday at Kildonan). As he lifted one of the large lozenges and examined again its geometric pattern of lines picked out in dots, he suddenly remembered that it should have its electrical properties, like amber. After rubbing it quickly on his sleeve he brought it near a tiny piece of paper. The paper stuck.

What magic this power of attraction must have been to them of old!

As he stared through the window, wondering how they explained it to themselves, he quite suddenly became one with them. He had indeed a flashing memory from early boyhood of a piece of chaff being picked up by the amber mouthpiece of a pipe. Two boys' faces and his own, in wonder, laughing. It had felt like some magical trick; and not until he had carried out a surreptitious experiment with his father's expensive silver-mounted pipe was he convinced, with an even profounder wonder (for he was now alone), that it was not a trick. He had put the pipe (after a few empty sucks at it) back in the ornate smoker's cabinet and stolen from the room, and the yellow transparency of the amber in the curved mouthpiece was still one of his clearest colour memories.

No doubt, he now thought, it was from this simple boyhood experience that he was able long afterwards to get some notion of primitive man's *apprehension* of an invisible spirit. It was like the potency in the amber rather than any *shaped* thing. And, quite literally, it had power. Between the spirit in man and the potency in the amber there was an unsearchable communion; an attraction in wonder, a repulsion in fear.

And beyond attraction and repulsion, what did man know to-day? He might coin electrical names for the potency (though even then *electron* was merely the Greek word for *amber*) but the *why?* was hidden as ever. What he gained in names he lost in the old *apprehension*. Equations were the chambered cairns wherein the ancient magics were buried. He was nodding with pursed lips when Mrs. Cameron knocked.

When he had her seated, he sat down himself, saying cheerfully, "Yes, I wanted to see you about—well, you know, my first week is up and we haven't yet settled what I owe you."

There were a few reluctant, friendly remarks, and then she said, "I'll just tell you what happened with Mr. McArthur, who was here two years ago. I asked him if twenty-five shillings would do and he insisted on paying me thirty. I hope——"

"That's fine," said Mr. Grant. "That's grand. Of course things have gone up a bit since then." He turned to the mantelpiece and then placed his payment in her hand. "And I am very pleased here; delighted, in fact. So that's all right."

But she stared at the three pound notes and then at him.

"Not a word," he said. "Shush! Wait till this tourist business gets properly going and then! . . . Oh, and by the way, I wanted to tell you, too, that I'm going out for dinner to-morrow night. But as it's Saturday, I'll be home for lunch. Must give my employees their half day!"

"It's too much," she said quietly, sitting still.

"If you're satisfied I am. Could anything be more perfect than that?" He laughed and rallied her.

When at last she was going out, she said, "If you're late to-morrow, or any night, you'll always find the door open."

"I do believe it's that kind of door," he replied. "But I shan't be late. I'm only going to Clachar House."

There was a perceptible arrestment, a momentary steadying of her eyes on his face, then "Good night, Mr. Grant," and she was gone.

He stood in thought for a little while, then turned to his beads.

13

In the last hour of the morning's work, they struck the peristalith, and the reason for the extra depth of the cutting was suddenly and excitingly revealed, for he perceived that the circle of uprights seemed here, on the south-west side, to be dented inwards.

There were two kinds of cairn, the long cairn and the round cairn. The ends of the long narrow cairn had an inward curve or bay, coming to points, like the thrusting horns of an immense snail. But the peristalith of the round cairn was always more or less circular. Some archaeologists considered that the long cairns with their horns were the older type. Grant now perceived that in his own roundish cairn there was, apparently, one feature of the long cairn. Anyway, here again would be something that might, when fully revealed, give his work an argumentative value! He was really so excited that he abruptly stopped operations for the day, for if they went further and found something like an entrance he knew he could never stop, and at the moment at least everything remained covered up from prying eyes over the weekend. Then on Monday morning! . . .

Mrs. Mackenzie had asked for five shillings a day. He gave her ten, saying he always paid on Saturdays, shushed her to silence, and marched home, laughing inwardly. For well he knew that he was a hard-headed shrewd business man. Three pounds a week for lodging, three pounds for labour; total, six pounds. They paid seven guineas a week in Kinlochoscar Hotel. Robbing the poor he was. Of course they could go fishing for brown trout at Kinlochoscar (and pay ten shillings a day for a gillie). Fishing! he thought. Just fishing!

His good spirits accompanied him to Clachar House.

"Archaeology a dry subject?" His coffee spilt over before he could set the cup properly in the saucer and have his laugh out. It had been an excellent dinner, with lobster salad, preceded by a glass of sherry which he knew as a bumper. "I should say it's the most interesting subject on earth!"

"And that's flat!" said Martin with his dry smile.

Grant laughed more merrily than ever. "Flat as a pancake," he agreed with a generous irrationality. "All the same, it is!" he declared. "For at least it does one thing to us: it gives us some small sense of proportion. It puts our problems—or our self-importance—in some sort of perspective. And that's something—these days."

"You mean," suggested Martin, "it has all happened before?"

"I do."

"And you think that interesting?"

"Interesting enough to control the fuss we make about the—the wrong things. Not, of course, that it ever happens exactly as before. There is a difference, I suppose, between a stone axe and an atom bomb."

Mrs. Sidbury smiled. She was a generous hostess and had clearly set herself to charm her guest. "You haven't tried the liqueur yet."

Gallantly raising the small glass to her, he tried, was stung, and coughed. "I—I forgot." He forgot it was a liqueur and had taken too much. He wiped his eyes and his waistcoat, thoroughly amused at himself. "A—a vodka basis?" he suggested.

She nodded. "We are nothing if not international."

She was a capital woman! The mad sort that throws her bonnet over the banister. He felt like throwing a few things himself at this stone-faced brother of hers, not but that he was acting the host with a certain automatic grace. But there was a fundamental lack of interest in the fellow; a burial urn from which the bones had been filched. He was not even supercilious. And now he was waiting for his guest to speak. Why couldn't he say something himself?

"And you have really found nothing yet, beyond the general shape of things?" Mrs. Sidbury asked.

He glanced at her with twinkling eyes, stirred his coffee, and glanced again. "As a matter of fact, I have," he said, overcome by temptation; "only I—don't want it to be known."

"How exciting!" she cried. "Do tell us."

"Well——" He hesitated still; then looking at her, a brightness in his eyes, said clearly, "As a matter of fact, I have found two skeletons."

Her brows knitted as she leaned back. "How gruesome!" she declared. "Phew!" and she shuddered.

"They're not really," he said, taken with the frankness of her manner, "when you get to know them. Personally I am rather attracted by skeletons. But I realise that others aren't. That's why I would rather you didn't mention it."

"I shan't! Do go on."

"As a matter of fact," he said, glowing inwardly from the liqueur that had gone the right way, "one of my first loves was a skeleton."

But now he caught her eyes on him. The room was suddenly skinned. He had gone too far. Yet it was remarkable to see the way the inner dark knot of her sanity held while she wondered if he, too, was a hidden neurotic. Her slight psychic shock touched his heart.

"It's really nothing out of the way," he suggested. "Perhaps I shouldn't have mentioned it. It's our fundamental condition, the thing that endures. I mean there's nothing morbid in a skeleton for me. Far from it. On the contrary, once you have gone so far—you can hardly go farther, so there's nothing more to worry about or be afraid of. You have the whole story—the physical story anyway."

"What sort of skeletons?" asked Martin.

Grant turned to him. "Actually, very interesting. As you know, in the chamber of the cairn I may find several skeletons. It may have been a sort of communal burial place —there were only very small pockets of humanity in those days—or it may have been a family vault, perhaps for the original Clachar House—or headman's hut! But, as I told you, we haven't yet found the way in. These two skeletons were found in a short cist, a built-in stone coffin, which had been intruded well into the edge of the cairn. These cists were the new style of individual burials, brought to this country by a folk who arrived on the east coast. Roughly speaking, that is——"

"The individual beginning to supplant the communal even then, you mean?"

"Perhaps!" said his guest.

Martin lit a fresh cigarette. "But why did they intrude it into the cairn? Or should I say infiltrate it?"

"Even the fifth column *then*, you suspect?" Grant was amused. "Who knows? But archaeologists have imagined that they settled down together rather reasonably. We may think that strange now—but it seemed natural enough when I was a lad. There *may* have been reasonable people, you know, once upon a time!"

"You think so?" Martin's eyes had their cool disintegrating smile.

"Why, yes," replied Grant. "Anyway, they weren't stopped when infiltrating the cist."

"They had probably left none alive to stop them."

"That's possible. But why then did they do it at all, why infiltrate without reason?"

98

"Once you develop—a peculiarity—you go on glutting it, without reason. Possibly that is even more fundamental than the skeleton."

"Can no story be told without argument?" asked Mrs. Sidbury with elevated eyebrows.

Grant turned towards her with a smile that warmed his face in the shy humour of a boy who has been caught out. "I sometimes think," he suggested, "that the story exists nowadays only for the argument."

"How true!" she exclaimed, reassured in a moment by her glimpse of the boy in the man. "Do go on with the story."

"In this short cist, then, I found the two skeletons—not, I may say, without some excitement."

"Two in the one cist? Is that usual?" asked Martin.

"No. In this case there is the extra and peculiar interest that they are the skeletons of a mother and child. She is a young woman, I should say in her twenties, and the child about four or five." In a complete silence, he went on, "I could find no trace of anything having happened to them. Sometimes, you know, you can tell whether a person had been suffering from an abscess in a tooth, or from arthritis, or other troubles that affect the bone, while of course anything like a brutal attack with a stone weapon," he added lightly, "leaves its story writ large." He looked at their faces and felt slightly disconcerted. Mrs. Sidbury's attention was white and extreme; Martin's sensitive features were expressionless in a carven aristocratic way, and the eyes, as always, seemed to see only what they were looking at—in this case Grant's face. "Of course," Grant continued with a slight gesture, "they knew quite a lot in those days. We have remarkable instances of surgery, of trepanning—cutting out a piece of bone from the skull, an operation that is still one of the most delicate and difficult to our modern surgeons. And successful operations, too, as the subsequent healing over of the bone-edges shows. With stone tools they did it. So perhaps they weren't quite so brutally dumb as we are sometimes inclined to think!"

"Such an operation—then?" said Mrs. Sidbury with polite interest. "How extraordinary!"

"Almost incredible when you really think about it," her guest agreed in his effort to lighten the atmosphere. "For they only had bits of flint, and presumably they would have to begin by shaving the appropriate part. Then the operation itself—but surely they had some knowledge of anaesthetics or drugs, otherwise their stoicism was more remarkable than all? Yet it was not an unusual operation. One late Neolithic skull," continued the archaeologist, warming to his subject, "found in France, had actually been trepanned in three places and quite successfully. And I must say I very much appreciated a learned colleague who wrote solemnly that the operation may have been performed in some cases to relieve chronic headaches."

Mrs. Sidbury smiled now.

"However," said Grant, with his own smile, "I have also found some treasure trove."

"Ah!" Light came back to her face.

"Yes. A jet necklace and a bracelet—of gold."

"Really?"

"Yes. I am particularly pleased with the bracelet," he admitted modestly.

"Well, you have been lucky so far," she said. "I am very glad. Some more coffee?"

"Please. Thank you."

"How do you account for the double death?" asked Martin.

The coffee-pot shook in her hand as if she were about to protest, but she remained silent.

"I don't know," said Grant. "The chances that they would both die naturally at the same time are unlikely. It may be that the child died, and, with no one to look after it in the next world, it may be that the mother—went also. Or vice versa. Who knows? Only," and his brows gathered, "I am inclined to think that their human attachments, relationships, in those days were of a peculiarly intimate kind, an intimacy that we have, perhaps because of our civilised interests, in some measure lost."

"An animal intimacy?"

But Grant was not put off. "Partly, perhaps," he said thoughtfully. "But also with something more to it—possibly—than your implication would suggest."

"In what way?"

Grant turned his face to his hostess. "Are we about to argue again?"

"You are!" she said, and he laughed, for more than a vague discomfort was now growing in him.

"You left the skeletons in the cist?" asked Martin.

"No. Oh no. I took them home in a box to Mrs. Cameron's, but of course they don't know that they are in the house. That's why I asked you to say nothing about it. And there's nothing really to be—well, to be upset about. I mean, it was all so very natural. Even the position of the two figures—frankly, I was touched. Oddly enough, the very day I arrived I went to the cairn to have a look at it," he continued, with a smile for his glass as he turned its stem between his fingers, "and then I came on Anna—you know, Mrs. Cameron's grand-daughter—asleep with her child in the shadow of a small rock, and their position was identical——"

Mrs. Sidbury arose and abruptly left the room. It was so dramatic an exit that Grant got up. "I'm sorry. I seem to be—saying the wrong thing."

"Sit down," said Martin coolly, and he drank his liqueur not with haste but completely.

"It's really time I was——"

"My sister is a trifle highly strung. Sit down. Some more liqueur?"

But his guest would have no more and insisted that it was time he went. "I have some things to write up, and it's a law with us that we write them up at once, otherwise the objective facts may get twisted."

He felt rather ashamed of himself as he left the house. He hadn't said good night to his hostess, hadn't thanked her, hadn't supported her against that brother of hers, damn him! The fellow had wanted to talk, yet had made no further effort to detain him. Sitting there, he would have analysed every statement to its fibres, until there was no life left, nothing. Not with interest, much less with passion, but with that sort of deadly automatism. He's either an ego-maniac or a walking death, he thought with a sudden mounting anger, for he realised that his own reluctance to stay had something to do with fear.

This so upset him that he could not go straight home. Veering right he presently reached the cairn, and its tumbled stones, the evidence of his labours, worked amusingly on his spirit. To have done; to do: that is the question—solved. My God, yes, he thought; it takes you out of yourself; it takes you out of that jungle. The stones were silent and grey-clean, and the alley between those removed into a mounting pile and the cairn itself was like a place which children would use in a game. He was pervaded all in a moment by the extraordinary feeling that he had brought lightness, friendliness, to the two whom he had found in the cist. This was an intuition so strong that he could not disbelieve it. He felt it was true, because it was true in the very essence of himself, yet an essence apprehended outside himself, like the evening light. Then in the same still moment he caught the silent dramatic removal of the shadow of an arm; faint, very faint, something that was there like the shadow of a hair in the corner of his eye but not there when his eye blinked and turned. He turned right round and saw that the sun had set—in a line beyond a standing stone in the surrounding circle.

His heart was pounding so strongly that his chest could not expand enough to hold all the air it needed. It was getting on for midsummer, and the sun did set late, what with extra summer time. Despite a low bank of grey-blue cloud, edged with salmon-pink, he could in fact see that the sun had just set. Had it, for one moment, pierced a veil, an interstice, and cast a weak shadow, slantwise, towards the point they were working on?

He walked to the stone and stood beside it, staring at the colour from the vanished sun. Turning, he looked back. As a stone circle it wasn't impressive; little more indeed than a ghost-hedge of modest-sized stones except for the tall one in the south-west; but it, he decided as he was drawn towards it, must be all of ten feet high. Then suddenly he realised that when the sun was setting in the south-west, poised on the edge of the ocean, it should cast the shadow of this tall monolith so that its tip would land a little to the right of the upright in the peristalith where he had stopped working. Would the entrance be there? From the entrance, would the sun be seen, when about to set, as a great golden ball sitting on top of the stone—and sending its shadow, like a phallic symbol, into the passage? Mid-winter and the dying Sun-god—touching the Earth-goddess of fertility!

Gorged with excitement, he put a hand against the stone, and his fingers, pressing the hard gritty surface, brought the strength of the stone into him. Glancing up its breadth to the top, he then had another illusion; he thought that certain curves, whorls, had a human semblance. This, of course, was pure phantasy, because it was completely and obviously an undressed slab. There were whorls of lichen, and there were lines—perhaps weathered, flaked—but, as he faced the monolith squarely from a little distance, he recognised sensibly that there was nothing intentionally human about it, not even in the outward swelling into hump-like shoulders a few feet from the top. He swore that this was perfectly clear. He laughed—and was suddenly silenced by his own sound. He turned and walked back to the cairn. These intuitive glimpses that always landed him in a mess!

He sat down on the cairn by the covered cist. The reality of the cist should keep him sober! he thought, with erratic humour. He looked back at the monolith—and held its stare. Remarkable the power of a stone—for how many civilisations over what immense periods of time! It had never struck him as it did now how extraordinarily remarkable this was. He thought of the Maya civilisation, with its terrific stone monuments—the most advanced Stone Age culture that the world had known, now lost, overgrown, in the malarial jungles, the impassable forests, of Central America. Trust America to do things even then on a large scale! he thought in an effort to relieve his mental stress. And all at once he heard Sheena ask her granny if the Stone walked about at night. Looking at the monolith again he saw that it was not the stone that walked but the spirit which was locked up in it. The spirit left the stone and strode over the moors, through many places, past silent houses, came back and was locked up once more and inscrutably. . . . Because this was an "impossible" notion, had they in time changed it to an urisk that lived in the cairn? The human accretion. . . .

But this was too much, for whole theories now beset him of life, death and after-life in all the religions of the world. Out of this vast spirit jungle, the Maya jungle stood out as something physically clear and tangible, and then in a moment—as if Martin all the time had been pursuing him— he had again the concept of Martin's mind as a jungle, but now he saw that as a jungle it was not alive, it was dead; the contorted branches, the twisting creepers, the very snakes, were dead. He actually had a forest image of this, and it was strangely horrible. It was the end of mind, like an end of the world.

He stirred by the cist, put a hand over it to make a contact. He had seen the two figures, in sleep's illusion, on the floor of his bedroom, alive. Life. The sun and its long shadow from the stone. Sex as the sun's shadow. The sun's warmth and life. . . . The warmth of Mrs. Cameron, of the welcome he got, the care. That kind of eternal household where life was. Anna and Sheena . . . why had Mrs. Sidbury walked out of the room?

In an instant, his mind intuitively encompassed inner meanings from the inflection of Mrs. Cameron's voice to all the things he had never quite heard, and he knew, as clearly as though Mrs. Cameron had just finished her interrupted story, that Martin was the father of Anna's child.

He stood quite still. Mrs. Sidbury had abruptly left the room when he had drawn the parallel between the two skeletons in the cist and Anna and Sheena . . . She obviously was abnormally taken up with her brother's condition. She would not want him to marry Anna—possibly for more than social reasons. Yet if Anna and Sheena were to depart this life in the way he had suggested the two skeletons in the cist had done, the effect on Martin might be such that— she had not dared think of it, had got up and left the room . . . something really desperate must have happened to Martin. . . .

14

He struck the passage to the chambers in the cairn on Monday afternoon. On Sunday he had taken an imaginary line from the setting sun at midwinter over the top of the standing stone with the shoulders to a spot on the cairn which did in fact prove to be the entrance. This culmination to an intense period of theoretic activity did not allay his excitement, and all unknowing he answered Andie in his own tongue when that ardent employee grew vocal at sight of the first flat slab. Besides, the dent in the curve of the orthostats was now beyond doubt, and though revealed only in one short section, it was yet enough for him to estimate the whole length of the dent. Moreover, the orthostats towards the centre of this inward curve grew taller and reached their greatest height in two that, like doorposts, flanked the passage. A fine symmetrical bit of work. No rushing now! He measured and jotted down findings and notes. The cultivated instincts of the field-worker held back the central attack on the passage with a self-denial that was an active delight.

At last everything was ready for the lifting of the flat slab that was the obvious cover or lintel to the low passage. All three of them got round it; heaved it up and over. Even Grant laughed at Andie's open-mouthed dismay, for there was nothing underneath but loose stones as if the cairn had poured in there. "No skeletons!" he rallied him with great jocularity. Andie's reactions were always slow, and now in his jerky way he looked at his employer and looked at his mother and couldn't quite make it all out. "Gu—gu—?"

"Ga!" replied Grant; "You wait! We'll get some fine bright things for you yet!" Then Andie's face creased up in its silent laugh that all but closed the small round eyes and emphasised the pink in the lower eyelids.

When the loose stones, which the slab had covered, were removed Grant found on either side the coursed walls of dry-stone masonry upon which the outer edges of the slab had rested. The height of the passage was barely three feet and the width half-a-foot less, but he did not wait to measure, for the passage continued to be blocked, and the next lintel had actually fallen in. This meant a renewed attack on the cairn above; a long tedious job, at which all three of them worked until the archaeologist's fingers were on fire. But in the end they triumphed, and although they could not lift out the lintel, they were able so to angle it that Grant, flashing his torch up the dark hole of the passage, saw that he could go ahead.

"You wait here," he ordered them, "until I come back." Then slipping down onto all fours, he left them a vision of his heels.

His beam of light shot along the dark low passage, but he went ahead slowly, examining the walls and particularly the lintels, with care. When he focused the slit between two uprights which must be the entrance to the chamber itself, his breathing grew more laboured and a trickle of sweat made him pause to clear his eyes, for he had fancied he saw a ghostly head guarding the doorway. But it was no ghost; it was a skull. He went on, trying to keep his eye on it, but this was difficult, for the beam of light was continuously moving with the movement of his hand which had to act as a forefoot. But at last he was almost beneath it and as he stopped and angled the beam full upon it, it frowned at him with an almost visible gathering of eyebrows. The effect was striking. He had never seen a skull look with such concentrated anger. The beam of light travelled up; the roof had receded; he could stand. So he stood and put the beam fair on the skull at eye level. Then he smiled. The beam travelled down to the limb bones leaning against the wall. Extraordinary! he thought. For the skull had obviously been poised on an edging of stone to the right of the upright. On closer examination he saw that a piece of stone had been hacked off to give it room. Moreover it was tilted forward slightly, which explained its effect of meeting the living eye at a lower level. A real artist was on this job, he decided, careful not to touch anything, for a flashlight photograph from the spot where his eye had first encountered it should be decidedly interesting! After examining the bone structure of the eyebrows with particular care, he slowly flashed his light around, and then passed in between the uprights, which were hardly more than eighteen inches apart. But here was no more than a small ante-chamber, and only when he had again passed between uprights did he enter a chamber some twelve feet long, eight feet wide, and seven feet high. Its walls consisted of broad uprights with coursed masonry between, which supported a roof of three huge undressed slabs that seemed to bulge menacingly down on the slim figure who moved the questing beam of light.

A stillness, a faint charnel smell, and the beam was among the bones of the floor. They lay about in a riot. They had been trampled upon and scattered. The dome of a skull lay in a corner like a ball at rest. Picking his steps he moved to the centre of the chamber and, stooping, inspected the ashes of a wood fire. Slowly he cast about him, touching, picking up. Many animal bones. Two axes, one with a reground edge. A calcined flint barbed arrowhead. A spear-head of flint three inches long. Many of the bones were partly burnt. A thin disc of talc with two holes near the edge. A fragment of pottery with ornamentation—like thumbnail marks in a row. His fingers caressingly felt the texture of the dark-red gritty ware before putting the fragment in his pocket. Another fragment. A third, too large for a pocket. . . . But he had now passed outside time.

Erect again, he cast the beam around and saw, what he had already seen, that this was not the only chamber. Passing between the two uprights on the west side, he entered a shorter chamber narrowing slightly towards the end wall, below which three skeletons lay side by side, fully extended. There were few signs of disorder here, but again only fragments of pottery, like those already found. But there were a couple of scrapers, three bone implements which interested him closely, leaf-shaped arrowheads and flint flakes. . . .

He came back into the centre chamber with the solemn face of a sleepwalker whose eyes glittered and vanished as the beam swept upward and on. His feet followed the circle of light on the floor and he stood in the east chamber. At once, as if magically drawn to it, the beam shone full on a complete vase. Forgetting to pick his steps, he stumbled on a hammer stone and the light circled drunkenly, but it came back to the vase, before which he reverently got down on his knees. Because he was greatly moved now, he was careful, and unknowingly muttered, "Leathery Atlantic", with that air of conviction which yet held a note of reservation finely responsible. He studied the ornamentation that went round the vase in bands. "Like the edge of a limpet shell," he whispered. "Finger-nail again." . . . Then he touched it, caught its rim, tilted it on its rounded bottom, and something rattled softly inside. The very sound of the rattle declared the vase to be whole. "It's whole," he intoned. "It's intact." The eye of the torch looked inside and white quartz pebbles looked back. Just pebbles, five white polished pebbles, and two with red markings. He looked at them in his cupped hands and shook his head. Merely mystery, pure mystery, and he was touched by an incommunicable grace of young womanhood in games, of bright young life. . . .

He put the pebbles back, lifted his torch, and a skull smiled.

Simon Grant knew that at first there is always something sinister in the smile of a skull, but after a time, when the mind has got used to this sinister element that dogs our bones, it can penetrate beyond to the spirit behind the domino, the allure to that which is known but never quite found, however eager and bright the immortal glance.

The skull, cocked up on the leg bones, looked over the edge of the pelvic girdle not without a certain residual dignity, an element of guardianship, of surveying the scene. The humour of this was profound, and still, and almost questioning. Had the body been placed seated against the wall, and the skull, like a fallen fruit, taken up its new position in the potent centre of man's strange anatomy? The very stones behind threw a momentary suggestion of design, of an arched frame, before the beam moved and picked up five skulls in a row. . . .

He pulled himself erect outside and blinked in the astonishing brightness of the sun so that for a moment or two the world took on a peculiar arrestment, a knowingness that was not a smile but was for him alone. The idiot's gaping face was mythological, the woman's closed face was alone in time. Then Andie broke into shambling movement and sound, and Grant perceived that Mrs. Mackenzie had had some trouble keeping him outside.

"Have I been long?" he asked and looked at his watch. "Half-past six!" He put his watch to his ear. "Good heavens!" He laughed.

"Gu—gu——?"

"Yes, yes! I'll take you in next time. Look, Mrs. Mackenzie," he said with impressive earnestness, "we must hide this opening somehow. There are days of work inside. Nobody must *ever* know, not until I'm finished. . . ."

They sealed it simply enough with a few artfully placed stones.

But at home, even after much writing, he could not subdue his excitement, his restlessness. The chambers were now in his brain as he moved about the floor, and when he stopped they swelled into their own size and he saw himself move about in them. They had the nature of a perfect illusion, yet they were real. He had come to Clachar thinking only in terms of a possible report for publication by a certain distinguished antiquarian society! For moments he was lost in a profound quietism.

It was out of one of those moments that he awoke to find himself regarding with a steady detachment the arch-like pattern of stones behind the skull in the east chamber. Had he been deceived? Stones took on such fantastic shapes in the travelling beam attended by its shadows, and his interest had been immediately taken up by that peculiar arrangement of skulls like an audience or bodyguard. Were they in fact guarding *something*? Had an intelligence so placed them . . . ?

His restlessness overcame him and, like a conspirator, he listened and peered out of the window. It was getting late and he must not be seen. Slipping the long torch into an inside pocket, he went quietly out and strolled towards the byre. From the byre he drifted away, crossed the stream, and, once round the rock, increased his pace.

The cairn was silent in the soft grey light. The wind had fallen. The sea was flat and vacant and the islands had settled down for the night. A gull cried from the cliffs, a sinking cavernous cry.

When he had removed the stones from the entrance to the passage, he paused to look around. Everything was quiet, including the monolith in the south-west, which was so still in its regard that he smiled back and even raised his hand a little way in salute. Then he disappeared.

15

He kept cool by counting the forward movements of his right hand and by the time the skull frowned down on him he reckoned he had come about twenty-five feet. More clearly than ever he saw how dramatic would be a photograph of that angry frown and moved his head and angled the light until he got what he considered the perfect elevation for the camera. He knew he was playing with time, playing with his own precious discoveries, and even did a little more reassuring research in the central chamber, before he stepped into the east chamber and flashed his torch on its east wall. There they were, waiting for him in a row, with that remarkable head in its pelvic girdle like a collapsed Buddha. Was it this conjunction of brain and pelvis, soul and sex, that had induced the notion of a smile, of ineffable, final irony? With the ultimate grey bone saying, Behold! The notion no more than flicked him, but it had its heightening effect. It was that which was not seen that lived on! But he was moving forward and the beam was searching the wall behind; it steadied, went slowly from stone to overlapping stone, up to the top of the curve, and down the other side. There was no doubt about it: here was a corbelled arch which had been filled in with carefully built-up stones! Subsequently filled in, of course, by a later hand. . . . *Why?*

His excitement bewildered him and his breath panted. *It's enough! Wait till to-morrow!* . . . but he could not wait. *Take a photograph of it or they won't believe you!* He got down on his knees, laid the torch on the ground, and tried to insert his hands under the girdle at opposing sides in order to lift the lot away without disturbing the arrangement. But the bones underneath tilted and slipped and the skull rocked in the girdle, first to one side with a hollow *nok!* then back again *nok!* then more quickly *nok! nok! nok!* in a laughter so surprisingly loud that he all but dropped the lot. At the same moment his conscience attacked him, for he was destroying the original disposition of the bones without having made even a note. On his knees he stilled the hollow laughter and regrouped the bones, his fingers slippery with sweat. My God, that laughter had been terrific! He refused to glance at his audience as his hands went flying through his pockets, but all they found was an envelope. Slitting it at either end, he opened it out into a fair-sized rectangle of clean paper, and with the spare stub of pencil which he always carried in a waistcoat pocket he began making a drunken sketch. . . .

Rough but 'twill serve! he decided, gathering reassurance as he folded the envelope and put it in his inside breast pocket. Then he lifted the skull out of the girdle and put it to one side, before also removing the girdle and the bones, and stood back a pace to consider his method of attack.

There were no uprights facing him in this back wall. The two huge uprights, which helped to support the immense lintel directly overhead, were flush with the opposing walls and came up to the corners of the back wall. But the tops of the uprights were not nicely squared off, they were visibly peaked, and the lintel also rested on this built-up back wall. If the corbelled arch retained still its original strength, then he could knock out the stones which had been subsequently built into it without any fear of a general collapse; but if it hadn't, then "flat as a pancake" would be a modest simile for anyone upon whom the lintel dived.

Every stone was stuck fast and immovable. With the hammer-stone upon which he had stumbled, he was about

113

to tap the top stone under the apex of the arch when the light, close up, showed that it was chipped. After careful examination, he decided that this very hammer-stone had been used to drive home the final stone and had chipped it in the process.

It shook time together. It telescoped it into a phantasy that was yet as real as the sharp taps with which a new human hand now tried to loosen the chipped stone by alternate blows at either side.

In and on that wall nothing moved except his own shadow, which sometimes magnified the close-cropped pointed beard to a warring pertinacity of the age of Fionn and Cuchulain, that last Heroic Age before the coming of the news of Christ. With the sharp acrid of brimstone in his nostrils, he but toiled the harder; sweat rolled from his brows as he swayed and struck, swayed and struck. Sometimes he staggered back and cast a look at the bulging lintel so short a space from his bared head; but the sight did no more than exhilarate him, drive him on. His eyes were beginning to smart, his ears to buzz, when just perceptibly the struck stone moved. Nothing more happened; the chamber waited. Within two minutes, he drew the stone out and the arch held, the lintel moved not. He stood panting like one who had run a long race.

Stone after stone he withdrew, dropping them on the floor behind him. The arch was little more than three feet in height and less in width, and in no time the opening gaped. Picking up the torch from the side of the wall whither he had shifted it for safety, he turned its beam on the dark cavity, and in an instant the darkness vanished and the cavity became a magical cabinet holding plumb in its centre a shapely urn.

Had he at last stumbled on that dish or vessel called the Holy Grail it could not have taken his breath from him more. His eyes drew nearer; it was a cinerary urn, an urn for the ashes or burnt bones left after a cremation, like that urn into which the Trojans had gathered the bones of glorious Hector, tamer of horses. But it was not made of gold, nor yet, more wonderful, of clay. It was carven in one solid piece out of stone. He touched it: steatite. But the nearest place for steatite, as he knew, was the Shetland Islands or County Donegal.

And what was a burial urn doing here? Neolithic man of the chambered cairns was not in the habit of cremating his dead. Cremation came later. Nor was the urn inverted; it sat upright and uncovered. Fully eighteen inches high and over a foot wide at the lip; without panel or overhanging collar, it had a clean elegance; from the lip its outline curved gently in and out again to a shoulder some three inches down, then sheered finely to a six-inch base. He brought the torch to the rim and looked in. But what he saw was not the grey of burnt bones. Straightening himself to come better at the matter, his head hit the top of the arch so sharply that for a little time he swayed, dizzy and sick, and with the extraordinary delusion that a figure had moved somewhere within the chamber or within his head. But he never took his eyes off the urn, and when his vision cleared he got to his knees and lifted a hand up and in.

The hand drew forth a thin metal collar or gorget of what was, to him, the *lunula* type, for it had exactly the crescentic shape of the jet necklace which he had found in the cist.

But the metal was pure gold.

It was not a unique find; five—perhaps six—of these had been found in all Scotland, but, with its engraved patterns, he could see that it was a distinguished, a lovely specimen.

His shaking hand went in again and brought forth a thin gold disc, like a miniature shield, several inches across, and patterned finely within concentric rings.

The next dip brought to the beam an ear-ring some four

inches long, curved like a scoop or miniature flower-basket, with the handle in the middle. It, too, was of gold.

As his hand went in once more, he could hear the trampling surge of blood in his ears, for he knew now that he had found a hoard of gold, that he was not only discovering treasure trove but creating archaeological history in his own land. Hoards of bronze had been found, but never a hoard of gold. His hand brought forth a penannular gold bracelet —with a second bracelet dangling from it, swinging, swinging towards the opening and just about to slip through when he made a grab at it and caught it, but the lunula slipped from the fingers of his other hand and for a moment he was entangled and confused; as the torch fell to the floor he cried out and was hoarsely echoed. But the light did not vanish. In a mad urgency, as though the spirits of the cairn like fiends were about to jump on him, he began dropping the ornaments, clasped against his breast, back into the urn, so that he could lift the urn out, the whole urn; which he should have done at first, in order to have the chamber in front of him, in order to have time to examine the incredible riches, this colossal find, and to defeat what might spring at his throat. Unaware of the knocks and thrusts of the stones, he got his arms round it. Staggering he turned—and faced the figure which had walked out of the monolith.

It stood beyond the beam of the torch, a solid darkness, on the sway, with dark-brown face and a glint of eyes. Sounds came from it of breath passing harshly in the throat. "Get out!" Grant yelled, for now he felt it coming upon him to envelop and crush; saw the wing-like lift of the arms. "Get out!" he screamed with all the fighting wrath that was in him.

As the claw-hands came into the shaft of light, he side-stepped and staggered. The arms followed the hands, the shoulders, the face. It was Foolish Andie!

Dizzied he yelled out of a face that was a sheer flame of intolerant wrath.

But the hands came on, came at the urn; the eyes gleamed red, the mouth frothed and jabbered, and the features moved in an idiot's smile.

Because of the urn he could not use his head to butt, but he did his wild mad best. Andie grunted and doubled over him, but his hands kept going round the urn. In a tearing effort at a sidestep, the archaeologist's feet hit the loose stones and he went over backwards, with urn and Andie on top of him. His head encountered stone with a sickening whack and life went out like light from a smashed bulb.

16

The electric torch had so fallen that its beam was directed towards the south corner of the east wall and had thus without more ado provided a light suitably angled for the removal of the urn from its corbelled cell. But now that the action was over, it continued to shine on a front-row audience waiting with the inscrutable humour which knows that the action of a play is not the main thing. One face only, leaning lightly against its pelvic girdle, was uptilted to the bulging lintel in an eternal mirth. As time and the outside world declined, the light would die and the bundle on the stones assume its skeleton shape, its proper and conventional dress of bones. No artist had ever contrived a different ending to this play.

But the bundle moved, it groaned, and in time it sat up, with a hand to the head in a gesture that held as the eyes roved. The skulls watched with so peculiar an intensity that when Grant met their black eyes his fingers came upon his face and so pushed into the living flesh that his jaws were forced apart. His wide eyes roved again, saw the torch and the gaping hole in the wall. . . . But there was no Andie; and there was no urn.

There was no urn. He shot the light everywhere. He stumbled about the stones like a madman in a drunken dream. Into the middle chamber he went and then into the west chamber, searching for his urn, crying wildly, "Where are you?" Anxiety and fear, fear that he would never find the urn, blotted out the pain in his own skull; old bones clattered about his feet like sticks in a petrified forest. "Wait!" he cried desperately and stood. Everything waited. "O my God!" he cried, and through the passage he crawled like a wounded demented animal.

The grey light of the fallen night met him; its watching silence communicated the lapse of the hours; the monolith in the south-west held an ironic reserve more impervious than its own stone. Everywhere was the indifference which hid the eternally lost. Through it the urn had shot and vanished and sunk forever out of sight.

He started running round the cairn, hardly feeling his feet so light was his head. He's hiding it somewhere! he thought. He's burying it! This impression was so strong that it was a visualisation, an enlarged view of Andie burying the urn. But where? Where? Where the landscape and the spot? Only after he had made two sweeping circles round the cairn did he come to his normal self sufficiently to realise that Andie in his simple way would have carried the urn home. Of course! My God, of course! Belief so invaded his mind that his head throbbed. He started off on a stalk of Andie's home. Wading through the burn, he slipped, and the cold shock cleared his head, but after he had climbed out he began to tremble with a sickening weakness and pain knocked its knuckles on his skull. As he rounded a knoll to the road a figure loomed out of the deep dusk—and stopped. Automatically the torch came up and Grant saw a face he knew, the face of a local young man whom he had met somewhere.

"I'm looking for Foolish Andie," he said, dropping the rude light from the puzzled face. "You haven't seen him?"

"No," said the man.

"I was looking for him," he repeated, with an overwhelming feeling of helplessness, of being lost in a strange place.

"What's wrong?"

"He's stolen my urn. An urn, with treasure in it. I must find it. It's—it's important, terribly important."

"Where did he steal it from?"

"From the cairn. I must find it before it's lost."

"Have you been to his house?"

"No. I'm just going. I thought you might have seen him."

"No, I haven't seen him."

"I'll go to the house." And off he set. But when he had gone some distance it suddenly came to him that he should have cautioned the man to silence. He stood, uncertain, feeling the whole night charged with conspiracy, then began to retrace his steps, breaking finally into a trot. But the man had vanished. He listened but heard no footfall on the road. Perhaps he has gone to the cairn? he thought, and once more he waded through the river, climbed, came to the cairn, stood, listened, and, with the dreadful feeling that time was just tricking him, started for Andie's home again.

The place was lightless and silent. A small thatched building stood over a little from the house. It had two doors, and when he had pushed one open, his torch shone on the beaded eyes of roosting fowls. The cock straightened himself and protested in a few hard notes of outraged dignity. The beam searched the orange-box nests and the dung. He closed the door and went to the next. A small barn full of the most amazing junk met his eyes. Closing the door behind him, he began his search. Straightening himself once, his head hit something and as he swiftly glanced up the blade of a scythe came whizzing down past his face. He had dislodged it from a rafter. When he stood on the teeth of a rake, the handle came up and hit him a crack on the forehead. By the time he had finished, he was swaying like the sole survivor on a battlefield. There was no urn.

Standing outside, he realised that all this time Mrs. Mackenzie would know. She would know certainly whether her son had been on the prowl. Not that he was now doubting the whole happening in the cairn; only it was difficult to keep his mind clear. And his head throbbed. Like one stepping on the moving edge of the phantasmagoria, he went to the door, hesitated, breathed, and knocked.

"Who's there?" called the woman's muffled voice.

"It's me, Mr. Grant."

Silence, followed by a clatter of chair legs. "Wait a minute. I'm just coming."

At last the door opened.

"Andie? Yes, he's in his bed." The warmth of her low-toned astonishment hit him.

"Has he been in bed all night?"

"Yes, ever since he went to it. Why—is something wrong?"

"Is he in bed now?"

"Yes. He's in here in the room." It was a two-roomed cottage.

His legs began to give. "Can I come in for a minute?"

"Surely—but it's a mess it's in. If you'll just wait a minute I'll get a light. Will you excuse me?"

He fell against the door jamb until she came for him, then he followed her, arms extended in the short passage, and sat heavily in the chair which she prepared for him. The atmosphere was warm and thick and the kitchen, with its wooden bed, was full of shadows from the swaying flame of the candle which she placed on the floor as she got to her knees before the smoored peat fire.

"Don't bother with a fire," he said.

"Are you sure? It won't take me a minute." Without the shawl her head looked curiously naked; the strong hair had been twisted into a simple knot behind. Her face was fleshy and gross but dignified in its calm anxiety. Life had prepared her for anything. She had put her skirt over her flannel nightdress and the shawl over her shoulders and breast.

He told her what had happened.

She stared at him and shook her head slowly. "I don't understand it."

"Has he been in all evening?"

"Yes."

"Quite sure? Take your time. It's very important."

"We were a little later than usual going to bed, but he's been in bed a long time now."

"Does he ever get out of bed at night and go away by himself?"

"Very seldom. And I know he didn't go this night because I never fell asleep myself."

"You're sure of that?"

"I'm quite sure. Sometimes the thought of things will keep me awake." Her solemn tones were touched with a mournfulness, as though all the time she was profoundly troubled by what he had told her. She was like one caught again in a familiar and fatal mesh.

"Then you are not going to help me at all?"

"How can I? What am I to say?" Her body moved in a dumb animal-like distress. She was sitting on a small stool and her eyes went to the grey peat ash again.

"Tell me this," he said, in tones suddenly clear and searching. "Was there never a time this evening when Andie left you? Think. I'm not against you. I would never harm you or Andie. If you can help me to find the urn, I will be grateful and—and pay you well."

"Oh," she said, "it's not the pay. You have been too kind. I couldn't go to sleep, thinking on the way you treat him, all the fun you make. To think that we were of some use, to a gentleman of learning. It came over me." She controlled herself.

All the time he could see that she was thinking of something, of some small thing. He waited, striving against a darkness that would blot him out.

"There was only one time since we came home," she said, "that he was out of my sight for a little, and I will tell you the whole truth of it, for indeed if I can help you it's me that will. It's before we went to our beds. I was sitting in the chair you're in now and Andie had gone out—as he always does, just before going to his bed. I was a little drowsy and nodded in my chair. When I came to myself, I wondered if he was in and went to the door. There was no sign of him. But just then he came round the corner of the house. I thought nothing about it, for I was wanting to my bed, though when I did get to my bed the sleep went from me. That's the only time he was out of my sight."

"How long were you asleep in your chair do you think?"

"It seemed to me just a minute or two, but I couldn't say for certain."

"He had nothing with him at all?"

"No, nothing. He was breathing a little heavy, and I thought that maybe he had been after the rat that came to the barn the day before yesterday. But I knew he hadn't got it."

After a further question or two about the length of time she might have been asleep, he asked her, "You are quite sure he's in his bed now?"

"Oh yes. I'll show you if you like."

"I should like to be certain."

"Very well." But she hesitated. "If he's asleep, maybe we shouldn't wake him. For this is what I have been thinking. If it's him that did take it, then he will have hidden it somewhere, and some time he will go to that place, and I will follow him. In that way we will find it. But if we frighten him now, then he will be hidden, for often he is cunning about little things."

"Why do you say *if* it was him? Don't you believe me?"

123

"Yes, oh yes, I believe you. I did not mean that."

"There's no other one like him, is there?"

"No, no. It's just—it's just overcome me."

"Very well, Mrs. Mackenzie. You do as you say."

"Thank you, sir. If it can humanly be done, I'll do it."

He got up and she followed him, but at the door she continued towards the other room, the flaring candle in front of her, turned the brass knob and entered.

"Are you asleep?" she asked quietly.

"Gu—gu——"

He heard a drawer being opened and shut, then she came back, carrying some article of clothing. She nodded to him from behind the light, and without a word he went away.

Through his physical weakness in the house, his mind had kept astonishingly clear, but now his body felt like collapse again. *If it was him. . . .* A note in the woman's voice, a strangeness. Did she think it was the urisk or what? he asked of the night with a drunken bitterness. *If it can be humanly done. . . .* Did she think it was not human? He conjured up the face in the chamber. At first he had had the extraordinary conviction that the figure had come out of the monolith, but that was because of its solid darkness, outside the beam. And he hadn't heard it come in. Why—how—hadn't he heard it? Because he was too busy. But the face, hadn't it breathed on him! And the hands, the arms, good God, didn't he know them!

This self-questioning in its maddening futility weakened him still more. He missed the path, misjudged the height of a low stone dyke, and on his back saw the moon look over the mountains. A faint glimmer in the deep dusk of high summer spread the earth under the moon soft as a cat's paws, and as he turned to get up, it tilted in a bewitchment; then hadn't tilted but was there, waiting. A figure moved up at the corner of the little field. Even as he watched, it faded away, was withdrawn. As he came by the corner of the garden wall, an animal sprang into and out of sight. The cat. The door was unlocked and he blundered through it noisily, paused, then knocked on the kitchen door. In a couple of minutes he found himself on Mrs. Cameron's chair while she, on her knees, was drawing the red embers from the ash and blowing the dry clods of peat to a flame. "One jug of water in the kettle and I'll have a drop of tea for you in a jiffy." She was nimble on her feet, so great was her anxiety.

His head now ached dully, stupidly. He was going to let go when he saw Anna in the doorway. She looked extraordinarily beautiful in the soft shadowy light of the hand-lamp now on the mantelpiece. The tawny hair, the pale wonder, the eyes grown large. She came in slowly as he watched her. Then he smiled.

Mrs. Cameron explained that Mr. Grant had had a bad fall. "I cannot find my spectacles," she added in a worried voice. But Anna didn't need spectacles, and as Mrs. Cameron held the lamp, Anna examined the back of Mr. Grant's head. "There's a slight swelling," she said. Her finger-tips explored under the hair. "The skin is not broken."

"That's fine," he said. "Thank you. I'll tell you what happened." And he told them, as though the suffocating burden had at last been lifted from him and his voice found it easy to speak on its own. Mrs. Cameron was at once full of assurance, of resource. She would see Mrs. Mackenzie first thing in the morning. "Don't you worry, Mr. Grant. We'll find the treasure, that's sure." She got the bellows once more on the peat until the flames enveloped the kettle and it began to sing.

"It means so much to me," he said. He told them how wonderful a hoard this was, how unique in the history of their country's antiquities. Usually in his voice there was a laugh or energy of some sort, but now he spoke simply and Mrs. Cameron glanced compassionately at him as she would at a woman who had been bereaved of her dearest on earth. The heart so moved in her that the first spout of water from the kettle missed the teapot.

"There's nothing like a wee bit of oatcake and butter for putting the heart in you," she said, buttering half a bannock.

And the tea refreshed him, brought him still more to himself.

"Only closed her eyes for a minute or two!" Mrs. Cameron scoffed brightly. "I have closed my own for half a minute and found it half an hour. Haven't we all? But she's anxious, poor woman, for her son. He's all she has, when all is said. And he's as fond of bonny bright things as a bairn. Do you think he will be able to keep away from them? Not him! Did ever you know a bairn that could?"

He gave an involuntary shiver and felt his knees.

"It's not wet you are?" asked Mrs. Cameron.

"No," he answered lightly. "I just came through the burn."

"Dear me! It's to your bed you'll go this minute. I'll fill a bottle." She had come half-way to feel his legs before she stopped herself, for his grey face worried her.

But he said he wasn't going to his bed; in fact he was going back to the cairn. Dismayed, almost angry, she did her best to persuade him against this exceeding folly, but he answered that he had remembered something, and she saw that he had a hidden will as tough as wire.

"In that case," she said, "you'll change yourself first, and Anna will go with you. I'm not going to have sick folk in my house."

On the way, he said to Anna, "I'm sorry to trouble you, but I could hardly let your mother come!"

Anna answered that she didn't mind at all and walked beside him down to the footbridge. Her companionship, her nearness, so moved him that he suddenly wanted to take

126

her arm or her hand. The deep dusk of the middle night had lightened under the moon. "What I'm afraid of," he said, curbing his desire, "is that someone might go into the cairn and take things. If you helped me to block up the entrance after I came out—do you mind?"

"No," she answered, "it's a pleasure." Her restraint was soft as the moonlight.

"You're a dear girl," he said impulsively, and added practically, in a sincere voice, "If there's ever anything I can do for you at any time, you ask me. And for your grandmother too."

"Thank you," she said, with a quiet embarrassment that moved him more than ever.

"I'll tell you what's really worrying me," he explained. "When I was making for Andie's home I met a man and told him I was looking for Andie and why. If he spread the news. . . . It was silly of me, but at the time I could only think of getting hold of Andie."

"Do you know who he was?"

"I know I've met him. He's a local fellow. But where?"

"What was he like?"

He did his best to describe him. She did not answer.

"That conveys nothing to you?" he asked.

"I don't know."

Then in a flash it came to him, and in his astonishment he stopped just short of the cairn. "I remember! The first day I came here . . . he was driving Mr. Martin's car."

She was silent.

"You know him, of course?"

"Yes."

"Now look, if you could possibly see him first thing in the morning and tell him for heaven's sake not to mention what I told him, I should be very grateful to you. Would you do that?"

But she hesitated. "We'll let him know," she murmured.

He stood still, looking at her. She plainly did not mean to speak to the fellow herself. Something of disquiet touched him and strengthened him.

"Thank you," he said soberly and led the way to the passage.

"You're sure you don't mind waiting here for me alone? I'll only be a few minutes."

She said she didn't mind and he went into the cairn.

17

As he crawled along the passage, he was aware that the cairn was coming alive. This did not worry him; he simply knew it happened. Nothing could irritate him more nowadays than talk about time, time as the fourth dimension "and all that sort of stuff". When he was intolerant he was inclined to be very intolerant, even perverse. For the truth was that time had become something other to him than a symbol in a mathematical equation. He even believed that an intuition was different in kind from anything logical or mathematical. Fundamentally it was an experience, and if the other fellow hadn't had the experience how on earth could he discuss it? It was a blind presumption on his part, literally blind. What on earth do you know about ghosts if you have never seen one? If you haven't experienced the psychic density of a place that was, over a long period of time, a centre of tremendous human emotions, what can you have to say about it that isn't irrelevant? With such questions he had pursued his opponents even through their laughter. When he knew what he knew, he had a remarkable tenacity about it.

Moreover his physical experiences of the whole evening had now and then released his mind in a light and unusual way. This lightness could even stand away from the thickness in his head, from the clogged brain, with an effect of clarity that heightened apprehension. In the electric beam the angry skull was now not quite so bare. But he didn't care much for the fellow. A warrior could be great-hearted. This guardsman hadn't been; though no doubt he had been loyal enough. All the same he was a fellow mortal who had done his job, so he nodded to him, friendly enough, and passed on into the east chamber.

The hole in the wall gaped with a false suggestion of rape. It should never have been built in. But there had been strong on-goings here. These severed heads had never been set in that row by pious hands. . . . Severed—could it be possible? he wondered.

His expression pursed as he stood in vision, nodding now and then very slightly. There had never been any doubt in his mind but that the urn was an "intrusion", possibly from the age of Gaelic myth and heroic legend. The intruder had found the passage into the long-covered tomb, and, for reasons which were not unimaginable, had concealed it here. In troubled times in all countries, people used holy places, places of worship, for hiding their treasure. In this last war an altar in a Balkan church had been used by the underground movement for storing dynamite. . . . Two or three levels of thought turned in his mind with a delicate jugglery, their planes tilting over in a visionary light, in a subtle game of fearful delay; then he walked to the spot where he had stood when he had withdrawn the ornaments from the urn, cast his light on the floor, among the stones, paused, stooped, and came slowly erect with the gold lunula in his hand.

It was real! The whole experience had been real! Weakness flushed his head and he sat down unable for a little time to get enough breath into his lungs. In Mrs. Cameron's kitchen, while he had been telling them his story, he remembered the ornament which had fallen from his hands when he had tried to grasp the dangling bracelet. This was it.

His weakness suffused him with an insidious sleep. His eyes closed and faintly he heard voices, clear voices but distant, coming down far corridors. At once he lifted his head, listened, put the necklace into a poacher's pocket, and started for the passage.

"Who was speaking?" he asked.

She stood against the moonlit world with an extraordinary authenticity, a drawing together of all meaning into her still body. "Mr. Martin," she said.

"Where is he?"

"He's gone home."

"What was he doing here?"

"He was just passing." Her voice was simple and remote; it was cool and fatal; but he knew that any instant she might break down.

"What were you talking about?"

She did not answer.

"Did you tell him I was in the cairn?"

"Yes."

"What did he say?"

"Nothing."

"Did you tell him about the treasure?"

"No. I told him you had forgotten something."

He stood, hardly aware of his questions, wondering if he would rush after Martin. But in another moment he saw such urgency as meaningless. Then the relationship which he had imagined between Anna and Martin came full upon him.

"I found what I was looking for," he said quietly.

"That's fine," she answered in her polite friendly way.

"Yes," he said. "This is it. It's pure gold."

As she tilted it in her hands the moonlight spilled off it.

"It's beautiful," she said. "What was it for?"

"For putting round your neck. Wait."

He took it from her. She was wearing a green woollen jumper open at the throat. He caught the lunula by the horns, lifted it towards her throat, and paused as she involuntarily swayed back a little.

"Perhaps I had better not stretch it," he said, "until we see if it's quite whole."

She was silent, but he knew that her recent moment of stress had passed.

"And now we'll have to fill in the opening."

She helped him with an intelligent eagerness, handing down stones until the entrance was completely blocked. She had a pliant strong body, and her hair fell about her face and was tossed back.

"That should about do. Thank you, Anna." As he got up out of the passage he staggered and she caught his arm. "So strange a night, I feel a bit dizzy," he excused himself, smiling. As they were getting clear of the stones, he saw that she was watchful of him. A deep generosity towards her moved him in a light incorporeal way. The odd thing about this condition was that it appreciated essences, the unspoken word, the quality behind the act. What was undying in her was known to him. He patted her shoulder gently. "I'm all right," he said in a light laughing voice. "And now for home."

He rested once, stretching himself on his back and closing his eyes. Anna sat beside him. But he could not find utter peace because he wanted to ask her some questions. Also he wanted to go to sleep. If she spoke to him frankly, he would tell her the way. He felt full of a wisdom as old as the cairn. But he could do nothing. You never can do anything at such a moment except *be* there, he thought. I must stop wandering, he decided, or I'll go away altogether. He sat up and felt faint.

"You go home, Anna, and I'll just wait here a little while." He hung his head.

"Don't hurry," she said to him. "It will pass."

They seemed remarkable words to him, full of so profound a knowledge that the faintness began to ebb. He lifted his face.

She put her arm under his to help him up.

"One minute. . . . Tell me, is it growing lighter or am I imagining things?"

"The dawn is coming," she said.

"Is it?" It seemed such extraordinary news that he looked about him in wonder. Then she helped him up.

Mrs. Cameron was waiting for them. There was bustle and concern and he was soon in his bed. But he couldn't sleep. The thoughts he had been choking back came out in hideous guise. No recent illness, no holiday feeling, could ever excuse his appalling rashness and ineptitude. He had almost behaved like an amateur. What his fellow archaeologists would think—dear God! The loss of a find of such historical significance *in such a way!* He writhed in mental anguish. . . . But in time, when bleakness came, he got control. There was only one thing to do now: carry on with coolness and cunning. Whatever happened he would keep a calm sough and be damned to them all! This final fighting thought exhausted him completely and he fell asleep.

18

Awaking to the strong daylight he looked for his watch on the chair by his bed. There was no watch and his head ached. A child's voice laughed distantly and abruptly stopped. His watch was still ticking when he pulled it out of his waistcoat pocket. Five past ten! He began to dress hurriedly. As he went round the corner of the house towards the byre, he saw Sheena by the peat-stack on his right. Her back was to him and she was speaking to her home-made doll. "Shshsh," she was saying mysteriously, "you mustn't waken Mr. Grant."

This simple innocence lightened his misery and on the way back from the byre he spoke to her. Her round-eyed solemnity, with the shy hands up towards her mouth, moved him to a smile and he remembered the letter to his craftsman friend about the Silver Bough. Mrs. Cameron met him at the doorstep. He wished her good morning and said he was very late.

"I thought I would let you sleep on," she answered, scanning his face.

"It's all right," he replied with a forced smile, "but I would rather you had knocked me at the right time."

"I'm sorry, Mr. Grant, but you needed your sleep."

"Doesn't matter," he muttered going into his sitting-room, his head suddenly throbbing with annoyance. He felt anxious and wretched.

Anna brought him his porridge.

"Did you manage to send word to Mr. Martin's chauffeur?" he asked her.

"Yes," she answered, and added, "Grandmother went to see Mrs. Mackenzie this morning. She told her you might be late."

"Oh, did she? My head is a bit thick. No news, I suppose?" He looked at her.

"Grandmother will tell you herself."

But Mrs. Cameron hadn't much to tell, though she warmly conveyed the impression that Mrs. Mackenzie and herself were his cunning and confident allies. Hope stirred in him, and after Anna had produced a small bottle of aspirin, he set out with his camera and gear.

As he approached the cairn and saw the two figures, their queer forlornness only made him clamp his teeth. How was it that he always got into impossible arguments and idiotic situations? Physical weakness turned his forehead cold. He greeted them, smiling obscurely, then turned abruptly on Foolish Andie and demanded, "Where did you hide it?"

Andie's mouth opened wider, then he became excited and as he rocked on his feet his arms opened and shut like wings, the hands slapping the thighs. "Hug—goo—ha—ha. . . ."

"But you do know! Dammit, where did you put it?" His voice rose shrilly, but at the end of the argument he was no further forward. The cunning look in the small eyes and the fat creased smile—heaven alone knew whether they meant anything or not. He did not question Mrs. Mackenzie, who all the time stood silent, for he felt angry and a little ashamed. This was not how he had meant to behave and his stomach sank as he felt he had merely increased the primitive cunning and fear.

Andie removed the stones with ardour, and Grant set about the business of taking photographs of the interior by flashlight. But it was difficult working alone, and his nerves soon got ragged. There was an unusual stillness in the chambers, too; not that everything was without life, but that something had receded, leaving behind a sinister aspect.

He had had a similar experience before when excavating a Roman villa; but now it was not a premonition of a brutal act; it was the presence of the annihilation after the act. It would not strike him; it would drain him through death to the negation of stone; and even then he would not be the stone, he would be the darkness.

He became aware of himself counting and recounting the bones, sitting on the floor by his electric handlamp. He stirred, got up, and muttered. After all, he *was* an archaeologist and this was essential work in the endless process of man's knowledge of himself and his creation of culture. Why be so upset? For the chances were almost certain that they would find the hoard. It only needed time—and for such a hoard he could wait for months, for years. Andie would go for it as certainly as a child would go for her doll.

Then he stood for an appalled moment listening to the dark whisper, the dark whisper that the hoard didn't matter. He could hardly breathe. He wanted to turn and vanish. *But you know it doesn't matter.*

He cast about him. He said aloud, "It is quite clear that in the chamber area the earth had been skinned to the rock. There is an inch or two of fine soil, probably from pulverised rock edges and pockets of earth left in cracks. . . ."

The echoes of his voice sounded lunatic; his brain throbbed through the cushion woven by the aspirin. Since his arrival he had been only once touched by this kind of fear; it was when Martin had asked him to stay after dinner. He suddenly saw Martin's face as it was then, and its aspect was *this* aspect. Why not? he said to himself with a stirring of wrath, a movement of his body to repel. Isn't the fellow Neolithic?

He went on with his work; but in a few minutes a whisper suggested: You'd better make a rough count in each chamber lest you are never allowed to finish this job properly; record the main things; hurry up. This suddenly seemed sound advice, and with a conscious sense of proportion he proceeded to act on it.

By lunch time he was all in and knew it. When he saw three hikers or tourists appear on the crest behind, he watched them for a moment or two with sharpened eyebrows, then suddenly ordered the closing of the passage. He was munching his sandwich again by the time they drew near. A mop-haired young woman with her hands in the pockets of her very short shorts, a solemn-faced young man with spectacles and a slung camera, and a handsome dark-haired fellow with a frank engaging manner who passed the time of day. The girl's eyes travelled from Andie's face to his mother's and then on to Grant's with the air of not believing it.

"Are you doing some excavating here, sir?" asked the dark fellow.

"Yes," replied Grant shortly.

"Any luck at all in the way of finds?"

"Luck is not the idea," he answered coldly, giving the fellow his shoulder.

"Sorry if we intrude," came the response at once in friendliest apology. "My friend had the notion that he would like a photo of this old pile. We hope you don't mind?"

"I do mind," Grant said sharply, glancing at him.

"Oh, sorry," he murmured, his intelligent eyes drifting over the excavations. There was a click and Grant got up and turned. The spectacled young man was winding up his shot.

"I should be obliged," said Grant angrily, "if you would stop doing that."

The expression behind the spectacles grew even more solemn; that was all. The girl stood now with her legs apart.

"We had no idea you would mind," said the dark fellow. "We are all very interested in archaeology. My friend here was in Egypt and Crete. We thought we even might be of some help, as intelligent amateurs."

137

"No, thank you," replied Grant, who, however, had once been an intelligent amateur himself. He felt confused and wretched, for he had a natural loyalty to all workers in the field, and Crete and Egypt were conjuring names.

"In that case, we'll make ourselves scarce," said the dark fellow agreeably. "Sorry for intruding."

"Very good of you to offer," replied Mr. Grant. "But, as it happens, I'm finished for the time being."

"Oh, really? You did manage inside?"

"Yes."

"Ah. How interesting!" He looked at the closed passage, then smiled and saluted. "We shouldn't have minded being with you!"

"The proprietor doesn't care for people on his ground," Grant explained with a difficult smile.

"Ah—ha!" The fellow nodded with the air of one to whom no more need be said. "May we sincerely hope you didn't draw a blank altogether?"

"You may."

"Goodo! And apologies once more."

As she passed him, the young woman gave Grant the unexpectedly sweet smile of a girl in a crinoline. All three saluted Andie and his mother and went off towards the cliffs.

Feeling he had behaved with outrageously bad manners, Grant found all taste for his sandwiches gone. With an intelligent young fellow like that, what a job he could have done! Not to mention intelligent companionship. He could not look at the idiot and busied himself getting his gear together. Then he told Mrs. Mackenzie that there would be no more work for the day. "First thing in the morning," he said. He had meant to speak to her privately but couldn't. As a last thought, he had some more stones piled against the passage entrance.

In the afternoon he wrote up his notes but couldn't

138

conscientiously guarantee even his total of humans buried in the cairn, and there were certain bones he would really have to do something about. And the soil would have to be sifted. And—O God, he had forgotten again to remove the vase!

But it didn't matter. Like the lean cattle and the fat cattle and the women kissed before, the things in the cairn didn't matter. They had all been found before. It was the urn, the pot of gold. . . .

The words "pot of gold" went through his head like a fairy legend. They were, in fact, a fairy legend. The pot of gold or the crock of gold, hunted all through northern legend but never found, because the fairies had buried it at the foot of the rainbow. And he had found it!

Wild gleams and echoes went through his head, swirls of the little folk in a green light, eddies of laughter, and the winking gold in the pot. He ravished their world, lifting the pot high above their heads, and they danced around, thrusting up their hands, but not disliking him, because he was in their world. . . .

He groaned aloud. He was of their world, sinking so low that his intelligence quotient was pre-logical; he was in Sheena's age group. He had heard of softening of the brain; this is what it was like before softening could happen to it.

He took the floor, walking it within the cage of the room. For he was not deceived. He had resolved the fairy story, had turned the archaeological key that opened the hidden chamber, had removed the stones of intrusion from the corbelled cell of legend or myth. All this he had done—to be foiled by an idiot in the guise of prehistory.

Out of this mental extravagance, one small terrible thing did remain. Unable up to this moment to understand why he had felt so hopeless about finding the urn, when common sense suggested there was every hope, he now realised that his subconscious had decided on its own that finding it was not in the logical order of things. And if this was more fantastic than any legend or myth, it was none the less of a persistence that had the teeth of a dark rat.

As he swayed in his tiredness, for his heart should have given out on him long before this—though actually it had never given him a twinge—he decided he would go to his bed. He would go to his bed and get up when the sun had set and then in the half-light, through the deep dusk of the summer night, he would stalk the idiot's cottage, he would wander and watch, for he suddenly saw with complete conviction that it was only in that light, when the logical was asleep, that the crock of gold could be found.

19

The sounds increased. He listened for a while, looked at his watch—it was noon, closed his note-book and crawled back along the passage. Two legs stopped him at its end and he shouted. The legs rose up, and he rose up after them. The legs had belonged to Andie, who was defending the passage against the public. The girl in the shorts continued to wind up a camera while at least a dozen pairs of eyes concentrated on Mr. Grant.

"What's all this?" he demanded, his eyes flashing. At such moments his pointed beard gave him a distinguished intolerance.

"I was only wanting in to have a look," said the man nearest to Andie, a mouse-haired fellow in slacks.

"Well, you can't have a look," Grant told him.

"And that's that!"

"Yes, that's that! The work going on here is private. It is being carried on by—by special permission. It's important that nothing should be disturbed. Absolutely important." The camera clicked and his eyes flashed to the girl. She smiled to him in a melting sweetness within a small nod and hitched her pants.

"Ladies and gentlemen," said Grant, with such control that his face visibly paled, "I appeal to you to go away."

Even children don't like to be told to go away. Some faces grew stony, others smiled in a peculiar way. They were doing nobody any harm and it was a free country—so far. Someone laughed. They began to move away but not as if they were really doing it or had to. And now obviously some curious things were being said, some esoteric joke touched upon. The laughter caught at good humour. Some sat down at a little distance.

Mrs. Cameron had told him that tourists often came to look at Clachar but that as the cairn was out of sight of the road they generally missed it. "There isn't much else for them to do, poor things." And he had actually taken a note of her next remark: "It's a favourite place for the Sunday School picnic." At the time that had held for him a subterranean interest. But he had been miraculously free of visitors until yesterday and now these three, whom he might have asked to be discreet, had blabbed the news. There would be a spate from Kinlochoscar henceforth. They had found a fellow who was actually doing something on his own. At last the Highlands had provided a spectacle for their entertainment. They could stand and gape.

Bitter as his thoughts were, he did not lose his cunning. At the right moment he slipped into the cairn again, leaving Mrs. Mackenzie and her son as a human screen. This would have to be Andie's last appearance on the site, for his gape value was obviously tremendous. Presently he called to Mrs. Mackenzie from the passage. She bent down. "I want your apron," he said, "but don't let them see you taking it off." He crawled out into the light, carefully placing the vase once more in front of him. It had been a laborious business and he was sweating.

But when Andie saw the vase he became tremendously excited and vocal.

"Shut him up!" said Grant hoarsely.

"Andie, be quiet!" she ordered with a calm intensity. His flappings and staggerings eased, but the younger visitors drew near again, two of them indeed all but ran up, while the mouse-haired fellow definitely sauntered.

"Gu—gu—gu——" continued Andie, for it is doubtful if any archæologist had ever had so enthusiastic an assistant.

"Andie!" Her voice had the remarkable effect of turning off a tap that drips a few final mutters. Grant had the apron round the vase.

"I'll give you something to do," he said to Andie with a social and vindictive smile as he came erect. "Get that slab against the opening." He deposited all his gear, including the swathed vase, safely out of reach. Mrs. Mackenzie interpreted his order with a single discreet gesture and Andie set to work. But though his neck swelled alarmingly, Andie could not upend the slab, not even with his mother's unobtrusive but powerful help. However, they got it so angled and tilted that Grant was satisfied. "Now for the stones," he said. And it was to be no light affair this time, it was going to be a complete block-up.

"Carry on the work," he said to Mrs. Mackenzie presently, "and stand by until I return." Then hung about with his gear, and carrying the dark-swathed vase like a funeral offering, he set off for his lodging, followed by many eyes and a few feet.

As he rounded the rock where he had found Anna and Sheena asleep, he glanced down towards Clachar House and saw two men who had obviously just left it and were now making for the cairn. There was no mistaking the black head of the enthusiastic amateur nor the movement of his companion of the spectacles. They had been interviewing Martin!

By God, there's treachery for you! he said through his teeth, and his whole body momentarily locked in rigor. Hell's bells, what would Martin think? Mass invasion! The vase slithered as in collapse. His heart swole up and choked him. He went on blindly for a little way, then rested. "I'll carry this for you," said Anna. He looked at her, then slowly looked about him. "Take off the apron," he said, "and see if it's whole. Very careful." "It seems all right. Yes, it's quite whole."

He nodded, "Thank God," and breathed more lightly. "I wish I had stuck to you entirely."

She glanced at him, but obviously he was not being personal. She slung the strap of his bag over her shoulder and lifted the clothed vase. "You can trust me to take care of it," she said.

"I would trust you with anything," he answered with a slight resurgence of vindictiveness. Then he got up and, walking beside her, told of the invasion.

Mrs. Cameron was hopeful as ever. "It'll all pass in a day or two," she prophesied. "Just something new for them to wonder at." When she saw the vase on its rounded bottom: "Well, well, to think it was the best they had, the creatures!" Sheena wanted to see and Mrs. Cameron lifted her up. "The kettle is boiling, Anna," she called; "make Mr. Grant a cup of tea." "I'm just making it," answered Anna from the kitchen. "Now come away, Sheena," said Mrs. Cameron. "Look!" said Mr. Grant to Sheena, and, putting a hand into the vase, he brought out three of the white quartz pebbles. Sheena looked steadily. "Now what would they be for?" asked Mrs. Cameron. "I wish I knew," answered Grant. "Are there many of them?" she asked. "Seven," he answered. "That's a good number," she said.

Sheena put out her hand and Mr. Grant placed a pebble in it. She looked at it and at the other two; then she looked up at her granny and lifted her face. Mrs. Cameron stooped to listen. "Ach you!" declared Mrs. Cameron. "She says they would be nice for playing five-stones."

"What's five-stones?"

"Och, just a lassie's game!"

"Indeed," said Grant. "Have you ever played it yourself?"

"Many's the time that. As sure as the spring came in, we would be at it."

"That interests me very much. You couldn't let me see how you played it?"

"I could not then!" She gave a small laugh and called Anna.

Anna came in with the tea on a tray, and when the round table in the centre of the room had been pushed to one side, she sat down on the floor with five white pebbles in her right hand. She scattered the pebbles, then, lifting one, threw it in the air, touched the floor, and caught it; threw it again, grabbed the next pebble off the floor and caught the falling one. As the stone came down for the fifth time, it clicked against the four in her hand and there were all five and not one had been missed.

Grant was staring at her. She was slightly flushed, but the whole swaying movements of her body, the swift flash of the blue eyes down and up, the tumble of red hair, the very sitting on the floor, had a feminine enchantment about it, innocent and invigorating as spring's own self.

"Why seven?" he wondered.

"We played with three, or with five, or with seven, but seven was difficult," said Anna.

"Ah!" He got up out of his chair.

"Come away," said Mrs. Cameron, "for Mr. Grant must have his tea."

"My chance," said Sheena for the second time.

"No, no," said her granny.

"Yes," said Sheena. "My chance."

"Certainly," said Grant before the small eyes could fill with tears, and when she missed her catch he said he could not do it better himself, so he tried and did worse. She gave up the pebbles absolutely, but with so continuing a concentration upon them that he said, "You wait till you see the present that I'll get you!"

Then she looked at him and something still as her soul hung between one wonder and another.

She kept looking back at him even after Anna began to lead her away. Alone, he stood quite still, for in the little face

145

he had glimpsed, beyond all doubt, the ghostly presence of the owner of Clachar House.

As he drank his tea, he felt quiet and detached. The turmoil had passed from him. What had to be done inside the cairn could safely wait. He could work for a few hours, very early in the morning, any day. For that matter, it could be done during the dead of night. Perhaps he had better go and see Martin, express his regrets at the mass intrusion, and say that he would have the stones put back on the cairn at once, so that the public would think the whole affair was over.

About four o'clock that afternoon, as he drew near Clachar House, he saw the chauffeur come down from the garage carrying a parcel and a newspaper. "Excuse me," he said, intercepting him, "but I just wanted to thank you for not mentioning our meeting the other night."

"It's all right," answered the chauffeur in an embarrassed way.

"You didn't in fact mention it, did you?" There was something a trifle stormy about the fellow's eyebrows that troubled Grant.

"I did meet two friends of mine, just after you left me, and I asked them if they had seen Foolish Andie. They said no. We scouted round a bit. That's all I mentioned it."

"Oh. I see. Thank you. . . . Would the other two, do you think——?"

"I shouldn't think so, but it didn't seem at the time that it was something to—hide."

"I understand. Believe me, I am not trying to blame you. Only, I don't want the public crashing in here. I don't want Mr. Martin to be troubled."

The chauffeur said nothing, then glanced quickly over his shoulder at Mrs. Sidbury as she drew near. After she had greeted Grant, she called, "I'll take them, Norman." Norman handed her the parcel and the newspaper and returned to his garage. "Please come and have some tea." As he hesitated, she added, "I do get tired of having tea alone."

"Actually," he said as they went to the house, "I was coming to see your brother. The public have got wind of our doings up there, and quite a few were on the site this forenoon. They are still wandering around."

"We heard something about that. Does it worry you?"

"I was frightened it would worry you—especially your brother. And I wanted to tell him that I am finishing up—for the time being."

"You're not going away?"

"No. Not for a little time. Tell me, is your brother annoyed?"

"Not more than usual!" She half swung round with an amused smile, then entered at the front door. "Have a chair. I'll see about tea."

She was back in a couple of minutes. "What's all this?" She held the newspaper in her hand.

He looked at her face, then took the newspaper. The large headlines stared at him:

CROCK OF GOLD discovered by SCOTTISH ANTIQUARY.

In a mounting tumult he read: "The most remarkable discovery in the whole history of Scottish archaeology has just been made by Mr. Simon Grant. The site is a remote cairn in the Highlands and the circumstances attending the find are already as fabulous as the Gaelic legends about the crock of gold which the fairies were alleged to have hidden under the rainbow. . . ." The print began to dance under his eyes as they moved down the column. Sub-title: THE CROCK VANISHES. "Working alone amid these old skeletons in the dead of night, Mr. Grant found the pot of gold. Exactly what happened at this extraordinary moment is not clear. But some of the young men of Clachar, returning home at a late hour, were waylaid by Mr. Grant and asked if they had seen his assistant, who had just run away with the treasure. Very naturally the archaeologist was at the time labouring under a considerable degree of excitement. The young men had not in fact seen the assistant and on their own joined in the hunt until the deep dusk of the summer night was lightened by the moon, when it was found that the assistant was in his bed. Strange as this story may seem, it now takes on a truly fantastic kinship to a midsummer night's dream, for the assistant was, and is, no other than the village natural who is incapable of expressing himself in articulate speech. Admirable at hurling stones from the cairn or similarly assisting in the work of excavation, he possesses no language other than obscure guttural sounds and is directed in his labours by his widowed mother of whom he is the sole support. His childish passion for bright ornaments that gleam like gold is well known in the district, and the plain assumption is that he has buried the crock of gold in some private cache which one day may, or may not, be found. When interviewed the following day at the cairn, Mr. Grant showed a marked reserve and would neither confirm nor deny. . . ."

But Grant could read no further. His hands shook. He said, "My God!" He sat down.

20

Mrs. Sidbury showed remarkable tact and Grant wiped a drip of tea from his breast in a quietened manner. "You can leave Donald to me. You need not worry about him," she said, thrusting the newspaper behind the cake stand.

"Thank you." He put his handkerchief back in his pocket with a shaking fist.

"I'll talk to Norman and find out exactly what happened that night. If the urn could be found before there's any more fuss, then it wouldn't really matter so much."

"Not so much," he said automatically and got up.

As he went on his way, he experienced a series of involuntary physical spasms. To think that I could have mistaken that black fellow for anything but a journalist! But the thought merely covered a much deeper one: Colonel Mackintosh, Blair . . .! Archaeological circles everywhere! The British Museum to Egypt! . . . He groaned quietly. The fabulous crock of gold—stolen by the village idiot! . . . Hush! he said to the universe. Be quiet! He shook his stunned head.

As he went in at the door, he called to Mrs. Cameron, and when she appeared asked her if anyone had interviewed her.

"There was one dark young gentleman—and very nice he was, I must say—who asked me what I knew about the pot of gold, but I said it had nothing to do with me and he better ask you."

"You didn't give him any particulars?"

"I felt it was not my place to do it."

"What questions did he ask you?"

"He asked me about Foolish Andie and about life in the Highlands. He was very pleasant and gave a little present to Sheena—just to bring him luck, he said, for he was trying to do what he could to make the Highlands better known to the world, for that would help the tourist business, he said. He was so nice that he took a cup of tea."

"Why didn't you tell me this?"

"I didn't think of it. Besides, he said he had been talking to yourself a little while before up at the cairn. So I thought you would know all about him and I was just doing my best. He said you were a very clever man and that warmed me to him."

When he had told her what had happened, she was very concerned and not a little amazed at the strange ways of the great world. "And he asked me if you were very tired when you came home late that night after Andie had stolen the pot of gold. And I said you were. Shame on him!"

As he went up the road, he realised how attractive the simple detective work must have been for the journalist who would enjoy it all the more because of the way he had been foiled at the cairn. Norman and his friends had talked of the midnight encounter. The story had reached Kinlochoscar the following morning. . . . He became aware that three tourists were watching his approach. They stood by the side of the road and followed him with their eyes as he passed.

He saw heads on the western skyline (no doubt keeping the movements of Andie under observation) as he turned off the road towards Mrs. Mackenzie's cottage. Andie was breaking peats at the stack and putting the clods in a wicker basket. He paused in his labours to regard his employer with a face like a mythological joke. Mrs. Mackenzie took her visitor into the kitchen.

Yes, the dark young gentleman had called. "He was very nice, and said that you were the one who would never get Andrew into trouble for stealing the pot of gold. And I said it was very hard on us that it should have happened for you had been so kind."

"You told him all about it?"

"There was little need to tell him, for, as he said, he knew all about it himself. Everyone seems to know about it." Her tone was mournful. "I told him nothing but what was the truth."

He sat in silence.

"He asked me, too, about Andrew and—and about the past. He said I had had a hard life of it. I am not complaining, I said, though I should feel it if shame came on me now. He said he was sure that would not happen. I hope he is right, for I have tried to do my best."

"Don't worry, Mrs. Mackenzie," he said quietly and hopelessly.

"I have tried to bear my burden."

"You have borne it nobly," he answered.

The tears started into her eyes, ran down her strong solemn face. "It's them watching the house!" she cried in a breaking voice. But she controlled herself and with shut mouth drew breath noisily in through her nostrils. It was not an easy grief.

He got up and patted her on the shoulder. "When they speak to you don't tell them anything. Tell them to go to me. I'll deal with them." He smiled wanly. She had brought a lump to his throat.

Before leaving he said lightly that though work would be suspended meantime, they would both remain on the payroll. For the rest she was to answer no questions. All she had to do was to watch Andie and try to find the hidden pot. If she found that she would not only do a service to him but to the whole learned world.

151

As he went down the road he felt quietly murderous.

It seemed to him that Mrs. Mackenzie and Mrs. Cameron carried on a way of life that was the essence, the traditional inheritance, of long periods of human living. It was the invisible good, the selfless kindness, that had kept the living going. Without it, all systems of thought, ideologies, intellectualisms in a hurry, scientific constructions, all would have collapsed. They collapse anyhow damn them! he thought in spiring anger and cast his eyes up to the ridge on his left. There were a couple of torsos on the skyline. He swung left off the road, making for the cairn. Women like them are simple; poor ignorant creatures, immediately vulnerable to the attack of the massive intellect. Figures of fun. Destroy millions of them so that the massive intellect may flourish—at some future date. Don't tell me! he said.

One of the torsos came into full figure and tentatively approached the archaeologist. "You haven't found the pot yet, sir?"

"What pot?" asked Grant, tugging one lapel of his jacket with a gesture that increased the eye-flash.

"The pot of treasure you found in the—the chamber over there."

"The chamber pot?"

The man laughed awkwardly in face of such devastating concentration and Grant stalked on.

That was the proper way to treat these curiosity-hunters, he decided. That was the kind of pot they understood. Enlivened somewhat, he ignored remnants of humanity still moving around, and contemplated the work which his labour staff had accomplished. They had certainly done a good job in the time. It mightn't be a bad idea if they spent a few hours of the very early morning finishing off the complete replacement of all the stones so that the cairn would then be restored to its original condition. Meantime the entrance to the passage was satisfactorily masked.

Before a somewhat flamboyant lady, whose long teeth were already showing in propitiation, could get her words out, he turned away.

Five small pebbles met him on the doorstep, telling their dumb tale while waiting for Sheena and to-morrow morning. A little later, he heard some questions that forced him to a forlorn smile, for he had got into the guilty habit of leaving his door ajar the better to hear the bedtime story.

"Perhaps, Granny, they were the five-stones of a princess?"

"Indeed and why mightn't they be? For a princess would have pretty stones if anyone would."

"Was she a beautiful princess?"

"Of course she was. A very beautiful princess."

"Are all princesses beautiful?"

"All the good ones are beautiful whatever. For if you are good then you become beautiful."

"And are all bad princesses ugly?"

"Ugly enough," answered her granny.

"Do you think Mr. Grant would show me them again?"

"Well, now, we mustn't be troubling Mr. Grant, for he has many things to think about and many things to do."

"Would like to see them."

"Hsh, now! I'll ask him, but not for a day or two."

Silence. "Granny?"

"Yes?"

"What's the present he's going to give me?"

"I've told you often enough I don't know. Content yourself, and you'll see that the present will come."

"When will it come?"

"How do I know? We have just got to wait."

"Maybe it will never come."

"It will come all right if he said so. Now it is high time

153

you were at your sleep." She began to hum the Silver Bough as she moved around.

Later, Grant called her into his sitting-room. Having seated her, he said in a friendly voice, "I want to tell you my news." And he told her of his talk with Mrs. Mackenzie. "I'm not blaming anyone but myself, but you can see how awkward it is for me that all this should be appearing in the newspapers? It's making a fool of me, because if the pot of gold is never found, what are folk to think, especially my friends?"

"I understand you," she said with feeling. "Never a word will I say to anyone now."

"Tell me this. Did Anna see Norman, the chauffeur at Clachar House? Did anyone tell him not to speak?"

"I saw him myself. But it was a little late in the morning. And Jimmy Sangster, who has the old Ford car, he had left for Kinlochoscar. And he was one of the two Norman ran into on that night. So maybe he said something. I don't know, but I could ask him."

"It doesn't matter now. Anna didn't care about going to see Norman?"

"No." Mrs. Cameron stirred in the silence. "They were friendly at one time, Norman and Anna, and she didn't care about going to see him herself."

"Ah, I see. I just wondered."

The room gradually became charged with feeling.

"He lives in the cottage by the stables and eats in the Big House, so it would have meant going there, too," she said.

"I see."

"Maybe you will have heard things about Anna, and maybe what you will have heard is true."

"I haven't heard anything, for I wouldn't listen," he answered. "I can see that she has a child and that she is not married. But I think so highly of her that I would let no one gossip about her in my presence."

154

"There are not so many gentlemen left now," said Mrs. Cameron simply.

But somehow he shied again at the nearness of Anna's story. "I was talking to Mrs. Sidbury this afternoon. Where is her husband?"

"They say he's still out East, in India or somewhere. He's a brigadier in the army."

"The regular army?"

"Yes. A big solid man. He's been here often enough."

"I should say that's the kind of man she needs."

"You would think so," she said. "All the same, she's a nice lady. When her heart is touched, her hand will give you anything. She was a sprite of a little one and would dance like a fairy. But I never see her now."

"You think she's not happy in her marriage?"

"Who can say? She's that taken up with her brother and the old House."

"She seems very concerned about her brother."

"She always was. Though it may seem a strange thing to say, I think he was always nearer to her than any man. That sometimes happens in families. When it's in the blood nothing will get the better of it."

He sat quite still, wondering just how far her meaning went, for certain relations, even marriage relations between brother and sister in ancient societies, like Egypt, were known to him. "I'm not sure that I understand," he said at last.

"It's just in the blood," she said again. "And when a sister is like that, there's nothing she won't do for the brother."

"And does the brother feel the same?"

"No, that's different, very different," she said.

He could not follow her, and felt that this old woman had an understanding of a blood relationship working through the sexes that was beyond him; yet he sensed that it belonged to this place and came out of it in a refining that was at once more elusive and more potent than any straight-forwardness of a Mediterranean culture, however archaic or introverted. The picture of the sunlit cairn and the two figures in the short cist flashed through his mind, from yesterday unto to-day, in the one pattern of time, momentarily apprehended. But in the very clarity of this he was somehow lost.

"Anna was only about eighteen when she went to work in the Big House, just before war broke out. Mrs. Sidbury had come home from London and there were some guests and she came and begged for Anna's help. Anna had been a year in the hotel at Kinlochoscar and was doing well. Maybe she had had her lads, like any other bonny young girl, and Norman, who was driving one of the hotel cars then, managed to run her home many a time. He was a well-doing lad, and och! everything was fine. Anna didn't want to go to the Big House, but it seemed a poor thing to me if we couldn't help Mrs. Sidbury. Anyway, she went. Then the war broke out, and everyone went away, and Anna herself went into the A.T.S., and soon she was in London."

Mrs. Cameron paused in her story-telling. Her face, with its finely etched lines, held her eyes as a lamp its light. A quiet light, in which all that had been written in her life was read. The eyes lifted to the window, to the light outside, quiet, too, before the coming of the night.

"In London, she met him again, met Mr. Martin. She wrote and told me of it. She was touched that he was so glad to see her and was so kind to her. Because of their uniforms, for he was a captain, it was not much they saw of each other, just once or twice when he was on leave. But after Dunkirk—I don't know." She paused again. "It's difficult for me to tell you, but after a time she came home, and the child she had here was his child."

"I saw that," he said.

Her lips fell apart and she stared at him.

He nodded. "It was last night; when you were taking Sheena away after she had seen the quartz pebbles. She looked at me in so still a way that he came into her face."

She heaved a big breath and removed her eyes. "I'm glad to hear that," she said in a curiously final way.

"Why? Surely no one doubted Anna?" He was watching her narrowly.

"Who knows what anyone will doubt? They were saying it was a queer time in London then."

Some sinister something of the ways of gossip touched him for an appalled moment. "But surely a girl would never blame—would never say it was someone if it wasn't?"

"You would think not," she answered quietly.

In a moment he saw that his question had been terribly naïve. For a girl to have more than one lover round about the same time was not unknown! Particularly then!

"Good God!" he said abruptly, and she didn't stir.

"But surely you were never in any doubt yourself?" he asked.

"No," she answered quietly.

"And even if it was a queer time as people say—and it was bad enough, heaven knows—why, why would Anna land on Martin if there was any mortal doubt at all?"

"He would be in the best position likely."

"But—but surely there are no people here who think like that?"

"There are people who think like that everywhere."

"Even in Clachar?"

"Even in Clachar, though I will say that all who knew Anna would never think that—because they couldn't."

"But who in Clachar?"

"There's one woman who lives by herself. But I'll say no more."

"What's wrong with her?"

"She never had a man," said Mrs. Cameron simply.

He laughed. "That's about it," he agreed with some bitterness, and added, after a short silence, "I don't want to appear curious, Mrs. Cameron, but why didn't Mr. Martin stand up to his responsibilities; I mean, why didn't he acknowledge the child?"

"That's just it," she answered, "that's the trouble: Anna never told him."

He gaped at her. "But surely——" His amazement stopped him. "Why?"

She looked out the window. "I don't know," she answered almost automatically. "He was out in the Far East, she said. And it was bad out there. Seemingly he said he would write to her, but she never heard. And the time went on. Then it was reported he was missing."

"Yes, but after he came back?"

She shook her head. "She wouldn't say anything."

A deep exasperation so got the better of him that he half rose out of his chair. "But why not? And if she wouldn't say anything surely you would? Didn't you do anything at all?"

"I'm not good at the writing."

"But—but Martin himself? How was he to know? Shouldn't you at least have given him a chance?"

"He knows," she answered. "And Mrs. Sidbury knows."

"How do you know?"

"I know."

He looked at her. Her expression was quiet and strangely resigned. He had the feeling of things happening in regions of fate beyond his comprehension, yet not altogether, so that he would have torn the regions apart like so many maddening webs. "Oh well," he said, "I give it up. All the same, I think it ought to have been put to him straight. But you know your own business, Mrs. Cameron."

"I thought so, too," she said, "but she wouldn't hear of it. She has her pride. She said she would leave me."

"I have heard of Highland pride," he answered, "but this is surely its limit." He refused her point of view.

"Do you think so?" she asked.

He looked at her. Her eyes were on him with so simple, so natural, an expression that they might have been asking him to repeat what he had said for her comfort, as if he were a man wiser than she and she wondered.

It was too much for him. "I don't know," he murmured.

"I didn't know either," she said. "I didn't know what to do. And the time came when you could do nothing."

He was silent. Then in a new, objective tone he asked, "Do you think it was Mrs. Sidbury?"

She took a little time, as if going over something in her mind. "No," she answered.

"But in view of what you said about her attitude to her brother——?" He waited.

"I don't think she would stand in his way, if she thought it was for his good. To be fair to her, I don't think she would."

He appeared to consider. "Do you think it was the difference in your stations in life?"

"There was that," she said; "there was always that."

"Supposing," he said, conscious of a tonic cruelty in his objectivity, "it had been Norman, his chauffeur, the one she used to go about with——" He stopped abruptly and turned his gaze on her. "If Norman really cared for her, how could he come back and be his chauffeur—in the circumstances?"

Her eyes went to the window. Her still face looked as if it had taken, in the inner places, an unsearchable punishment, if not now then long ago.

"You talk of your Highland pride," he said, for he could not overcome the anger that was in him.

"Norman," she said in her even voice, "is the one whose life he saved when he got the decoration."

In the silence, Anna passed the window.

"There's Anna back," she said, "I'll not be keeping you." She got up and smiled. "Thank you for the nice talk we had." And she went out, wishing him a good night in her kindly way.

21

He stood for a while before the window. Anna's voice could just be heard in the kitchen, doubtless giving her grandmother news of where she had been. The muffling of the voices set them in a distant interior, a far background that was yet a world of its own. His avid concern for his golden ornaments, his archaeological treasure, so sank away that it left no more than its gleam in front of that background. An intuition of the meaning of his labours came upon him, an apprehension of history that was profounder, it seemed to him, than any philosophy of history could contain. Warm human voices, muffled, and in front of them the gleam of gold. The one pattern, indivisible.

It passed, and he was left restless, upset. . . . That fellow Martin was beyond him. That he shouldn't want to marry the girl and that sort of thing—all right. Good enough. Sex was always number one mess anyway. He took a turn on the floor. And now, my God! this newspaper business. He looked at the sky. Grey; it had been grey all day.

When the gloaming was deep he went out. But he did not go in the direction of the cairn; he wandered inland towards the hills with such cunning that presently he found himself able to command Mrs. Mackenzie's cottage and any solid shadow in human guise that might sally forth from it. For a while he was all ears, wondering just how many pairs of eyes might be intent as his own. Extraordinary how the hunt for buried treasure had always obsessed humanity. Was there more to it than the simple greed for gain? Clearly there was. In simple fact, there was the gleam. An ironic expression regarded the involuntarily evoked image of Colonel Mackintosh. The sharp-pointed beard tossed a trifle. But you, too (he said to the image), follow your gleam, and he was not put out by the Colonel's effort at a withering smile. He felt subtle and diverse. Just as, he thought, the music of the Silver Bough was more than music. And then, in a moment, like the key that fits into a lock, like the forgotten word suddenly remembered, what the Silver Bough really stood for came back to him: it was the passport in those distant days to the land of the gods. As he stirred, he got the impression that something had stirred with him—over on the right and a little higher up. There it was again! a dark stooping body, hauling itself up the hillside. His breathing stopped altogether, for the action, the movement, of the body made him think of Foolish Andie.

Then began the wildest feat of shadowing that he had ever undertaken. It was a warm close night and the sweat runnelled. His shirt stuck and his eyes smarted. When for intermittent periods he lost the figure altogether, he suffered anguish. Once he nearly gave himself away, for he had got to his feet and was running lightly on when all at once there was the figure only a little way in front. He stopped in a sickness of surprise. But the figure could not have heard him, for now it rounded onto the old drove track going into the hills. When it left the track and he found it again going up the Robbers' Glen, something more than wonder touched him.

It was pretty dark now in the deep hollow of the glen and often he stood and listened, waiting for the click of a footstep. But the time came when definitely he knew that he had lost the figure. Either it had arrived or it was sitting down and resting. This created so harrowing a state of suspense that he actually found himself going forward on hands and knees. He's near the top of the glen by this time, you fool! said common sense. But there was another sense, which had no faith in common sense now, and it kept him to hands and knees like a tracking dog trained not to whimper. His eyes watered from the sweat of bitter vexation. Then he heard a sound.

For a little while he wondered if he was the victim of hallucination. After all, his particular trade did call for the use of imagination, for a certain capacity to reconstruct the past at least, to visualise it at ritual and ceremony, and he had found that occasionally he was able to do this so concentratedly that he could both see and hear. But the rumble of muffled voices which now reached him from the earth beneath had something other about it, while yet it seemed as real as the grass beneath his palms. If the long-dead robbers had been talking in their den. . . . As his thought was suspended, his head turned slowly upon the fearful air. The thing he had been following mightn't have been solid. . . . There might be others of them about. He remembered that figure which had appeared from *nowhere* near this very spot. . . . There was a rumble of laughter. He backed away with the feeling that it had hit him in the belly.

With a native pertinacity there goes a caution which can swallow the gulp of fear. He backed away and hid, but when no more things appeared he crawled out again. More than that: when at last he was satisfied there was no visible entrance to this underworld of muffled sound, he crawled back to his hidey hole, determined to wait on daylight and reason. He was a scientist and for his creed must, if need be, go down fighting.

Also he found now that he could give the sound almost any effect he liked, while there was certainly nothing about the tumbled ground and odd boulders or stones to distinguish this part of a glen from hundreds of similar parts. The affair was not merely mysterious, it was quite definitely abnormal. He assured himself of this abnormality in order to keep himself as near the human norm as possible. The sweat dried. He smothered a sneeze.

The deepest dark of the night passed and when at last he was certain that the air was faintly lightening, he heard a quite distinct thud. A head and body appeared coming up out of the earth perhaps thirty yards down the glen. When his full length appeared there was no doubt it was a man, though quite impossible to distinguish him. Another came up. In all, four; then the thud was repeated and the four men, talking in quiet human voices, walked away and were quickly lost to sight.

Crawling forward he listened. The subterranean rumble had ceased. When he reached the spot of their emergence, he found only tussocks and boulders and a stone slab. But a slab had a special significance for him. He did not leave the slab alone. It was not lying flat but tilted against the earth. One or two stocks of old heather grew over its edges. When he put forth his strength he made no impression on its apparently rock-bound solidity. But once he had removed the cunningly placed flagstone on which he was standing, the slab gave under his pull and if he hadn't been nimble it would have pinned his left leg when it fell over with a thud against a hump. A black hole yawned.

As he went into this hole he clicked on his torch. It was a covered passage of about the same dimensions as the one in the cairn. But he could hardly have gone more than twenty feet when the passage entered a low chamber. As the beam shot here and there, the archaeologist thought that he had stumbled into an earth-house, an underground place of refuge, a dug-out of the Late Bronze Age, but as it more methodically disclosed a circular chamber, with radials of drystone masonry, he decided that here in unique fact might be a working specimen of the prehistoric wheel-house. This so astonished and excited him that at once he felt danger must lurk somewhere, in the black corners, behind the dykes which projected radially from the containing wall like spokes from the rim of a wheel whose bush has been widely cut away. When he put his hand out to crawl into the dwelling it sank a sudden foot and he landed on his head, but the bulb in the torch did not snap and he picked himself up with more of a snarl than a yelp. Nothing came at him, however, and he sat on until his heart-beats grew less fierce, then he warily got to his feet and found that he could just stand erect. A pungent odour came through a tobacco thickness like the very smell of the beast of danger. The torch isolated a white enamelled jug with black chips. He stood very still, listening, and for a moment or two fancied that he heard footsteps until he assured himself they were his own heart-beats; then he began to move.

Old dried heather in sacks; a raised flagstone for a table with wet markings; a small recess or ambry in one of the radials containing drinking glasses; he lifted one of the glasses, sniffed it, and got the faintly pungent odour, not of the beast of danger but of vodka.

Fear began to lift. A drinking party, a secret brotherhood! His mind flashed across Europe. Here was mystery stranger even than the prehistoric. Behind the next wall, in a built-in recess, he found a small cask, upended, with a copper tap a few inches from its base. He sniffed it, knocked with his knuckles, and nodded. Backing away, he swung the beam round until with a jerk it stopped on the figure of Martin leaning against the wall by the passage entrance.

A ghost face and glittering eyes. The figure never moved and the beam wobbled, but it came back to the face again. Grant dropped the beam and stood speechless; then he jerked it up again. The fellow was still there.

"Hallo," he called.

Martin did not answer. But after a moment or two his voice came level and dry: "Are you quite finished?"

Grant could not answer.

As Martin came away from the wall, his torch clicked on. He began looking around the stone table, then stopped and lifted a wallet, examined its contents, and put it in an inside pocket. "Making a long stay?" he asked.

"No, I'm going," replied Grant, "I'm just going. Did not mean to intrude."

"For one who did not mean it, you managed very well." He stood with his head lowered and turned slightly towards Grant, upon whom he now set the beam of his torch which travelled slowly up the body to the face, where it rested with an inhuman curiosity.

"I happened on the place. That's all." Grant shifted his feet.

"Blind chance."

"Not altogether," replied Grant, whose voice was distinctly firming. "But I was not looking for this place. I was looking for something else."

Martin did not answer. Then as if the whole thing hardly interested him, he said in the same cool tones, "Seeing you are here, you'd better have a drink."

"No, thanks."

"No? A small one might do you some good." Without paying any further attention to the intruder, he set about lighting a candle and producing two glasses, a cut-crystal decanter of the colourless liquor, and the chipped enamelled jug which he shook, saying, "This water is quite fresh." He poured out two large drinks and added water. "Try that."

Grant took the glass with a mutter of thanks. He was confused because he had been caught in the wheel-house like a spy and angry because he smelt something deadly in Martin's even manner. Martin raised his glass in a just perceptible gesture and drank a mouthful, whereupon he deliberately waited until Grant had drunk.

"You still think it's vodka?"

"I don't know a great deal about drinks," replied Grant, gasping slightly.

"You are inclined to judge by colour, perhaps."

"Not entirely."

"It has been matured in plain wood: that's the whole mystery."

"I cannot say I feel enlightened."

"No? It's an interesting subject. Won't you sit down?" He got onto a stuffed sack, his back to the wall and his legs out, and indicated another.

"Before the war a certain man hereabouts made his own whisky. Being a crofter he had not the wherewithal to buy the hotel stuff. The bother about making whisky in that fashion is getting it matured. He thought this an excellent place for leaving the liquor to mature. It has matured rather well, don't you think?" He drank again then took out a pipe and began to fill it.

"So it wasn't vodka?"

"Disappointing?"

"I just wondered."

"Things are not always romantic." He lit up. "Even if this particular fellow had a rather romantic end. They trussed him up, then slowly, with a peculiarly deliberate art, they bayoneted him. He felt it was coming to him, he said, so before the actual event he told me of the existence of this place and its drink." His sensitive mouth drew and exhaled smoke with an easy precision. The pipe was going well. "In these times, when whisky can hardly be bought, we who had helped to sustain the Empire thought we might reserve this map-reading for our exclusive—uh—use. Won't you? . . ." His left hand, palm up, indicated Grant's glass in a gesture at once elaborate and negligent.

Grant's hand shook a trifle and as he drank he was aware of the eyes upon him, of their cold gleam. Replacing his glass on the stone table, he said, "I was looking for something

167

and—and heard your voices underground. I thought it might be—I thought it might have something to do with my discovery which was stolen, removed, from the cairn."

"Your crock of gold?"

"Yes," replied Grant, experiencing a sudden stinging blood heat.

"So it was quite genuine?"

"Quite."

"You had no idea of the existence of this place?"

"None." His fumbling hands found his cigarette case. He felt passionately angry and drew the smoke in short puffing smacks. "I wouldn't spy anyhow."

"Spying is a wide term—now."

"I don't care whether it's wide or narrow; I don't do it." He puffed. "I was indebted to you already."

"For giving you permission to spy—to investigate the past?"

"You may call it spying on the past: I call it extending the range of our knowledge."

"All spying does that—in war it's essential."

The sinister implication did not help Grant, who replied, "You may mix your categories if you like. I am not impressed." His eyes now had their own flash.

Martin's eyes travelled over Grant's face. "It is perhaps not clear to me how disturbing the bones of the dead helps —what kind of knowledge."

"Knowledge of ourselves."

"A rather gruesome sort of knowledge, don't you think? And particularly gruesome in its beginnings. Not that I stress the adjective, but I should have thought it would be wearisome, messing about in it."

"We see things differently. I find it neither gruesome nor wearisome."

"You don't think that a man's bones—and even his crock of gold—should be left to moulder in peace?"

"No. And your question, if I may say so, reflects a personal attitude which—to me, at any rate—is defeatist. Even peace is not achieved by mouldering."

Martin smiled. "Neither, according to the profoundest, is it achieved by action and interference, particularly in the process of acquiring *material* knowledge."

"Perhaps. But some of us go on finding knowledge—leaving it to others to philosophise upon it."

"That may be a somewhat superior retort, for it implies that knowledge is only of one kind, namely, your kind. Before a man achieves the peace that passes understanding, he presumably has acquired a knowledge other than your material kind of knowledge. Or would you say not?"

"I can only speak for myself."

"Naturally."

"Well," said Grant, with a sharp tug at one lapel, "have *you* achieved the peace that passes understanding?"

"I should doubt it," replied Martin with a smoothness of infernal humour. "However, you really have evaded the point—perhaps characteristically. I referred to the peace of the skeletons and the crock of gold—not *your* peace or the *future* peace of someone else. I know we are cannibals, but is it worth while labouring the point? Why go on chewing up the dead bones and the bloody acts?"

"Man is man because he has thought and investigated and found out. That's the process. If you don't like it, that's your concern. Personally I know no other way for man to exist at all. If he hadn't existed in that way he wouldn't, in fact, have gone on existing at all."

Martin looked at him so steadily that Grant unthinkingly finished his glass. It was really a belligerent act.

"It's the vagueness of your words that's so—extraordinary. Think, investigate, and find out. . . . Old bones and bloody acts—with a clear prospect of many more old bones and very many more bloody acts. I should have thought you would at least have found it boring."

"You contort the whole business."

"But you do in fact hunt out skeletons and stone axes and arrowheads and so on and try, I presume, to reconstruct their bloody acts and ceremonial sacrifices. I admit we have progressed in performing bloody acts and sacrifices on a universal scale since the days of your prehistoric cairn, but it does not seem to me that it's anything to make a fuss about, much less build your edifice of knowledge upon."

"You think humanity took the wrong turning?" And Grant's eyes shot a sudden irony.

"That wouldn't matter," replied Martin with eyes that made Grant's restless again. "It's when you keep on along the wrong turning that, it seems to me, the whole thing becomes stupid, literally bloody stupid. However, it doesn't interest me very much—apart from a question of discrimination involved, and that question being insoluble there is left only the sound of our voices. It generally comes back to that. And an analysis of the voice-sounds does not take you very far—at least no further than any other analysis, for it is characteristic of an analysis that it should analyse away. Let me help you." And, ignoring Grant's protest, he filled up both glasses.

Grant had a poor head for alcohol and what he had already absorbed would normally be more than enough, but now the effect upon him was singular in that his flesh, instead of clogging his brain, seemed to lighten and thin away, leaving the mind to rise up into a subtler freedom than he had experienced even in a secret hour of twilight. His head was a reservoir full of millions of words and thoughts. The only difficulty was this fellow's power of damming him up; for he did not seem to believe in anything, not even in his own curiosity, penetrating as it was. He appeared to be using talk to fill a vacancy; and his reference to bloody acts was a perverse reference to the annihilation that followed them. And this stillness about him, this living in his eyes, might, in an ultimate moment, use the death-thrust as a temporary full stop.

The suggestion of fear or danger generally induced in Grant a certain daring or even recklessness; not calm courage but a fiery pertinacity. In high accents he now carried the war directly to the enemy, his head clear as a whistle, and the dam burst.

22

The words, the visions, grew ever more fantastic. There was a time when the local schoolmaster would have applauded Grant very strongly for the striking way in which he sustained the British mythology against the Roman, Scandinavian or even Hellenic, not to mention the Hebraic. From his high horse, the archaeologist commanded the knights of the Round Table, set the whole Arthurian epic to the splendid movements of chivalry. What other body of myth in the history of the world, the whole world west to east, he demanded to know, had produced so lofty a concept of human behaviour or so wonderful an expression of it in literature? Romance that was poetry in essence; Irish colour and craftsmanship and saga; Welsh legend and poetry; all these islands, indeed, as the original home of the druidic mystique, beautiful and precise, magical and living. And if that was so—and who could gainsay it from all the evidence?—then at least the root of the matter was in us, and surely therefore the exploring of so potent a root was something more, and higher, than a futile spying or indulgence in curiosity, even if it took a no more distinguished form than the opening of a chambered cairn in a Highland clachan.

Martin watched the coloured procession with a detachment that at moments almost seemed interested. The word druidic even brought a smile. His eyes moved about the archaeologist's face and steadied once upon a fume of bubble at the lips, curious to observe how small specks of it were liberated upon the air.

"I thought these druids performed in oak groves," he said, "not at cairns or in stone circles."

"We know little enough about how or where they behaved and then mostly from foreign sources. You might as well say that people were silent in their ceremonies at your cairn in Clachar because we do not know the tongue they spoke."

"Wasn't it some kind of Celtic tongue?"

"The Neolithic people did not speak even any kind of Aryan tongue, much less a specific Celtic. It was an archaic tongue of which we know nothing."

"And it died with them?"

"No. It just died, but not with them. They took the invaders' tongue, perhaps Pictish; but they lived on."

"I thought we didn't know much about the Picts' language?"

"Neither we do, because there were more invaders and a new tongue called Gaelic. And you, who are still Neolithic in your bones, literally in your bones, actually speak yet another invaders' language called English."

"The bones remain but the languages die?"

"More than the bone remains."

"And how are you so sure about my bones?"

"Because to be sure is part of my business as an archaeologist. I see the bone of your skull as I see the bones in your ankles."

"And all this amounts to—what?"

"To knowledge." And Grant lifted his glass and drank.

The analysis of the meaning of knowledge produced a considerable amount of arid sound, though the archaeologist achieved one or two interesting arabesques even here, until at last he swept the whole thing aside, including his glass which he retrieved unbroken from the earthen floor, and said that for him all this had yet a profounder significance, for knowledge qua knowledge was but the tools and the material.

"A moral significance?"

"Yes," said Grant like a shot. Then he waved a dismissive left hand. "I am aware of the inflection in your voice. Let us dismiss the word moral. We can dismiss any number of words; if an abstract word offends you we can cut it out. There is nothing abstract in the significance I mean. There is, on the contrary, all that which, being alive, is potent and life-making, not life-destroying. The chivalry to which I have referred, the literature, the song, Arthur and Ossian, the craft of the hands, the colour, the greatness of the body in its tragic bearing, the courage—the courage that does not give in, that—that takes its gruel and fights on and pursues the high thing and the right thing though the heavens should come down in small bits."

"A moral lesson?"

Grant stared at his glass, in no way self-conscious, but as one brooding a little over the greatness he had heard, even while its echoes passed away. Martin filled the glass once more, spilling a little of the liquor on the stone. The spilling produced a momentary wavering in Grant's vision so that the stone tilted. He realised for the first time that he was getting drunk, but this drunkenness was a peculiar phenomenon, like a transparent screen between one world and another, and it shivered like a screen, wavered, so that what was known to be there was not quite seen, but did not need to be seen because it was known. He became aware that Martin was talking. With a peculiar deliberation, strangely in contrast with his recent visionary flights, he listened, looking at the face before him and seeing it with a remarkable clarity, so that it was no longer strange to him and unknown, so that even its death instinct was not a positive thing, a destructive force, but simply that condition which

174

had been left when the positive had ebbed away. It was a face stranded on the modern shore.

"These primitive Celts, they ate each other," Martin concluded, "they were cannibals."

"That may be," answered the archaeologist with profound solemnity, "but if so, at least they ate each other formally."

Martin did not laugh. His face was arrested in an extraordinary, an involuntary stillness.

"All primitive peoples," continued Grant, "have such formalities, such courtesies. If they eat the body it is always the body of the enemy, never their own bodies, and they do so in order to acquire his virtue and his strength and his valour."

"This they do in remembrance of him," said Martin.

Grant met the eyes and cried wildly, challengingly, "Yes! Why not? Why shouldn't they? It might be better for us if we still remembered. But we don't. We have lost the love of God and the understanding of sacrifice. We destroy Christ's body. We smash it to smithereens and dissipate it from our sight. We truss it up and bayonet it and leave it for the jackals. We destroy because we hate. We hate. We hate ourselves all. And because it feeds on itself, hatred is the ultimate cannibal that eats its own body." He stretched for his glass and missed it, but caught it at the second attempt. The stone, however, tilted further this time. The liquor from the glass ran over his hand as he assumed a completely recumbent position. But he was growing weary of all this talk, and not without dignity he composed himself on the yielding softness of the hard floor and closed his eyes.

He opened them on the bare hillside.

23

The hillside, the glen, was vacant of life, had the frozen appearance of being on another planet. As he held his head still, this impression of otherness grew. Distance, distance itself up the glen, was a very remarkable thing, for it existed in a new strange time and yet had all the astonishing attributes of space. His head moved and a jeweller's hammer hit the grey matter; the flush of pain went forward to the bone of his forehead, knocked, and sank to the pit of his stomach. The skin of his face was sweaty, greasy, and hot. He shivered suddenly and sneezed and was blinded. Then rearing himself with care, he looked at the hillside again.

When, quite close at hand, he saw a flat slab leaning against a bank, he approached it. The heave set the flushes to a dark reel, so that this time the slab did pin his leg as it fell over. He wriggled like a half-smashed snake till he got his leg free. The shin bone ran blood beneath the rent in his stocking. Where the slab had been, however, were no more than dark earth, a large hieroglyphic red worm, and one or two centipedes that fell as if his eyesight had suddenly hit them. There was no hole to a passage. He stared at the spot until he heard the gurgling laughter of the water in the small burn.

The water stung him then ran out of his beard and eyes; it sizzled in his mouth and astonished his stomach. Its innocence was, indeed, so cool and healthy that his stomach did not know what to do about it, then tried to heave up and couldn't. The dark pain knocked on his forehead again, this time more firmly.

He lay back till the blood on his leg should stop running of its own accord, for it only ran all the faster when he tried to stop it. On this strange morning of the world things were apparently like that. But they could bamboozle him as they wished, he knew he had been in a wheel-house. For if he hadn't been, how could he be like this now? He failed to hit a horsefly that landed on his leg, hitting the wound instead. After he had wrung out his handkerchief in the burn, he tied it round the wound and got up.

It was the usual kind of tumbled ground, with more boulders and hummocks than could be seen from a hill-top. But he had no desire now to investigate further. It took him a little time even to hear the ticking of his watch, which registered seven hours thirteen minutes. Martin had no doubt hauled him out and away like a sack in order to defeat his curiosity. But perhaps—to leave him in the sun? Heaven alone knew. As he finished winding his watch, he started unfastening his collar, paused, looked towards heaven and found it bland and blue.

As there could be no question of climbing he began to drift down the glen, with a stagger now and then and even an eye for a slab, but presently he was just going on "alone and palely loitering". The words came to him from the poem with so peculiar an aptness that, for the first time, he smiled, if wanly. But it wasn't exactly *La Belle Dame sans merci* that had had him in thrall! And yet for the life of him, by the dark gods for a moment, something flicked somewhere, and he realised that Keats was not only a great poet but a poet of many dimensions. Keats had rattled the Silver Bough!

This seemed so enlightening, so superb, a description of the poet that he had to stop; a private revelation which he hung on to through the blood flushes. The young magician had shaken the Silver Bough upon our earth and gone away.

He saw him going.

He went on himself again. Perhaps, he thought, with a sere humour, it's that ancient and innocent cold water rousing the grey alcohol. . . .

I see a lily on thy brow
With anguish moist and fever dew . . .

The magician knew about it. Grant nodded carefully, the humour softening his eyes. Suddenly birds *were* singing; chirping at least; wheatears. They, too, were innocent as the cold burn water. Remarkable the amount of innocence there was on the earth, sheer innocence, bright grass, clear air, immemorial freshness, everywhere, except in this spot of meandering clay, for which he could feel pity were he not so profound, so obliterating, an ass. But he must have dreamed a lot of the stuff he had said. Surely! O Lord, surely! he hoped. For suddenly he remembered the lingual knot. Neolithic, Pictish, Gaelic, English. Then Martin and his infernal eyes had asked, "What language next?" and he had replied, "Vodka." High Heaven!

Debouching from the Glen of the Robbers, he turned right and followed the gushing Clachar; rested and went on; then, pulling himself together, started on a slanting down-hill stalk of his lodgings. When he found himself being tracked by what looked like the black journalist he got to his feet in a blinding anger.

Little Sheena saw him coming, backed a shy step or two, then turned for the front door and met her mother. After a moment, they both went into the house. Anna was standing in the kitchen, visible to him, if he wanted her.

"Anna?"

"Yes." She came quickly forward.

178

"Tea," he said. "Just tea. A whole potful."

"At once," she answered.

"And would you—and would you take it up to my bed-room?"

"Yes."

He nodded and smiled, looked at the steep stairs, then began to mount them.

24

It was late afternoon when he woke to a thrush singing in the garden. The thrush stopped and the world listened. He felt light as the listening and dwelt in it for a little time, then his eyes wandered about the bedroom and saw the teapot. The feeling of convalescence was distinctly pleasant until in a small snuggle of luxury he moved a leg. The leg not only pained him but had grown a shaggy hide, which turned out, however, to be no more than an unremoved stocking. Otherwise he was more or less undressed. He saw the face of a colleague who on occasion would admit: "I had a skinful last night." He had never been quite sure whether the man had been ashamed or otherwise. He wasn't quite sure yet. Sheena began to chant and was abruptly stopped. Had Anna really seen what was wrong with him? His breath must have been eloquent!

She was really a fine girl, but removed from Martin by exactly another world. There was no point of contact. This had nothing to do with social differences at all. Martin was beyond any human contact of the kind. The fellow had reached the end of everything, where there was nothing. This might have been remediable if he hadn't possessed an intellect. Things can be done to the sick mind. Nothing can be done to the sick intellect, which at once and without effort analyses away the word "sick" and what is being done, exhibiting both elements as without meaning and futile, then waits for anything more to analyse away.

He tried to recollect one occasion during the night, even a passing moment, when Martin had shown a trace of real emotion, even argumentative emotion. He couldn't. Yet Martin had clearly wanted to speak, and would have gone on speaking or listening for ever. Surely that was something, a *desire*? Moreover he had gone with his war cronies to that place to drink. He wouldn't have gone if he hadn't wanted to go, if drinking didn't give him *pleasure*?

And then, in this present rarefied condition of his mind, Grant made what seemed to him a subtle psychological discovery. Martin would speak, and Martin would go, and Martin would drink, purely and automatically to *do* those things, because once he stopped doing *them* there was nothing left but to die, to cut the throat, to slip down into deep sea-water.

This was so strong a thought that it pressed the bone inward between his eyes. He got up and light-headedly began to dress.

Mrs. Cameron knocked and came into his sitting-room, asking him if he would like his food now.

"Thank you, I would, if you don't mind."

"Dear me, you've caught a cold!"

"No, no, just a trifle hoarse." He cleared his throat. "The night air, you know!" He smiled.

"We were that anxious about you," she murmured, "and the potatoes will take a while to boil. There's some nice soup——"

"The very thing! Never mind about the potatoes. And if Anna makes some of her strong coffee, we can have a cup of tea later. How's that?"

He often discussed the food position with her and knew in considerable detail the idiosyncrasies of the butcher in Kinlochoscar. As she was hurrying away he said, "I hope you weren't too anxious?"

"No, it's just that we thought you might have fallen and hurt yourself. Anna—but it's all right."

"Anna what?"

"Nothing—she just had a walk." Anna was behind her. "Oh, there's this telegram; it came in about midday," and the old lady took it from Anna and handed it to him. As the door closed, he burst the envelope:

"Hoping to arrive to-morrow Mackintosh."

His face went bleak and a small throb was resurrected. Blair, the petrologist, would be driving him up in his old Bentley. Probably a whole carload of them!

Anna came in with the soup.

"Have you got to-day's paper?" he inquired, for he had asked her to get it.

She hesitated a moment. "Yes."

"Will you fetch it, please?"

It was unlucky for the archaeologist that his striking discovery had happened in one of those rare brief intervals when international relations did not threaten immediate world disaster. A powerful foreign leader had actually used the words "not unhopeful" on the day Grant had uncovered the short cist, and in sheer relief there was nothing that the British public could hug more closely to its heart than a crock of gold. A prescient editor at his conference board had clearly, and gleefully, said "Feature the Fabulous." The world was going young again. Even the fairies were popping out of their gestapos. Man might yet laugh once before he died. The careless journalistic rapture of the old piping days of peace then ensued.

There were two photographs. The first was of Mr. Grant, Foolish Andie and Mrs. Mackenzie, with the cairn itself as background. The archaeologist bore a hatchet-faced look of intolerant worry which contrasted oddly with the drunken tilt of his tweed hat; he was also holding at arm's length the wooden handle of a pick-axe as if he had but that moment grounded the sword Excalibur. Andie was grinning under his fringe in a manner that definitely, even astonishingly, looked the schoolbook picture of prehistoric man. Mrs.

Mackenzie, a yard or more in the rear, seemed folded slightly upon herself in a shrinking emotion. But it was the second photograph that knocked Grant's chin up, for it was a photograph of the interior of the cairn. It was moreover a very good photograph and showed not only the corbelled cell from which the immortal crock had been removed but also the row of skulls. The way in which one skull eerily stared from its pelvic girdle fascinated the eye. Clearly there was no fake about all this. Here was the real stuff. And that the crock should have been "secreted away", allegedly by the gentleman in the first photograph who replied "Goo-goo" and again "Goo-gar-h-h-h" when questioned by a correspondent, added that touch of genuine mystery which had become all too rare a commodity in these scientific days. The sub-editors (among whom were three young Scots poets) had so distinguished themselves in the matter of simple captions that. . . .

The door opened and Anna came in with kidneys on toast. "Oh," she murmured, "I thought you would have finished your soup."

Grant looked at her and at his soup. He dropped the paper on the floor, sat down, and began to sup his soup.

When Mrs. Cameron came in later, he had his elbows on the table, and the fine point of his beard dipping into his coffee cup, as he stared out of the window.

"I hope the kidneys were tender," said Mrs. Cameron. "Archie was in a good mood to-day, maybe because he had more in his van."

"Fine," he answered, getting up.

"I'll just clear away, then. Anna had to go up the road."

"Been talking to Mrs. Mackenzie?" he asked.

"Yes, oh yes. I was there this morning when you came home." She shook her head. "The poor woman is getting demented with them."

"With whom?"

"The visitors, spying on her. Two of them—one was a girl, I'm sorry to say—got hold of Andie in the barn and gave him things, bonny things."

He stared at her. "What for?"

"I don't know, unless it's to keep in with him."

"Do you mean," he asked, "that they are trying to tempt him to disclose where he has hidden the—the urn?"

"Maybe," she answered. "Maybe too—it's only what I was fancying—they'll be thinking that he might go and hide the bonny things in the same place."

His lips parted but no sound came. Then he turned away, walking over the paper.

Mrs. Cameron picked it up. "I did not want Anna to bother you with this until you had enjoyed your food. It's a poor photograph of you, whatever else."

"I suppose the policeman at Kinlochoscar is the only one in the whole district?"

"Yes. He was here to-day. And it's him that was important, too, for he had a busy time."

His brows gathered.

"There was that many cars," she explained. "Never before has so many been seen in Clachar, and as he was saying to myself, in these days of petrol restrictions it looked very suspicious. I heard just a few minutes ago that he has got two or three cases that he will be prosecuting."

"What were they doing?"

"All to see the cairn and hunt for the crock of gold. And they made a fair mess of Alick Cruban's young corn and flattened Donald Willie's potatoes as flat as this floor. I told the policeman——"

"Was he here?"

"He was. But I said you had been travelling all night and was not to be disturbed and he could see you to-morrow—or this evening itself if his business was very urgent. He said he had no formal business at the moment—that was his word, for he likes an important one."

"I want to see him."

"He'll be here to-morrow to direct the traffic, he said." There came a distant roar of two or three cars starting up, "You should have heard it earlier," she commented.

Quite silent he stood.

She stole a glance at him. "Not that you can believe everything you hear," she said.

"Can there be anything else to hear?" he asked.

"Plenty," she said, "for rumour has a tongue longer than next week." She spoke cheerfully, as one amused. "But at least I made nonsense of the story about melting the gold, for I saw Tom Alan of old Fachie's myself, and he laughed and said 'You never know', so I knew."

"Melting the gold?"

"The gold in the crock. For they're saying that gold is now three times its own price; and they're saying that if someone found the gold and melted it down, then no one could know where it came from and you could make a fortune out of it. I'm only telling you this to prepare you, for the lies that will be going about would make Beelzebub blush—and he's not the one for blushing." She added the last words inconsequently out of her compassion.

"Who is Tom Alan?"

"Grandson to old Fachie. He happened to be one that Norman-at-the-Big-House ran into on that first night, so a yarn folk had to make. Just blethers. Don't you be bothering yourself about that."

He had nothing to say.

"I'm very hopeful yet," she added desperately.

He looked at her.

"For with all their spying they'll keep Andie from going to his hiding place. He's not so foolish as many of them—selves, stravaiging about as if grown people had nothing better to do in this world. Donald Willie says he will have the law on them for his potatoes."

A faint smile came to the archaeologist's face, but it faded as, a little later, he set out for the cairn. The finding, the melting and the selling of the gold would be the simplest matter in the world, particularly in these black-market days with advertisements for gold in every newspaper. The exhilarating feeling of the treasure hunt would wilt before the face of the money shark. The youth of the world had been eaten up by the sharks. The youth and the beauty and the fun. Devoured by the grey monsters.

He went on more firmly and didn't cast a glance at odd watching humans. The world was a sea of sharks' faces. The faces came up into the light and the teeth snapped.

They had even been poking about in the cairn, holes here and there and boulders rolled away. But the passage was still covered, intact. The ground itself was getting burned up by their feet. This was really going beyond the limit. For the photographs to have been in the paper to-day, they must have been taken two or three nights ago. He tried to think, but time was the one thing which seemed beyond fixing. Its fluidity came about him like invisible water. Ten yards away, her legs apart, stood the girl in the short shorts, a thumb about the strap of her slung camera, contemplating him. As his gaze steadied upon her, she smiled her unexpected melting smile.

Dizzied a trifle with wrath, he went straight to her. "Did you or your—your friends take the photographs inside that cairn?"

She looked at him and her expression caught a certain archness. "You would really like to know?"

"I would."

"Well, I could tell you a whole lot," she admitted. "But —what are your intentions?"

"Intentions? What do you mean?"

She pivoted perceptibly without moving her feet and glanced at him sideways. "Supposing I told you—what would you do about it?"

That momentarily stumped him, for clearly it would be witless to inform her that he would convey the intelligence to the police.

"You see," she said, "your technique of handling the press has not proved very very good. Has it?"

"Better than the press deserved." He managed to stop himself abruptly.

"Perhaps," she agreed. "But I have found it pays to speak nicely even to a wild dog."

He could have spanked her. "I haven't," he said. "And what pays you is no concern of mine."

"Are you sure?" Her raillery was gentle.

"Dead certain!"

"Well—all right." She gave a shrug that was a bodily pout. "I merely thought you wanted information."

"Breaking into private property and photographing private belongings—it's actionable by the police, and I shall see that the proper action is taken. I don't need your information. Your newspaper will have to provide that. And you can tell your friends that; and you can tell them that if they don't make themselves scarce——" He stopped once more and tugged a lapel. Having to talk like this to a young woman made him angry beyond measure.

"I doubt if photographing distinguished men—or even an old cairn—is actionable," she said. "I should hardly think it's even a moot point. But it's a wealthy paper. And at least, so far, you have been treated with the respect due to a distinguished archaeologist."

The impertinence of her! The damned impertinence!

She smiled shyly and attractively. "If only you would be nice, we would be so willing to help. And at the moment we *are* rather at a loss." Then she looked at him with really

187

intelligent reserve. "Would you be able to recognise certain articles of prehistoric make—if you saw them?"

In a flash her self-confidence, her superb bargaining position, was made plain. They had found the urn!

"I should," he said, unable to say more, for a tremor had come to him.

"You would recognise certain ornaments—a bracelet, for example, or a necklace?"

"Yes," he said, "I—certainly."

"Anything else?" She looked away to give him time, for though she was a gentle girl she had to be reasonably certain in so important a matter.

"Gold discs," he said, "with ornamentation inside concentric circles."

She nodded. "Gold torcs?"

"I didn't examine all the contents of the urn. I hadn't time. It was nearly full and I—in the circumstances—I hadn't time."

"Is there anything unusual in the make or—or—material of this cinerary urn?"

"Yes," he answered, his excitement mounting intolerably, "it's made of soapstone, not of clay."

"And in height about——"

"Eighteen inches."

She nodded. Then she smiled to him in the friendliest, most helpful way. "How *did* you let your assistant make off with it?"

He was just about to tell her the whole story when there came an awful pause in the universe. He took a step nearer to her, his head lowered, shooting forward slightly, his eyes like blue-hazed steel. "Have you found the urn?"

"Well," she pivoted again, "not exactly, not yet, but we shall, and when we do we'll—know it now." Her eyes lifted. "Oh, there's Arthur. I must go." She flashed the

archaeologist her sweetest smile. "Thank you very much."
And she went.

Presently he became aware that there were faces quite
close, looking at him as at one bereft of all inwardness.
Automatic as wrath, he followed the direction the girl had
taken. Presently he saw her running, the scanty shorts giving
her bare legs a flashing ease. The dark-haired Arthur was
running with her and she was shouting her news to him as
she ran. He could hear the high pitch of their gleeful voices.
Suddenly she fell and could not get up, but apparently she
was overcome by no more than laughter. Arthur hauled her
up and gripped her hand and they ran on. Their small racing
two-seater went out of Clachar as a comet with a dusty tail,
though there was still ample time to get their full description
of the urn and its contents, as conveyed to them in an
exclusive interview by Mr. Simon Grant, over the wires
from Kinlochoscar for the early morning edition.

25

After lunch the following day, Grant decided to escape. The policeman and himself had walked the lands of Clachar in high and purposeful striding during a forenoon that had looked like the prelude to some immense gala performance, charged with colourful humans and with motor cars which manœuvred so expertly that up until 12.37 (policeman's time) only nine of them had got bogged in wayside ditches. The correspondents of five different newspapers had approached Grant before the reporting fraternity as a whole decided that the archaeologist was disinclined to be helpful. But the amount of material for comment of every kind was so great, and newspaper space so restricted, that the need for selection engendered the happiest devotion to their art, while the staffs of two weekly picture papers so manipulated their expensive cameras that they achieved for their wondering public a higher synthesis of a civilian rout in war-time, Miami Beach, and a nostalgic throw-back to the far-away innocence of Bali in the ancient days of peace.

Craning out of both sides of the rather small window in the thick wall, Grant got a crick in his neck, rubbed it in an anger which smouldered with guilt, went to the door, jammed his tweed hat on his head, and walked away uprightly but without haste towards Fachie's cottage. Within half an hour he had won out on the track which went beyond Clachar to no inhabited place. Twice he hid as research parties returned to Clachar, hurrying as though in their out-field work they might have missed something.

What peace it was to come on this tiny deserted beach, this break in the cliffs, this haven! But for some cigarette cartons, a scattered newspaper, thrown balls of lunch wrappings, five empty beer bottles, one lemonade bottle, two broken bottles on the edge of the tide, and similar artless evidence of the playfulness of a modern day, the haven might have lain in the hazed sunlight undisturbed since native feet had left the solitary crumbled ruin in its green fold of ground by the little stream that tumbled over ledges to meet the great sea.

Grant stood for a while looking on this scene and was so obscurely moved by conflicting reflections or emotions that he went to the stream and got down on his knees and drank. Then, without further thought, he left the place, climbed up the steep face beyond, and moved down towards the edge of the headland, from which he could not only see the haven itself but also the walls of cliff which stretched on either hand, the northmost point of one of the three islands off Clachar, and outward over the ocean to what seemed, low down on the distant horizon, either a purple band of cloud or a fabulous land. He stood like one who, having escaped from all behind him, might at last take off. And for a little while something in him did take off, so that presently when his eyes saw the cormorant sunning itself on a spit below and the calm sea turning snow-white on the spit's point, these objects appeared of so primordial a freshness that they might never have been seen before. Moreover the refluent movement of the brimming green water that lapped the cliff or broke in small thoughtfulness on the shore rose up towards him and he experienced the singular sensation of moving with it. So finely heady was it all that he sat down and, after further gazing, lay down, whereupon the peace and wonder of it rose upon the air itself and up to the sky.

The cleansing sea, the great sea that could cleanse forever the utmost human refuse. But even that thought was too thick or too sticky. The movement itself was so thoughtless and divine. He perceived, with an effect of astonishing discovery, astonishing not in a disturbing way but merely with a divine lucidity, what the philosophers were arguing about when they discussed the abstruse concept of subject and object, the knower and the thing known, being one. Only, unless he had ever been a blind fool, most of the philosophers whom he had read on the subject had themselves never achieved this wordless fusion, this momentary oneness of the seer and the thing seen. Doubtless that was why they had been so arid. How divine, in yet another moment, to let that thought go, and once more take the sea upon the air and float to the high blue that did not need to smile.

He was wakened by a shout. The sky stared down at him as he pulled the tweed hat from his face. He rolled over on his side and saw a man on the grassy slope above the shingle of the small beach. It was Norman, Martin's chauffeur. A little child ran out from under the slope and stood at gaze. The fair head and the tartan of the diminutive kilt told him it was Sheena. All at once she ran back out of sight again calling "Mammy!" Norman followed her slowly and as it were doubtfully. By crawling a few yards through the heather, Grant brought the small party into view.

Anna was sitting by the wall of the old ruin, pushing back her hair, while Sheena was gripping her off shoulder and peering round at Norman, who was now standing a few yards from them. He was asking her something and as her hands came away from her hair she answered him. He looked about him for a moment, then clearly spoke again, but Grant could not hear their voices. They obviously had not much to say, and for the watcher the whole scene had something strangely static about it. Norman neither advanced any farther nor went away and Anna sat where she was, turning once to the child who was excited and inclined to climb up on her.

At last Sheena grew so restless that she left her mother, but spasmodically, inclined to walk sideways so that she could keep her eyes on Norman. As she tripped and fell headlong, he heard her scream. A few long strides, and Norman had picked her up. Anna was beside them at once. Sheena had clearly hit her head on a stone and Anna finally got to her knees to chase the hurt away.

"It was that nasty stone that did it," said Anna in a raised voice.

Sheena looked at the stone and yelled, "Yes!"

Norman kicked the stone and heaved it away, an act of retribution and justice which so astonished Sheena that it silenced her. As she looked up at Norman, her eyes caught a stranger sight beyond him and she called, "Boat!" They followed her pointing hand. Rounding the small headland from Clachar came a row-boat with one man in it, his back to them as the oars dipped and rose in creaking rowlocks. When he realised he was in the tiny bay the man rested on his oars and turned his body round while the boat moved slowly on.

It was Martin. Anna got up from her knees. Norman still stood motionless a little while before walking down over the crunching shingle. Then he called in a voice which Grant heard very clearly, "Mrs. Sidbury wants you. Visitors have arrived."

Martin sat on, his forearms to the elbows flat on the oars, like one enchanted by the scene. Then he straightened up, nodded, and, dipping an oar, slowly pulled the boat round and gave way with both oars to the same easy rhythm as that with which he had appeared. Before he had gone far, Anna turned away with Sheena towards the ruin. Norman stood alone, watching Martin until he rounded the point; then he looked over at Anna and Sheena, went slowly towards them, said something, and took the path up the green slope. When he had gone over the crest, Anna stopped gathering her belongings and sat down.

She sat with her hands not on her lap, but abandoned to the grass, looking out to sea. Sheena, however, had not received enough attention and Anna took her on her lap, examining the sore spot on the fair head, soothed it, kissed it, put both arms round the small body, and rocked it gently, gazing over the head at the sea again as she quietly sang.

Perhaps because of his previous interest in the sea and of what he may have dreamed in his sleep, Grant had the feeling of having witnessed an act in a strange and enigmatic play. It had meanings beyond what he could formulate, beyond the players themselves, though he knew their story. He lay flat on his back with a suspense in his breast which stopped thought altogether.

He did not want to lose this curious sensation of pure suspended being, as if somewhere beyond it there was something, a something which would explain it, not in words but in an enlightenment, like the light waiting on the sea. But all in a moment Norman was before him, kicking the stone and heaving it away, transferring the hurt from the child's head to the stone, and this contained within it so much of man's story, his ritual and magic, that the archaeologist heard the clear thought: That's the man for Anna. Their very grouping, while the other man rowed away, was the significant core of the whole little drama.

Sheena's cries made him turn over again. She was running about the small foreshore, picking up the cigarette cartons and other treasure trove which the visitors had abandoned. Anna was still sitting gazing out to sea, and with her green jumper and dark-red head looked like a creature that might have come up out of that element.

He lay flat once more and smiled, wondering if perhaps he was "escaping" too far. The word "visitors" (called by Norman) came into his mind and along with it the figures of Colonel Mackintosh and Blair. They must have arrived! The feeling of guilt, from which he had run away into such extraordinary dimensions of thought, stung him sharply. He should have been at home to receive them, to find accommodation, to help in every way he could.

Sheena saw him coming and ran to her mother. Anna arose and smiled. "Some visitors have arrived and are looking for you," she said.

"Have you been hunting me?"

"Someone came and told me. They are at Clachar House."

"That's all right. Been picnicking? And how are you, Sheena? What a lot of bonny things you have got!"

Sheena was shy, though her eyes never left him.

"Well, I suppose I had better go." He stretched a hand towards Sheena. "Coming?"

Sheena looked at her mother.

"We won't go so fast as you," Anna said.

As he went on his way, he thought about them. There was something in Anna, some deep secret life in her, that warmed him. A man could spend his whole life with a woman like that and grow richer in himself.

Mrs. Cameron's eyes steadied on him for a moment, then her face cleared and she gave him the news of the last few hours not without a dry humour which he relished. After he had washed and combed his hair, he hunted for his special pair of scissors and trimmed his beard. He liked it very short. With the nervous excitement of one prepared for battle, he set out. For well he knew that at last the dread hour had come, the bitter hour of arraignment before his peers. There was only one thing to do and live: carry the war to them.

26

"**Y**ou're a fine fellow," said Colonel Mackintosh, his deck chair creaking and staggering as he heaved himself up, "I must say."

"Why, what's gone wrong now?" Grant asked, laughing, as he shook hands.

"Wrong? Good God!"

"Our great new publicist," declared Blair. "Let me congratulate you."

"Thanks very much," replied Grant modestly.

"I'll get you a chair," said Mrs. Sidbury, and Grant went with her into the hall.

"Did you see Donald?" she asked him.

"Yes . . . well, at least—I saw someone in a boat, heading this way."

"I sent Norman——"

"I think they made contact."

She gave him a dark flash of understanding. "It would be so nice of you to help me entertain them. Colonel Mackintosh and my father were old friends."

"I'll do everything I can," he said, lifting the folded chair, and they returned to the gravel in front of the house, where the two visitors were waiting on their feet.

Colonel Mackintosh was a big, straight, thick-set man with so short a neck that his shoulders seemed permanently hunched. His face was fleshy and his brown moustache so thick and droopy that his voice would have sounded like a growl from ambush if it hadn't been husky. He wore a blue cap over a full head of faded brown hair, was sixty-six, and liked stories of a salty humour. His small eyes were now on Simon Grant.

"Do sit down," said Mrs. Sidbury, and as they sat down she added, "You'll stop for supper, Mr. Grant?"

He got up again. "No, thanks. I know how difficult rations are and my supper will be under way."

"I have warned them they'll only get fish, but there is plenty of that, fresh from the sea——"

"Thank you, but, if you wouldn't mind, I must not overdo my irregular appearance——"

"Huh!" interrupted the Colonel, and Mrs. Sidbury withdrew, leaving Grant to change his mind.

"Irregular!" repeated the Colonel. "I should think so. What's all this menagerie about?"

Roger Blair, a lanky thin-haired man in his fifties, wearing gold-rimmed spectacles, stretched out his legs with a laugh that threw his head back.

"What menagerie?" asked Grant.

Colonel Mackintosh waved an arm over hillsides on which humans moved. "That."

"I can't help that."

"No? Who then has produced this colossal spectacle?"

"Cnossal, you mean," said Blair.

"My God, you would think it was," agreed the Colonel. "Out with it! What's the big idea? I thought you had some notion of the—the amenities of archaeology, if not the dignity."

"Are you trying to make some point?" inquired Grant.

"Do you think I have travelled up here *not* to make one?"

"That's for you to say. If I have given our normally arid subject some publicity, I should not have thought that altogether reprehensible in these days. But I may be wrong."

"Normally arid!"

"From a public point of view. I have always maintained that there is a conception of archaeology which is not only scientific but also human. In a modest way, I have been trying to exemplify this."

The Colonel's humoured sparring got a check. His chair creaked as he tried to focus Grant more clearly. "You don't mean the whole bloody thing is hocus-pocus?"

"You are referring, I presume, to the reports in the press?"

"What else would I be referring to?"

"I thought," said Grant, smiling to his hat, "that I had managed those rather well."

"Look here, Grant. For God's sake don't tell me that I shouldn't have let you loose alone. I meant it for your health's sake more than anything; a small-scale affair." The Colonel, hitherto in holiday mood, had now let a note of real concern invade his thick voice.

"It may be a small affair but at least it's my own."

"Right down to the crock of gold?"

"Even to the crock of gold."

Blair laughed. "I was right," he said. "I told you the whole thing was too fantastic."

But the Colonel was still inspecting Grant. "Why?"

"Well," replied Grant, "it happened that way. And for the rest—we fought pretty well in the last war, well enough anyhow to be weary of barkings and snarlings from India and Egypt, not to mention Russia and the Holy Land. Don't you think we were due some light relief?"

"A cnossal spoof to cheer up the great British public?" said Blair without a laugh, with almost a note of marvelling.

"Don't you think the great British public has earned some fun?" inquired Grant with a sharp glance at him.

"I didn't think you had it in you!" declared Blair.

"I beg your pardon?" Grant eyed him.

Blair laughed in a high echoing way, the throw-back of his head being so sudden that his felt hat fell off.

"But——" said the Colonel and paused, and he didn't often pause when all set for the kind of elaborate inquiry or fooling that tied another man in knots. His blue eyes were small, shrewd, and penetrating.

"You think perhaps I have overdone it?" inquired Grant with open innocence. "I admit I have wondered myself. But then—people are clearly interested when the subject is presented to them in the right way. I think I may fairly say I have proved that. Now what I have been really wondering is this: why can't we get some experts to deal with various aspects of the whole matter, as it appertains to the cairn, in a truly human way? If we can show man's continuity on our own soil, in a human way, over thousands of years, his work, his arts, his ceremonies, his ornaments, show his thought and his courage, wouldn't it help us now? Our island story has its inspirations as well as its splendours."

The Colonel was manifestly beyond speech and even Blair had an odd look in his eye.

"As for myself," Grant continued, "I am prepared to take up the religious aspect."

"Religious," croaked the Colonel.

"Yes," said Grant. "I have had time to give it considerable thought. We are inclined to think that the crock of gold in legend just meant a pot with gold in it. And so it did. But it also—and here we touch subtle duality—it also meant something more. The crock was at once, as it were, both real and symbolical. This raises the whole question of the meaning of the symbol, both in religion and art, not only *then* but now, in fact especially now: again a continuity which we should work out, and this time a spiritual continuity which might have a profoundly meliorating effect upon our present over-indulgence in materialism."

"Phew!" blew Blair.

"I'm sorry if I have been monopolising the conversation," said Grant with an apologetic smile, "and though there is much that I might usefully add, perhaps I have said enough to indicate my general attitude."

"God it's warm," said the Colonel on a gust of solemn breath and mopped his forehead with his handkerchief.

"The weather has been exceptionally fine," Grant agreed as one who knew it had gone out of its way to favour his designs, but secretly.

Blair put a finger inside his collar and pulled it outward to let air pass to his chest. "Subtle duality," he murmured.

"Schizophrenia," muttered the Colonel; and added, "This is even more than we had bargained for."

"Speaking for yourself," said Blair, and then he began to laugh his high-pitched laugh.

The Colonel started with a wheeze, but his head went up and such surprisingly forceful gusts came from his shaken body that the old canvas of his chair burst and the wooden struts cracked like a gunshot as his posterior found the gravel. Then Grant began to laugh and Martin came out of the front door.

The chair clung so tightly to Colonel Mackintosh that in the end Grant had to pull it off him from behind as Martin and Blair heaved him to his feet.

"Ho," said the Colonel, "hm. Is this the kind of crockery you keep nowadays, Martin?"

"Sorry it could not stand the test," answered Martin, with a smile. "It's pre-war."

"So long as Grant did not find it in the cairn," said the Colonel, dusting his behind.

Amid the restored good humour Mrs. Sidbury came out and the Colonel apologised for breaking her chair. It was decided, on examination, that the canvas had perished from old age.

"It's what we all perish from," said the Colonel, "when we're supposed to be lucky," and refused any of the other chairs. "Once bitten," he explained, and added with a glance at Grant, "or should I say twice?"

"Do come inside," invited Mrs. Sidbury. "You'll find something firmer there."

"You'll have to excuse me," said Grant, "but we feed rather early at the cottage."

"Oh." She looked at him. "If I cannot persuade you, would you come round later for coffee?"

"Thank you very much."

From a little distance, he heard Blair's laugh as they all moved into the house. But he did not mind. He was indeed quite pleased with himself, having led them up the garden path more successfully than he had thought possible. In the next bout, he could not expect to come off so well, but at least he would surprise them! Then he began to marvel a little at the words which had come to him, and as he went on they seemed to contain an inner truth. Otherwise, presumably, they would not have been effective! But he could not laugh the matter off entirely, and all at once, and with an effect of piercing sincerity, he said: It's true. There's Martin. He's suffering, not from materialism, but from the *end* of materialism. He is what it arrives at. And that means woman, child, and everything.

His footsteps quickened, his eyes flashed.

27

"Now this is a somewhat serious business and we have got to get down to it. Apart from the invasion of Martin's land——"

"I'm sorry about that," said Grant, interrupting the Colonel, "and this morning I took what steps I could with the police about it." He looked at Martin. "I wanted to see you, for the law of interdict is an involved and slow business, with its proof of individual damage and so on; I wondered if it would help if we got a notice put up."

"Trespassers will be prosecuted?"

"I know it doesn't mean much," Grant admitted, "but I thought we might say that steps could be taken to prosecute anyone who interfered with the cairn or trespassed to the damage of this land, something that would make it clear to reasonable people that they mustn't just damage things wantonly."

Martin's face held its still smile, then he shook his head slightly as if the suggestion were hardly worth discussing.

"I'm very sorry about it," said Grant. "All I can say is that the policeman will make a difference. He reckons he has already got several petrol prosecutions on hand. By the way, Blair, I hope *you're* all right?"

"Certainly," answered Blair, with the smile that always provoked Grant. "It was not difficult to get a special supply of coupons from the Petroleum Officer once I had persuaded him of the national importance of your discovery of the crock of gold."

The Colonel smiled. "Don't be so cocky, Blair. You may yet be prosecuted for getting coupons under false pretences."

Through the laughter, Mrs. Sidbury asked, "Is this a veiled attack on you, Mr. Grant?" and he knew that at least he had one ally.

"The veil is so thin that you needn't notice it," he answered.

"Martin tells me that in a way he was responsible," said Colonel Mackintosh, "for your first extraordinary step, namely, engaging the village idiot."

"Mr. Martin was good enough to effect the introduction, yes."

"And you engaged him? Odd thing to do, wasn't it?"

"You imply that a village idiot is not qualified to be an archaeologist's assistant? I think I see what you mean." He was thoughtfully judicial.

Mrs. Sidbury laughed.

"But *you* found him all right?" asked Blair.

"I found him a very good worker," answered Grant, "and there seemed something familiar, too, about the cast of his mind. He is remarkably fond of stone implements, though not a trained petrologist."

The Colonel could not restrain a soft wheeze over this thrust at Blair, who laughed also and said, "According to all accounts he was even fonder of your crock of gold."

"That, unfortunately, is true," agreed Grant, "but then, being an idiot, he probably thought it was worth being fonder of."

"Wait a bit, you fellows," said the Colonel, "we'll have your sparring afterwards. Now tell me, Grant, what on earth made you think of inventing a crock of gold?"

"I didn't invent it."

"Then who did?"

"I wish I knew. All I know is that a crock of gold was there."

After staring for a few seconds, the Colonel asked, "Where?"

"In the cairn. In the small corbelled cell, which you saw pictured in the press."

The silence lasted a little longer this time. "I'm not fooling now," said the Colonel.

"Neither am I," said Grant, holding the Colonel's eyes.

"You mean you found a funerary urn full of gold ornaments?"

"I did."

"In that cairn?"

"Yes. There was a false wall blocking the cell; I removed it and found the urn there."

"And then?"

"Then it disappeared."

"How did it disappear?"

"It's the only part of the story the press doesn't know. I had rather intended to keep it to myself, but if you would be good enough to respect my confidence, I'll tell you."

Then he told them the story of the discovery, the struggle with Andie, and his loss of consciousness.

"How long were you unconscious?"

"I don't know. But it might have been anything up to an hour. I just can't be certain."

"All this took place about midnight? Wasn't that a strange hour to have had such an experience?"

"You think the whole thing might have been a dream or hallucination. I understand that," he assured the Colonel simply. "However, it wasn't. Though the press might have got to know little about it, if I hadn't, after leaving the cairn, met Mr. Martin's chauffeur and asked him if he had seen Andie who had run away with the treasure or whatever I called it to him. I was rather upset at the time."

"Then you found Andie in bed and his mother had never missed him?"

"That is so."

"You know me well enough, Grant, to know that I have always respected your work, but—I'm not doubting you went to the cairn—even at that hour—but, I put it to you, is it possible that while inside the cairn you may have slipped and got a crack on your head and fancied things?"

"Only one difficulty about that. I remembered that one of the ornaments had fallen out of my hands when I was surprised by Andie. I went straight back—and found it."

"You mean you still have it?"

From his poacher's pocket Grant took a small flat wooden box, which usually held some of his drawing instruments. Very carefully he withdrew what was inside, unwound handkerchief wrappings, and there was the lunula, gleaming in the light. As he walked with it to the west window and laid it on a small mahogany table, they all followed him. Without a word, he handed Colonel Mackintosh his pocket magnifying glass.

The Colonel's examination was minute, then he straightened himself and turned to Grant. "I suppose you know that this is the finest specimen of the lunette extant?"

"It's the best I have seen."

"Uhm," said the Colonel and stood staring out of the window, the magnifying glass drooping from his hand.

They all followed his gaze, past some pine trunks, to the western ocean which had upon its evening face a mingling of light, a curious crawling effect like a marvelling. The horizon was very remote.

The Colonel turned his head and looked at Grant. "A whole urnful?"

Grant nodded, a faint smile on his face. "A gold hoard."

"My God."

"Congratulations," Mrs Sidbury murmured, like one restraining with difficulty the airiest laughter. It was as if she had said: I did support you! "May I?" and she lifted the lunette in her fine nervous hands, delicately as though it were made of glass. "How wonderful! . . . To think of it then! How long ago?"

"Goes with the food vessel, Food Vessel complex. Bronze Age," muttered the Colonel.

"How long?"

The Colonel heaved his shoulders slightly. "Who can say—in the absence of the total contents?" He swung round on Grant. "What are you doing about this?"

"What can I do?"

"Do you mean you're doing nothing?" This was the Colonel at last in earnest.

Grant heaved his own shoulders. "What do you think the —the whole menagerie is doing, including the members of the press?"

"Good God—what made you tell the press?"

Grant was silent.

"Heavens above, surely that was the last thing on earth to do! Why broadcast it to the public, if you ever hoped to find the urn?"

"There is a more real danger," answered Grant simply. "Talk is going around that if the urn could be found the gold could be melted down, secretly disposed of, and a small fortune realised." And he had the satisfaction of seeing the wind knocked completely out of the Colonel, who for a little while indeed did nothing but gape; then he took the floor.

By an hour later, Grant had given them a fair account of his whole work at the cairn, and Colonel Mackintosh, realising at last that his subject, which was his life's devotion, had neither been lightly handled nor traduced by vanity, was simple and direct, appreciative and full of resource.

With a gleam in his eye, he even complimented the gentlemen of the press. "That's their trade as this is ours, and
seeing the beans have been spilled in spite of us, I'll get hold
of that fellow Arthur and talk to him, on the record and off,
as an ally. We have only one thing to do now—get hold of
the hoard. You certainly had a bit of damned bad luck,
Grant, even though you did go out at midnight!" He
turned to Mrs. Sidbury. "I'm talking in Edinburgh in three
days' time. Do you think you could manage to put us up
for a couple of nights. Blair here can live on winkles."

"Delighted," she answered. "That will be splendid."

"Thank you. I didn't know the Highlands had started to
crawl with tourists." The springs of his armchair protested
faintly.

Two hours later, when a further supply of coffee was
exhausted and the more intricate archaeological aspects of
the discoveries in the cairn had been discussed in minute
detail, the atmosphere was friendly and warm enough for
expressions of probability and even of wonder. The past had
come into the room in an almost palpable way.

"It's not so difficult to imagine yourself living two
thousand years ago," said Mrs. Sidbury.

"It's often easier," said Grant.

"How?"

"Because you can live and move the way you want. You
can make a story of it, and every movement in that story
means something—as important as you would like it to
mean."

"Have you been making any stories?" asked the
Colonel.

"A few. Efforts at reconstruction, shall we say?"

On the command to fire ahead, Grant gave a quite vivid
description of the ceremonies accompanying and following
a burial in the chamber when it was "the cathedral of its
time". He borrowed from recent anthropological field

work among primitive peoples in Eastern archipelagoes, from Homer, from extant religious practices, but without parade of knowledge, for he had been thinking the matter over, or rather—though he did not put it like this to the Colonel—the matter, the reconstruction, had flowed into his mind. This had been one of the most remarkable things that had happened to him. In odd moments, before going to sleep, during a pause in his writing, on his back outside, while his mind was passive, there flowed into it scenes of a remarkable clarity. It was as though some invisible director had emptied his mind, as he might have emptied a stage, and then let his players flow in upon it in a drama which the archaeologist, as spectator, followed with surprise and profound understanding.

When cross-questioned by Colonel Mackintosh, he had, of course, his factual answers ready: the music, the pipe, the primitive stringed instrument, the women with ornaments and make-up, the crowd, the dancing. On the dancing he was particularly effective, giving it a vastly wider range and variety than we dreamed of, borrowing here in particular from recent knowledge of native African dancing which had been praised in such extravagant terms by some European masters of modern ballet. And when the Colonel said that this was altogether too extravagant, Grant switched to the religious basis of dancing, the mimetic art that persuaded the gods, and wondered, anyhow, with an innocent smile for the Colonel, where the Neolithic people came from. He was ready even for Blair, who had been hoarding up the word "cathedral". And when the Colonel said, "I suppose you can now answer the question: was the chambered cairn a communal burial ground or a private mausoleum for the head man and his family group?" Grant answered, "I could have a shot at it." Even Mrs. Sidbury laughed, but with pleasure.

"It seems simple enough to me," said Grant. "At first, in

the early stages of arriving, settling, hunting, it would be communal, but as the settlement grew, became stabilised, it would tend to become the private mausoleum."

"As simple as that?"

"Human nature is always as simple as that," replied Grant. "Economic conditions would merely tend to swing the thing either way."

"The motives never change?"

"Not the deep-seated ones."

"You were going to tell us," said Mrs. Sidbury, "and I hope I am not upsetting your argument, how the crock of gold came to be there, I mean the story about it."

"I'm afraid, for the first time, that might be a bit fanciful."

" 'For the first time' is good," said Blair.

"I rather think," said Grant, "it has something to do with the woman and the child in the cist. But it is difficult here to link the whole thing up because there may have been a time interval. Not that there need have been. Terms like Neolithic Age or Bronze Age are, as Colonel Mackintosh has made so clear in his distinguished published work, convenient working terms, but there always are in different places overlaps of centuries in tools, practices, cremation, inhumation, and so on. Even to-day in the world there are people still in the Stone Age."

"Let's hear your story," said the Colonel.

"The trouble is," said Grant, "it isn't yet quite clear. But it very nearly came to me last night. I got a sort of preliminary feeling of the whole thing."

Blair threw his thin face up in genuine amusement. Grant smiled in good humour, but with a light in his eye. Colonel Mackintosh's face seemed to have grown slightly fatter, his eyes smaller, in a puckishness that blew through the hairs of his moustache. Martin had spoken very little but was unobtrusively one of the company; when he did speak his voice was natural and at ease. Mrs. Sidbury's eyes had flashed on Grant when he had mentioned the woman and child and, without looking at her, he had been aware of the momentary tension.

"Leaving the question of feeling alone—in deference to Blair—I think a few simple facts do come through. In the first place, the woman *and* the child, if skulls and bones mean anything, are of the same family or racial group as those in the cairn." He looked at the Colonel. "You can check that to-morrow. In the second place the bracelet which I got in the cist is exactly like the pair of bracelets which I pulled out of the urn and had a look at. You must take my word for that—meantime. Also the jet necklace bears a marked resemblance in design to this gold lunette. There is thus in the workmanship a definite relationship of period and place. Third: manifestly this was a woman of importance or she would never have possessed gold. Obviously it was a rare metal or we should have found more of it in our field work. The notion of a crock of gold did not become a legend for nothing presumably. Fourth: it seems to me that the grave gear of a woman of such importance is pitifully slight. Remember, too, a woman *and* her child—and I am not sure that we know enough about the constitution of their society to say *only a female child*. Taking all these points together, I submit it is not too fanciful to assume a relationship between the woman in the cist and the gold hoard."

The Colonel leaned back. "Your points are interesting, decidedly interesting—but your final assumption!" He shook his head. "But you would first have to do some jugglery between burial in a chambered cairn and burial in a short cist."

"Well of course," agreed Grant. "That's where the drama comes in. We take it as established that the individual cist burial was a method of burial introduced by a round-headed people invading us from the Continent and landing on the east coast——" He paused.

"Well?" The Colonel waited.

Grant smiled also. "I agree it's difficult. But let us assume for a moment that this woman's man was the headman of this settlement. For gold to have been about at all, raiding must have been going on, either raiding or trading. Let us assume he was away on a raiding—or trading—expedition."

"What would he trade with—from a place like this?" asked Blair.

Grant nodded. "You may be right."

"And if it was a case of a sudden invasion of a peaceful people—how had they managed to get the gold?" asked the Colonel. "You'll have to assume, I'm afraid, that they were a fighting raiding lot, not unlike the clansmen of a later date." The Colonel was enjoying himself.

"Very well. Let us say the headman was away fighting, and while he was doing this Clachar was invaded by round-heads from the east coast. The local home guard would do their best, rallying round the woman and child, but in the end they are overcome and the woman, to avoid capture, decides to pass out, taking the child with her—poison or drowning, something like that, for I can find no evidence at all of violence to a bone."

"And the roundheads buried her cist-fashion in the cairn out of respect for so noble an enemy?" suggested Blair.

"They might," said Grant. "It's the kind of thing they did in those days."

Blair laughed in enjoyment of his scepticism.

"And in the hurry and alarm, the aged medicine man would block up the urn in the corbelled cell?" suggested the Colonel.

"He might," said Grant. "It would certainly be the best place to hide it."

"Why?"

"Because if the old boy was then done in and the headman came back and drove out the invaders, the first thing he would notice when he had opened up the passage and entered the tomb of his forefathers was that the corbelled cell had been built up. Investigation would reveal the urn, and the headman would bless the memory of the aged priest."

Colonel Mackintosh laughed. "You seem to have thought it all out!"

"I admit I thought of that bit only this minute. Actually I am not at all sure that it happened like that."

"No?" The Colonel eyed him.

"No. You see, a rather extraordinary thing is taking place in my lodging just now. I have the two skeletons in a box in a small room—a cell—just off my bedroom. The first night they were there they came out while I was asleep and were . . . very much alive . . . on the rug in front of the fireplace. They appeared a second night. The third occasion was last night, but last night, for the first time, they saw me."

All eyes were on him and in the silence the summer night came into the room, for the curtains had not been drawn.

"Did they get a shock?" asked Blair, but no one laughed.

"Well?" asked the Colonel.

"That's all," said Grant.

"You mean you woke up?"

Grant hesitated. "I terminated the interview by coming to my ordinary senses."

"You think the woman might have spoken?" probed the Colonel.

"She might."

"In English?" asked Blair.

"I don't think it would have mattered whether she spoke in words or not. An experience is an experience—not speech."

"But you can't communicate it without speech."

212

Grant looked at Blair. "Can't you?" Then he got up, apologised for stopping so late, and in a few minutes was on his way home, wondering in the light-hearted aftermath of parting whether he understood the silent look Mrs. Sidbury had given him.

28

For two days Colonel Mackintosh took control and things got going. To his solid body was added his solid reputation and all irrelevances and foolish speech bounced off him. He joked with the policeman, and if anything further was needed to draw the law to his heels, he unconsciously achieved it by mentioning the Home Office as if it were his private club. The passage in the cairn was reopened, and as the Colonel's extensive hindquarters slowly disappeared the policeman started an eagle-eyed patrol which had small consideration for human curiosity even in its more cunning guises.

For naturally the public, not to mention the press, were in a state of suspense about what might be happening inside a cairn peopled at the moment by three archaeologists and the village idiot. But Colonel Mackintosh was quite simply in his element. He snuffed the air, he handled the bones, he lifted a skull as it were an apple. His manner was off-hand while he spoke to no one in particular. He ruminated, squatting like a buddha. The outside world of time was no more as he dredged the dust of millennia and ordered Blair to hold the light to it. When Blair spoke out of his knowledge, the Colonel said "Hm" or "Hmf" through nostrils fashioned to blow such knowledge away. He poked here and scraped there. His finger of electric light travelled so deliberately from door-jamb to lintel that it wrote the architectural story as it advanced. When Blair felt called upon to indicate the more fascinating aspects of that story in plain and even excited English, the Colonel still contented himself with sounds that may have been Neolithic. At last he entered the eastern chamber, and before the raped cell his features gathered, lifting the moustache bushily and closing the eyes to slits. Grant had laid his hand-lamp on a stone on the floor. Blair withdrew his torch from the cell and straightened himself. The Colonel turned to Foolish Andie, who was by his right shoulder, and stared at him.

As Andie held the stare, his mouth opened a little more; as his head moved his eyes glistened. "Gu—gu——"

"Gu gad!" said the Colonel sternly.

Andie's shoulders began to move. His eyes swept to Grant, who was by the Colonel's left side.

"Gu—gar——"

"By gad you did! And this is what you did!" roared the Colonel. Whereupon he swung round and embraced Mr. Grant with such unexpected violence that that slim figure lost its balance and grabbed at the Colonel.

"Look out!" yelled Blair.

The Colonel felt his shoulder wrenched by a paw, but Grant tore in, and forced Andie back with imperious shouts.

Andie stood flapping his arms like great wings, gabbling in tremendous excitement, but dominated by his employer, who continued to address him sharply until the eye-glistening rage subsided.

"That was a near thing!" said Blair and blew a chestful of air.

But the Colonel, though breathing heavily, did not seem put out. "He did it all right," he muttered, watching Andie. "Point is: does it convey anything to him, does he remember?"

Through the flying dust of the centuries, Grant said, "I'll give him something to do." He turned to Andie. "Come on; we have got to shift these stones—from here—to there."

The Colonel watched Grant shifting the first stones himself, then turned away, and did a minute examination of the cell.

"Odd that this should have been the only place," said Blair, still shaken with amazement, "where this overlapping—this corbelling—should have been done."

The Colonel straightened up. "I don't know," he muttered. "I once had a dog that buried bones in the garden. I came to the conclusion that he had forgotten where he had buried some of them, if not all."

Blair looked at him. "You're thinking of the crock of gold?"

"God knows what happens inside that mind," muttered Colonel Mackintosh as he watched Andie stack the last of the loose stones against the off wall; then he proceeded to examine the row of skulls.

It was after lunch when the Colonel was tackled by Arthur. Blair and himself had gone back to Clachar House to eat, for it was no great distance and Mrs. Sidbury had alleged that it was easier to spread something on a table than wrap it in paper.

"And you are Arthur——?"

"Arthur Black, sir," replied Arthur with a smile.

"Hm," said the Colonel with a glance at his black head. "What do you want?"

"I was wondering what you thought of the cairn?"

"Why, is there something you think you could learn about it?"

"From you, sir, everyone could learn."

"So you brought everyone to the spot? You think that's helpful to us?"

"I can't help that."

"Can't you? If you brought them here, you can drive them away? Surely you don't suggest that the press is not omnipotent as well as omniscient?"

"Do you imply, sir, that it's omnipotent enough to get an exclusive interview from you?"

"I might imply even that."

"I am prepared to obey all instructions and, where necessary, submit copy for your approval."

"You looked an intelligent fellow." The Colonel turned to Blair. "Tell Grant I've been waylaid by a man who wants to grind his own stone axe."

Then Colonel Mackintosh seated himself and prepared to speak to the young man.

Before returning to Clachar House for supper the Colonel thought he would like to have a few words with Mrs. Mackenzie. "She seems a nice simple stupid woman," he said.

It was his use of a word like "stupid" at such a moment that made Blair smile appreciatively and got Grant a little on the raw, though he smiled also, for he knew it was an indirect way of baiting him.

"We don't want to crowd the poor woman out," the Colonel continued, "so perhaps you'll tell Mrs. Sidbury I'll be along presently."

"Very good." Blair saluted.

As the two men approached the cottage, the Colonel asked, " I suppose she's quite *compos mentis*?"

"Quite," replied Grant.

"You say she resents all this intrusion?"

"I suspect she thinks it's bad manners, but that's merely because she doesn't know any better."

"Not a radical defect in intelligence, you suggest?"

"Possibly not."

As Mrs. Mackenzie appeared in answer to his knock, Simon Grant, at once smiling and friendly, said, "Here we are troubling you again, Mrs. Mackenzie, but Colonel Mackintosh was saying he did not have a chance of speaking to you properly to-day with all the people about. I hope we're not intruding?"

"Would you please come in?" Her grave face hardly smiled and her voice had a smothered note of distress. They followed her into the kitchen, where she hospitably saw them seated.

"Is all this getting a bit too much for you?" asked the Colonel.

"It is," she admitted. "Too much."

They thought she was going to break down, but she swallowed and pressed her lips and then was calm again. She obviously had been having a struggle with herself before they appeared.

"I asked you and Andie along to-day, because I did want you to meet my friends and we needed some help for opening the cairn," Grant explained, "and your son is a capital worker."

"Excellent," said the Colonel, watching her.

She made a neat fold of her apron on her knee and then looked up at Grant. "If you don't mind, sir, I would like that we stopped now working at the cairn."

"Why, what's gone wrong?" asked the Colonel before Grant could speak.

"Everything," she said.

"Nothing's happened to Andie?" asked Grant quickly.

"No," she answered.

It was the reticence of one who did not wish to trouble them with personal explanation, who was tired and wanted to be left alone, who knew that she may have let them down but could in herself and in her son do no more.

"Surely you are not bothering your head about all these silly gaping people?" asked Colonel Mackintosh.

"We are not used to it."

"You're lucky," he said heartily. "Mr. Grant and myself have got used to it long ago."

She did not answer, sitting quite still, her face to the fire. The slight movement in her hands, pressing against her knees, drew Grant's attention, and he saw them intimately and isolated, and read their lines and colour as he might some ancient script. He glanced at her face. The skin had the texture of the skin on a plate of cold porridge; a heavy face, with graven lines which he had not noticed before; her eyes had a strange glisten in them as though a weight pressed on her forehead.

"Have you been keeping your son from going out at night?" asked Colonel Mackintosh.

"Yes."

"You're quite right. We'll have to see that you're not troubled any further."

Grant heard the remarks, but vaguely, so lost was he in apperception of her being. His eyes had withdrawn to the fire.

"You have no idea at all, from your son's behaviour, where he may have hidden the urn?" continued the Colonel.

"None," she answered.

"If Mrs. Mackenzie had any idea she would have told me," said Grant suddenly, as though the words had been surprised out of him in anger, but when the Colonel glanced at him he was smiling.

"Once we have got all these people cleared away, you'll find everything will come all right," the Colonel assured her.

But Grant got to his feet with the unbearable feeling that she was going to break down in a way no stranger should witness. "I must get along," he said briskly, afraid now to address even one word of sympathy to her.

"You're in a hurry." Colonel Mackintosh looked up at him. To end the interview was surely his prerogative.

"I think we should get along," said Grant smiling.

"People round here are very restless," said the Colonel to Mrs. Mackenzie, but he got up. With a cheerful good-bye, Grant turned for the door.

Behind him he heard Mrs. Mackenzie say, "No, thank you. We need nothing." He felt pierced between the shoulder blades.

There was a slight confusion on the Colonel's features as they walked away. "An independent sort of woman, too."

"But stupid," said Grant, relieved now, drawing in the outside air, prepared once more to give as much as he got.

The culminating episode of the Colonel's short visit occurred the following afternoon. The girl in the shorts appeared before the cairn and said to the policeman that she must see Colonel Mackintosh at once. But the policeman, who had already had cause to measure his resources against those of the press, was not impressed, and even less impressed when she said that she was prepared to crawl up the passage in order to deliver her urgent message in person.

"I have heard that one before," he suggested, stretching his six feet in sarcastic ease.

"You go in yourself then and tell him," she said.

He perceived now that she had been running, that she was breathless, and that her eyes were very bright.

"What's your message?" he asked.

She looked at him with such earnestness that she was plainly tempted to tell him. "I can't tell you," she said. "It's for Colonel Mackintosh."

"He is not to be disturbed by the public."

"I am not the public." She spoke with such penetrating force that one or two hovering members of that great body drew a little nearer. In the desperate moment she took a step nearer him herself. Involuntarily he lowered his head. "We have found it," she whispered.

As his head went up again his lips parted in astonishment. "You mean the crock——"

She stopped him with a swift nod. "Hsh!"

His expression slowly narrowed as his eyes searched her

face. Still far from being completely reassured, he got into the opening himself, stuck his head up the tunnel and roared, "Ahoy, there!" Grant's figure wavered distantly against swinging lights. "That newspaper woman," bellowed the policeman, "says she wants to see Colonel Mackintosh."

The Colonel rose out of the passage and as the girl was imparting her intelligence in a low swift voice his legs were butted by Blair who was followed by Grant.

"Just see that no one goes in there, constable, till we come back," said the Colonel, and the three scientists, with the girl in their midst, walked away. They passed the tall monolith in the south-west of the circle, dipped with the ground, went up between two shoulders of land, rounded the inland one and came into a tiny valley whose watercourse was dried up. From a swath of tall bracken Arthur Black's head reared up. He waved to them.

The Colonel's brows gathered, his moustache lifted, as he gazed not only at a short cist but at a baked-clay cinerary urn.

Arthur's eyes were brighter even than the girl's. "It's quite genuine," he said and smiled at the Colonel's puzzlement.

"You mean it's—genuine?"

Arthur's smile deepened. "Quite genuine." He snatched a coloured silk neckerchief from the top of the urn. "Have a look."

Colonel Mackintosh got down on his knees, looked inside the urn, withdrew a burnt bone, examined it, withdrew another, looked inside again and put the bones back. Then he examined the exterior of the urn. It was an excellent specimen of the Overhanging Rim type, with decoration not only on the collar and the inside bevel of the lip, but also right round the shoulder below the collar; a particularly tall specimen, too, not much under two feet if his eye could measure anything.

"You found this—here?"

"Yes," answered Arthur. "We saw him coming out of this valley fairly early this morning."

"Who?"

"The idiot. We have been prospecting ever since."

"How early?" asked Grant.

"Before eight o'clock."

The Colonel stepped to the edge of the cist, which was the usual affair of four slabs on end, from which the covering lid, some four feet by two, had been heaved over.

"Find anything else?" The Colonel was staring at Arthur's jacket which covered part of the interior.

"Yes. We have found a hoard."

The Colonel's mouth came adrift.

"It surprised us, too," said Arthur, reluctant to move. "It tells the story of a whole age."

"Where is it?"

"Under that jacket." He still could not move.

Blair stooped and lifted the jacket, thus revealing the hoard. Items: a broken electric torch, five brass army buttons, a silver-bright Seaforth crest, a motor horn with perished rubber bulb, and a cheap cigarette case containing —of all things—a one-pound Treasury note.

"My God," said the Colonel more in awe than anything.

"They're coming," said the girl quickly.

Arthur glanced over his shoulder, then swiftly covered the mouth of the urn with the girl's kerchief.

"Will I give them the dope?" he asked Colonel Mackintosh.

The Colonel glowered at some members of the public who were slowly, circuitously, but certainly, drawing nigh. "I should have liked a photograph of this."

"I have taken six," said Arthur.

The Colonel looked at him with an enigmatic humour. "The play is more realistic than we had hoped."

222

"We hadn't counted on such a stage-manager."

"By gad, we hadn't! Or should I say Gu gad?" The Colonel's humour was dry but flavoured.

Blair carried the draped urn past many staring eyes as the three learned men headed for Grant's lodging. "The meaning of the play," the Colonel explained, "is this. The crock of gold has now been found and will be conveyed south for expert examination. The cairn will be completely closed up this evening. Colonel Mackintosh and his associates are leaving to-morrow. Everything is over. Let the public depart in peace and Clachar return to its ancient somnolence."

"Is that what Arthur is telling the world?" asked Blair.

"It is," said the Colonel, "with some ambiguous embellishments. It was the best I could do for you, Grant, in the way of getting rid of the menagerie, especially its scavengers."

"Not too bad," Grant allowed.

"There's a way of handling these fellows," suggested the Colonel. Blair so appreciated the remark that he glanced at Grant and stumbled and the old bones rattled in the urn.

"Of course, Arthur being a bright young man," proceeded the Colonel, "had his price. In the first place, I promised him one of your prints of the lunette and one of the jet necklace. That all right?"

"It might be managed."

"Secondly, when we return here to open up the whole cairn in a week or ten days, we shall countenance him as a sort of press agent in chief, or vague words to that effect." He negotiated an awkward cleft, puffing as he hauled himself up. "Talking about handling the press, did I ever tell you the one about the tomb and the mummy?"

"You did," said Grant.

The Colonel cocked an eye at him and laughed as they continued on their way.

29

With the Colonel's departure the weather broke, wind and rain from the sou'-west drove flapping curiosity before it, and Grant stood looking from his little window as from a newer kind of earth-house. His feeling of seclusion was deepened by a fragrant warmth from the peat-fire which Mrs. Cameron had insisted on lighting. "The bit fire is friendly," she had said.

The green of the grass was greener, fresher, as wind and rain swept along under the hurrying sky. The grasses flattened themselves, wiggled, in a green mirth that held on. The rowan tree was a more solemn riot, full of convolutions of itself and high bursts of abandon, but sticking to its own root at all the odds. For a miraculous moment the cat appeared on the garden wall. A blackbird whistled and was gone. Between the bursts he heard the pounding thunder of the sea.

He took a turn about the room; he stood before the fire looking at the lazy flapping of the yellow flame. *Friendly.* He turned his face over his shoulder and looked about the room, alert and welcoming, wondering, and glanced out of the window where the riders drove fast. His smile broke into a soft laugh. It was amusing; it was gay and intricate and extraordinary. The landscape had been swept clean of all the chatter. The sea was having a thunderous holiday, smashing the rocks, roaring tumultuously into the caves.

A vision of the Monster Cove came before him; in an instant submerged contacts were made and he saw that the electric torch which had been found in the short cist was the torch which he himself had dropped in that cave. There was just no doubt about it. He hurried upstairs and hauled out the hoard, unscrewed the cap of the torch, and found the piece of cardboard which he had used to keep the cell from rattling inside the case. There might even be some juice in it yet. He transferred the bulb from another torch and produced a red thread of light. Proof positive.

He had gone back to the cave and looked for the torch; had failed to find it and decided it had got covered over by wrack or shingle; had promptly forgotten it in exploration. Now it was not only clear that Andie had found it but had found it in the dark. Which means he had used a light. Andie liked striking matches. He enjoyed pressing the button of a torch and producing the magic in so novel a way. But here was a use of light in a prehistoric cave for a definite purpose —or—at least—from a definite urge.

He put the hoard away and went downstairs. As he left his sitting-room Anna happened to come out of the kitchen and stopped at sight of him.

"I thought I'd have a turn out," he said.

"It's stormy, isn't it?" She smiled.

"It will do me good. And how is Sheena to-day? I have hardly heard her." The child's voice had drawn his attention but now it was silent. As Anna looked back into the kitchen, he took a step or two forward and saw Sheena sitting under the table, her face pale in the dim light.

"She's been having a game with herself," murmured Anna.

But Sheena's face exhibited solemn wonder at the new vision of their guest in oilskin and sou'wester, and when the guest stooped and spoke she continued to gaze at him with grave reserve. He laughed and went out.

As the wind staggered him at the corner of the house he laughed aloud. He had instantly understood what Sheena was doing under the table. Even when quite a big boy of

225

seven or eight he himself had been fond of odd corners, of
going into hidey-holes. A certain piece of the attic had been
Aladdin's cave. Suddenly he wondered if these early centres
of the brain were those which still actuated Andie. If the
later centres were inhibited, would the earlier deepen much
as a blind man's hearing sharpened?

The rain pattered noisily on oilskin and sou'wester; it
stung his face, it was cold as well water, it was fresh, it
became fresher, and as he stood for a moment on the other
side of the little bridge, where the wind's force was broken
by the slope, he felt exhilarated, as though there was no joy
like a clean cold joy, no colour like this colour, no dancing
wildness like the world's own.

He kept low, avoiding the upward paths, and was soon
in sight of the sea. Beyond the pines that surrounded Clachar
House, his eye caught the white plumes tossed from the
south-west corner of the southern island. Breaking seas to
the horizon, an inward rushing, a roar of surf on shores, a
deep booming from cliffs.

As he came low by the boathouse, he saw how the islands
sheltered the sea-way to Clachar, how boats in a storm
would run for the islands, and knew that thus it had been
since man first hollowed a tree-trunk and adventured upon
the waters. Clachar was old. No wonder he was sometimes
confused by the centuries, even by the millennia! Confused
with the humans rather, who were the millennia, so that the
woman and child from the cist in the cairn. . . . His thought
passed into a visionary warmth and press of life. But Donald
Martin's face came expressionless and old as the grey rock.
All at once he was aware of someone beckoning to him from
a corner of the boathouse. He stood for a moment as before
some illusory trick. Then he saw that it was in fact Mrs.
Sidbury.

She greeted him with her usual cheerfulness, her restless
fly-away manner, but he saw that she was quivering.

"It's the cold," she said. "Phoo-oo!" and she shivered right into the core in an exaggerated way that was at once frank and friendly. Her dark eyes looked at him and flew away. Her yellow oilskin was buttoned across her throat and the strings of a yellow translucent head-cover were tied under her chin.

When he suggested that if she got colder it mightn't do her any good, she laughed and asked, "What brought you out?"

Suddenly he felt warmly attracted by her, dangerously because he felt she needed handling. There was something worrying the woman and once again he got the impression that her bits might fly asunder. But now this did not embarrass him, though it induced a certain excitement. When he found the most sheltered corner she jumped up and down in a light dancing movement, trying to throw off the shivering cold.

"Anything gone wrong?" he asked normally.

She shook her head as if he had asked about the weather. "Just that brother of mine."

"What's he up to?"

"I wish I knew. It's the sea."

"You don't mean he's been trying to go to sea?"

"He would try anything with the sea." She danced and shivered and shook the cold from her face. "After the last few days he'll feel like it."

"Why?"

"The extra depression, following on visitors."

He thought for a little and asked, "Does he get depressed?"

"Perhaps it's not a good word. There's nothing left in him."

"After visitors, his mind is drained grey as that rock."

The continued casualness of his words must have been like a gift to her, for she glanced at him with a quick smile and nodded.

227

"Why do you invite them then?"

"I must do something. There is always the hope that he may be taken out of himself."

"And you're always wrong. Tell me this: what did you really mean by mentioning the sea?"

"It's the last element," she said lightly, and glanced at his thoughtful expression as he now stared before him. "He goes more and more to the sea. He catches all the fish. He has lines and nets."

"You mean——" He hesitated.

"It's the way he's going," she said.

He did not look at her. It was tragic, but for a strange moment, beyond this woman, in another light, he thought: It's a good clean way. And for the first time he got an austere vision of Donald, of the final element in the man, and it touched him deeply and fatefully. He could not speak.

"Colonel Mackintosh—I like him," she said. "And that man, Mr. Blair. There's an ordinariness, a normal way of living and working—I thought if only——" She went stuttering and hurrying on but he had nothing to say. Even the warm personal impact she had made upon him passed away.

Presently he began to speak quietly. "I was in the first big war. I remember what it felt like when you come home and find that you have no real contacts, you have been shifted outside them, you are outside and cannot get in—and—perhaps—in your silence, for you cannot speak, cannot tell—don't want to get in, want to stay out, to go away and wander—where the ghosts are—remembering those you knew. . . . That was common." There was no emphasis on any of his words, no warmth; his memories seemed automatic.

"How did you get in?" she asked.

"Work. I started working. Gradually new human contacts were made and the memories went farther and farther away."

"Donald has no work."

"Oh yes, there's always plenty of work," he answered, as if that were not the trouble. Then he turned his face to her. "Does he—do you—believe that that girl up there, Anna Cameron, has his child?"

The lightness, the impersonal manner, fell from her. She squeezed the cold out of her hands. She looked startled and frightened. "They say so."

He remained silent but his face hardened.

"Do you?" she challenged him.

"Yes."

"You think he should marry her?" she cried a trifle wildly, broken by his quiet sternness.

He took his time. "Would you be against it?"

"Why should I? Why should you think that?"

"I am only asking you." But his voice now was gentler.

"I would not be against anything that was for his good. Surely you believe that!"

"I do." But he could not add anything more though he was aware she was struggling against an obscure accusation.

"Do you think it would be for his good?" Her face was white and challenging.

His silence seemed to torture her so that she cried, "Why don't you say what you think?"

"No, I suppose it wouldn't," he replied in a quiet almost downcast voice.

"You know it wouldn't!" There was a sharp triumph in the bitter voice and this affected him somehow to a deeper silence, and he became aware that in some mysterious way he had been brought still nearer to Donald, to that plane where all words were a distraction and without real meaning.

"He is not ready for it yet," he said. The words "probably he never will be" formed in his mind but it was as if he could not be bothered speaking them aloud.

"You know there is nothing I would not do for him. Nothing!"

And he knew it was true, but he also knew, in the case of what they had been discussing, that it was true *as a last resource*. But, one step farther on, *a last resource* would always be too late. She knew this also. He decided he had better say something. "I had a long talk with your brother one night. I think I know a little about how he feels." He paused.

"Did he mention her? What did he say?"

He looked at her, for it was astonishing to him that she could even imagine they had discussed so personal a matter. Instantly he apprehended a profound distinction between man and woman. She moved restlessly and her face flashed away. "No, we didn't talk about that. About other things," he answered. "But I should say that he simply has no interest whatever in Anna or the child. Just none. That's the trouble. And even if he tried to get an interest it wouldn't come. He knows he would be of no use to them. Not that he tries to justify himself in that way. If he did, there would be no final difficulty."

"I know!" she cried. "That's just it! And he won't go away. What can I do?"

And now it was almost as if there was hope in the woman's voice, certainly the craving for hope in a new line of action, some other bright way out of the awful despair.

"I don't know," he said, and added, reflectively, "I'll think it over."

Her gratitude touched him. He had liked her from the very beginning and now he told her of the torch which he had dropped when they were together in the Monster Cove and which he had found again in Andie's hoard. She became enthralled with interest, as if their talk had lifted her into the happiest state of expectancy, and asked if he thought Andie might have buried the crock of gold in the cave.

"It's possible," he said. "He may have more than one hiding place and the cave might strike a deep memory."

When he left her, he became consciously aware of the smell of the sea and its tossed tangle, looked back and saw the white-smothered waves and the thrown spume. As these were shut off, the freshness of the earth came upon him, out of the long-parched ground, and the colour, the wet vivid green. The wind flattened and combed the irrepressible grass, the drenched wild flowers, and the rain was a driving mist against the dark-brown mountains. All at once he saw old Fachie by the sheltered gable of his house, his left arm outstretched and his dog rushing low to the earth to round up a cow or stirk that had got into the young corn. There were no other figures to be seen and in a moment the little drama with the old bent figure might have been of any Age back to Neolithic times. When he had watched it to a conclusion and was going on again, words dropped into his released mind. He had quoted them more than once from the Preface to Frazer's *Golden Bough*: "Compared with the evidence afforded by living tradition the testimony of ancient books on the subject of early religion is worth very little." "And," as he himself had often added, "not only of early religion."

He smiled, aware of still carrying the remarkable quietude which had so strangely come upon him by the boathouse. *He won't go away* she had said. Nothing was keeping him, of course. He would want to see people less and less . . . no one . . . until the sea got him. He stood for a little while, quite unaware that he had stopped, in a curious mindless wonder, then went on to the cottage.

30

As he entered at the door, Mrs. Cameron came to help him out of his wet oilskin, to hang it up to dry in the right place. "Wait you," she said when she saw his hands at his face, "and Anna will get you a towel." As he was turning to the stairs, protesting, Anna came with a towel and he began rubbing his beard vigorously. He refused to do anything about his feet and legs, and now he was in the kitchen, assured that they had just been on the verge of making themselves a cup. "I don't think I would swap a teapot for any bottle yet invented." His back to the fire, he was stretching himself, warming his hands. "And what does Sheena think of this weather? Not much! Eh?"

But Sheena was shy, and Anna took the blind hand that reached towards her while the eyes remained on this mysterious stranger.

"Sheena, is it?" said Mrs. Cameron, lifting the peats under the kettle until the flames flew up. "I have given her such bad lear that when she is tired of her own stories she will be at me for mine. Indeed she was wondering if you had any stories yourself!"

"Me! What stories could an old bachelor have to tell a little girl like Sheena?"

Sheena had now put one hand to her mouth and was looking up from under her brows as he continued to smile to her.

"If I may say so, it's not but that you have plenty of time left to learn."

He glanced at the old lady and laughed. "You think I might come at it yet?"

"Indeed I sincerely hope so."

This banter delighted him and he confessed that the only stories he knew had to do with old cairns and ruins, and they weren't real stories at all but a dry-as-dust which learned men made up into stories for themselves, great rigmaroles which they solemnly wrote in books. Sheena just wouldn't bother her head with them.

But apparently he was wrong, for Sheena, it seemed, had a consuming interest in archaeology, and particularly in that esoteric aspect of it which concerned the Man in the Stone. This had touched her much more closely even than the Man in the Moon, and she still remained unsatisfied despite the ingenious efforts at elucidation by both her great-grandmother and her mother.

When Grant was seated, with his cup of tea beside him, and Sheena at last almost by his knee, he was suddenly overcome by an extraordinary access of uncertainty, if not of shyness, for it was a literal fact that he had never told a story to a child. He now groped for a rag of that confidence with which he had addressed learned societies. "The truth is," he said, in a flash of inspiration, "the story about the Man in the Stone isn't finished yet. But when it is, I'll tell it all to yourself."

"Now!" said her granny. "Won't that be fine?"

But the small grave face lifted and asked, "Where is he?"

"Where is he?" repeated Grant, and when the cue didn't come from the void he added mysteriously, "Ah!"

As this deception was beneath consideration, a small thumb poked at his knee, and then the grave face regarded him again in silence.

"It's a long story," he said. "It's so long a story that— that it begins with a dog."

At once a living interest dawned in the small face.

"It was a wonderful dog," said Simon Grant. "Indeed it was the first real dog that ever there was here. Before then, they were all wild dogs, wolves, and they wandered in the mountains and the woods, and they lived by killing beasts, and when they were very hungry they would kill men, too, and women, and even little children."

"Was that long ago?"

"Yes, long long ago, thousands of years ago. It was even before they put up the standing stones over there or made the cairn. And the people then they hadn't knives like our knives: they had only sharp stones. And they hadn't sheep, and they hadn't cattle, and they hadn't horses. What do you think of that?"

"What had they?"

"They had just their stone knives and their stone axes and their bows and arrows, and with them they went off hunting the deer. They were great hunters and could run as fast as fast could be. Well, one day there was a man and he had no food, and he had his mother and his granny and a little girl living with him, and he had to go off and find food for them."

"Were they living here?"

"Yes, but not in this house, because this house wasn't built then. At that time the people would be living mostly in the caves by the sea. Anyway, one fine day off went the man from whatever house he had here then to see if he could catch a deer, and when he was away up behind in the mountains, going through a lonely glen, what should jump out on him but a great wolf with long white teeth. But if the wolf jumped out on him, he soon jumped to one side, and when the wolf jumped at him again, he swung his stone axe to hit the wolf, but he didn't hit him properly that time. So the wolf came at him again, and it was a terrible fight they had, the man and the wolf. But the man had one thing which the wolf hadn't got and that was his stone axe, and with his stone axe he at last killed the wolf and so won the fight. But now the man was very tired, and when he went over to sit down—what should he see lying before him but a deer! For the wolf had just killed the deer. And now the man had a deer. Wasn't that lucky for him? And that wasn't everything, for now comes the strangest thing of all. For you wouldn't believe what the man saw next. Do you know what it was? It was a little puppy wolf!"

"What was it like?"

"Well, it was just like a puppy. For a wolf is only a wild dog. Do you understand?"

"Was it like old Fachie's puppy?"

"Exactly! The very one! So there it lay, where the old wolf had left it, in a nest of wild grass. And when the man saw it, he understood why the old wolf had fought so hard, because she had fought to save the puppy's life. So suddenly he thought he would take the poor puppy home with him. But when he came to lift it, it was not so easy."

"How that?"

"How did he lift it? Like this." And Grant lifted Sheena onto his knee.

But before Sheena could become self-conscious Mrs. Cameron said, "That's as good a story as I have listened to and I hope you will go on with it." He replied equally seriously that he would be happy to continue; and Sheena, not too pleased about these outside interruptions, pulled very slightly at the top button of his jacket. And so she learned how the puppy growled when robbers came one night and thus warned the man in good time, and learned moreover how the puppy grew up, and went off one day with the man, and pulled down a deer which the man had wounded with an arrow, and many other interesting and astonishing things.

When at last he found himself in his own room he could not sit down, much less attend to his long neglected correspondence. I have let myself in for it now! he thought, for he had promised to relate how primitive man tamed the horse and the cow and learned to grow crops, all on the lands of Clachar.

But he could not conceal from himself that he had enjoyed it. He had not dreamed he was so inventive. O lord, if the Colonel and Blair had overheard him! Sheer softening of the brain! With Blair rising to the comment, "You've found your true métier at last!" He shook with mirth. But at the same time his intelligence was suggesting seriously that it might be better to deal with the pig next because, after all, he had heard about the three little piggies that went to market. Was Sheena too old for the accompanying traditional action directed towards her toes? When his mirth found itself suspended in solemn questioning, it mounted in a higher wave than ever and drowned him completely. As he lay in his chair and lifted his heels, a last shred of sense tried to clack them noiselessly.

At fifty-two a man was no doubt growing senile, was reverting to his childhood. And a little child shall lead them. . . . Suddenly he saw Sheena, as he had seen her the other day, playing at "making a housie" by the peat stack. Her utter absorption (for she had not seen him) had kept him quite still. Only a creator, like an artist, was ever absorbed in the same way. Now he had a profound intuition of the meaning of what he had seen, of the self at once being lost in, and being part of, the very act of creation. He saw that that was *precisely* what the absorption meant. Whenever he had moved and Sheena had seen him, her self-conscious-ness—and his own—had destroyed creation. *And a little child shall lead them.* My God! he thought, feeling Sheena still on his knee, against his breast, under his chin.

After supper, the rain moderated into occasional showers, the wind into squalls. He grew more restless as the hours passed. The whole place had become a complex in which

236

he was meshed and caught. After all, he was an archaeologist. His business was to find the crock of gold and detail its contents with scientific precision, not get entangled in human affairs. And even if his experience did in some measure deepen his understanding of his subject, still archaeology was an exact, and exacting, job of practical work. It was for poets to follow the gleam of the crock to the tune of the Silver Bough; their peculiar minds ran that way. That an idiot should have stolen the real crock from him was an ironic judgment on him. He would go to bed, have a good sleep, and get going early in the morning. It was early in the morning that the practical Arthur had seen Foolish Andie.

From his bedroom window he looked on the world. The light was fading. The house was very quiet. Suddenly he was afraid to turn round. So he forced his head over his shoulder. There was nothing on the mat, no one. With beating heart and quickening breath, he went to the small room and pulled the door open. Everything was motionless including the narrow box on the floor with the skeletons. Probably the wind had made a small noise on the roof, though he hadn't consciously heard a noise. He had the distinct feeling of a presence, something moving in the air about him. He closed the door without touching the box and went back to the window, but found he was facing the room.

He was definitely disturbed, far more so than he had ever been in a dream of the figures. For he had experienced no feeling of supernatural fear in the dream. He had been absorbed in watching them and only when the woman had turned round and seen him had something of inexplicable awareness drawn the air to such a tension between them that he had awakened. But it had been a tension of awareness, of inexplicable recognition, rather than of fear.

Now he was uncomfortable, and because it was all so intangible, so obviously psychic, he grew a bit annoyed, even angry, for dammit it was reducing things to a pretty low ebb if he was to lose his sleep over this sort of business. But "this sort of business" was merely a cover-up of what he actually felt—and almost saw, namely, that he was *between* the skeletons of the woman and child *and* the living Anna and Sheena (who were now asleep). He was between them, as between players at opposite ends of a court. It was not that the two women *played* him. But he was there. When a blatter of rain hit the window, he jumped. Look, he said to himself, fancy breeds this sort of idiocy; it's fresh air you need. He even remembered his illness. So strongly came this urge to go outside that he had to rationalise it by thinking: why not? This might be the very night for Andie! He turned to the window and saw that indeed it was the very night. The broken storm, the forming gargantuan cloud, the absence of every human from the landscape, the deepening dark and scurry of the wind: the elemental playground for the fellow. He listened, stole softly downstairs, got into boots and oilskin, and went out.

31

When he had crossed the footbridge, he held down by the stream for a little way to avoid going over visible skylines. In a country place there was always someone about, some sleepless face at a window, but apart from a skyline it was dark enough for any outline to be little more than a blur at fifty yards. The pines about Clachar House were a black pool and he could see no light as he came round the slope and began the ascent towards the cairn. The sky was overcast, but the fierce rain-squall had passed and the wind had dropped to a moderate breeze. The roar of the sea seemed louder.

The brute cairn squatted, amorphous, the piled-up debris of an age. He circled it with a feeling of fragility, a lightness that could be crushed like a gourd. Inside, the skulls kept their "lidless eyes apart". He needed a touch of macabre humour to steady him. But when he came by the covered-in passage and looked down towards the tall monolith, he could have sworn it moved. He broke out of the clutch of fear by walking slowly towards it. Again there was movement but now beyond the stone and he sidestepped to get a better view. It was a figure with lowered head, slanting away towards the sea, at once mysterious and uncouth. He fancied he saw the vague pallor of a face turned over a shoulder to look back, then the body began to merge with the dark. He quickened his steps and reached the monolith, caught a glimpse of something again, followed, lost it entirely and hurried. When he reached the steep slope to the sea, he paused and peered down, but could make out nothing. The sea thundered on the shore, for he was now above one of those narrow "faults" which broke the cliff line at irregular intervals. Through his mind flashed the thought: It's Andie, making for the caves!

There were distinct steps worn in the turf and he descended with care, pausing every now and then to stare. He knew he could dominate Andie and an eager cunning ousted fear. He had never tackled the caves from this end, for the approach from Clachar House was flat and easy. When he reached bottom a flick of spindrift from a breaking wave blinded him for a moment, but as he blinked he was certain he saw something move round the cliff. But the seas were running so high that before he could look round he had to step back, for the white froth came seething about his feet. It must surely be the very top of the tide. Anxiety swiftly got the better of him, for there were several caves and he might lose Andie. As he followed the retreating surf he saw a darkness some twenty yards along like a yawning mouth. After the next breaker had exploded he made a dash for it. But at a dozen paces the smooth stones gave on low broken rock; he stumbled; was soused to the knees by the next comber; jumped a narrow fissure; held on again; waded through a final gap to the thighs and had just got clear of it when a tremendous wave came piling in and swept him up the near cave wall; he had to cling to it against the sucking roaring recession before moving up the shingle.

Listening beyond his breath and his heart-beats, he stood against the rock, but no inner sound in the great sounds came to him. His mouth closed; his tongue between his lips was surprised by the salt and he was strengthened warily, even in the instant that he realised he was half-trapped. The inner darkness was more solid than the rock.

With one hand touching the wall he moved up the slope of shingle pausing at every other step to listen. His intense concentration increased the fearsomeness of the place until its reverberations opened up like dark petals of unearthly danger. The thought of Andie himself opened into nearer shapes until his foot was moving over the shingle like a hand before taking his weight. Amorphous bodies with smothering arms and invisible eyes. . . .

By its very excess his imagination steadied him and his features sharpened. When the rock suddenly left his hand, he stumbled but was swiftly upright again. He felt for the torch in his pocket, but still could not switch it on, as though to be safe he must come invisibly, stealthily, upon what he sought. He got down on his hands and knees and at once felt more secure. As he crawled, he stretched each hand in front of him like a feeler, but his oilskin impeded him by getting caught under his knees. As he lurched, his hand landed on a smooth wet surface: it gave; it moved; he heard its astonishment, the crunching of the shingle, a flurry and threshing. He yelled as he reared and stepped back, but his hands could not get at his torch, could not find the opening in his oilskin, then found it, miraculously caught the torch as it fumbled out of his hands, and switched it on. The dark beast was flapping down to the sea. A barking cough came from behind him. Two eyes gleamed against the swinging light.

The floor of the cave began to heave with monstrous life. His legs were suddenly shot from under him and he fell backwards on a body that threw him with a skelp against the stones. Presently he realised that the torch lay yards away but still burning. When at last he picked it up and shone it around, the whole nightmarish upheaval had vanished.

Seals, of course, only seals, he thought, but he was trembling and slightly sick. He staggered on drunkenly. This cave, like the Monster Cove, took a leftward bend. When he had flashed the beam around its walls, he sat down and lowered his head, then threw his head back and breathed heavily. The sickness would not come out of him. As its flushes ebbed, he shivered.

Andie could not have come in here. No one had come in here. He had better get home. His head drooped again and he closed his eyes, no longer afraid of the cave. If one of these brutes had passed over him. . . . The cliff wall trembled and he felt the solid rock and the earth beyond about to crumble and avalanche down upon him. He got up.

As he followed the seething roaring downrush of the water and shone the torch on the outward cliff walls he realised two things: that the tide was still coming in and that he could leave the cave only by the way he had entered it. Towards the Clachar shore the water smashed solid against the cliff foot.

At first attempt he retreated before the oncoming surge; at the second attempt he was caught in the gap and the wave broke clean over him. He took some salt spray into his lungs and the agony of this was sharper than anything he had ever experienced. Trying to draw breath so obsessed him that he did not retain any very clear memory of how he got back into the cave. Indeed there remained a sort of false memory of the sea helping him, lapping him up the shingly beach of the cave, to lie with his head on his arms. From there he crawled up, and, in a dim state of being, found the sheltered wall where he stretched himself full length and lay with closed eyes and stertorous mouth.

Long after that the tide was still coming in and his mind was obsessed by a new danger: at full tide would the cave be completely flooded out? He knew now that he had never before been in this cave and he was beginning to suspect that it could be reached only at low tide. Certainly when he had visited the caves on the Clachar side he had gone along the shore as far as the sea would let him. This cave had been shut off and Mrs. Sidbury had presumably never thought of mentioning it to him. When his torch had been shot out of his hand he had found it still alight because it had landed amid old sea wrack. But now he realised that the wrack was up to the inner base of the wall.

He tried to keep himself warm by all kinds of exercises, including ploughing the shingle with a broken batten of timber. Between the gusts the wind died away and this was a little comfort, for its eddy got him searchingly even when he was crouching against the leftward wall. Time alone could answer the final question: how deep would the smashing seas swirl about him at high tide? At intervals he left his partial shelter to stare round the rock and flash his torch on the broken waters before they started their downward roar.

When the upper edging of froth was hissing on the stones before the inner bend of the cave, he had a short spell of horrible panic, struggled in the murky foredeath, yelled—not yet abjectly but in a blind self-piteous wrath, lifting his arms, staggering blindly.

This ebbed from him and he felt eased, more spent, as though he had actually vomited, and he became aware of a faint greying in the atmosphere as if the moon's dying crescent had suddenly risen over the hills—or, possibly, the morning itself was coming. As he stooped he even fancied he saw great shivering froth bubbles burst and vanish like bright mocking eyes. Very soon the water would be swirling about his feet. But his senses now were numbed and fear no longer physically active.

He squatted against the inner rock again, felt it tremble as the wave thundered, and his mind grew strangely passive in the darkness, and he became aware of himself as a cowering primitive man, a Paleolithic cave dweller. It was a condition quite different from anything he had imagined. Nothing wild, farouche, snarling—but squatting here by the rock, waiting, strangely passive, part of the roar and the

243

reverberation, at once inside them and penetrated by them as his jaw quivered, penetrated by the cold, and aware of *something* that rode the elements and flashed through them and yet was behind them as the mover. When his teeth were clicking he got up, switched on his torch and dug another bit of the floor, searching, with no sense of irony, for the crock of gold.

As the greying of the light increased it had a curious almost supernatural effect upon him, as though some sort of translation to an extra dimension were involved. For still a little time he denied the urge to step out and look at the hurtling greybacks, but at last he did so and was surprised by the amount of light on the waters. Then his eyes were held and his breathing stopped. There was a boat on that tumultuous sea, a small boat, with one man in it.

The boat was quite close in, its prow on the cave, but the man was not pulling the boat, he was backing it away, backing its stern against the seas, but now suddenly he was pulling, the boat rose high, coggled over and was lost, and the wave came rushing on, toppled over in a smashing roar, and the seething water swept his feet. But the boat was there, the man on the oars, pulling, digging in, holding against some undertow that gripped the keel, shoulders heaved and twisting at oars fixed like iron bars, then perceptible movement of the oars as the boat straightened, stern to the next one, and the next one towered, and up she went and out of sight. And she was coming again, knifing the back swing, the oars lifting the body off its seat; gathering way, coming, the wave mounting behind, the body flattening in every last ounce of strength for the final run. On the crest she came and grounded on the shingle in a smother of sea into which the man leapt. Grant rushed after the retreating water and gripped the stem of the boat already sliding away, fatally away, until suddenly she slewed and stuck, with Martin's face rising above his knuckles on the gunnel, yelling "Take that!", pointing to the painter in the bow. Grant staggered up the shingle with the painter, twisted it round his waist, and lay back on it, heels dug in. As the next sea lifted the boat, he at once fell flat on his back, cursing his ineptitude, but in an instant had heaved himself forward, and, as the rope gripped him in a violent jerk, ploughed the shingle like a dragged anchor. Next time, he was better prepared; and the third time he belayed the painter round an edging of rock. The painter held.

In a little while Martin said, "She's all right there." He stood looking back at the seas and Grant saw him smile, then he went in behind the boat which now acted as a windbreak to the inner part of the cave. "Put your torch on," he said. Grant swung the beam around. Now there was a metal flask in Martin's hands. He held the light as Martin poured. "Some vodka?" "Thank you," said Grant, down whose gullet the liquid went like cold fire. He gasped and coughed until warmth burst upon him. Martin helped himself and screwed on the cap. "We'll have a fire," he said in a voice casual and friendly, and from the boat heaved out a pile of sticks.

Martin moved naturally, at his ease, in no hurry. As he sat against the sheltered rock, he ran fine shavings four or five inches long with his knife from a piece of white wood, but did not break them off, merely tilting them over, one behind the other, until they bunched like a torch of feathers. When he had made five of these, he grouped them on the flattest stone he could find, and built smashed pieces of wood against them. They searched around for every extra bit of timber they could find. Then he put his petrol lighter to the wooden feathers and a tongue of flame ran up. With extraordinary care, as if it were an art or a ritual, he built the fire up. Grant's astonishment was complete when Martin leaned several whole peats against the crackling wood. "I thought you might be cold," he said.

"I was cold," said Grant. The boat seemed to lurch. "Is she all right?"

"Yes," answered Martin, "it's the top of the tide." He came back from the boat with a khaki haversack, which contained a flask of coffee and a brown loaf.

32

"It was Andie all right," Martin answered. "He seems attracted by that tallest stone."

"You've seen him there before?"

"Yes. It's the only thing I have ever seen him lean against."

"Did he come down this way?"

"I doubt it."

"Where were you?"

"At the cairn. I rather fancy I might have found your crock if you hadn't appeared." He leaned forward and pushed a slim log into the fire. The increased glow shone on their faces.

"You've been watching him?"

Martin smiled and gave Grant a slow, measuring, but quite friendly look. "I wondered where you had got to when you didn't come back. You were taking chances, weren't you?"

"How did you know I was here?"

"I happened once to see the flash of your torch."

"It was very good of you to—come."

"It was a gamble. I wasn't quite sure what the storm would do in here at the top of the tide. I tried earlier, but was beaten."

Grant was steaming warm, but every now and then his teeth chittered. There was a self-possession about Martin, a curious slow largeness, which seemed to come out of the storm and the night. A flowering of the man in unearthly danger.

"What do you think of Andie?"

Martin looked at him, then attended to the fire again, this time with extended care, building and balancing with a precision which the flames acknowledged.

"I mean, do you think he has forgotten where he hid the crock?"

"No," answered Martin, sitting back and lighting a cigarette. "He is merely extra cunning about it. Boyish."

"You mean primitive?"

"No. I hardly need to tell you that a primitive society is highly complex in its human relations."

"But you would think that he would respond to his mother. He must see the condition she's in—or does he?"

"Does a boy really appreciate his mother's concern about the secret he insists on hiding? Does he not, in fact, become more obdurate the more she pleads?"

"You think it's like that?" murmured Grant, staring at the fire. "You think his is just an arrested intelligence?"

"No. We live not in our intelligence but in something else. It's not the boy's intelligence that stops him responding to his mother."

"I understand what you mean."

"I wonder."

Grant glanced at him. Martin acknowledged the glance with a faint smile but said no more.

"Have you ever done any anthropology?" Grant asked, stirring from a vague uneasiness.

"Not in books. But I've seen a few things happen."

"You mean out East?"

"Among other places. But out East I perhaps had the opportunity of seeing it naked." He added, as on an afterthought, "Quite literally naked, in fact."

"Did you?" muttered Grant.

"Yes. She was a very charming woman, too; a white woman. Her husband was manager of a rubber estate. They had polished him off. They took longer over the woman."

"Did they?"

"Yes. There were five of them, and if you want to go one better than a sexual orgy mere killing isn't enough. The whiteness of the skin of her body obviously roused their perverse interest. It became clear that the little yellow sergeant coveted the skin. He took out his knife——"

Grant's body suddenly heaved forward in a retching spasm, but nothing came up. He straightened and, as he wiped his eyebrows, stuttered, "Excuse me—but—a man once described it—it's my stomach, I can't stomach——"

"Have a drop," said Martin.

Grant took a suck at the flask and presently in a husky voice added, "I was in the first world war. It's not that I—but——" He shuddered from the raw spirit. "You saw—the flaying?"

Martin was watching his face. In a light even voice he said, "I managed afterwards to break away. I shadowed that unit for a long time. I became knowledgeable in forest craft. In fact, I couldn't have done what I did do if certain dormant instincts hadn't come to life. That's what I meant by saying I didn't get my anthropology out of books."

Grant was grateful for the cool ease of Martin's voice, for an objectivity so impersonal that the man might have been looking on at what had happened to him. Moreover, the talking itself, the cool fluent talking, seemed as natural in this wild time and place as had his silence elsewhere. And yet, as it went on, he gave little away, came no nearer.

"You—you got away finally?" Grant said, craving this cool strength.

"Yes. But I did a few things before then. It was rather complicated, for I don't mean I merely got to know how to live in the forest. Something more abnormal than that. I lived mostly on their rations, as a matter of fact. These five men—they got the uncomfortable feeling that I haunted them."

"Did they?"

"Well, I had to get inside their minds. Which really meant inside my own. At that level we are all primitives, we possibly go back beyond the gods, before gods were, to a supernatural *something*. Isn't that the psychic picture? You have a name for it, haven't you?"

"Mana."

Martin nodded. "A Melanesian word, I was told, for the mysterious energy that comes from the hidden or ultimate source of power. Have you never felt it—at a moment of intense experience? For it is not so occult as it sounds. All profound religious experience is full of it. I rather fancy the magicians up at the cairn knew quite a bit about it—in their own particular way. Didn't they say that everything ultimately was *one thing*?"

"They did," said Grant.

"I began to understand. For a psychic experience is very different from a metaphysical exercise about it, different in kind. These magicians or druids or whatever you call them——" He paused and a slow ironic smile came about his eyes. "I believe you debate as to who the druids were?"

"We wonder if they came in with the first Goidels or Gaels or whether a certain aboriginal——"

"I know. The name is everything!"

In the silence the wave thundered and the cliff vibrated from a physical power which had in it something of exultance that seemed more than the water and the rock. When Grant moved and the shirt momentarily left his back, the skin there went clammy. The heat from the fire burned his shins and his face; sometimes his head jerked away from the smoke that stung his eyes. Rising above these physical sensations induced in time a curious mental sensitivity which was like another and heightened aspect of himself,

250

tenuous as a vapour that at any moment might pass away altogether.

"The words *power, energy* obscure the thing," Martin was saying. "They make us think in physical or atomic terms, whereas these magicians were probably searching for—what may yet be found in the sub-atomic."

Argument never failed to goad Grant and now he made a valiant effort. "Are you trying to tell me that these primitive magic men of the cairn tried to *identify* themselves with the original cause of things, that they were practising mystics of that profound kind; not only that, but that they were Eddingtons trying to penetrate beyond the symbol in the equation?"

"Well?"

"I did not credit them with such knowledge," replied Grant relapsing into a toneless voice.

"*Knowledge*? Of what?"

"Oh I see what you mean—the kind of knowledge, but the implication is," and his voice rose again, "that primitive man, before he even began to make gods, had an apprehension of God."

"O God," said Martin, pleased by the esoteric flavour. "You'll be asking next whether there hasn't been any *progress* in our notion of God. For it would certainly upset our scientists and psychologists to suggest that God was *given*, like a mathematical axiom, to man in the beginning."

"Do you believe He was?"

"He? What's He? You cannot get away from the anthropomorphic. Even legend has it that these magicians or druids got such an understanding of how the ultimate essence or power worked that they used it to change human beings into swans and fawns and trees. And even if that was no more than a piece of occult poetry to hold the ordinary mind in thrall—still, it took that shape. For the real druid was after real powers; he wanted to tap the source."

"Did you tap it, in the jungle?" asked Grant, a little combatively, for the horror of the operation Martin had witnessed stirred in his vitals again like a sickness.

"In my own way, yes. It took time." Martin's eyes considered Grant. "I also used certain small tricks, sounds, and after I had disposed of the second man of the five, I got a white sheet. By the time four were gone and only the sergeant left, I was becoming adept. The sergeant was now very jumpy, and he could not show it because he dare not lose face. Once the whole unit combined to comb me out—a very clever move it was—in broad daylight, of course, though it wasn't broad in the jungle. I poked my face through some creepers and a man saw me. He stood and I, quite motionless, looked at him. He decided—his expression grew uncanny with fear—that he daren't see me. He glanced here and there and made off."

"Did you get the sergeant?"

"I left him wrapped in the white fabric. There were eight bullet holes in it. They must have thought it very mysterious because there was no bullet hole in the sergeant."

Grant had nothing more to say. A curious malaise was getting the better of him; his body was sagging, slumping, but not in sleep. He felt the flask being put into his hands and took a swig. It revived him but with the effect of bringing the night and the storm about him in an unearthly way. "You still can use this power?" It was hardly a question, little more than a last politeness in conversation; for his mind fell beyond the question itself into the place where the horror lay.

"I dropped all that," Martin said.

"Did you? . . ."

Martin sat quite still for nearly a minute. The storm, with death in it, might have been his flower. Then he looked at Grant and continued, "There are psychoanalysts who say that when the aggressive or destructive instinct in you is

252

dammed up it injures you, and that you have to destroy other things, other people, in order not to destroy yourself, in order to protect yourself from self-destruction."

"Good God," said Grant, groaning.

"There is quite a lot in that—as far as it goes. You'll have noticed that the egomaniac in a big way always becomes a figure of public attraction, for he stirs up the unconscious urge in humanity towards destruction. Let the old be demolished, he shouts, so that new wonderful constructions may arise—*his* constructions. For all that opposes him, that might expose the pathological inferiority from which he suffers, must first be swept away in order that his prestige may then reign supreme. Psychiatrists have made the picture familiar; in the world to-day the *total* or totalitarian picture. They point in the recent war to a whole nation having come under the sway of such a psychopath or group of psychopaths—for men moved by the same mad urge are drawn to one another by a sort of psychic magnetism. Quite. . . . But . . . you only get to know the real motive—when you yourself have gone far enough in experience, in pure destruction."

"What motive?" asked Grant out of a darkening stupidity.

"You have to go far enough," repeated Martin quietly, "to know what happens when the destructive instinct has actually had its way."

Grant met Martin's eyes for an instant. Their dark concentration had yet about them something like a smile, something that came out of so much experience that they could rest amid the infernal knowledge they evoked with an ultimate calm; and yet they directly conveyed this knowledge; it came from them; Grant felt it piercing into and pervading him. In a sense he was outwardly blinded, so that meaning now swelled up inwardly. It was as if he had been taken to that vast inland country where all conscious analysis

253

ceases and the mad impulses are themselves seen at work, where passion is no longer passion but pure violence in action, where violence in action feeds on violence, feeds and grows ever more gargantuanly, until nothing ultimately is left to be destroyed but the destroyer himself; and then in a final upsurge the destroyer turns on himself and achieves his last obliterating triumph in a frenzy of self-destruction.

"In history it has taken many outward forms," came Martin's voice. "You know about the old races. Didn't the Aztec civilization, for example, didn't the old Aztecs become so obsessed with human sacrifice that they were destroying themselves, were actually in process of committing racial suicide?"

Grant groaned. He could no longer think.

"However, it might be interesting for a start to take this simple picture provided by the psychoanalyst, with its concealed self-destruction motive, and lift it from the individual case to the European level——"

"Do you mean," and Grant had the odd sensation that something was suddenly shouting the final question in him, "that humanity has got the wish to destroy itself, that—that the death instinct has got charge?"

He glared at Martin who considered him with the steady characteristic look which Grant had always felt as something palpable; it now came out of the jungle of cave and storm and sea.

Grant suddenly began to retch, as though the raw spirit were at last taking effect; but nothing came up. A wave of icy coldness went over him and he staggered to his feet. But his trembling was such that he could not stay on his feet and when he had stretched himself full length on the shingle, he let go.

Martin gathered all that was left of the fuel and built it into a final blaze. He took off his oilskin and threw it over Grant's body; went out and saw the clear light of morning on the sea. The tide had retreated a considerable distance. His weather-proof wristlet watch recorded 4.25. His eyes followed the waves and studied their impact, studied the formation of rock on the south side and the backwash. Then he went to the boat and began to examine the planking where the bilge had taken one or two heavy poundings. After bailing her out, he decided she was quite sound. She was only twelve feet long and even lightly built but of seasoned wood by a craftsman who had spared neither fine ribs nor copper rivets. He unhitched three wooden rollers, each about two feet long and ankle-thick, from under the forward thwart, and began clearing the shingle from under the after end of the keel.

The fire had died down to an ash-flecked glow and the grey light in the inner cave made Grant's face ghastly. It stirred as Martin stared down at it, then Grant sat up. He began to shiver violently.

"We'd better go," said Martin.

As Grant arose, Martin lifted his own oilskin over his arm and they went out to the boat, into which Martin dropped his oilskin and the haversack with the thermos flask.

Grant, swaying slightly, looked at him. "Are you going to tackle it?"

"Yes. But you needn't come, if you don't want to. You'll get out of here in two to three hours." Martin's voice had the ease of utter impersonality, yet his eyes remained in some remote way personal.

Grant could not gather his wits; something persisted in a sort of myth of danger and largeness; he was desperately cold and tried to control, to hide, the chitter of his teeth.

"We'll try to slew her off, if you give me a hand here," Martin said.

By a manipulation, at which he was obviously expert, of the three rollers, Martin at last got the boat moving, but it was a heavy and difficult job because he wanted her over towards the south wall of the cave. After an initial breathlessness, dizziness, and furious pounding of the heart, Grant began to feel a warmth in his body. The cave faced west but the seas were running from south of west and he saw that Martin had chosen the only spot for the push-off. The wind and the white-caps outside were almost gone but the seas looked big as ever and broke with an even greater thunder.

It seemed to Grant an impossible venture, a death-questing wildness. Pure green came through the curl of the wave. Martin was quiet and thorough, sparing and instant in movement; the pallor of his face was the pallor of the bone beneath.

"Will you give me a push off?" he asked.

Grant nodded.

They both pushed; Martin leapt over the gunnel and whipped the oars into the rowlocks; Grant pushed on, and when the water was over his knees he jumped but got only his breast over the stern-post; there he wriggled impaled, until he fell over into the boat; but the boat was swinging back and he put out his hands to fend her stern off the cliff, felt his palms scraped by the barnacles without pain, got a skelp from the momentarily shipped blade of Martin's oar, but now they were off on the recession, on the deep back-eddy. Next time he fended off with one of the three rollers which, glancing off his chest, ripped through his oilskin and, as the boat left the rock, he all but fell into the sea. A wild effort at recovery landed him in a heap on the footboards. But Martin now was hanging on both oars over the threshold where the waves tripped, losing distance to gain a little more. Grant glimpsed his face and saw a strength in its pallor that was cold and more than human; a bleakness that was more than deathly: it was stoical and everlasting, as if the fellow was not drawing on his mysterious *source* but was part of it. A curious quietness came on Grant, a commitment, a sense of relief in his own act that was a cold gladness.

They rose up over the wave and fell down into the swinging hollow, but they were leaving the cave.

Grant saw when Martin began to tire, when the swing of the oars lost a living quality and became automatic. Martin had never spoken; had nodded once commandingly to the floorboard on which Grant now sat beneath the stern seat; he pulled steadily with a side glance for a coming wave. The sky had cleared into great blue patches, fresh and vivid from a sun Grant could not see; only on the south-west horizon were the clouds still dark and lowering, as though swelling about the storm's root.

Martin was pulling away towards the southern island and presently Grant, looking about him, at the cliffs, the tumultuous shore, at Clachar, began to get an idea of how Martin had fetched the cave in the storm. From the sheltered side of the spit north of Clachar House, he must have made out for the north island, brought her through the seas into the inshore lee of the middle island, then holding into the storm and slipping with it, had finally come down on the cave. As his eyes lifted from the imaginary passage to Martin's face, he found Martin's eyes on him. They did not smile; but there was an intuitive recognition in them, so cool and remote in its understanding of his calculations, that he himself smiled, as though detected in a naïvety, and glanced away. But he now knew that that was in fact the route which Martin had taken.

In time, Martin brought her to run before the weather. The wind had died away and, as he baled, Grant for the first time felt safe from the lift and swirl of the waters. To begin with, he had waited for each towering mass to smash in on them, not in fear so much as in a sheer tension of expectancy, but now, in a queerly miraculous way, he felt safe. His mouth, losing its leathery dryness, was growing softly slimy. The wound-up tension inside his skull was easing.

They were making way now. Martin's pallor had taken a grey tinge. Grant, facing Clachar House, could see that the intention was to clear the spit and land on its lee or northern side. The final passage to the boathouse was too narrow, too shallow, for the swing of the seas. The waves were spouting on the broken rocks that ran out to the point of the spit. But once round the spit, there would be no trouble.

Presently Grant was aware that Martin's eyes glistened, that the man had come out from the blind automatic action of the will. Casting a glance over his shoulder, he saw that the dark clouds in the south-west had swollen up upon the sky; a flurry of wind spat a few sea-drops into his face; a darkness was coming racing over the sea with an edging of spindrift; Martin was almost rising off his seat in the effort to get power into his left oar; then the gust hit them.

For a few seconds it seemed to sweep them over the sea with a tremendous flattening power. It took off, but only as a man might pause to take a deeper breath. The next time its violence drenched Grant in a smother of spray. Martin hung on his oars, and when they shot out he dug them in again, holding to the solid sea.

Grant at last saw the danger that the rower had seen too late. With his back to the spit and watching the near seas, Martin had unknowingly been cutting his passage round the spit too fine. The wind was now driving them right on the spouting rocks, and the more Martin pulled his left to nose her seawards the more the wind caught her. Minute followed minute in iron tension until it was clear that, unless the wind's grip instantly slackened, they would smash. It was then Grant saw the figure of a man staggering over the spit towards them and knew it was Norman the chauffeur; and then he saw another figure, her skirts about her legs, swung this way and that, but lying forward on the wind, coming, and knew it was Anna. His body was whirled round and he was facing the oncoming seas. In a long trough, Martin had put her about and was trying to hold her, stem to the on-rush. Grant saw his eyes find the two figures and a white stillness of implacable concentration steady him in a last exercise of his strength. As though infuriated by this relentless obstinacy the wind rose to its last and final pitch. A scraping shudder, white spume, a heave and a wrecking crash, and Grant's body was thrown on a dark rock and the sea went over him.

33

A drumming in his ears, dimmed eyes, and, as the dragging on his crumpled pitching body eased, a bursting desire to get up for air; a cessation of the onward thrust, a brimming choking instant and the water was going back and his head was through; a jagged black edge of rock and his hands on their own had it and gripped while his mouth spewed and the recession roared and the air was sucked in a trickle of pain; drunkenly and dimly he saw Anna coming, but he could do nothing, could not move, for he had to get more air first, and the sea hit him, pitched him over the low rock, and covered him again. But the holding of his breath this time was easier than the time before because he was drowning; then a clutch was holding him against the recession and his head was through once more. Anna was hauling him too strongly, too harshly, but he was too stupid to tell her, so he crumpled up for ease, but she was merciless and would not give him the moment he craved; his arms were about her as they fell in the water, but she had no mercy, would not lie still for the life-easing moment, and he was being dragged like a sack, tied at the throat, choked; he was being carried and the pressure at his throat eased; he was alone, his body in a slow wriggle, squeezing itself, like a dark octopus. A formless spot inside him, that was his will, hardened, and pushed its thin spire like a screw upward through the desire for obliteration; it was merciless as the woman had been and told him that there were others.

What he saw, because of the condition he was in, must

260

always hold for him something of the nature of legend. First he saw the woman, the water swirling about her knees, leaning forward over the sea, the wind shaping her, and he thought she was crying wildly and imperiously at the waters, like a sibylline woman; then he saw the boat, her stern in the air, pierced through the side by a jagged rock, whole in her form but spiked and held in a dumb crucifixion; the shore came at him next, roaring and seething in a tumult that was beyond the bourne of life and extended far, streaming tragic eternal elements known only to the spirit; and beyond it, the waves, mounting, curling, incoming, onrushing, and he saw the boat shudder and heave as the smashing waters lifted, and he saw a hand lift against the boat and grip the gunnel and two streaming heads appeared; now the woman moved, going down after the roaring waters, and a great cry to her to go back choked him and he spewed again, blinded, as he tried to get on to his hands and knees. The woman, caught by the waters, held to a rock, and held to something else, and the two heads rose, and Martin's face fell over white and streaming red. Twice the sea got them after that, but the woman with Martin in her arms came at last staggering with him and fell to the ground beyond the sea's reach; but Norman was down, yet not defeated, for on fumbling hands and knees, like a wounded beast, he crawled two slow yards and lay, and when the next wave came it swirled to his thighs, moving his legs like roped weed, but his breast was anchored and he lay.

Grant's eyes came back to Anna on her knees beside Martin, her hands at his throat and breast, her hair plastering her cheeks, and he saw the sheer bone of her face and the strength of it. She was a little above him, against the sky, and her face lowered to Martin's face and cried something, but Martin lay with his head fallen over, a little river of blood on his face. Through a sick darkness he reached them. He wanted to take his oilskin off and made signs and muttered, "Under him". Anna understood and tore the coat off him, but he held onto it and began rolling it. She struck away his fumbling hands and rolled it for him in a trice; then he made her turn Martin over upon the coat and, getting to his knees, pressed the body above the waist; let it go and pressed again, in the way he had been taught at the swimming baths when a boy. But he was dizzy, sick, and presently became aware that Anna was on her knees astride Martin's body, pressing and relaxing, with a rhythm so natural that her head, as it lowered on the pressing stroke, seemed to be listening to what was passing inside Martin's breast. This affected him in so extraordinary a way that he stared, fascinated, and found himself listening also and waiting. She had put her scarf under the face, and the left temple, taking the weight, had turned the face sideways a little; the mouth was partly open and the trickle of blood which had been going in at the corner of the mouth was now running back into the hair. He looked utterly lifeless, dead as any mass of tossed seawrack, and the pallor of the face held the spent tragic essence of the man, remote now beyond its earthly remoteness.

Something touched Grant in a wild way and he reared up again. Anna's eyes were on him. "Keep on!" he cried. "Don't stop!" He saw her throat swallow and the face set again, but now with a quickening of light in the eyes, as though he had given her hope against all the chances. At sight of this he felt so weak that he could have wept, and a hot stinging behind his eyes enraged him and helped to clear his head and settle the involuntary urges to vomit up his inside. He caught Martin's near hand and began massaging it towards the heart. Norman came staggering up and got down on his knees by Martin's head, put the flat of his hand under the forehead and lifted the face just clear of the ground; then laid the head against the scarf and turned away to vent the spasm that had come over him.

262

Anna worked on and Grant thought he would get Martin's boots off and slap the feet. The fierce storm-gust had passed away completely and as his fingers fumbled with the laces a shaft of sunlight struck him. Suddenly Anna cried out in a wild heart-rending cry, "Donald!" Grant had never before heard the elemental cry of the woman to her mate; it so affected him that his skin crinkled and he turned back; but she was working on the body with the same rhythmic persistence as before. Norman slewed round and looked at her. "He moved!" she cried, the exultation in her voice high as a seabird's piercing note. Her face was quivering now and her tears blinding her, but her hands did not stop in their strong tender exercise.

When Martin was sitting up, she stood to one side. Norman was in front of Martin, two yards below him on the slight slope, his feet apart, his eyes on Martin's reactions with a narrowed intensity, his cheekbones smooth, swaying just perceptibly. Grant was sitting in a slump, his shoulders and head drooping. His eyes turned on Martin and saw the fine features, in their stone-like agelessness, with death and life as equal guests who could come and go. Martin's lips pressed, the nostrils flexed, the eyebrows gathered, and the breath that had gone in swelled his chest; he breathed again more heavily; his head fell back and he blew a great breath from him and stirred, the teeth showing between the drawn lips.

"Let us go," said Norman. "It's not far."

Martin said nothing, but Norman stopped by his shoulder, his hand arrested as though Martin had spoken.

A shudder went over Martin and his fallen head shook— and lifted. At once Norman put a hand under his arm and with a commanding look drew Anna to his other arm; together they helped him to his feet.

Grant got up and saw them stumble a few paces and stop.

263

Martin did not want their help; he wanted to be left alone so that his will would be free to take him in its own way. As he went on again, Anna walked alone but Norman was by his shoulder.

All at once Grant became aware of the warm sun, and a surface shivering went over his body and his jaw trembled. He felt light-headed, strangely freed, and his face turned to Anna and smiled. Her distant expression softened into a faint answering smile and he saw the glisten of life in her eyes. He thought she looked beautiful, with a beauty that inhabited her, and this he would remember, he felt, as one remembered a figure in the landscape of a legend. An extraordinary reality was given to her by the solid particularity of her features, her flesh. She was walking there drenched and moulded and he saw her, and his heart was moved and lifted up.

When Martin reached the first pine, he leaned against it. They all stopped and Norman's features gathered in a troubled impatience, but he waited, offering no assistance. Grant saw Martin coldly measure the distance ahead, slowly push the pine from him with his palm, and start off again. As he came at the front door, his body fell against it while his fist tried to turn the large iron knob. Norman shouldered up and got a grip of it, but the door would not open. Martin's forehead was leaning heavily against the wood as though he had let consciousness slip while still holding to his feet. Norman looked at the bell-pull. There was a clicking sound and the door opened from the inside. Martin rolled sideways but Norman gripped him as Mrs. Sidbury, in a red silk dressing-gown, stood slim and white-faced before them. Swiftly her flashing black eyes took them in, but Grant saw them stop for an instant on Anna, arrested in pure shock; her brother was stumbling forward and the blood on his face brought a small sharp cry from her even as she caught him and helped him into the hall. Norman went in after them and Grant was about to follow when he stopped to make way for Anna. But Anna was not moving; she was staring and listening. Martin's body had thumped into a chair; Norman's voice said, "Get some whisky, please." Then slowly, as one no longer needed, Anna turned away.

Grant watched her in a moment's stupor as if he could not for all the world either move or utter a sound. Then he started after her. She heard his steps and turned.

"Won't you go in and take something?" she said.

"No."

"Do go," she said. "I'll wait for you."

"I'm going with you," he answered.

She did not say more and they went on together. As he stumbled once, he explained, "I'm light-footed, but I'll get home, if you don't desert me."

"We needn't hurry," she said.

"Don't say you'll make a cup of tea."

"I will—at once," she answered and smiled.

"Now don't weaken me." He went on a few paces. "If anyone had said I could have come through last night——" He dared not risk shaking his head, yet the astonishing thing was that he did not feel tired: only exhausted to nothingness. He knew he was light-headed because he wanted to tell her that he owed her his life and that she was a very remarkable young woman. He wondered if he could tell her this without embarrassing her. But the thought of it weakened him and he had to stand still for a little.

"There's no hurry," she encouraged him.

"Do you think we could sit down for one minute?" A treacherous trembling had come to his muscles.

"No," she said. "We must keep going."

"You're right." And as he started on he added, "You shouldn't have mentioned the tea."

He stopped again and asked her, "Have you been hearing anything?"

265

"Just the birds singing."

He nodded and went on. But as they came at last to the little bridge he stopped and looked at it, and looked around him at the freshness of the morning on the world, and he did so openly and unashamed. It was something very exquisite and lovely to have come back into.

At last they entered the cottage and as she turned from closing the door, he smiled to her. "Thank you, Anna," he said, and he took her hand and kissed it in gratitude and homage, then turned to the stairs.

34

The afternoon was full of sunlight. From his pillows he looked through the window to the ridge which ran its course against the blue sky. His skin was so sensitive that he reckoned he had a touch of fever, but nothing of any consequence because he was quite certain his lungs were clear. He had inflated them powerfully several times and found them resilient as footballs. This added to the pleasure that had come out of dreamless sleep and stayed with him, for he was delighted at having come through what he had come through, and secretly proud, for it should have done for him; a still delight, like the secret life in the sunlight, which was everywhere without going anywhere. He was particularly proud of having leapt into the boat. A fellow did a lucky thing like that once or twice in a lifetime. The gods could be kind—in spite of themselves! Hearkening, he heard the muted sea, and his memories rode the waves to that fantastic shore. He also heard a foot on the stairs. How differently Anna mounted! He smiled as Mrs. Cameron came in with the tea tray.

Yes, he was feeling grand, he told her. "How's Anna?"

"Fine. She's out with the bairn a walk."

"You'll be blessing me for upsetting your household."

"About that—I don't know," she said.

He laughed and glanced at her as she arranged the tray on the bedside table. "The post has been," she said.

"So I see. Is that a wedding present?" he asked as she laid a long narrow packet by the tray.

"It might be better for you if it was."

"Instead of consorting with wild characters at all hours of the night. Perhaps you're right."

"It's no laughing matter. I'll say what's on my mind: we don't like you going out like that at night."

"I am sorry, Mrs. Cameron, to have troubled you so much; I really am."

"It's not the trouble to us at all: that's nothing. But I'll be open with you, for I have never been happy at the thought of you being out after Andie in the night. In the day it's different, with his mother there. But we have no right to expect from him what God didn't put there."

"You think he might turn on me?"

"He might. It's not my place to say what you should do or should not do, but I could not have it longer on my conscience that I didn't warn you."

"I appreciate that," he said solemnly, for he could see that she was moved and uncomfortable. "But he wasn't out last night, was he?"

"He was out, and out late," said Mrs. Cameron. "And his poor mother was in a state, and she's had too many trials in her life to get into a state easy."

"Did he defy her?"

"He takes turns, though seldom, and when he's in one of them she has to deal with him as best she can, for if he's crossed he becomes violent as an enraged bairn. You know his strength."

"He seems very good-natured."

"So he is. And she never knew him so happy as in the first days with yourself."

"Perhaps all these people spying on them?"

"There was that, it's true."

He looked at her. "You are thinking that if I came on him when he was secretly visiting the crock of gold, he might go for me?"

"I am sure of one thing: he would never let you take it from him."

"But how am I ever going to get it then?"

"You'll have to find out where it is and then take it away when he's not there. But you cannot do that alone by yourself at night."

He thought for a moment. "Very well," he said.

She began pouring the tea. "There's another thing."

Her constrained manner drew his eyes. "What?"

"His mother was telling me that he's taken a fancy for the girls."

"No!" He spontaneously chuckled.

"Oh yes," she said. "There was that Lizzie Duncan that dresses herself, and he went up to her on the road and he was twisting and smiling, she said. So she walked away, but he walked after her, and then she began to run. There was no harm done, but Lizzie said she knew what he meant."

He tried to keep his laughter in and shook the bed. "They're not blaming the crock of gold for that?"

"No. It was that one with the little short trousers on her that started him off."

"Oh no!" he cried. His laughter took control of him immoderately and his head waggled.

"Goodness knows what she did to him," said Mrs. Cameron.

"I wish I knew," he cried, beyond control. "I would like to see him t-tackle her."

His laughter was infectious. "Is she a bold one, then?" she asked.

"Bold as brass. Always trying to get a story for her newspaper."

"If she comes back this way and is not careful, she might get more than a story."

Presently he wiped his eyelashes and the door closed on a happier Mrs. Cameron. When he had drunk two cups of tea, he tried to unknot the string on the long stiff parcel, but his fingers were still shaking, so he tackled his letters. "Dear Sir, The recent reports in the press about your remarkable find of a gold hoard have a particular interest for me as I am——" He slit the next envelope—and four more. Only six about the crock to-day. The spate was definitely drying-up. He idly thumbed out the flap of an envelope bearing a penny stamp and unfolded an account:

	£	s.	d.
To one Silver Bough . . .	4	5	0
To one Oak Case for same . .		7	6
Total	4	12	6

Never before had an account seemed miraculous; he was out of bed and fumbling through his trousers for his knife; back in bed with the knife and slitting the string on the parcel. There emerged a polished oak case that might once have held cutlery. He pressed a small bright knob and the lid opened. Lying on velvet and over two feet long was a silver bough with nine golden apples pendent. He removed soft packing-paper and lifted the bough out by its simple handle. The golden apples hung along the slight curve of the bough, increasing in size from the small one at the tip to the largest by the handle. He struck one of them with a finger nail and it rang like a tiny gong. He struck another and another; then he transferred the bough to his left hand and found he could run up nine consecutive notes as on the white keys of a piano.

He started on the *Home Sweet Home* of an early piano lesson. He was utterly enchanted.

Out of enchantment came an eye that went over the workmanship and material with microscopic care. The craftsman, the artist!—and the fellow hadn't even written saying he would do it! Where on earth did he get these apples of sound with their clover-leaf openings underneath? Straight out of some medieval hoard, beyond doubt! In his original letter—the only one in the whole transaction— he, Grant, had suggested a fiver as the limit. To one Silver Bough: £4 5s. But the thing was too deep for laughter. He poked at the velvet—and saw a tiny rod, with a knob at each end, clipped to a side of the case. It came away with a click. One knob was covered with washed leather; the other was silver-bright metal. Lifting the Bough in his left hand, he struck the apples with the leather knob and the notes came soft and muted; he struck them with the silver end and they leapt on the air in a dancing gaiety. For one long moment he grew still and solemn, and from the spaces of the air came the remarkable words, chiming softly in his mind: "Dear God, there's hope for the world." But the next moment he was up in the air himself and his fist was knocking strongly on the bedroom wall.

Mrs. Cameron came round the door with a face prepared for the worst.

"Come here!" he called.

"What is it?" she asked, looking at what his hands covered as though it might jump out at her.

"Remember the Silver Bough?"

But she was bewildered, so he had to explain how he had listened to her telling the story to Sheena and singing the song, how he had written to a great craftsman who lived in a little shop in the city of Edinburgh, and how lo! here was the Silver Bough itself. He pushed the closed case towards her over the bedclothes, saying, "Press the button."

Her astonishment was so great that it was comical.

"Lift it out."

She lifted it out.

"Now, strike the golden apples with this," and he handed

her the soft end of the striker. She caught the soft end and struck with the hard.

"Dear me," she said, "dear—dear—me!"

She stood so helpless and entangled in the witchery that his delight swayed him, his blue-striped pyjama-jacket jerked from its moorings, and his navel had a quick bird's-eye view of the whole scene.

"Now!" he said. "Here, give it to me!" She handed it carefully to him. "Clear away that table and sit down."

When she had done this—for he had a very imperious manner when roused—he said, "Now I want you to sing the Silver Bough for me."

"But——"

"No excuses! Just as you sing it to Sheena." He had the Bough in his left hand and the soft striker ready.

She gathered herself, and cleared her throat, and gathered herself. Then she began.

"That's it!" he cried, interrupting her. "Wait now!" When he got the right starting apple, he sounded it steadily, humming "Ah-h-h . . . Ready!"

She started to sing again, and now the notes went with her, missing the way occasionally but tripping quickly on to it again.

"Not bad!" he declared. "Once more!"

By the third time, she had lost self-consciousness and was as interested as himself that there should be a full and harmonious rendering. Moreover the clarity that rang out from the hard end of the striker inspired her to a performance that recalled the Kinlochoscar hall where she had sung as a young woman. Her mouth opened, and her eyes opened too, and she looked far through the window.

"Splendid!" he declared. "I think I've got it!" And he went right through the tune on his own to make sure.

"You have it indeed," she said. "And beautiful you make it sound."

272

"Now for the last verse!"

"Dear me!" she said, but she got her hands on her lap again, looked through the window, and, as if time itself were no more than the sheet of glass, she sang to her own childhood.

"Wonderful," he said. "Just perfect. The next thing is to arrange about presenting it to Sheena."

"Is it for Sheena it is?"

"Well of course!" His eyes flew merrily upon her. "Did you think it was for yourself?"

Her eyes fell to the hands on her lap and through her smile he saw tears glisten.

Embarrassed, his own eyes dropped and he tucked in his pyjama jacket. Sounds came from the world outside. Sheena cried to the cat.

"That's them!" said Mrs. Cameron. "And goodness me! I forgot the pot on the fire; it will be over!"

He laughed.

She stopped at the door. "I would like Anna to see it."

"Send her up!"

Anna appeared and stood.

"Please sit down," he said, pointing to the chair.

She came quietly and sat down, a faint warmth in her cheeks.

"How are you feeling to-day?" he asked.

"Fine, thanks. I hope you are well?"

"Never better. Have you heard about the others?"

"Yes. Norman spoke to me. They're all right."

"Perhaps it's more than we deserved to be!"

She smiled but said nothing. Her presence affected him deeply, so he began at once, laughing lightly, as if it were now a matter of no great moment, to tell how he used to listen to the Silver Bough and how he had ordered one. "This is it here," he said, and added, "It's the only one in the world. Press the button."

273

She pressed the button and opened the lid, and it might have been jewels for her wedding from the way she looked and forgot him. Then her eyes rose.

"Take it out."

She lifted it out, but he took it from her. "Listen!" With the muted end of the striker he played the melody flawlessly.

"That's lovely," she said; her body seemed to burgeon; a brightness came from her on the air; her tawny hair had deeps like the music; in her eyes the yielding tenderness, so perilously characteristic of her, shone like stained glass in an inner place; but the firm smooth bone, that had faced the storm, held it all quietly.

"Try it!"

She took the Bough and the striker, and struck. He saw the reserve, the slight awkwardness, the deference, fade away, melt, and the country girl who was Anna come through with the smile which opened on a delicious little laugh. Her colour deepened to match the brightness in her eyes.

"Start here," he said. "Hit that one." He leaned over to instruct her.

She did not rush at it, but she was apt; there was a certain slowness, as though tenderness and strength needed time to mix. He felt a draught amidships and pushed down his pyjama ends, realising with an upsurging fondness that his hands could hardly be trusted to keep to themselves, for it would be good to tell this young woman how highly he thought of her.

He could see how moved she was as she went out, and felt strangely excited as he lay back. When the grey matter began to stir, he said to himself: I am not deceived; this is not being romantic: this is the enduring goodness of life itself. But even the words were opaque. The vision itself was everything.

It was outside him, and went on through the grey wastes. There came upon him an access of extraordinary assurance. His body grew still and his eyes were lost beyond the green ridge.

Sheena's reaction had something of this stillness when at story-time that evening he presented her with the Silver Bough. She could not move, and when her grandmother suggested that she should at least thank the gentleman she did not seem to hear and certainly did not speak. But the remarkable thing was that she apparently could not put a hand out, could not accept it; she even pushed herself away from it against her granny's breast; but her eyes never left it. He closed the case, laid it on her lap, ruffled her hair and with a laugh went out.

35

That night he was feverish and troubled with fantastic bits of thought and dream. Then all grew quiet and he was aware that a little girl of Sheena's age was sitting on the mat in front of the fireplace. She had black hair, wore a diminutive white linen nightdress, and was completely preoccupied taking pebbles from a painted bowl and placing them on the floor before her. She leaned forward to the bowl and then back, and had the air of communing deeply with herself though she was quite silent. Somehow this pre-occupation was more arresting than if she had been doing something full of mystery. He knew quite well nothing was going to happen. He knew it did not matter which pebbles she picked or how or where she arranged them on the floor. It was the concentration on the doing that was remarkable; it was beyond or behind everything that could happen; it was so complete that he himself with a feeling of infinite ease got lost in it, and his eyes moved behind the child—and saw the feet. They were the naked feet of a grown woman. Instantly his whole being was gripped, and he could not move his eyes from the feet. He knew he had to look up at the woman but he could not. In the struggle with himself, he awoke. The grey morning was in the window.

As he lay back, the thought came to him full-blown: why did they drive me out to the cairn—the cave—the storm with death in it? For it was no good denying that he had felt a compulsion to go out. He had been pushed out by the "influence" in the room.

He was wide awake now, with the sea-shiver tremulous in his skin. It was not a true fever. He knew that. And he argued that the "influence" could be only in his own mind. He made this quite clear to himself, but the logic of it could not blot out what had happened, could not destroy even now, at this moment, his apprehension of an invisible traffic between the long narrow box and the mat before the fireplace. His sensitivity became so acute that he got up, opened the door of his "dark room", felt queerly vulnerable as he stretched up and unpinned an edge of the black cloth which covered the skylight, looked down at the long box and around, closed the door, and got back into bed.

Inside his own mind: that's where it all happened. But logic now became uncanny and asked him: why did your mind produce the feet?

He saw the feet again, solidly moulded, clear in every toe-nail. He had been at ease, lost in the child's concentration and then—the feet, the clutch of fear.

Logic began to mock him, shifted its footing with every Why? until it became more evasive, more mysterious, than the "influence". He grew very hot, and when the blood-pulse became audible in his head took a sleeping tablet.

That afternoon he felt pleasantly languid and was amused at Mrs. Cameron's whispered references to Sheena who was still silent but utterly wedded to the case that contained the Silver Bough. It was as if something incredible and august had happened to the little girl. From hidden corners came an occasional note or two and once the voice had sung the melody with a pure solemnity, but during her movements through the ordinary world the box was shut.

Anna had gone to Kinlochoscar, and Mrs. Cameron was explaining with exaggerated humour that she dare not even make a call on a neighbour who was ill, when he offered to take Sheena out for a stroll.

277

To their astonishment, Sheena silently went to him and took his outstretched hand.

"Well! well!" said her granny. "But surely you are not going to carry the box with you, too? It might fall down and break."

Sheena looked at Mr. Grant.

"It would be safer at home," he said seriously. "I'll tell you what—we'll lock it up in my box and I'll carry the key away with me."

"Nobody would ever get near it in that case," said Mrs. Cameron.

"And we'll go away to the little shore and gather some pretty shells for your housie."

They had much conversation on the way, for Sheena, relieved of the sweet tyranny of possession yet with the knowledge that the Silver Bough would be safely waiting for her, came right out of herself. She expended so much energy that he saw her flagging going up the slope and asked if she would like a lift. She raised her arms so naturally that she finished her question with one arm round his neck. The warmth and smell of her little body, the whisk of her hair on his cheek, stirred him so profoundly that it stirred him to his brightest humour. He was sweating before he set her down and sat down himself, wiping his forehead and laughing. In time they reached the little shore, where she had been with her mother when Norman had come to them and Martin in the boat.

He was sitting on a low rock, watching her gathering shells, when he happened to look to sea and saw a row-boat coming down the coast towards Clachar. It was Martin and as he drew abreast Grant stood up and lifted an arm in salute. Martin lay on his oars for a moment or two then turned the bow to the rock, where Grant met him.

"Like some fish?"

"Nothing I like better. You've been lucky."

278

"There's a good patch opposite the White Shore," said Martin indifferently.

"Is that the white strip of beach you can see from the headland up there?"

"Yes. Can I heave them out for you or—I think I'll stretch my legs. You get cramped sitting." He took the painter with him. Then he stood, arrested. A small face was showing beyond the low rock.

Grant, who had completely forgotten Sheena, said at random: "I'm acting nursemaid to-day!" He laughed. "This is Sheena. We're great friends." Then he called, "It's all right, Sheena!" and went a couple of paces towards her. He did not know what to do, so went right up to Sheena. "How many shells have you got now?" He stooped; he inspected what she had gathered. "We'll need more yet for the path up to your housie." But her attention was distracted; yet he refused to turn round; and did not do so until she had been persuaded to gather more. Martin was sitting on the rock, smoking a cigarette, his face impassive.

"I have come to the conclusion that sea-water doesn't do anyone any harm," said Grant as lightly as he could.

"Depends on how much you get of it," said Martin.

"I got a fair amount," said Grant, holding to his smiling air.

But Martin was watching the child. Grant looked into the boat. "What are the fish with the red spots?"

"Plaice."

Grant studied the shape of the flounders and plaice carefully, the gear in the boat, a pipe, a tin of mussels, brown handlines on wooden frames. He suddenly remembered the boat that had been wrecked. This was a rougher, heavier one. "Was she a total wreck, the other boat?"

"She might mend, if we had the timber."

Grant could not look at him, as though something destructive or savage had come into the very air. When he did

279

look he was surprised to find that Martin's face was expressionless. His watching of Sheena was quite detached and Sheena at the moment was utterly absorbed with the mother-of-pearl shimmer in a shell. She was only a dozen yards away and they saw her try to scrape the shimmer off the shell with her fingernails but it wouldn't come. This was so wonderful that her face lit up with brightness and she cried, "Look!" and came with it at arm's length. Grant stepped down from the rock, took the shell and tried to wipe away the mother-of-pearl with the ball of his thumb; when he couldn't do it she jumped with excitement.

"It's a beauty," he said, putting it back in her eager hands.

"I found it." The tiny pink fingers with the transparent nails pressed against the mother-of-pearl; the brightness shone again in her face as she looked quickly up—and saw Martin. The brightness faded and the small face grew solemn and thoughtful.

"Perhaps there are more," suggested Grant.

Now she was looking up from under her brows and she came close to him; glanced at the shell and looked up again.

"Won't you try to find some more?" The position was becoming very awkward. "Run away now!" He turned to Martin, smiling. "We are keeping you."

Martin's eyes came onto his face; they walked over it and stared in, without curiosity; they shifted to the child, held for a little while, then with a slow easy gesture he took a pull at his cigarette and said, "Well?"

Grant went along the rock to the boat. There was the question of how he should carry the fish. Martin went into the boat and threaded eight of them on a piece of string, shoving it under the covering flap of the gills and out through the mouth with a thumb.

"This is too many," said Grant.

"Don't think you can carry them?"

"No, I mean—it's too much."

"I could take you to the spit if you like."

"That would be too kind, besides——"

"As you like."

"Well——" Grant looked back and saw the child's face staring at them over the rock. "If you're sure it wouldn't be a trouble?"

Martin didn't trouble to reply.

Grant put the shells in his handkerchief and carried Sheena over the uneven rock. She was excited.

"You get in first," said Martin; then he lifted Sheena in and Grant took her between his knees.

The sea was calm and the sun shining through a sky haze. Martin began to row away and Sheena's eyes grew round and looked at Martin and at the receding shore.

She could not understand Martin's face and turned sideways to it and Grant made conversation to her; but in a moment the lifting and falling of the boat over the slow impulse of the sea had her attention and she was looking at Martin again.

It was only then that Grant's inner acute embarrassment passed from him, for he realised that in Martin there was no awkwardness at all and had not been from the first moment. No abrupt talk, no stress, only that gaze in which there was neither curiosity nor indifference. He pulled a slow steady stroke; the seaman's oar. His face and shoulders had somehow an added distinction from the sea, an extra dimension of remoteness. When his eyes and Sheena's met, it was Sheena's that moved away. But he clearly did not frighten her. A slight wonder came upon her, a tendency to whisper: that was all; then she was looking at him again.

A small jetty pushed out from the northern shore of the spit and when Martin pulled alongside, Grant got out. Martin lifted Sheena out and then the fish.

"I can only thank you," said Grant; but as they moved away Sheena looked back, dragging a little at his hand, but

281

he did not care to turn round. He had thought he glimpsed Mrs. Sidbury in the pine plantation, and as they went along the avenue through the trees he saw her in the distance. She was standing in the middle of the avenue looking half over her shoulder and turned to them as they came up.

"Mr. Martin was good enough to give us a lift from the little shore," he said, smiling, "*and* present us with these fish."

She was pleased her brother had had such good sense and he presented Sheena. But Sheena had her right thumb at her mouth and curious eyes. Mrs. Sidbury had to take her hand and shake it politely. Sheena drew back and regarded her with a child's complete gravity, and for the second time Grant saw Martin in her face. He spoke laughingly to Sheena, for he did not care to look at Mrs. Sidbury.

As they went on again his embarrassment returned and he felt a fool. Mrs. Sidbury might think he was introducing Sheena to the family. Good lord! he thought. He had caught the tail-end of the piercing look she had given the child. He felt hot.

36

The whole involved business worried him. As if he had been a nursemaid arranging a sentimental tryst! And Sheena, of course, was full of the boat and the sea and questions to her mother and granny in the cottage; so there was also their aspect of the affair and heaven alone knew what thoughts. He had better clear out for a few days —but he couldn't do that because of the famous crock of gold.

Late that evening he walked about his sitting-room quietly, until the notion of escape produced its own plan. Each morning he would get his sandwiches and spend the day going far into the country behind Clachar; he would cover every glen and height in a vast arc from, say, the White Shore in the north to Kinlochoscar in the south.

With his large-scale map spread out on the table, he studied contour lines and place names. With compass and binoculars, he would get a sound general picture, and with luck he might happen on a particular find. As he narrowed the arc about Clachar, he had the notion that he was closing in on it, and this induced at once a feeling of clean satisfaction. It was the proper way to go about finding anything. These chance sallies in the night had always seemed futile, had gone against his scientific training.

As he folded the map, he felt freed and competent once more. By the time he had covered the ground the Colonel and his helpers would be back. They would quickly open up the whole cairn with a systematic perfection that did the heart good to think of, and when that was finished, he would

283

have his field plan ready for a systematic search of the surrounding terrain.

The archaeologist stood back from the bog of human emotion. He smiled at the nursemaid. As he lay on his back before turning over to sleep, he even indulged in a proper romantic solution of what he now called "the Clachar complex", whereby he would be the *deus ex machina* arranging the proper marriage to the tune of the Silver Bough, with Andie grinning over his present of the crock of gold, and Colonel Mackintosh, say, as best man! The irony was tonic and sent him to sleep, smiling.

He set off in the morning in excellent spirit and was hungry for his lunch by the time he had reached the White Shore. It was a fine sweep of pale brown sand and pulverised shell. The foreshore, grass-grown, was narrow; a thin waterfall dropped a sheer twenty feet, with black glistening rock behind and a boiling pot below. It was a beautiful spot, all light and lightness, and before eating he bathed and trotted along the edge of the tide and sat puffing until he dried. He could not put his clothes on. He went in again and came out. He caught a glimpse of the meaning of immortal youth and laughed. Tiny shivers rayed over his skin as, clothed once more, he munched; then the shivers left him and a divine glow took their place. Drowsy, he spread his legs and half-dreamed. Martin's face came before him.

There was nothing you could do with a face like that. It was death. Even the sea-fishing was automatic. In anger at its intrusion, he roused himself and got up, and soon the face, like any nightmare vision brought to the light, faded away.

That night he was full of a healthy tiredness and went to bed early. In his sleep, he saw Sheena sitting on the ground, exactly as he used to see the Neolithic child, but Sheena was making patterns with sea-shells on the black earth (black as peat dross). Sheena was utterly absorbed in what she was doing, but he could not enter into it because he was aware that someone was watching her. He knew this was not immediately dangerous to Sheena, but it so clutched him that he could hardly turn his head. When he did, he saw Martin squatting motionless on the ground, looking at the child. There was no expression on his face; it was bone-grey. His rebellious reaction to it awoke him. He had the feeling that he had cried out. Listening, he thought the house was preternaturally quiet. The grey half-light was in the window.

It was no good dodging this kind of infliction with sleeping tablets, he decided. He must face it out. The anger that had spired in him faded, and he was actually falling asleep when his mind came awake on a plain quiet as a meadow. In the same instant, without conscious change of scene, it was the jungle, and for a long time he followed Martin in his death-hunt through the jungle. Tree boles, undergrowth, festooning creepers, staring colours, the human body slipping round, vanishing; the mysteriousness of shapes, of patterns, and in the midst, stared at then suddenly seen, a face. . . . Sentries, men carrying buckets, smoke, sleeping bodies, shallow trenches, felled trees, rifle barrels. . . .

And now he is watching Martin; like an invisible eye he is following behind him, aware not only of what Martin is doing but why he is doing it. Martin is light on his feet, noiseless as a shadow, remorseless. Not hate, or other hot emotion in Martin's mind, simply a concentration so intense that it goes out from him to its object, its victim. A thought transference that the victim feels. It compels. . . .

Grant stirred, and when the vision faded he wondered just how much it meant. Psychic research; telepathy; the sending of a message from one mind to another at a distance. Hypnotism, with the compulsive action of one mind on another. Those authentic stories of friends of his, concerning African medicine men, Indians, whose power of the eye. . . .

Plainly the effect on Martin of the unthinkably abominable destruction of the white woman had been abnormal; it must have acted like some kind of mental catalyst before it could have produced that intense singleness of intention, that gathering of his total psychic powers into so ruthless a focus.

But the effect could have been abnormal only upon an abnormal sensitivity, an unusually high capacity to feel; and it could have been focused only by a mind of exceptional strength. And Grant thought with instant and complete conviction: That's the picture of him.

He remembered now something that Mrs. Cameron had said about Martin's early army troubles—with his colonel, was it? Martin would do his duty as a soldier, and do it all the more ruthlessly for his hatred of human killing, but to the sadist, superior officer or not, he would show that Neolithic face in stone.

Grant knew this so absolutely that he was moved to an obscure affection. He glimpsed the figure again in its stillness, its strength, its inner integrity of being. Martin's struggle to reach the cave had brought him so near death that he had flowered. Grant saw the cave-light on his face.

He turned over in his bed. Self-destruction. In Martin it would not come about in a sudden spasm of revulsion. He was not that kind. Grant groaned, for now he knew that Martin was the kind that went slowly down the road to a final nihilism, as slowly and remorselessly as he had hunted the yellow devils. All belief, all capacity for belief in human kind, had been slain at that horrible moment in the jungle, that culmination for him to all the meaningless slaughter in the world.

No one could help him now. His sister knew that; it haunted her, for she had an insight like his own.

In an extraordinary stillness of revelation Grant saw that

286

Martin could not be cured, he could not be cured unless he were *reborn*.

Anna would be of no use to him. She might save him from the sea, or he her. No use. Rebirth could not *start* that way. A woman like that might be his ultimate salvation, but he could not take the first steps with her. To look at her white body—good God!

No. It would have to start, if start it ever could, from the beginning, with a selfless absorption in some simple kind of doing or making. Like the absorption, the utter unself-consciousness, of the child arranging sea-shells on the black earth. Simply that. No more than that. No thought beyond. Doing that. . . . Let him lean over once and move a shell.

Let him lean over and move a shell! thought Grant into the silent reaches of the night.

Then he became confused, feeling that he had merely let himself be moved by his dream of Martin watching Sheena arranging the shells on the black peat dust by the peat stack.

Yet through this characteristic doubt there remained the uncanny conviction that if only Martin could lean over and move a shell something incalculable would be born in him at that instant.

For it could only now be something like that, something he could gaze at for hours, that he could help, without exercise of intellect, without question.

The child arranging sea-shells on the earth; pure pattern. Neither good nor evil; neither solid purpose nor self-conscious design. . . .

But there was a design: she was making a little house, she was "playing housies".

He could lean over and move a shell into this primitive magical sign of a home. Let him do that one *positive* act and what would follow *might* be incalculable.

For there was nothing fanciful about one thing at least: *Sheena was there.*

When overtones of meaning had faded upon the air, Grant experienced a curious quietening, wherein everything was interpretation or understanding. Without thought of outcome or ending. Then all at once he had the notion that he would like to see his friends in the narrow box. Without a moment's hesitation, as if someone like Anna had called to him, he got up and went into the dark room. But he did not open the box there; he took it with him to the mat, and, on his knees, unfastened the lid and lifted it back. The light was still a fine twilight; in the gloom of the box the two skulls were softly grey and the eye sockets dark and deep. After he had looked at them for a little time, he said gently, "When it's all over and they have gone away, I'll put you back in your own place."

37

After that night, Grant enjoyed his days on the hills. The feeling of liberation spread to his heels and he was often astonished at the degree of tirelessness in his energy. Certainly he was slim and of no great weight; there wasn't much of him to carry! He often smiled to himself, and once he had the odd notion that if he shaved off his beard he would come up through like a boy. Why had he grown the beard at all? He decided it was sheer waywardness . . . or a nascent atavism!

He discovered nothing of any importance and on the fourth day found himself in the Robbers' Glen. The last thing he wanted to do was pry into Martin's affairs, but he could not resist an elaborate scouting and spying and a final advance on the underground wheel-house with the feelings of a man poaching on his host's ground. Not that he was altogether doing this. In the name of science. . . . He chuckled.

Where so much was mental, he had at least to establish the actual existence of the underground dwelling. But when half an hour had passed in a close search on what he deemed the very spot, he began to be worried. The notion of Martin's head pushing above a skyline complicated the worry. Then suddenly he found the opening. From the low dark tunnel came a thick pervasive smell he remembered. With the utmost care and no little effort, he replaced the flagstone, redressed its edges with the old hanging heather, and stepped away. He did not feel safe until he was nearly half a mile lower down, where he rested, had a plunge in a small pool, and ate his lunch.

Perhaps some day, some year, he might do the wheel-house in style. It would keep! That made him think of Martin. As he stared into the small dark whirls in the pool and got lost in the sound from its throat, there came before him the cairn in the darkening night and the figure behind the monolith. Martin had been there! Then the astonishing thought came with an underbeat of excitement: Had Martin *called* Andie to that spot at that hour?

The significance of the question held him.... He was again in the cave and heard Martin say that he would probably have found the crock of gold if he, Grant, had not appeared.

At the time he had thought the remark no more than an acknowledgement of a chance meeting in the night—did not Martin often wander along the dark shore?—with no particular significance. But now....

With a deep conviction he realised that Martin was the only man who could understand Andie, who could command him in his own unusual fashion, and who could therefore find the crock of gold. This was as near a certainty as anything on this earth could be.

Why not get in touch with Martin? Why not call after dinner, and, at the right moment, put it to him?

But at once he saw he could not do this, not deliberately. He could not risk alienating Martin. When he found himself trying to understand this, a further astonishing question asked itself inside him: Supposing Martin had followed Andie and found the crock, *what would he have done about it?* And he found that he could not answer; he just did not know. He had no reason at all to suppose that Martin would in fact ever tell him anything about it. There was a dark place beyond the utmost reach of his intuition where Martin and the crock would be hidden.

There was an excitement in this, a penetration . . . and the possibility at least of a small extra discovery of oneself. And the more he penetrated, the more he discovered of himself, *the nearer he drew to the crock of gold*. That was no myth: it was simple fact. In a momentary wonder that it should be so, he laughed. He had never before seen, he declared, what myth meant. The sunlight danced on the dark swirls in the pool.

But he experienced quite a different kind of excitement the evening before Colonel Mackintosh and his party were due to arrive. It was his longest trip, and dropping into the Kinlochoscar Hotel for a glass of wine he found the manageress so pleasant, and the wine so pleasantly weakening, that he stopped for dinner. Yes, she told him, three rooms had been reserved for Colonel Mackintosh, a Mr. Blair, and a Mr. Scott—arriving to-morrow. These were the only rooms available and Colonel Mackintosh had booked them before he left. No, she didn't know of others. He explained that the Colonel was not a very good correspondent and a question of labour was involved. However, he hoped that at least there would not be so much publicity this time! . . .

On the way home he was in such good fettle that half-way along the road he left it to spy out some ground towards the sea. Every day there had been the possibility that he just might pick up with his field-glasses an unsuspecting Andie in some lonely place, and he approached the ridge, which should give a view of the valley in which Arthur had found the cist with the collar urn, more like a deerstalker than an innocent archaeologist. Then he saw the tents and his features so narrowed in wrath that his whole face, with its clipped pointed beard, gathered a tolerable resemblance to a Neolithic axe. The advance guard of the great British public had arrived! He could hardly take the binoculars from their leather case.

Four small triangular tents, a larger round one, and, at a little distance, a rectangular affair of brown sacking that was all too plainly a latrine. Seven young men were squatting like braves—round the cist.

As he approached the latrine, an eighth, with khaki shorts and bare legs, was shouldering a spade.

"What's all this about?" demanded Grant.

"All what?"

"Who gave you permission to camp here?"

"I thought permission. . . . Are you the landowner, sir?"

"No, I'm not. And if you haven't got permission to camp here, I'd advise you get it before you squat. You can't just dump your tents——"

"Good evening, Mr. Grant."

Grant wheeled. "What—you, Jim Dickson?"

"Yes, sir," said Jim, a smiling hefty young man. "We are the labour battalion sent on by Uncle James in advance." Uncle James was Colonel Mackintosh.

"Well I'm damned!"

"All budding field-workers, at your service." Jim half-bowed, half-hitched his pants.

Grant capitulated with a roar of laughter. He knew three of the lads well.

An hour later, he left them, smiling. From their apparently innocent questions, he could see that they had worked out a foolproof system of night-shifts and super-boy-scout stalking, with the crock of gold as their Holy Grail. The farther they had to crawl on their bellies the better! When he had done his best to warn them about Andie, one of them had replied negligently, "We have done some deer-stalking, sir. If you don't want him to see us—he won't."

He glanced at his watch: it was nearly eleven o'clock. Anna would be coming out to look for him again!

He came round the slope and saw a movement at the base of the tall monolith. At first, with a swift uncanny feeling,

292

he thought it was a black dog; but as he stopped and stared he saw a human being on all fours: it was Andie. His head was down, like an Eastern man in prayer. Or was he scraping, like a dog? Andie's head lifted and looked round the stone towards the cairn; then slowly he reared up and, one shoulder against the stone, kept on peering round at the cairn. All at once, as if something had touched him, he turned his head and saw Grant.

"Hullo, Andie," said Grant as he approached. "What are you up to now?"

Andie's face was a mass of grinning creases, the eyes reduced to thin slits. The ground at his feet was unbroken.

Grant spoke to him again, humanly, smiling, ready to take part in the game.

Andie spoke thickly and his shoulders began to heave. He was excited about something; but his grinning held also a sort of baffling embarrassment. Suddenly Grant wondered if Martin was about and his eyes travelled carefully over the cairn.

Andie's arms began to flap slightly.

• "Well, what is it?" asked Grant. "Want to go and find it? . . . Come on, then!" And he made a tentative but indefinite movement.

Andie, however, was equally indefinite, waiting for a lead, waiting to follow: clearly he had no notion of going to any specific place himself. He was looking at Grant now as a dog looks at a shepherd, but with something behind the eye that no dog has.

"Well, let us have a look," said Grant in his friendly employer's voice and started for the cairn. At once Andie was striding alongside, muttering away. A complete circuit of the cairn revealed nothing.

"Doesn't seem to be anyone around, does there?"

"Gu—gu——" answered Andie, his eyes on Grant, waiting for the next move.

293

Grant was completely baffled. But he did not want to give in. He rested against the cairn. The daylight was shadowed, easy on the eyes, a still grey silence. An oyster-catcher swerved suddenly above them, and was gone over the cliff. The sea-floor rose slowly in a grey glimmer to a remote horizon.

He must appear to Andie as a superior being, the myster-ious one who has knowledge. He came, opened up cairns, found skeletons and pots of gold. Andie would at once expect *something more* when he saw him. Not what had been, but the new bright thing that would be.

How was it possible to reverse this? "What brought you here?" he asked, hoping that something in his easy attitude would shake or confuse Andie. "Does your mother know?"

A definite pause came into Andie's being as if he had perfectly understood. He began to mutter and hunch his shoulders, then his mouth opened in a stare. Grant turned his head and saw Andie's mother approaching. Her shawled head and shoulders gave her the appearance of a woman coming out of a remote place or remote time. Her skirt was down to the top of her boots, obscuring the movement of her legs, though she was plainly walking. Once or twice Grant had been touched by the legendary, by a feeling of something archetypal, larger and more enduring than the individual. He felt the strange shiver of this now, got up from the stones, spoke at once, "Good evening. Are you looking for Andie?" He smiled in his friendliest way, making the moment normal, preparing for his explanation of how he had come on Andie. "Don't blame me this time!"

"It's time he was home," she said quietly.

"It's more than time we were all home," he agreed. But somehow he could not begin his explanation, his excuse for himself. Andie anyhow was muttering, and Grant saw that his face was congested, angry, like a wilful boy's.

"Come, Andrew," she said.

"Home, Andrew. Off you go!" said Grant cheerfully.

"Gu—gar—r—r."

"But we must. Good night, Mrs. Mackenzie."

"Good night, sir."

Grant found himself walking away. But once out of sight curiosity got the better of him. When he had rounded the shoulder of the slope, he held to his right for some distance and then lay flat. He saw them in the hollow, and mounting the next slope, on their direct way home. Andie was walking with his long uncouth stride behind her, bent, his hands behind his back. For a little while the sky held them in clear outline, then they slowly dropped beyond.

When he got home he found a telegram from Colonel Mackintosh: "Arrange camping ground for eight student helpers." As he took off his boots in the sitting-room, he heard Mrs. Cameron stirring. He went to the kitchen door and called gently, "It's all right, Mrs. Cameron. I was detained in Kinlochoscar and had my dinner there."

"I have only just lain down. I'll make you a cup of tea."

"No, no. Please. I'm sorry I could not let you know."

She told him of the telegram which had come in the forenoon and of the young men who had called.

"That's all right," he answered. "They saw Mrs. Sidbury. I have been with them."

"Oh then! That's fine! It was on my mind."

"Good night."

"Good night, Mr. Grant. I hope you sleep well."

38

Late the following afternoon Andie made a dramatic entrance into the whole company gathered at the cairn. The hour, five o'clock, had been fixed by the Colonel. Blair was in whipcord riding breeches, an open-necked khaki shirt and new spectacles. Mr. Scott carried flannel trousers of a remarkable slackness, a roll-topped seaman's blue jersey, a pipe and a rocking gait. Colonel Mackintosh wore plusfours that hung well and baggily, a collar and tie, and pre-war expensive hill boots. Grant had his tweed hat and the knickerbockers that appeared a trifle scraggy about the knees only by comparison with the Colonel's, so that young Armstrong, a student of such matters, wondered if he had borrowed the idea from Bernard Shaw or found them in the cairn.

The Colonel was establishing his leadership by making it clear that Mr. Grant was the leader in this ploy. He used the words "ploy" and "foray", and even got as far afield as "the Cattle Raid of Ulster", thus setting the local simplicities of their present venture over against the classic cultures of the Mediterranean, but with a feel for the words in his mouth that to the discerning suggested he would tolerate nothing but the most careful and earnest work. "With a name like Grant, or even Mackintosh, one finds oneself on one's native heath, and though dubious names like Scott, or even Armstrong, may have a lower or at least more Lowland connotation, still, if history may be credited, their knowledge of the cattle-lifting foray was hardly less than the Highlander's and perhaps more thorough."

With a decorous "Hear, hear!" Armstrong induced a round of applause. The Colonel blinked and blew through his moustache. The unrehearsed pleasantness of the moment —his simple if sudden intention had been to compliment Grant in a roundabout way—induced such friendly feelings that Colonel Mackintosh decided to cap the occasion with a yarn which might poke these young rascals in the place where it might do them most good.

"Talking of Highland forays," he began, "let me illustrate with an example which I am sure you will all appreciate."

But he had hardly cleared his throat when the screaming began. It was the high-pitched terrified screaming of a young woman who was being murdered. It so shocked and bewildered them that even Scott of the Navy was staggered where he stood. Then the screaming head was seen coming round the bend, the torso, and finally the very short shorts and the flashing legs. A few yards behind came Andie, with bent body, and the springing strides a hillman is inclined to adopt when he is being beaten in a walking competition. Scott only managed five gallant strides before the young woman threw herself solidly upon his protection. From behind the tall monolith, Andie thrust a grinning head.

Grant was the first to react. His person began to work as though the tail of a long eel had stuck in his throat on the way down. But he was unobserved, for younger eyes were concerned with the Navy's expert handling of the occasion.

"What happened, young woman?" asked the Colonel.

She straightened herself from a reluctant mooring. "He— he attacked me."

"What did he do?"

"He—he was going to——"

"But he didn't actually?" demanded the Colonel like a judge.

"Hang it, Colonel, you could see what was happening," said Scott who was thirty-five and knowledgeable.

"We all observed that part of it, Mr. Scott—right to the end," remarked the Colonel with excellent asperity. Then he turned to the lady. "He didn't actually lay hands on you, did he?"

She was trembling but looked at him. "N-no."

"Well, let that be a lesson to you," he said sternly.

Her eyes opened to the full and a glint of anger shone. She had become aware of the male audience. "I didn't——"

"Naturally." He nodded. "Where's Arthur?"

She had finally got some control of herself and with an intolerant mien turned her head as if Arthur might appear out of the blue; which he did.

"Come," said the Colonel to her with a small bow, "and we shall hold converse with Arthur touching matters of publicity." And she went with him like one striving to be unselfconscious in amateur theatricals.

Upon the watching silence, Armstrong murmured thoughtfully, "As a Highland foray, it had its points."

"You pipe down," said Scott. "Don't you think, Blair, the Colonel was a bit tough?"

"I rather suspect," answered Blair, "that he thought you might have been unequal to dealing with hysterics."

"By what warrant?"

But Grant was walking towards Andie.

Andie's embarrassment was that of a good-natured boy who cannot stop twisting and laughing at having been found out in something more unexpected than disreputable. His eyes glinted with light and his swayings and contortions were as remarkable as his laughter.

"Andie, I'm surprised at you!"

"He—he—he—e—e——"

"It's no laughing matter!"

"Whu—hu—hu—u——" And though the body doubled, the better to squeeze out the breath, the bright eyes were watching with a cuteness.

298

Suddenly a voice behind barked a laugh and Grant, swinging round, observed that three of the young men had come up and that the others were on the way. Jim Dickson had been unable to control himself, though he had had the grace to turn his back. Grant's eyes ran over the landscape, but there was no sign of the Colonel and the lady, whom happily the cairn concealed. But the other faces were also being infected by Andie's mirth. Scott stared at it, then he suddenly broke. "You d-dog!" he cried out of a rich fellow-feeling, laughing from the diaphragm. He took paces away and paces back; threw his head up. The boys let themselves go.

"Here—stop it!" Grant yelled. "Sc-c-cott!" Then he gave way also.

Presently the Colonel came striding towards them. "That's a fine way to behave, I must say. I expected more from you, Grant."

"Huh—he—e—e——"commented Andie, still enjoying the whole splendid performance.

"And you're the ringleader!" the Colonel shouted at him.

"Whu—ho—ha—he—e—e——" His face squeezed itself like a rubber ball at Christmas.

The Colonel's nostrils snorted, his stomach abruptly keeping time, then he laughed manfully where he stood.

Grant saw Andie home. To Mrs. Mackenzie he explained that he might be able to engage Andie on the same work as before, the young men, who were from a University, having greatly taken to him.

Mrs. Mackenzie thanked him, said it was very kind of them all, but there was work to do at the stone-breaking for the road and it was more suitable that this should be gone on with.

He saw that she was troubled and did not wish her son to have anything more to do with them. When he asked her to think it over, she said simply, "No, he is not fitted for your company."

"I think you are wrong. We all understand him."

"I am his mother," she said. As though to make it easier for him, she added, "The stone-breaking is what we mostly rely on. We must keep up with it."

"I quite understand," he said. Then he had a helpful thought. "In that case we had better square up for last week."

"But we have done nothing——"

"But that's not your fault. I didn't pay you off." By good luck he had three pounds in his pocket-book. He placed the money on the table.

"But I cannot——"

"And you consider yourself a business woman! I hope you are not so soft with the road surveyor."

She was moved. "It's very kind of you."

"Just business. And we'll be seeing you. So long just now."

She did not answer and he was glad to get out.

When Andie appeared at the cairn the following morning, he received an ovation from the young men. The preliminary work of opening up the passage had just started and Andie, wading in, began to hurl the stones behind him with skilled ease.

Grant spoke to the Colonel of his interview with Mrs. Mackenzie.

"Uhm," replied the Colonel. "We don't need him." His eye roved. "Though he might have earned his keep," he suggested in a rather loud voice, "if only by keeping the young women away."

It was clear, however, that Colonel Mackintosh did not really want him, that he was all set now to see the work go ahead in an intelligent way, without distractions. The whole affair must be a simple object lesson for these young fellows. When Mrs. Mackenzie appeared the position grew complicated. Andie stubbornly refused to budge.

300

"Just wait a bit, Mrs. Mackenzie," Grant said to her. "We'll fix it all right."

Meantime some of the young men had been murmuring together and Jim Dickson strolled up to his uncle, the Colonel. "Can I have a word with you and Mr. Grant?" The three withdrew.

"We were talking it over in camp last night," said Jim. "We understand from you, Uncle James, that the finding of the crock of gold would be of primary archaeological importance. Our feeling was that if we grew very friendly with Andie, then—anything might happen, naturally enough."

The Colonel eyed his nephew. "Uhm," he said. In his dispositions for the actual work, he had forgotten the crock.

"That is, if it is," said Jim.

"If what is?" demanded the Colonel.

"If the crock of gold is," said Jim with mild innocence.

"*If* is the operative word," said the Colonel, easing his suspicions.

"Some of them did rather suggest it was like hunting a fairy story," his nephew agreed.

"Hm! What do you say, Grant?"

"I think he's right," said Grant shortly.

"Very well. Fix the woman—and let the Fool carry on for a bit anyhow. And you, young fellow—no nonsense!"

Jim's face looked hurt, then it smiled.

A few happy days followed for both Andie and his mother. The lads were fond of him and treated him in a natural happy-go-lucky way. "Hullo, Andie, how goes it?" "Gu—gu——" "Fine!" They shared their sweet ration with him, and when Mrs. Mackenzie appreciated their astonishment at one basket of two dozen fresh eggs, she made arrangements with her neighbours for a daily collection. They also seemed to be able to drink immense quantities of milk, and did not appear repelled at the notion of a boiled fowl in a great iron pot of broth. They insisted on paying for everything and a price list was agreed upon. There were trials of strength over boulders or great slabs. Mrs. Mackenzie had never known her son so happy. Once Grant caught her, with knitting needles arrested, looking over at three of the lads working on a new cutting. One of them had obviously made some sort of joke, for he dug Andie in the ribs with his elbow, as if he were a sly dog. Andie swayed with mirth. Grant knew, by the way Mrs. Mackenzie's body moved upon itself, that she was touched in some deep maternal region where the line between happiness and tears is hardly definable.

But such extraordinary theories had been pushed upon them by Scott at dinner for four in Kinlochoscar Hotel the other evening that a car driver had had to be knocked out of bed to take Grant home and the Colonel was still suffering from a sort of general indigestion. Among those mentioned in the debate were Tylor, Schliemann, Valerius Maximus (who said the Gauls lent each other money repayable in the next world), Ra-Osiris and his god's liquid, Leucippus who founded the atom theory in the fifth century B.C., Pythagoras and the Orphic dogma of moral dualism, King Arthur, Robert Kirk, the Arab Avicenna who knew how the human mind could alter objects, and the Presbytery of Dingwall which took action against four Mackenzies for sacrificing a bull on an island in Loch Maree in 1678. And all this as a sort of general disposition of forces by Scott to confuse counsel while he made his main move on the tall monolith, for he had been more attracted by Grant's suggestion of a phallic symbolism than by his crock of gold. "The phallic has got more to it," he said, "and to think of it—in these parts!"

"Why particularly in these parts?" asked the Colonel.

"Because they had more time for it—obviously," replied Scott. "In the comparative absence of mere distractions like culture and its rituals, which still astonish any honest man——"

"But you can raise a culture on anything——"

"Exactly! That's my whole point. Here they had *something* to raise it on, something that still remains even more fundamental, thank God, than an ideology."

At 1.30 a.m. Scott had put his helm over and headed for the main objective. "At least we can have a shot at this: let us dig down to the base of the monolith. Supposing we find, for example, that it has been shored up in order to cast its shadow at the given moment into the exact spot! Wouldn't that suggest something? Once we are certain of the levels, the original levels. . . ."

And now this afternoon, as Grant turned away from his vision of maternal emotion, he heard the Colonel say, "For God's sake, keep that thing still."

Scott relaxed his grip on the handle of the pickaxe, which he had essayed to swing as a Highland athlete swings the sports hammer, and said, "Why not now? The chambers have been detailed and the levels taken. The boys are back at donkey work and——"

"I don't consider excavation donkey work. At least it should be supervised. Besides, as I said, when we have completely finished with the cairn——"

"But look, Colonel, I could get down to this thing myself in a couple of shakes. Blair is lost in the northern radial incision. You are both, Grant and yourself—aren't you, Grant? What do you think?"

"We believe in order," said Grant.

"Exactly! But what's order without inspiration? Assuming we establish a phallic significance, the effect on these youngsters will be noticeable in an added zest. It will give them an eye for everything. I have always maintained that archaeology should be cheered on."

Scott knew he could make the Colonel laugh in the end,

303

even if he had to stand on his head, which he had already done on three separate days. He had even laid level half-crowns with Blair that he would get Andie to manage it yet.

Before the Colonel and Grant knew rightly where they were they were before the monolith. The Colonel stopped and looked at the stone. Then an astonishing thing happened. His face quickened, his eyes opened. "Mighty Osiris, I've got it!" The voice was not loud; it was husky and intense.

The other two glanced at him in astonishment and closed in.

"The shoulders—look!—quite distinct—and see these lines, that upper whorl—it's the man in the stone," declared the Colonel. "It was meant. . . . Here, dammit, don't push me, Scott. What time is it?" He pulled out his gold watch. Then he kicked abrasions in the turf to mark the exact spot on which he had been standing, as sheer reactions from his scientific training.

Grant had got this queer "look" of the thing more than once, though he had been at pains to generalise it. Now Scott swore he saw it, got behind the monolith, and swung his pickaxe.

The Colonel did not care much for this brutal and amateurish attack, so when Andie appeared he asked gruffly, "What are you doing here?"

"The very man!" cried Scott. "Here, Andie, give us a heave."

Andie's excitement was stupendous. Scott and he collided like rams as they strove for foot room and a conjoint grip on what was either a great boulder or solid rock. Andie's neck and face so swelled that Grant thought they would burst. Nothing moved except Andie, from whose feet the ground had to retire.

"Wait," said Scott. "Wait, my boy. We'll have to get more of his clothes off." And he swung his pick. He paused and yelled, "Hey, Jim, bring that shovel and crowbar!" When they were brought, Andie scooped out the loose stuff. In the end, with Jim's help, the great slab was eased away from the monolith and tilted over.

"Stop!" cried the Colonel commandingly. "Come out of that!"

Scott gave him one look and immediately stopped operations.

"It might fall over," said Colonel Mackintosh. "Many of them are not so deep as supposed. It was a damned silly way to set about it anyhow."

"Maybe you're right," said Scott reluctantly but with the utmost good nature. He scratched himself. "I'll tell you what, Colonel. We can cut down three of the laird's pine trees and use them as shoring battens. That would make everything as safe as a church and would let us see——"

"We can discuss that when we dine there to-night," said Colonel Mackintosh, half turning away.

Scott winked to Grant.

"Gu—ga—ga——?" Andie was still in the trench, his face uplifted in wide-open expectancy.

The Colonel turned on him. "What are you hoping to find? Another crock of gold? Get out!"

Scott left pickaxe, crowbar and shovel tidily together, and as they followed the Colonel to the cairn he paused for a moment to feel Andie's biceps. Mrs. Mackenzie resumed her knitting with a smile. She had now eight orders on hand for stockings.

39

Grant awoke violently and held his breath. His eyes roved. There was nothing in the room, no one on the mat. Something had happened somewhere and he was afraid. The familiar grey of the dawn was in the window. When he reached it, he saw Mrs. Mackenzie going down by the little garden wall. She stood by the rowan tree, turned her face and looked at the house. He shoved his head through the window opening; the piece of wood that held the window up fell over the sill and with the back of his neck he heaved the frame higher. "What's wrong?" he called.

She did not move; her voice was quiet and strange: "Andrew hasn't come home."

"Wait for me." At once the window-frame lowered on his neck. He struggled to draw his head back; as at last, half-strangled, he jerked it in, the frame fell like a knife, but by good luck his finger-tips had slipped and he was clear. He was coming out of the sitting-room with his boots on when Mrs. Cameron called. "It's all right," he answered and closed the front door behind him.

"I don't know where he is," Mrs. Mackenzie said. Her voice was still quiet but it had a tremor, an under-surge.

"When did he go out?"

"About eleven o'clock before going to bed, as usual."

"And he never came back?" He hadn't his watch with him but it must be two or three in the morning.

"No."

"Don't worry. We'll find him."

She did not answer.

"Have you been looking far?"

"Everywhere."

"You're sure he's not back?" He was wondering where to go first. The caves, he thought.

"No. I went home a little while ago," she answered, "but could not rest."

"Let's go this way."

When they had crossed the footbridge, he kept low, making for the beach. About a hundred yards from the boathouse he saw Martin come out of it. "Wait here," he said quietly and went on.

Martin had been a good host at dinner, friendly in his impersonal way, and this for some reason had been a relief, until Grant had felt that Mrs. Sidbury's gaiety covered an extra anxiety. She had tried to get him alone but had only had time to whisper that she would like to see him to-morrow (now to-day). From that moment he had realised that Martin's extra ease had been the ease, the quiet competence, he had shown in the cave at the height of the storm, with death in the offing.

"You haven't seen Andie about?"

When his eyes had finished with Grant's face, Martin said, "No."

"He's been missing all night. That's his mother up there."

Grant followed Martin's eyes to the shawled head and still body against the slope. In the grey light it looked ancient and statuesque. He felt a queer hot surge in his breast.

"What I can't understand——" he said and stopped.

"What?" asked Martin.

"These fellows in the camp—at least two of them were supposed to keep a watch."

"Two of them were after a salmon in the Sea Pool."

"Were they?" said Grant in bewildered astonishment. "Did they see you?"

"No." Martin was still staring at the woman.

"I was wondering if he mightn't have gone to the caves."

Martin looked at him curiously. "Why?"

"I don't know," muttered Grant, his thoughts rocketing from him like pigeons.

"It was all too much for him," said Martin, and Grant instantly felt he should have known that.

Martin began to walk up towards Mrs. Mackenzie. He did not greet her nor did she him, but they looked at each other for a moment. Then they started up the slope to the cairn.

Nothing was spoken, nothing was said at all, and Grant felt that something was drained away and the moment strengthened. The quest was fatal but it was calmed.

When they came round the cairn Martin stopped and stared. Grant followed his stare and saw that the tall monolith was down. Never before in waking thought had he experienced the certainty, the inevitability, of nightmare. Had it not been down, fate would have been absent from the universe.

Martin was going forward. There was something pale against the dark earth, rounded, like a face, a foot or two from the side of the fallen monolith. A harsh cry came from Mrs. Mackenzie. Martin stooped, put his hand on the face, then he straightened slowly and stood quite still, giving way as the woman got to her knees. She put her hands about the face, she cried aloud.

Grant saw that the monolith had caught Andie's body at the base of the chest and crushed it flat as his hand against the edge of the trench. Instantaneous death.

The woman was now clawing at the edge of the stone, trying to free the body. A wild impulse came on Grant to tear and help. Martin's hand stopped him. She scrabbled back, her face lifted to them.

"He's dead," said Martin clearly.

"Andrew, my son!" she cried. "My son! O my boy!"

"Get the fellows from the camp," said Martin, and Grant started off running, the terrible keening cries of the mother pursuing him.

As he returned, the lads racing up behind him, he saw Martin move along the stone with the pickaxe in his hand. Mrs. Mackenzie was sitting bent over her son's face, her cries quietened to quivering moans, her head shaking in bouts of sorrow, of negation.

Martin put a hand under the woman's arm. "Come away, Mrs. Mackenzie. We'll get Andrew out and take him home."

The young men had never seen lamentation of this kind before; they had only known a decorous grief. They had never seen hands on a face.

She got up and went with Martin. In a few minutes he came back alone.

"We'll dig away the edge of the trench here," he said, "and drag the body out. The stone is supported fore and aft."

After clearing a way through to the trench on each side of the body, they began digging under it. One of the lads started to retch and Martin sent him with another to fetch a gate from a field. The bloody squelch that was the centre of the body affected most of them as they drew Andie away until the feet stuck. In a few minutes they had him on the gate.

"Three to each side," said Martin, taking a grip forward.

Walking behind, Grant observed the averted looks of the white-faced young carriers. He saw Andie's protruding mouth, the head that swayed with the gate, the blood-sodden mess. He told Armstrong, who hadn't got a place, to fetch some sacking from the cairn. Armstrong ran at top speed and soon overtook them. "Hold on!" called Grant. He spread the sacking over the body.

Martin beckoned to Armstrong to take his place and fell behind with Grant. "I think," he said, "you should go and tell Mrs. Cameron."

"Yes," said Grant at once and hurried off.

When he reached the door, Mrs. Cameron met him, fully clothed.

"Andie is killed," he said. "The big stone fell on him."

She stood quite still for several seconds, as though hearing or understanding something at a distance. "Poor woman," she murmured. "Come in," she said.

"We wondered if——"

"Yes, I was just going. The kettle is boiling. You would be the better of a cup of tea."

The running seemed to have sickened him a bit; he was feeling squeamish.

"No," he said. "Not just now. They're carrying him to the house."

"Very well, I'll be going. I'll knock on Mrs. MacLennan." And she set off.

He went upstairs to his bedroom and gulped down some cold water. As he was coming out, Anna's door opened. She had an overcoat over her nightdress.

"It's Andie," he said.

She nodded. She was pale and did not seem able to move or speak. Her eyes looked extraordinarily deep. "Do you need anything?" she asked.

"No, I'll be off," and he went downstairs.

They had reached Andie's home by the time he got there. Mrs. Cameron was going in as the lads came out. Then Martin came out.

"That's all we can do," Martin said to Grant. "I'll phone the policeman in Kinlochoscar and he can get in touch with the doctor."

Grant thanked the lads and suggested they should go home

and brew a strong pot of tea; then he started down the road with Martin.

For a little way there was silence. Grant said, "It's a pity. It's a pity it should have happened like that."

Martin did not answer.

Grant knew there was nothing to say, but still, the human being had to speak sometimes. However things had conspired to happen, he was at the root of them; it was he who had drawn Andie in. Suddenly he remembered that Martin in the first instance had sent him to Andie. Hostility hardened his face and he thought: I'll keep my mouth shut, too.

"It's more complicated than that," Martin said thoughtfully, without a trace of emotion.

"What?" asked Grant, feeling lost.

"Your remark about its being a pity."

"How do you mean?"

"It's all over for her now."

"Good God I should think so!"

"Otherwise there was the future," said Martin in the same voice. "It must have worried her, because she was getting on in years." As a peewit swooped and rose, his eyes followed it.

"You can hardly mean she's relieved he's dead—or do you?"

"You're being obtuse, aren't you?"

"Am I?"

But Martin did not seem interested in the last question. Had he been self-complacent or cynical, one could have been irritated and wholesomely aggressive. The fellow was just nothing human. Like the pervasive light. The sun had not yet topped the mountains. The peewit was a materialised spirit that had lost something and couldn't rest. The air was an immaterial sea.

"Anyway," said Grant, "I hope there's someone to see to the funeral arrangements." Even to his own ears the words sounded wholesome and solid. They made him feel better.

"Oh yes," remarked Martin lightly.

"Who?" demanded Grant.

"The neighbours. They may be depended on to bury their dead."

Grant managed to stop himself asking: aren't *you* one of the neighbours? The words that came were: "In that case I don't suppose she will be pleased to see any more of us."

"On the contrary," said Martin in that voice of his which could be so cool and fluent, "it would help her if the whole lot of you turned out to the funeral."

"With a wreath?"

"Two, if possible: large ones."

Grant shot a look at him, but as he saw the head beginning to turn he looked away. Here was the path down to the cottage. He would have to say something as they stood and parted. Martin simply went on. At the corner of the gable, Grant stopped to get complete control of himself. The blackbird was singing on the rowan tree. The cat came picking its steps through the dew-damp grass, leapt onto the bottom wall of the garden, had a slow look around, its tail twitching to the song, steadied its sphinx-face on the human for an indifferent moment, then leapt down behind the gooseberry bush.

Anna was in the kitchen, fully dressed. He had the extraordinary feeling of going into a predestined place where they were alone. She smiled, inviting him with silent understanding of the tragic moment, remote a little even in her smile, but warm and tender-hearted. His tray was ready and at once she began pouring hot dark-amber tea into his cup.

"I'm just in time!" he said, striving for lightness.

"I saw you coming."

With a sense of waiting and watching, of service, of being part of the need and the hour, her simple words affected him deeply. He rubbed his hands, turning from the fire, and gave an involuntary shiver.

312

"You're cold," she murmured and glanced at the fire.

"No, I'm fine."

He would have to watch himself. The moment was treacherous. A few nights ago, after he had heard Sheena play the Silver Bough faultlessly right through, with an incredibly light touch, light as a fairy's, he had found a part of his mind, as he sat alone, the house quiet and the wind fallen, making a small phantasy on its own. For in fact he had a city flat, an inherited flat. An old woman came in and kept it indifferently clean. His principal meals he ate in a restaurant or at the club. . . . Sheena was obviously musical. She should get piano lessons from Miss Boyd or—perhaps, later, from Old Antonio. Almost the only kind of housekeeper to be got nowadays was the woman with the child. Accepted as normal among his friends. The thing could be done. Anna was young, and there might be a club joke here and there for a time, but it was really quite normal. . . . When his whole mind woke up and got the scheme, he had felt a bit awkward and hot, but laughed. Still, before he was going away, he *might* say to Mrs. Cameron, only to Mrs. Cameron, that if Anna ever wanted a job, he *might* arrange something, and Sheena—it would be a pity if she did not get piano lessons. . . .

He sat down and began to drink the tea. His hand shook and a little slopped over onto the saucer, but she was attending to the fire and did not notice.

"Was Andie—did he suffer?" she asked.

"No. Oh no. He was killed instantly."

"Was he by himself?"

"Yes. It was the big standing stone. We had been digging there. He must have come out all alone—to finish the digging. He was perhaps wondering what—what we were digging for." He lifted his cup again and without a word, unobtrusively, she placed a clean saucer under it. "Thanks," he said, "thank you. This is good tea."

313

"You should eat something," she suggested politely.

"No, I'm all right. A bit chilly. We got the young fellows from the camp. Across the body it got him. He must have been so keen digging that it tilted over on him before he got clear. He seemed to like that stone."

"You would often find him there," she agreed quietly.

"Yes. Anything special about it, any story?"

"No—well—I remember, when I was a child, stories about the cairn being haunted, about a man. It had something to do with that stone, too."

"Locked himself up in it, did he?"

"Something like that," she said with some confusion. She brought the teapot and filled his cup again. He looked at her hand. It was a firm capable hand, with fair smooth skin. The fairness was part of her colouring. The hand withdrew.

"Sheena never woke up?" he asked.

"Only for a minute."

"She's very musical."

Anna was silent.

"Don't you think so?" he asked. "The way she plays—and picked it up so soon."

"She worships it," she said, smiling.

"Does she? Who knows—what's your grandmother's story?—about leading the owner of the Silver Bough to some wonderful place? I—I am very fond of Sheena. I should like to think it might bring her luck—and you too." He put his cup down. "I am quite sure it will." He turned his head.

She looked into the fire, one hand on the mantelpiece. She was shy, but there was something else in her expression, a troubling he did not understand. Had he suggested anything uncanny? He was feeling nervous and excited, confused. He wanted to get up and go over to her. Then something in that troubling reminded him of the foreshore when Martin and himself had been rescued, and he actually felt the quivering, the shake in his arm, ebb away. He stared out of the kitchen window, then got up.

With his shoulder towards her, he said, "I owe you a lot, Anna. If ever there is anything I can do for you—or for Sheena—you have only got to ask me."

As she did not answer, he turned his head. "You know that?"

"You're very kind," she murmured, warm and confused but with the troubling now like something obscurely tragic.

The whole morning and its tragedy came upon him. "You'll go to your bed, won't you?"

"I'll see," she answered. "Perhaps Granny might need something."

As he got into bed, he thought of how men retired and left it to the women. They would have to take the clothes off Andie. At the end of man's bloody day, the women stripped the naked body. His inner eye saw Mrs. Cameron at her task. Then the women would stand aside, unfitted for the religious words and the nice ceremonial job of committing the body to its eternal home. What tragedy was in Anna's heart God alone knew.

40

Andie had been very fond of funerals and never missed one. His own would certainly have been a wonderful show for him. Colonel Mackintosh had told the young squad that they must button their shirts to the neck and put a tie on, and they had gone one better by getting black ties cut out of a camera cloth by a woman in Kinlochoscar. They also collected red cottage roses and made a magnificent wreath.

The Colonel said to Grant, "We'll hand in one from the rest of us. What flowers do you suggest?"

"Oh, I don't know."

"What about something original," suggested Blair, "say, a small crock of forget-me-nots?"

"You have a macabre sort of humour, Blair," said Scott.

"Perhaps we can leave it to the hotel gardener," decided the Colonel. "And I think, as a touch of respect, that we'll give the cairn a miss for that day."

The wreaths overflowed the coffin and filled up the hearse. Some obscure feeling of sympathy drew the largest crowd within living memory to any funeral from Clachar.

"If only Andie could have seen this!" said old Fachie sitting in one of the hotel cars, which Grant had privately ordered.

"It's more nor you or me will have, Fachie," said Davie Munro, his gnarled hands on his stick.

"Indeed that's true. And we don't grudge it to him. So long as there's something in man, if I may take it upon me to use the words of our Lord, that would do it unto the least of us, there's hope for us all."

"Indeed and I back you there. It's a brave show for Clachar whateverway. And the laird here himself, too. Boy, boy!"

"A fine thing to see. It is that. And a fine day for it."

"And the minister spoke ably. He has the understanding in him and he says it to a turn. You can rely on the Reverend Mr. Mackenzie. When he used the words 'our simple fellow clansman', I thought it was nobly said."

"Yes, there was something behind the words that should travel high," said Fachie, a glimmer of beatitude in his eye.

"We're all the one clan at the end of the day."

"Fellow clansmen—ay, even to the Munros," said Fachie. Davie laughed. "The widow's dram has gone to your head, boy."

"It was where Himself meant it to go," said Fachie. "Where she got it I wonder; though I'm thinking it will be Mr. Grant, for a nicer gentleman you couldn't meet, and able. Man, I'll tell you a thing he told me no later than yesterday and it will astonish you, clever as you may think yourself."

"Let us hear it, and we'll see."

"It's about the bones of animals that were eaten and that they'll be finding in old prehistoric places like the cairn over there. In the case of the cattle, he was saying, it's mostly the bones of young beasts, calves. He took over one bone to show me. And right enough it was a calf's leg. Now how would you explain them eating the young?"

"How long ago would that be?" asked Davie to gain time.

"Thousands of years ago; ay, thousands of years before the birth of our Lord; and it's his own words."

"Boy, are you telling me there was people in it here then?"

"There was. But you're not answering my question. Why was it the young beasts they killed?"

"They would know no better likely, for it is ignorant they must have been," answered Davie.

"We'll leave ignorance to where it may belong. Well then: they killed the young beasts for just the same reason as you and me must sell them—because there wasn't the winter feed for them!"

"No!" said Davie.

"Oh but yo," said Fachie. "For there was no buying and selling then, no markets to send young beasts to. So, being wise, they just ate them."

"They would have to indeed," Davie agreed, and laughed in pleasant wonderment.

Thus they continued to discuss happily the unchanging problems of man's estate as the procession wound its way to the churchyard.

When the undertaker, a heavy whispering man, with thin grey hair and his bowler in his hand, came and breathed confidentially, "You'll take a cord, Mr. Grant?" Mr. Grant hesitated, strangely confounded on the edge of the mysteries. "It was Mrs. Mackenzie's own wish, but only if it should be agreeable to you." He found himself whispering his reply and following the undertaker to the inner ring. This had a markedly solemnising and uplifting effect upon him, as though a concealed sense of guilt were being freed by some hidden agency. He could see he was the only stranger who had a cord. The feeling of taking part in an immemorial rite grew strongly upon him and he was aware, deep in the heart of man, of a profound brotherly ordering and responsibility. This was good, and he knew it instantly as more ancient than the Neolithic cairn. Hitherto he had fancied that one could conceive of prehistoric man only imaginatively. Now he knew better. As the pressure came on the brown cord, he lowered away with care and knew the mutual burden of

318

mortality. The plate on the coffin, declaring that Andie was "aged 29 years", went down into the long cist. The undertaker's assistant pulled up the supporting bands. The cords dropped.

He found himself turning away, slowly, with the other men, when the brown earth was falling quietly. Now he was talking to two of them. There was no haste. Incuriously he saw Martin's car drive away. The Colonel, Scott and Blair were standing beyond the gate. He didn't mind. Men should stand occasionally, just stand, and talk together humanly and let time go over them. Some of the young squad from the camp were wandering around, reading the tombstones. Armstrong must have said something, for three came round him like fowls round a titbit. Their humour was decorously concealed and Grant found himself smiling. The lads were moving on when one of them stopped and pointed: "A rainbow." There had been rain during the night and an occasional narrow white curtain still passed away to the north. Sun and shadow, massive cloud-banks white as snow, with a tendency to group towards the north and show a dark under-belly.

"That's where the crock of gold is buried," said Armstrong.

"Where?" asked Jim.

"Under the rainbow."

"Go on!" said Jim.

"It's a fact. That's the Gaelic legend. The crock of gold lies buried under the foot of the rainbow. How masterly! And now how apt!"

They laughed in soft wonder, staring at the coloured arc.

"Which foot?" asked Jim. A young elbow nudged him and he turned round.

"The left foot," said Grant, who had paused on the path to greet Davie Munro; then he went slowly on in Davie's

319

company, smiling, and finding time, as he spoke and listened, to wonder exactly which foot it was.

Colonel Mackintosh invited him to a late lunch, but, after thanking him, he said, "They are expecting me at home."

The Colonel's eyes twinkled. "They have taken you into the inner chamber."

Grant smiled.

"I think it was a great gesture," declared Scott. "And dammit I confess I was glad."

"I was pleased myself," said Grant simply, and Blair, who had been about to say something, thought better of it and only laughed lightly.

He drove home in the hotel car with Davie and Fachie, and had some interesting and even merry conversation.

Mrs. Cameron greeted him at the door. "You must be starving! Go in, now, and I'll just bring your dinner."

Between the broth and the chicken, she said, "It was a beautiful funeral; the largest I have seen since the old laird himself was put to his rest from Clachar House."

"Yes, it was a very nice funeral," he agreed.

"And such beautiful flowers! Mrs. Mackenzie felt the honour of it and it did her heart good. Indeed it did my own the same."

He was astonished to find that he was not uncomfortable before this expression of sentiment, that he did not fear even more of it. On the contrary, he was at ease and lifted up into that quieter air where responsible men met and buried their dead. This feeling of freedom was remarkable, as though he had been blessed. "I am glad to hear it," he said.

"And did you—did Mr. MacGrowther, the undertaker—did he say anything?"

"He asked me to take a cord. So we saw Andie to his long home. And I confess, Mrs. Cameron, that I appreciated the honour."

"God bless you," she said. "Now everyone can rest at

peace. Dear me, your food is getting cold," and out she bustled.

He liked cold boiled chicken. He smiled, and now a faint irony came into the smile. He remembered Martin and his remark about the two large wreaths. The fellow had been right.

As he was stirring the cup of tea which Mrs. Cameron brought in he conveyed something of his underlying thought.

"Ah well, poor woman," she answered sensibly, "there was the other side to it too. So long as she was alive she might manage to look after him. But the picture of him some day, when herself was no more, being taken to an asylum——" She shook her head. "Many thoughts lie in a mother's heart, and because Andie may not have been all in it, did not make it easier for her, indeed it made it the harder in a way."

He nodded, saying nothing.

"And lately, too, she was sore troubled about him, for it would have broken her heart if he had to be lifted and her still alive. Then you took him back, and though she was afraid and it was against her will, yet she saw him being happy with the young men, and she saw, too, that they grew fond of him, scholars all of them, and Colonel Mackintosh would be strict like a father, and she liked that best of all. And there was that big gentleman, Mr. Scott, and him standing on his head." All at once the tears came and she went out.

But in a little while she was back with the teapot itself, wondering if he would like another cup, and he told her there was nothing he would like better. "The house is very quiet to-day surely," he added. "Where has the music gone?"

"Och, out and away and the Silver Bough with her, herself and her mother. Take it she would, and there was no denying her, for she has found a new way of it now."

"A new way?"

"That she has! And bonny it is, too, I must say. She sort of tips the Bough up, and the notes run down one on top of the other as fast as they can go, so there's a tumble of them on you, yet each as clear as clear can be. You would think they were laughing, and indeed you laugh yourself. He was a clever man who made yon."

He laughed with pleasure. "I must hear that."

"You will! And more than that. Though where she got this new notion just goodness knows. Someone must have been talking of the White Shore. I can't remember myself talking of it, though och! you'll say a thing and not notice it, but a child will notice it. Anyway, it must have a strange sound for her, like a place in a magic story, and I'm fancying she thinks that if she tips up the Bough, away off somewhere, it will be like the young man shaking the golden apples before the king and she will find herself on the White Shore."

He was lost for a few moments as she gathered the dishes.

"Where did they go?" he asked.

She seemed to hesitate. "Maybe they went the way of the little shore, though I wouldn't be sure."

He looked up at her sideways. "They could hardly go as far as the White Shore?"

"No," she said. But her good spirits seemed to have faded. Her hands grew busier and she did not look at him.

"You're not worried about them, are you?" he asked lightly.

"No," she said, about to lift the tray away. But again she hesitated and he saw that she needed someone to speak to.

"What is it?"

"Och, it's nothing to trouble you with, Mr. Grant. Only, Anna—I just don't know what's happening to her. I just

322

don't know at all. I overheard her tell the vanman that she could not go to Kinlochoscar yesterday. It wasn't like her, but I never let on I heard. She's troubled, I'm thinking."

"You had better tell me," he said.

"It was the other day," she said, "the day after poor Andie was killed. She was tired because she had been up most of the night, as you know, so she went out in the afternoon with the little one, who was anything but tired, and it seems they went as far as the little shore, for Sheena can think of no other place, and since she gathered the shells with yourself there, it has fair gone to her head." She paused. "It's difficult for me to get the rights of it, for Anna herself would never have said a word about it, and didn't say much at the best, only the little one couldn't tell me enough. What seems to have happened is this. Anna fell asleep and Sheena went to the little strand to gather shells. Mr. Martin then came up in his boat and saw Sheena all alone. Sheena saw the boat. I asked her if she was frightened when she saw the boat and she said No. For she had been in the boat, as you know."

"She liked it," he said thoughtfully.

"So he must have come in and grounded the boat. Anyway, Anna suddenly awoke and saw that Sheena was missing and she got up and ran over the little rise of ground—and there was Mr. Martin and Sheena by the edge of the tide, and he was sitting on a rock and Sheena was showing him her shells. How long they had been there together there's no way of knowing surely, for the child does not know time, but it must have been a little while."

"What happened then?"

"Anna says nothing happened. But I can see she was terribly upset at having been caught asleep and the little one alone by the tide. I asked her didn't she tell him that she had been up all night but she said No. So they came away, and that was all, she said."

He was silent.

"I think she might at least have told him or said something," declared Mrs. Cameron.

"She's not that kind."

"Don't I know it! But that will get her nowhere ever. As I've told her before now. You can't just stand dumb and life going by you."

"I'm not even sure of that—in this case."

"Oh I don't know," she said, distress now in her voice, "but it showed me one thing at last, and it is that she's eating her heart out. It's terrible, and her so young."

He nodded, and when she had gone out, he went up to his bedroom and changed into his old knickerbocker suit.

It seemed to him that the bedroom was extraordinarily quiet, full of peace. Emotion was a heady food! I'll go out for a walk, he thought, and lie on the earth in a quiet place. You'll go to the little shore, he said; he was sitting on his bed, fully clothed, and with a smile looked at the mat, for it was as though the "influence" had spoken in him. Amused, he went and opened the door of the dark room, saw the black cloth hanging from the skylight, and on the floor the narrow box caught in a musty sun-warmth that came against his face. He closed the door. The "influence" was so obviously nothing more than his own unconscious promptings! But he might as well go out.

41

Aware of some obscure internal argument about the direction his feet were taking, he really paid little attention to it. Old Fachie was sitting at his gable corner, a cloud of smoke rising like incense from his head. Comfortably fed after a very enjoyable funeral, he would be indulging in reminiscence and reflection, wondering with solemn appreciation how and why he had been spared so long. "Many's the change I have seen in Clachar in my time," he would begin, but Grant's footsteps did not deviate, though he acknowledged the ancient's salute with the full length of his own right arm.

He had enjoyed the funeral himself. There had been a wonderful sense of balance about it somewhere. An integrating influence. Social or communal primarily, no doubt, but personal in actual effect. To abide sentiment solidly on your two feet made you feel wonderfully competent, and wise. The people who sneered, who ran away to protect their skinned sensibilities, missed something, something much larger than their own egos. That was perfectly clear and extended the scope of the world, allowing things to happen under time and chance with a certain naturalness.

Though how rarely they happened as each individual wished them to! And clearly they couldn't, or the over-all balance would be lost. For the whole had this balance, which was extra to the sum of its parts. Having arrived at this conclusion from living experience, he paused to look back and take a breath. The cottages, the little fields, the winding stream, the road—and on the road two figures, a man and a woman. The woman was Mrs. Cameron beyond doubt. She would be getting all the news of the funeral in detail. God bless her! he thought, and laughed softly. His eyes roved over the slopes and the ridges and came to the cairn. Curious humans were moving around it like ants round their ant-hill, but two of the labour squad would be on guard by direct order of the Colonel, who did not believe, he had said, in skulls as souvenirs. For a little while his eyes rested on Clachar House, then he continued up the slope.

No, things did not happen to romantic order. In that sense, nothing had "come right". Andie had been killed and the crock of gold had been buried under the rainbow. Not actually under the rainbow, but near enough to give immortal sense to Keats and the figures on his Grecian Urn:

> Fair youth, beneath the trees, thou canst not leave
> Thy song, nor ever can those trees be bare;
> Bold Lover, never, never canst thou kiss,
> Though winning near the goal—yet, do not grieve;
> She cannot fade, though thou hast not thy bliss. . . .

The crock of gold seemed to have brought Keats to life in him after many years! And it would not help much now to be jealous of the rainbow! After all, a crock of gold under the rainbow would be only an urn in a museum. Even irony had its over-all balance. The poets needed a myth to feed on. It was their secreted honey. Keats took over from the archaeologist.

And his brave hope that he might be able to show some connection between the crock of gold and the lady in the box in his bedroom! . . . She had been asleep to-day, quietly. Or had she turned over in her sleep and smiled—and set his feet walking?

How fantastic a being was man in his secret recesses!

There was nothing mad enough for him secretly to conceive—even Anna as a housekeeper and Sheena getting piano lessons! A faint squirm touched him now. He had been suppressing in himself the cry that Anna had given over the body of Martin on the storm-driven foreshore. He nodded, and went on.

Nothing had certainty in it to anyone . . . except to Sheena playing her Silver Bough. Quite literally, that was the fact. He saw it with such absolute clarity that he laughed again. And presumably here was the "influence" that had been directing his footsteps!

Heady stuff, this sentiment! He had not got quite used to it yet. The funeral had helped; and afterwards, with Mrs. Cameron . . . she had really deep down been quite cross with Anna for not knowing how to handle a man! He laughed for the third time, and then his thoughts fell from him, for he was coming over the ridge and he should see in a moment if the two of them were on the little shore.

It took full five seconds for his wits to gather enough sense to make him lie down. Martin was leaning against the stem of his boat which he had grounded on the shingle by the dark skerry. Fleeing the funeral concourse to the fishing grounds, he had presumably been attracted once more by the same figure on the strand. Grant saw the Silver Bough glisten in the sun. She was showing it to him. It flashed as she tipped it up. Anna was standing at a little distance, quite still.

No sound reached him as Sheena played her melody. Everything was arrested except the just perceptible movement of her hand. The playing seemed to go on beyond time. But at last it stopped, and now everything was absolutely arrested. Slowly Sheena's head tilted up. Martin straightened himself. He looked at Anna and called something. She went down towards them slowly. He turned and heaved the boat afloat, holding the gunnel firmly while

Anna stepped in from the rock. Then he lifted Sheena in and finally the Silver Bough. Pushing off, he got both oars going and headed outward over the tranquil sea; then gradually her bow came round, and to the watcher above it was clear at last beyond mortal doubt that a strange and adventurous journey had begun to the White Shore.